FREEFALLING IN THE MOONLIGHT

AUDREY LYNDEN

PENSKE

For more information, contact:
tricia@audreylynden.com

Cover Design: *Okay Creations - Sarah Hansen*
Editing: *All that Editing - Lynne Pearson*
Proofreading: *One Love Editing - Sandra Dee*
ISBN: 978-0-9973400-5-1 (paperback)
ISBN: 978-0-9973400-6-8 (e-book)

Published by Penske Publishing

For my dad, Alfred Penske. Thank you for teaching me to stay steady and stand tall in a world of tough men. Your patience and integrity guide me every minute. I've been fortunate to inherit your extraordinary listening skills and sense of humor. And because of you, I'm able to shoot for the moon while knowing how to crash land safely.

AUTHOR'S NOTE

Dear Readers,

Freefalling in the Moonlight is a contemporary love story that dives into some gritty matters while infusing hope into these messy situations. There are strong characters who find themselves face to face with the darker forces around them. In total, this story is a romantic adventure of love, hope and empowerment.

Please be aware that this book contains: an on-page scene with sexual harassment, the death of a brother and a mother (off the page), a misogynistic villain without a conscience, and the challenges breast cancer survivors endure.

The characters in this story strive to overcome adversity, take care of their mental health, and ultimately find their happy ending. However, if there is a possibility that any of these subjects strike you negatively, it may not be the best read for you at this time.

Freefalling in the Moonlight is an escape where you'll find that honest and true love triumphs.

Artfully yours,
Audrey Lynden

HOLLYWOOD CUE

APRIL

TOP STORY

Chris Wagner Reclaims His Title! Once Again Proclaimed...*Nicest Guy in Hollywood!*

HOLLYWOOD ICON CHRIS WAGNER IS RIDING HIGH AFTER ALL ALLEGATIONS AND ACCUSATIONS AGAINST HIM WERE DROPPED. HE'S BEEN EXONERATED OF ANY WRONGDOING AND IS READY TO GET BACK TO WORK NEXT FALL AS THE LEAD IN SCORSESE'S LATEST MOB TRILOGY.

BY GEMMA GARNER

APRIL

No script was needed as Chris Wagner, Emmy-winning star of TV's *Case Closed*, left the Chicago courthouse. His blue eyes, often compared to Hollywood icon Paul Newman's baby blues, sparkled in the spring sunshine. Arising from what was initially dubbed the end of his career, Wagner, bookended by his wife and two daughters, told reporters, "It's true. The justice system works. In today's toxic environment of celebrity slander and cancel culture, I've fought hard to be a voice of reason."

Well-known for his role as a downtrodden FBI agent solving 1960s cold cases, the actor is also known to industry insiders as the *good guy* in Hollywood. A self-proclaimed feminist, "thanks to his two tween daughters," Wagner has generously donated to the #MeToo movement and other female empowerment causes. He strongly advocates, demands equal opportunities, and nurtures the women working around him, once stating, "The show writers are familiar with my script changes. I'm a nag. Many of my lines can be given to co-stars, so when I see a chance to bolster the careers of my female colleagues, I make a stand."

Wagner celebrated his victory with fellow thespian and long-time acting coach Gus Reid. The two actors share roots in the Midwest, and Reid has given his full support to Wagner. Reid's brother, Robert, headed up the prominent Chicago defense team that ultimately cleared Wagner's name and reclaimed his reputation.

When asked about the women who accused him of sexual assault and workplace harassment on the set of *Case Closed*, Wagner dropped his head, visibly shaken. "They are lovely women with a passion for drama. Creative souls are what make this industry thrive. Unfortunately, miscommunication runs rampant in the film industry and leads to misunderstandings. I have nothing but hope for the two women who falsely accused me." Wagner's voice broke in the emotional response. He wiped away a tear, and his wife became his crutch as they went down the stairs.

After his family was tucked into the back seat of a waiting SUV, Wagner's husky voice returned. "The tremendous support from my fans has been lifesaving. Thank you to all the true crime enthusiasts who make my job a delight every time I step onto a set. I'm here and free, thanks to my die-hard followers. I'll never forget **#freeWagner** and **#welovewagner**." After blowing several kisses toward the press, the tinted window closed, and he drove off. **{GG}**

ONE

May

Rob Reid wanted to throttle his older brother's famous, million-dollar neck. The *Effing Hollywood Wanker* was asking for another favor? Glancing above at the restaurant's fake grass, fairy lights, and white trellises adhered to the ceiling, he ruminated over Gus's last request. The favor had turned into a nightmare and evolved into the current situation playing out in the upstairs banquet hall. Sitting at the first-level bar of the Hamptons Social, Rob wondered how long he could avoid the party or its vile host, Chris Wagner.

Rob scanned the message from Gus again.

Really NEED you to babysit the dogs.

The Wagner fiasco was the only favor his brother deserved, so Rob ignored the message and opted to make Gus wait a little longer. Let him sweat it out. Although, the actor extraordinaire probably wouldn't actually sweat because megastars rarely did, and there really wasn't any drama to be had. Rob would acquiesce and take care of Humphrey and Bogart because the dogs were like his own and because he needed a hit of fresh hometown air in Wisconsin.

Behind the bar, the waitress cracked open another bottle of Whispering Angel Rosé—the signature drink in the Hamptons-themed restaurant and served at many swanky East Coast galas. She filled the glasses on the tray and went up the stairs to hand them out to Rob's colleagues, who were celebrating the biggest win the firm had seen all year. Unfortunately, the successful case was due to the machinations of Chris Wagner—the world's worst client and a despicable human being.

"Rosé?" The bartender held out a pink bottle.

"No, but..." The restaurant wasn't anywhere near a balmy ocean but instead a mile away from Lake Michigan in Chicago. The breezes coming off the water hadn't yet hit sixty degrees, and it was already May. "I'll go with the bourbon old-fashioned."

Rob counted the seconds before Fran was recognized and gawked at when she entered the restaurant. In tonight's crowd, it took less than ten. A professional, probably an attorney, approached the supermodel of swimwear and introduced himself. Rob watched patiently for his good friend Fran to appease her fan and then waved at her to hurry it along. He had to get upstairs before Wagner's thank-you speech kicked off.

She caught his eye, winked, and gave him the one-minute finger. After taking a selfie with another fan, this time a woman, Francesca Marcheti, jogged up and wrapped Rob in a familial hug. Their friendship was as hard as a rock, and she was doing him a solid by being his plus-one to get him through this dismal event. Hugging her, he leaned close but not too close, attentive to her chest. She looked beautiful, but the double mastectomy last February was still fresh in his mind and undoubtedly in hers.

"Ciao. Here I thought I would be waiting for you," she said, sliding onto the wicker-backed stool beside him. "Weren't you volunteering at the Y today?"

"I went, but another volunteer took the kids on a field trip to the Art Institute. So, they dove into art instead of a pool. I did some laps and had a good workout." He leaned toward her. "Did I get all the chlorine off?"

Fran inhaled deeply. "All I smell is bourbon. Are you sure you want to get all liquored up before facing the ass?"

"Yes. Again, thanks for doing this for me. This is the end. One last time to see Chris Wagner. And I'm vowing, here and now, never to read another article written in the *Cue*."

"Finally, I get to help *you* out," she said, tipping her head toward him. "Like the new wig?"

"Seriously?" It was the exact color of her real hair, dark chocolate. "I'm impressed. But I thought everything had grown back?"

"Slowly, but surely. Still coming in too patchy." She took hold of his hand and yanked him to his feet. "And tonight, to take off the pressure, I wanted to look my absolute best for you. The king of popsicles."

Rob shook his head. He would never regret the hours he'd spent with Fran as she went through chemo, radiation, surgery, and more chemotherapy. The combined stress of Wagner's case and Fran's health care was finally ending, soon to become a distant nightmare.

Draping his arm over her shoulders, they strolled up the stairs side by side. Close in height, he knew, especially when the crowd of suits swiveled to look their way, that he and Fran were a good-looking couple who appeared to be in love. Thankfully, the depth of their friendship, which began because of a mutual interest in fast cars, remained a mystery to the outside world. Besides, he'd fallen in love once and didn't relish the idea of doing it again. Or if it was even possible. Maddie Logerquist had supplied his life with the proverbial troubled waters without any bridges.

With Fran next to him, Rob made the obligatory rounds of handshaking with the other partners in the firm, introducing them to one of the most famous swimsuit models in the world before cancer forced her to retire early. All of his colleagues congratulated him on his victory in court and then showered his *date* with compliments.

Rob scanned the room for Wagner while talking shop. When he spotted the "Nicest Guy in Hollywood," as proclaimed by the *Cue*, he clutched Fran's hand and took in a deep breath. More than a month ago, Rob left the courtroom to run as far away as possible from the prize ass. While Wagner schmoozed with the firm's president, Rob discreetly stared at the TV star, noticing a sheen to his forehead. Even his celebrated blue eyes were bloodshot. Rob wondered how many drinks Wagner had downed before this party of his making. Or if tonight's dinner started with an appetizer of some illicit drug.

"Heads up." Fran elbowed his rib cage. "He's coming over."

Rob caught Wagner's attention and gave him a quick nod of recognition. On cue, Wagner strode up to him and Fran. Wearing a navy suit, similar to Rob's standard work wear, he looked civilized, but outside appearances were often phony. In this case, Rob was certain the man clothed in an expensive suit, probably a Tom Ford, was a complete fake.

"Rob. Good to see you," Wagner said, eyeing Fran from head to toe. "You look familiar? Were you an extra on *Case Closed*?"

Protectiveness overcame Rob, and he tightened his grip on Fran's hand.

"No," she said, lifting her eyebrow. "Francesca Marcheti. From Chicago's Luxury Autos. "Have you purchased a Ferrari recently? If so, you may have met my father."

Rob swallowed a chuckle. It was true. Fran's family owned the only Ferrari dealership in the Midwest, but she had been on the cover of *SI* multiple times. For Wagner not to recognize her celebrity proved he was as narcissistic as he was predatory.

"Where is your better half?" Rob asked seriously. "Or the girls?"

Wagner cleared his throat. "Back east in the Hamptons. For the summer. Starting vacation early."

"Sounds lovely," Fran said. "What are your daughters' names?"

"Trudy and Natalie," he answered while scrutinizing Fran's face. "Wait a minute. You're the model, aren't you? Who had her boobs lopped off. Like Angelina."

A loud rush of blood coursed through Rob's head. "Don't be so bloody vulgar."

Wagner leered at Fran. "Hey, I'm the client. Paying the overpriced lawyers. I can say whatever I want and however I choose to. Right, babe?"

"Better lower your voice," Fran said, giving Rob a look of cold calm with a hint of sinister. "I'm from a *famiglia* with a lot of *bada-bing*."

Her Italian family may have been Old World, but nothing close to mob-related, at least Rob thought. Seeing the glint in Fran's dark eyes made him wonder. Maybe all the times she'd had to look warm while posing in swimsuits during the coldest time of year gave her a formidable and slightly terrifying side.

Wagner was oblivious to Fran's *empty*, or maybe not, threat.

"I think you owe my friend an apology, Chris. There's no need to be so crass."

"My apologies. I didn't mean to offend you." Wagner widened his eyes. "I was just shocked at how good you look. Considering..." he said, clearing his throat. "You no longer sport your most delicious and famous assets."

Rob wanted to take him down and pound his smug face into the ground. Instead, he crossed his arms over his chest and let out a long, windy breath. "Now you're the nicest guy in Hollywood again. I gave you a second chance." *Never again.*

Shaking her head, Fran said, "You're lucky for a complete d-bag."

Wagner strolled on, moving among the other staff with a polite smile, quick hug, and an occasional selfie. The selfies, Rob noticed, were taken with only the blonde women who worked in the office.

"Well, that went well. Don't you think?" Fran observed, leading him to the bar.

He made sure no one was within hearing range. "If I did have another chance, I'd sink the asshole and take him for all he's worth. No questions. No deals. And no NDAs."

"What do you think is really up with his wife and kids?" Fran asked. "Last month, they were one big happy family."

"Not anymore. I hope she stays in the Hamptons. For good. Then the daughters will have a chance for some normalcy," he said, staring at his drink.

Fran laid her hand on his shoulder. "Speaking of normalcy. When are you coming to Elkhart?"

Racing his sports car at Road America, his retreat each summer, couldn't come fast enough. Then he remembered about watching Gus's dogs. "I'll be in Wisconsin by July, if not sooner, for my brother."

"Only Gus?" Fran gave him an unnerving and perceptive smile. "What about Maddie?"

Recently, Rob's thoughts kept wandering off track and toward Maddie. The last time he'd seen her—February—was disastrous. They'd been pushing a god-awful sleigh bed in a race on a frozen lake in Baileys Harbor. Tense and perturbed by the

Wagner case, he'd been unable to function naturally around her. Or was it his frustration over being in the friend zone?

"My schedule is tight, and I'm anxious to get the Triumph from the shop."

"Your precious car isn't moving anywhere. When you get to Wisconsin...at least call Maddie."

"When did you become so pushy?"

"I'm Italian. It comes with the territory. And Maddie figured into every story you told me while I was going through chemo, dude." She clutched his shoulders and shook. "I want to meet her. *Per favore.*"

"Sì, sì. I'll keep you posted. I suppose I should thank you, or maybe not, for getting me hooked on watching *Summer Haven.* Never thought of myself as a reality TV watcher."

"Watching a bunch of thirty-something New Yorkers partying and living it up in a Hamptons mansion all summer long is my idea of a perfect escape. And your Maddie makes them look good while dressed in bikinis."

Laughing, they headed toward the door. When Fran took time to pose for a couple of photos, he scanned his phone for messages and clicked on another one from Gus, again asking about the dogs. He jotted a response, then closed his eyes and pictured Maddie.

It seemed like he woke up and fell asleep with her on his mind every day for the past decade, but his heart wasn't sure how to process this part of his daily routine. Focusing on work made the loss of his one true love somewhat easy to forget, but who was he kidding? Whether she knew it or not, Maddie Logerquist was immersed in his deepest desires, and there would be no way to avoid her or their history when he returned to Wisconsin. Their roots were tangled, knotted, and deeply entrenched together.

TWO

June

Maddie crunched over the carpet of discarded needles from the canopy of evergreens, the earthy scent making her nose itch and eyes water. She would have preferred sitting at her desk and inhaling the luxurious pine-scented candle she'd just bought at Wicks & Balms, but the day had arrived. A trip into the woods of Toft Point was required. Tightening her grip on the urn, she ran face-first into a spiderweb. Pawing at it, she groaned. Up ahead, a snake slithered around the corner of the chinked log cabin, where her brother was peering into a filthy window.

"This is disgusting," she yelled. "And watch out. There are snakes."

"No big deal. I'm not Indiana Jones." Brady pushed open the cabin's decrepit wood door and stepped inside. "Do you have Ma's will with you?"

"Of course." Keeping the urn safe, she cocked her hip to show him the black binder jutting out of her summer tote bag. Inside the abandoned cabin—once used as a dorm for men who'd worked at the long-gone quarry owned by her family—

she said, "There are several pages describing Mom's last wishes if you want to take a look. Double-check, but she only states Toft Point."

"No, I trust you. And you're the organized one." He shined his flashlight around, illuminating the dust motes floating about the stuffy space. "Not gonna lie. It's been great having you home."

"Aw, you're just being nice," she said, tripping on a loose plank of pine. With a huff, she stepped closer to her brother. "We just have to spread Mom's ashes in...some...area. Since the ground is finally soft enough."

"Complicating word, *area*. Toft Point is over seven hundred acres." Brady kicked branches and debris out of his way, then inspected the hearth and the mantel. "Our mother, the Dame of Baileys Harbor, Wisconsin. She never missed a detail. Except when it came to her final resting place."

"Elsie Logerquist made specificity an art form," Maddie said, "but maybe she wasn't capable of making this one decision. Because of the cancer." Maddie still recoiled at the speed of her mom's death. The diagnosis came, and two months later, she passed.

"An old receipt. Damn. I hoped, like an idiot, it was a map." Brady crumpled up the piece of paper he'd picked up and shoved it in the back pocket of his jeans. "Let's go outside. This place is giving me the creeps. Reminds me of Crystal Lake."

"Ha. My brave brother, a member of the Coast Guard, is frightened by dilapidated bunk beds?"

"Aren't you?" He led the way out of the dank cabin. "Ma had a way of making everything about our small town bigger than life. A never-ending hunt for treasure. It's like she's still here and hiding in the bushes. Ready to jump out, scare the shit out of us, and lecture us on the importance of moss in the environment. I'm not interested in pissing her off."

"As if," Maddie scoffed. She'd been the one who had, without a doubt, utterly disappointed their mom when she moved to New York a decade ago. "You have nothing to worry about, golden boy."

"Golden, my ass." He circled around the remains of a lime kiln. "Do you think she'd want to be laid in this thing? A lot of moss covering it...what's left of it."

"How morbid. And redundant. She's already been in one oven."

"Right, sorry, Ma. Wasn't thinking."

Maddie held out the urn, growing heavier by the minute. "The answer is here. An urn shaped like a lighthouse means, possibly, she wanted to be near or around a lighthouse?"

He shaded his eyes, gazed west, and pointed at the water. "The closest lighthouse to Toft Point is over there, a small island only available by boat. It's called the Birdcage."

"Why the hell did Elsie buy an island with a decrepit lighthouse?" She trembled as cold dread shimmied along her spine. "It's not mentioned in the will."

"No idea. Maybe Ma wasn't completely...*there* when she purchased it. The tumor may have been working on her brain before we knew about it. But since Birdcage Island isn't a big concern, let's not worry about it. At least for today."

She tipped the brim of her sunhat to get a better look through an opening in the woods. Unlike the lighthouse on Cana Island, the lighthouse on Birdcage Island had a weird metal birdcage perched on top of it. She sighed. Since packing up her life last fall and returning to her hometown of Baileys Harbor, all Maddie seemed to do was worry about everything.

First, the hospice, then the funeral, followed by an endless list of responsibilities as she'd assumed her mom's multiple community positions. Maddie had created a spreadsheet to keep track of the many details revolving around the conservation work and the Logerquist legacy. She plodded on and tried her best to take over Elsie's role—essentially a twenty-first-century Rachel Carson for Baileys Harbor.

While Brady tossed pinecones around, she wiped her runny nose and wandered to the hiking path. There was an inscribed plaque welded onto a tower of limestone boulders.

Those who visit Toft Point to enjoy its wild, untamed beauty and rich biodiversity should be deeply indebted to the Thomas Toft family, whose great fondness and respect for this land eventually led to its permanent protection.

She kicked the rock and felt sixteen instead of thirty-four.

As the daughter of Elsie Logerquist, granddaughter of Vivian Toft, and great-granddaughter of Helen Bailey, Maddie was dealt a fortunate hand. A family located in a lakeside town where she had absolutely no desire to live.

She settled the urn on the ground next to the monument and checked her phone for messages. The service was still sketchy. She added *cell service* to her notes, a list for the next Chamber of Commerce meeting. After jotting several other reminders for herself, she returned to her surroundings—uninhabited nature with an unwelcoming vibe. Maddie scanned the woods and looked hard between the towering white pines to see Brady, but he had disappeared. Slipping her phone into her bag, she trudged onto a path leading closer—too close—to Lake Michigan's rocky shoreline. "Ahoy? Brady?"

Only the dreadful sound of the lake's crashing waves from beyond the trees answered her. The safe and peaceful presence of her brother had evaporated. Maddie closed her eyes and shook off the awakened and awful fear she'd been struggling to bury since moving home from New York. She shouted for Brady again, shivered in the blazing heat of a midday sun, and laid her hand on the back of an Aldo Leopold bench to keep calm.

"Hey. You okay?" Brady jogged toward her. "Sorry. Just wanted to check the water levels."

Maddie exhaled. "Yes. No. Not really. It's June, and there's so much going on. I *literally* just turned the agenda for the next Commerce meeting into a novella."

They hiked back inland, a safe distance from the water. She plopped on the ground, pressed her back against the cool stone commemorative, and tapped the urn. "And, of course, the funding for the lighthouse has to get cut by the state. Oh, joy of joys."

Her marketing skills and influencing had been honed from living a gig life in a tough city, but Maddie continually wondered if her more modern approach to work would be enough to keep her mother's projects going forward. Especially since one of the two darn lighthouses was more like a doomed dirigible.

Brady sat on the ground across from her and crossed his legs. "You're a badass. You can take this town and blow the roof off. I know, when the time comes, you'll be on a plane back to the city. And your buddies on the cast of *Summer Haven* will be celebrating your arrival with whatever cocktails they'll be stirring up on the show."

Maddie wouldn't and couldn't let herself think about the past. Leaving New York and the Hamptons last summer was a complicated mess. More factually, she'd been unceremoniously asked to leave by the reality show's producer, who happened to be her ex. "Thanks, but I need to get through this summer in Wisconsin."

"You have a network of friends here in Baileys and all of our complete support."

Maddie pictured her hometown friends Kat Orlov and Lucy

Maxwell, both of whom owned successful businesses on Main Street. Graham Bilby was her steadfast volunteer at the lighthouse. And—

"Don't forget about the one and only Gus Reid," Brady said, reading her mind. "He's a celebrity. You get his world."

Startled, she shook her head hard. "You're comparing me to an A-list TV star. Gus Reid is around-the-world famous. I'm a C-list, no, D-list, onetime reality TV show *guest*. Hardly onscreen and mostly behind the scenes as the stylist."

Five years ago, landing the gig as head stylist on the popular TV show *Summer Haven* had put her on cloud nine. One of her model friends from FIT had introduced her to Alex, the main guy on the show where a group of a dozen New York professionals gather on summer weekends to blow off steam after a grinding work week in the Big Apple. Airing the parties and shenanigans at the Hamptons mansion had developed a devoted following of fans.

"But you know the drill. Fancy folks live a certain way. How much money does the lighthouse need?"

"A quarter million," she said, considering the amount. She had definitely learned about the peculiar and luxurious needs of the rich and famous while spending summers in the Hamptons. Two hundred and fifty thousand dollars was pocket change for many of the resort-loving Easterners.

Brady fell back on the ground and groaned.

"The lighthouse prism has to be replaced." Maddie put her hand protectively on the urn she'd set beside her leg. "Couldn't we sell the Birdcage lighthouse and the property to a private party and use the proceeds to pay for the other lighthouse?"

"Who would buy it?" Brady stood and held out his hand to help her up. "Not even sure what's going on over there. No one has stepped foot on the island in years."

"We're dealing with too many darn lighthouses for this tiny

town." Shrugging, she cradled the urn and stood up. With her free hand, she brushed off the debris of needles and leaves from the back of her silk shorts. The university's purchase of Toft Point was pure luck. The board members of another one of her mom's babies, the Sanctuary, were constantly adjusting the budget. Donations were tough to rely on.

"Gus Reid has a lot of Hollywood connections and well-known friends," Brady said. "People love that shit. Seeing famous folks and snapping selfies with them. You need to find out how he can help. Besides, it's not like I'm suggesting you go talk to Rob."

"If you weren't so strong, I'd wrestle you into a headlock."

Rob Reid. The younger brother of Gus and the only guy she'd completely fallen head over heels for. Except Rob barely remembered her. The last time she'd seen him, inches apart and pushing a sleigh bed across the ice during Winterfest, they'd barely made eye contact. "He's a high-powered Chicago attorney. I don't think he has time for us."

Brady dropped his arm over her shoulders, and she nearly caved from the weight of it.

She relaxed. "Okay. I'm on board with Gus. Utilizing his star power is a solid idea for fundraising. But Rob? He's probably focused on his latest case or hanging with..." She stomped down the image of Rob with Francesca. A swimsuit model so famous she only used one name.

Her brother waited for her to finish, ignored her, and then continued. "Rob was extremely close to Ma. And to all of us. His perspective, and history in Baileys, may come in handy. The point is," Brady said, arching his eyebrow, "there are folks in town who would go to the moon for you and back. And then hand you a platter of cheese."

"I believe they call it a charcuterie board these days." Maddie took off her sunhat, fanned it across her face, and then placed it on top of the urn. "I'll figure out something for this overload of lighthouse responsibilities," she said. "What about Mom?"

"For now, let's set her on the dining room table in her house." Brady gently took the urn from her. "Then Elsie Logerquist can look out the window facing Moonlight Bay."

"Good idea." She extended her arms and shook out the cramped muscles. "And a great view of the water."

Her mind wandered as they hiked back to the parking lot. She tried to focus on the dilemmas, her mom, the lighthouses, but all she kept thinking about was Rob. Picturing him in her head—from long ago—on the cliffs of Cave Point Park. Maddie winced. Sometimes, from out of nowhere, she sensed his touch.

After jumping off the bluff and into the water, they'd climb onto a boulder and soak in the sun. While lying on the limestone landing, Rob would lightly caress and then kiss the inside of her arm. She shivered at the memory, hugged herself, and rubbed her forearms.

Don't let the past drag you down. Just keep moving.

THREE

June

Pure dread stifled Maddie. After moving back to Baileys, she'd been able to dam up the flow of memories by staying clear of Elsie Logerquist's estate—a museum filled with too many triggering artifacts—until now. Shortly, all twenty of the decisionmakers most embedded in the community would arrive to hear Maddie's pitch to save the Cana Island lighthouse.

In the center of the dining room table, her mother's urn commanded a presence, but it was anything but calming. Maddie adjusted her laptop for the millionth time, then closed the window shades to cut the glare from Moonlight Bay. Elsie's view of the water had had a good run the past week. Scrolling through her PowerPoint images, Maddie wondered if twenty-five photos of the decaying beacon were too many.

Kat opened one of the french doors from the kitchen. "Decaf and regular are brewing. Once you finish your presentation, we can eat outside on the deck. Do you want anything?"

"Is there tequila in the freezer?"

"I think so. You've got this, girl. Do you wanna do a practice run?" Kat strode around the room and checked the dining room table as if it were in her restaurant, the Beacon. She straightened Maddie's arrangement of binders—color-coded—and then pulled out the head chair. She admired the ornately hand-carved wooden chair back. "This furniture is beautiful. Are you sure you don't want to move in here? My apartment is so small."

"I love sharing your place, Kat." She adjusted the image of the lighthouse projecting on the blank wall above the sideboard. "It's spacious compared to my shoebox in New York. And a lot more...relaxing."

"Okey-dokey. But since most of your belongings are stored here, don't you think—"

"Simplifying, Kat." She quashed the dismal feeling that surfaced daily. "Sorry, didn't mean to be curt. It's...this place can be overwhelming. I can't stomach it. I'm relieved Brady's been able to take care of it since my mother passed."

After a kind smile, Kat ducked into the kitchen and returned with a silver serving tray. "Here's to the past and the future." She poured the Silver Patrón into a shot glass and handed it to her. "Fresh limes. Lick, salt, and shoot. Have at it."

"Perfect." Maddie sprinkled salt on her thumb, then licked and downed the ice-cold tequila, becoming calmer as the cool burn melted.

The Fourth of July holiday was a month away, plenty of time. She'd worked on tighter deadlines. True, this incoming group of leaders needed to make pivotal choices quickly, and Gus Reid, with his fame and notoriety, would make or break this plan. However, all were Baileys Harbor fans and would do what it took to ensure the success of her proposal.

Brady came into the dining room, barreled around the table, and wrapped her in his arms. "Hey, sis."

While she was swathed in brotherly love, Michael Powell—Kat's boyfriend—came up and jokingly joined the hug.

"I think your fireman is here to save us," Maddie said, unsure if Kat heard her.

"The band's back together," Gus chimed in, piling onto the group hug.

Swarmed by burly men she'd known forever, Maddie's overwrought nerves relaxed.

"Are you okay in there?" Lucy pushed the men away. "She needs air, guys."

"I'm better now." Maddie finger-combed her hair to smooth down the mess and took in her posse. Gus was as Hollywood-gorgeous as ever, and his fiancée, Lucy Maxwell, looked great, but was it Maddie's imagination, or had her stomach grown a bit? Brady was Brady. And Michael looked fireman fit with every one of his dreads trimmed to perfection.

"Evening, mates," Graham Bilby shouted as he walked in. The uncle of the Reid brothers was her right-hand man at the lighthouse and looked dapper in a crisp polo shirt and Madras golf shorts. "Lovely to see you all."

With few memories of her dad, Maddie felt a deep surge of fatherly love when Graham tugged her into his chest. "Glad you're here."

The noise in the dining room escalated as others arrived—the mayor and her assistant, the police chief, members of the C.O.C., and various business owners. After greeting one another, the group took their seats around the dining room table, and Maddie turned on the screen. The wall behind her was illuminated with a vintage photograph of the lighthouse. Most of the people in the room could be spotted in the photo, only they were about fifteen years younger. "I found this pic and thought it was a solid reminder as to the meaning of the lighthouse."

Gus craned his neck toward the image. "Damn, did I really have a mullet?"

"Hard to believe it, but yes," Michael said. "We could probably blackmail you with this pic by sending it to *People*. How important is your title of Sexiest Man Alive?"

"Okay, folks," Maddie said, "While we're waiting for—"

"Rob," Graham stated, looking at his phone. "He just texted. He's on his way."

"Right, of course." Maddie smiled hard and wondered if the one shot of tequila would be enough to keep her nerves from jumping overboard when Rob joined them. "Well, ah. Let's remember the true celebrity is the lighthouse. At least it was. We need to give it a makeover—a sleek and sexy look for the twenty-first century. Unfortunately, the state won't be helping with funding anymore. That's why I called this emergency meeting."

"No delays, Graham," Gus said. "Lucy has to get home early, so if Rob's a no-show, he'll have to get updates from you."

Lucy blushed and kissed her fiancé's famous jawline. "I'll manage, no worries. This is important, and it's the lighthouse we're talking about."

"What's going on, you two?" Kat asked. "Some celebrity stuff we should know about?"

"Maybe. We'll be in Malibu for the month of July," Gus announced. "I have some news. There's another show my agent has lined up for me, but we'll see."

Maddie's stomach twisted, then flipped. Her entire presentation and pitch for the fundraiser was hitched to Gus Reid. And now, the hometown celebrity had just torpedoed it. "Holy... But I thought—hoped you were going to be here for the Fourth of July. For the month. The holiday."

Gus patted his heart. "Damn, sorry, Maddie."

"Let's go through all the fundraising ideas," Brady suggested with a thumbs-up. "We'll figure something out."

The rest of the group concurred with nods and smiles.

"Okay." She stood away from the table and wrapped one arm around her stomach. She barely kept the remote from sliding out of her sweaty palm. "Ladies and gents, the topic at hand is the Fourth of July. As I said, the state has cut the funding at the worst time ever, summer. The lighthouse needs dollars." She clicked the remote, and the photo of the lighthouse prism flooded the room. "This is working, but it needs an upgrade. And some high-tech fixes." Staring at the image on the wall, she adjusted the ankle strap of her sandal. "My most recent estimate for the lighthouse updates stands at a quarter million."

Murmurs rumbled through the group.

"What I was going to propose—" Maddie caught a nod of encouragement from Brady. "Is or was...kicking off a fundraiser the week before the Fourth and then continuing for the rest of July and possibly August. With Gus, I had planned a series of events to celebrate. Similar to our Winterfest last February. I mean, thanks to you, Gus, Baileys Harbor has turned from a sleepy Midwest small town into a thriving vacation destination."

"True." Gus wagged his well-manicured eyebrows in jest. "Go on. I'm thinking about how to make this work."

"A doppelganger?" she asked despondently.

"Maybe." His million-dollar smile sparkled like a darn cartoon.

Maddie cast off the sinking feeling, cleared her throat, and continued. "My thought is to coordinate exclusive fundraisers where people, for two hundred fifty dollars apiece, sign up for an evening tour at the top of the lighthouse with a four-star dinner afterward. Dessert would be a chance to meet Gus Reid in person. One-on-one. If all the spots sell, we could raise twenty grand a week."

"I'm already on board," Kat said. "The meal planning and catering will be organized by yours truly."

Michael raised his hand. "I'll be available for security concerns."

Brady gave Michael a high five. "I've spoken to the Coast Guard team patrolling the lake. We can double up on the safety. I told them about the lighthouse situation."

The mayor and her assistant were taking notes on their devices and nodding.

Emboldened by the positive reactions, Maddie changed the image to the numbers chart. "My original thought...was that by summer's end, with money from Gus's Hollywood cache, the funds might close in on the two-hundred-and-fifty-thousand-dollar goal, and if not, we could look into a loan for the rest."

She tried like hell to sound upbeat, but without Gus, this plan would never get off the ground.

Michael crossed his thick arms across a chest that could rival the pecs on Terry Crews. "Gus, here's the deal. We need fireworks and a famous face to get money for the lighthouse. What's your plan?" he asked.

Maddie displayed the photo on the wall—the friends around the lighthouse years earlier—to muster up a sense of nostalgia. Sighing, she collapsed into her chair.

With dramatic flair, Gus retrieved her remote, tapped the keys on her laptop, and resumed the meeting. He pulled up the image of a man who was equally, if not more, handsome than Gus. One of the famous *Chrises*, the actor Chris Wagner. Since April, he'd been splashed over TV talk shows, online celebrity gossip, and fodder for Hollywood insider columns.

"Him?" Maddie heard the depraved, *gushing* tone in her voice. "Chris Wagner? Really?"

"I don't like him," Graham said, crossing his arms and harrumphing. "Rob worked his arse off in court defending the wanker."

"Uncle Graham, I know." Gus gave his uncle a quick grin. "But I've been working with Chris for a few years, and he's been completely professional. His career is hotter than ever, and he's on the cusp of a great deal with Scorsese. And thanks to my little bro, Chris has to fulfill a court order, so he'll do anything I ask him to. Even if it's parasailing across Lake Michigan to get to the lighthouse on the Fourth."

Maddie scanned the others' expressions. They all seemed as starstruck as she was, and she'd actually met Chris Wagner when he made a cameo on *Summer Haven*. She distinctly remembered hoisting up her jaw before the star came up and said hello to her. "Are you sure Chris Wagner is free to come here? Or if he even wants to."

"He will because he owes me, and especially Rob. Chris has to complete some community service, per the legal system, his agent, and studio."

"Isn't Chris Wagner the douche accused of sexually harassing his co-star?" Brady asked.

"Exaggerated by the tabloids," Gus said. "Even if Chris Wagner is the lech they've made him out to be, he deserves a second chance. Hey?"

Graham shook his head. "I don't know about this. I heard he's still playing about and ignoring the rules. Cheeky bastard."

She assumed Graham had more accurate knowledge because, of his three nephews, he was closest to Rob. But Gus had rehabbed his own tattered image, so a lot of what he was saying made sense. Besides, having Chris Wagner come to Baileys Harbor for the lighthouse would be a windfall.

Gus retrieved his phone. "I'll call him. Right now. What do you all think?"

Maddie nodded while prayers crept into her thoughts. Rob was the only missing voice, but since he wasn't currently living in Baileys and hadn't bothered to show up...*you snooze, you lose.* "Do it. Call Chris Wagner." Maddie's voice was one octave higher, but she couldn't help it. Chris Wagner would solve all her problems, and then she could return to New York.

FOUR

June

"I had no choice but to wait for the judge," Rob rehearsed the excuse for being late and pressed the Audi's gas pedal. With such short notice to get to this meeting, he questioned his sanity. Except Maddie had sent him the message, and even though the timing wasn't convenient, he had to get up north. Once again, they'd be together in Baileys Harbor.

Nearing the Logerquist estate on Moonlight Bay, he chuckled. Originally, the area had been called Mud Bay, and developers found it a hard sell. The wrought-iron entrance gate was open, so Rob drove in and parked next to Uncle Graham's Aston Martin. Before he slid out of his car, he eyed the sleek automobile to his left, and Road America begged for his arrival. Maddie came first though.

He jogged up to the arched doorway and knocked. When no one answered, he let himself in. The posh Logerquist house was like a second home to him. After his own mum had died, Elsie Logerquist was an amazing proxy mum. What a loss, such a tough woman and an incredible conservationist.

"Hello?" Multicolored binders, a signature Maddie move, and empty coffee cups were cast about the dining room table. He kissed his fingers and planted them on the urn—a silver-plated lighthouse—centered on the table. "Miss you, Elsie."

Voices filtered in from outside, so he glanced out the window. The moon shone over the water, and strings of light-bulbs dangled across the deck where everyone had congregated.

He strode through the kitchen to grab a beer and noticed the wall. The spot where all the awards and photos had once been displayed, celebrating the three athletic Logerquist siblings—Maddie, Brady, and Tyler—was now blank, empty, and sad-looking. A sense of gloom swept through him.

What a miserable tragedy. Rob would always miss the dare-devil and prankster one of the twins. Tyler was Loki to Brady's Thor. Shaking his head, he held up his bottle of beer to the blank wall and wondered. Had Maddie spoken Tyler's name since moving back to Baileys Harbor? Or since the day he died?

What a horrific situation. All four were exceptional swim-mers, but Brady was the strongest. And if Tyler had any chance of breaking free from the lake's riptide, it was his brother who could do it. Not him. Not Maddie. She'd been desperate to jump from the boat that summer evening to find her brother, but Rob had held her tight in his arms. It was one argument he wouldn't lose. Then Brady returned without Tyler.

Rob strode away from the empty wall and went out the back door and down the stairs, taking them two at a time. Outside, he scanned the scene. Gus, the FHW, smiled brighter than the moon. Michael, of course, was standing close to Kat. When would those two get married? And Maddie. Taking pictures and shouting at the guests with her usual propensity for cursing.

Uncle Graham shouted, "Bloody 'ell. Snap the picture."

"Done. Okay," Maddie yelled. "Finish your whiskey, old man."

Lucy laughed.

A cool lake breeze woke him up.

Home.

"Evening, all. Sorry for the tardiness," he said, approaching the group. Immediately, his closest friends cheered and jeered him, lovingly, of course. Brady pulled him into a bear hug, and Rob slapped his good friend's back.

Graham and Maddie were in a head-to-head discussion, but his uncle gave him a knowing nod. Before he responded, Gus punched his arm. "You missed a meeting of the minds, bro."

"Sorry, couldn't be helped. Judges, you know, like to keep tight control on the wheels of justice. And their golf schedules. Good to see you."

Lucy gave him a peck on the cheek. "Thanks for taking care of Humphrey and Bogart for us. The dogs are looking forward to summer camp with their Uncle Rob."

"Not a problem. I have plenty of jogs and swims lined up for them as their camp counselor. I'm glad to be out of Chicago. The air and humidity, it's been thick as a jungle."

Uncle Graham and Maddie parted. While his uncle checked on something in the brick pizza oven, Maddie headed his way. Finally.

Her long black hair had disappeared. Now, she sported a short cut, probably cropped shorter than his own, which was overdue for a cut. Her beautiful face and open smile, like he'd seen on screen on *Summer Haven*, were on full display. But in person, Maddie, as usual, stunned him. As she came toward him, he forgot to blink. Instinctively, he fast-tracked his steps to get closer to her.

"Howdy, stranger," she said. "What the hell took you so long?"

A rampage of passionate memories threatened to swallow

him down. He shook his head to clear them out. "The glacially slow court process. I had to wait to file a brief."

"I hope you weren't wearing those tattered shorts and dingy T-shirt." Maddie scanned him with her sea-blue eyes from head to toe. "A little shabby, dork."

"It's summer, and I'm officially off the clock." He pulled his phone from the back pocket of his oldest, threadbare, favorite khaki shorts, which he'd thrown on with his Tom Petty T-shirt. He held up his phone to show off his calendar app. He'd drawn *Wisconsin* over it. "I'm here and comfortable enough to run up the stairs in the lighthouse."

"Cheers, sonny." Graham came up, clutching a tray of pizza fresh out of the stone fire oven, and offered them a slice. "It's lovely, this setup out here. Did you tell him the bloody awful news?"

"Give him a chance to finish his beer." She scowled at his uncle.

"*Grazie.*" He grabbed a slice of heavenly scented pepperoni pizza. "What's going on?"

When Graham opened his mouth, she shushed him.

"It's about the lighthouse." She stirred her cocktail and bit the cherries off the stick. "We met earlier, as you know, to figure out some fundraising ideas."

He resisted the urge to stare at her lips.

Graham snorted. "It's all your brother's fault."

"You both know Gus can do no wrong." Rob glanced about to make sure his brother was out of earshot. "What has he done this time? Win another Emmy award?"

Maddie took a gulp of her drink. "We're in a dire situation. The money to fix the lighthouse has been cut, and you know how Elsie loved the thing. I'm doing what I have to do for her," she said, then scowled at Graham.

The determination in Maddie's voice cut him to the quick.

She could be obstinate; some might say pigheaded. His debate skills were polished by their high school arguments.

Her shoulders stiffened. "I developed a fundraising plan. Unfortunately, it hinged on your brother's celebrity, and he won't be in town. So—"

"Chris Wagner is filling in," Graham sneered. "The wanker."

Rob almost choked on his pizza, then coughed to clear it. As a defense attorney, he'd learned to fine-tune every one of his expressions to disguise all of his appalled reactions, but this time, his facial muscles froze. It took a full second before he smiled, swallowed, and spat out one word. "Oh?"

With Graham and Maddie both clearly upset, he knew his anger or frustration would make everything worse. He set his pizza down and took a long swig of beer. "What did you all come up with? Sorry to make you repeat yourself, Maddie. Elsie and the lighthouse are important."

Graham huffed and strolled to the pier.

Maddie rewarded him with a sisterly hug and a chaste peck on his cheek. Her typical MO, when they crossed paths these days, once again reminded him that they were in the dreaded friend zone. He reconfigured his emotions and let his lawyerly side prevail. "Tell me what's happening."

"I need to come up with a quarter mil for the lighthouse. Starting with July Fourth, and using the star power of Chris Wagner, we're planning a series of fundraisers."

"Has he agreed to it? Were you in contact with him tonight already?" The sound of the d-bag's name was painful to hear and impossible to say. Again, Rob regretted he'd been unable to get Wagner's arse thrown in jail.

"Yes. Yes!" Maddie's voice trembled with excitement. "Gus talked to him directly. No agent or PR person was involved, and

Chris Wagner agreed to come here next week and stay through August. Isn't it great?"

Rob didn't know whose neck he wanted to wring tighter, his brother Gus or the devil himself, Chris Wagner. He took in a deep breath of cool lake air. He couldn't come up with one "great" thing about this situation. Once again, he would be dragged into the toxic circle surrounding Chris Wagner's life. The last thing he'd expected, as he made his escape to Baileys Harbor only three hours ago, but there was no way he'd leave now. His hometown, and especially Maddie, couldn't navigate the vicious human being alone.

"I'm staying at Gus and Lucy's, and here and there, I'll be taking off to get to the races at Elkhart. If you need me for anything, you know how to find me."

"Oh, right, the vintage car races, they're happening. Graham mentioned it."

Once again, she used the overly concerned *big-sister* tone he despised.

"I'll stick around for the Fourth. Sounds as if a lot will be happening then."

"Sure, sure," she said, patting him on his back like a loyal pet. "It's all good, and I'm grateful you'll be here."

Brady came up to them. "You guys okay? I got word Wagner is an asshole."

"He's not my favorite," Rob announced, "but the 'asshole' will bring in the funds for Elsie and the lighthouse."

"Wagner can't be all bad," Maddie protested. "You defended him and won. Right? And he is a good friend of your brother's."

"Not exactly friends. They're both actors and very good at what they do. As for my role, it was simply doing a job to the best of my ability with this client." He added, "If there's a camera around, Wagner is an all-around perfect guy. Unfortunately, when no one is watching, his Hollywood smile disappears. Just make sure you aren't alone with him or that there's a camera always in the vicinity."

"I sort of get it," she said. "Working behind the scenes on *Summer Haven* taught me a lot about the eccentricities of reality TV celebs and famous A-listers."

Scratching his jaw, Rob gazed out at the water. "I did watch a couple of episodes last February, but my caseload was intense. My TV time was severely cut back. I managed to see you romping through a Hamptons vineyard though."

"That was fun. We did a wine-tasting episode. Unfortunately, soon after filming that episode last August, I was asked to leave the show, and Brady called me back to Wisconsin for my mom."

"I'm sorry," he sighed, staring at the boathouse at the end of the pier. Without a doubt, Tyler's sleek red Barracuda racing boat was still docked inside.

He dragged himself back to the present. "Have you ever met the megastar? In person? Talking face-to-face?"

"One time at the Hamptons house while filming. He was very gracious."

"He lied to me, and I was his defense attorney." Rob combed his fingers through his hair. "Keep *liar* in your mind at all times. Even if you go all starstruck, remember, the ass is married with two young daughters. Don't let him convince you otherwise."

"I can handle him. While at FIT, I modeled for some of the world's sleaziest photographers, and I've learned many ways to mitigate depraved and horny goats."

Brady hugged Maddie. "We've been through worse. It will come together."

"I was thinking about heading to Elkhart tonight to meet

with a mechanic about my car in the morning," he said. "But it's late. I'll stick around and keep the schedule open."

"Thanks," she said, gazing at him. Her eyes seemed to shimmer like the lake's surface before he dove into the water.

"Whatever I can do for the lighthouse."

And you.

TOP STORY

Chris Wagner Hugs the Heartland

The Hollywood icon turns into a small-town hero with his latest role: fundraiser and savior of a crumbling American treasure.

BY GEMMA GARNER

JULY

Two months after sexual harassment allegations against him were dropped, Chris Wagner is once again facing the cameras and making appearances to reconnect with his unwavering and adoring fans. Wagner was spotted in Baileys Harbor, a small town tucked in the middle of Door County. The Wisconsin peninsula is an exclusive resort area referred to as the "Cape Cod of the Midwest." No surprise the megastar headed to this idyllic vacation spot, as it's home to his good friend and colleague, Gus Reid.

The star of the now canceled show, *Case Closed*, wore khaki shorts, a red polo shirt, and Birkenstock sandals as he stood on the front porch of the Harbor B&B. Surrounded by an entourage, he greeted fans and the local press.

"Fundraising and philanthropy. It's my mantra. The good people in the heart of the country need me," he said, pulling a small flag from a pot of red geraniums and waving it around. "Happy Fourth of July. With a fresh start, I'm focused on making America a better place for everyone."

Big news! The greatest place is on Lake Michigan.
#lightupdoorcounty #savecanalighthouse
7:18 PM · July 1 ·Twitter/X
603Retweets 42Quote Tweets 5,805Likes

Only last April, Wagner celebrated his win over the "toxic environment of celebrity." Seems he's moved on to greener pastures and confirmed it by the lackluster tweet. **{GG}**

FIVE

"I'm a celebrity stylist who swears like a Foo Fighter and never puts up with shit from anyone," Maddie muttered under her breath while watching Chris Wagner lead his entourage in a stroll around the lighthouse grounds.

"Parading around like he's a king at a castle. Wanker," Graham said. "He's a right prat."

"Give him a chance. This is huge." Maddie closed her eyes and envisioned the check made out to the Cana Island Lighthouse Fund. Like on TV, it would be one of those old-time pieces of cardboard passed to the Publisher's Clearinghouse winner. "And so worth it. Come on, let's see if Kat has any food for us to sample while Mr. Wagner is surveying his temporary stage."

A white canopy tent had been installed beside the light-keeper's house. Maddie joined Kat at one of the many round dining tables and fiddled with her handiwork. Over a decade ago, her mother had given her a beginner's sewing project. After Maddie finished sewing and embroidering over twenty tablecloths, they were used at every fundraiser hosted by Elsie Logerquist. Luckily, Maddie found them in the estate's pantry.

Three tall glass jars—red, white, and blue—shone as centerpieces. Fresh wildflowers sprang above the rims, and sparkling glass confetti, also red, white, and blue, was sprinkled on the tables.

"Can you spot Wagner's table?" Kat asked without hiding her annoyance. "There will be a lot of fireworks, more than we bargained for, if he's not happy this weekend."

"Hear, hear," Graham huffed. "I'm going into the souvenir shop to make sure it's stocked up. Text me. Warn me when he's getting close."

"I know his type. I can handle him," Maddie said. "I mean, *we* can deal with him."

Wagner could bring the lighthouse into the twenty-first century because of his celebrity, and Maddie was going to do everything in her power to create a spectacular and welcoming vibe for him. Then she spotted his table. A tall, high-backed chair covered in gold silk fabric towered like a shiny phallic symbol. "Maybe he's taking this role seriously, like royalty?"

"And his peen needs a gold wrapper?" Kat snorted.

"Think big...I mean outside the box...I..." She gave up. "All of tonight's spots sold out in less than an hour, and the next three nights have waiting lists."

Rolling in cash by the end of July was her first goal, but Maddie knew she'd have to plan for a backup. So far, the FundMe account for donations had gained followers on Instagram, and dollars were trickling in. Her list of hashtags was developing nicely. The two most popular so far were #lightupdoorcounty and #savebaileyslighthouse.

"Wagner's supposed to weigh in on tonight's menu, and he's late." Kat folded a napkin as if perfecting an origami swan. "Please stay with me."

"Relax, your food is outstanding. You have nothing to worry about. I've dealt with this stress while working on *Summer Haven*. As the head stylist, I had to make sure that not one string on anyone's swimsuit would move at all. Even when the stars were swimming or smooching." Maddie pulled out her phone. "They expect perfection, and we've gone above and beyond."

"God, it's great to have you here. I've missed you."

A smidge of guilt slid through her. Maddie couldn't tell Kat. As much as she liked being in Baileys and closer to her biggest client, Sunkissed, she really wanted to get back to her life in New York.

"Wagner will lead an exclusive tour of the lighthouse on the Fourth and pose with guests at the top and then dine with them because they've donated extra dollars. The stats are looking fantastic."

"You sound just like Elsie! She would be incredibly proud of you." Kat grinned. "Following in her footsteps?"

"Hell no. She's like a goddess in Baileys. I'm a mere Earth dweller."

The day Maddie left her hometown to attend FIT for her second degree, all her mother said was, "Have a nice time." As if Maddie hadn't been accepted into the prestigious Fashion Institute of Technology to top off her business degree from Madison with another degree in fashion design. But it was in fashion and not even close to the realm of her mother's earthly causes. It was like Rachel Carson had given birth to Stella McCartney.

"Is Rob coming tonight?" Kat handed her one of the embossed menus.

"No, I doubt it. I haven't even seen him since the council meeting." Maddie stared at the menu until the flutters in her stomach settled. Just hearing Rob's name turned her to Jell-O. How she'd remained so composed the night of his return, she'd never figure out, or maybe the tequila *had* helped. "The mac and cheese with lobster looks delicious. When can I get some?"

"Not until tonight." Kat sat up straighter. "Uh-oh. Here comes His Highness."

As Chris Wagner strode closer, Maddie spotted his signature ocean-blue eyes. Wagner had been compared to (both in talent and looks) the classic Hollywood actor Paul Newman—her mother's favorite. Not because of his eyes but because of his charities.

She stood, smoothed down the lap crease in her shorts, and strode over to meet him, relieved she'd worn her three-inch platform espadrilles. Added to her stature, she almost came eye-to-eye with this bigger-than-life man.

"I'm Maddie Logerquist, Head of Baileys Harbor Chamber of Commerce and organizer of this fundraiser. Pleased to have the opportunity to meet you, Mr. Wagner."

"It's Chris." He shook her hand efficiently. "All of these arrangements have been procured and signed off by Nina, my PR director. So far, it looks adequate."

"It's been a pleasure." Maddie gritted her teeth and smiled. She'd barely slept the past month to get this kickoff weekend organized and every seat filled. Not to mention finding a host of sponsors from all over the peninsula. She turned toward Kat and lifted her brow. "Dinner for tonight will be relaxing. We hope you'll enjoy your time in Baileys Harbor."

Two men dressed in black suits strolled around the tent.

"Nice, I see you brought Agents J and K," she said, for an infusion of humor.

Only Kat laughed.

"Those are my bodyguards. Which reminds me. Who should I speak to about my sleeping arrangements? I've been given a room at the Harbor B&B, and it stinks like old lady perfume. Besides, I need more space for—" He pointed to the guards and the others in his entourage wandering around. "—them. They're too crammed in their rooms."

Maddie overlooked his pompousness, but the presence of his bodyguards alarmed her. She didn't recall their presence while filming *SH*. But the set of a reality TV show was chaotic, and Chris only appeared on one occasion last summer. But better to be safe than sorry when dealing with celebrities and their adoring fans who often went overboard.

She gripped her phone and scrolled through photos of the house. It was secluded on Moonlight Bay, far from prying eyes. She'd been staying with Kat to avoid the estate—rife with Logerquist history. Here was an opportunity to alleviate her guilt since leaving it empty for so long. She showed Chris the pictures. "There's a house not far from here that belongs to my family. There's a hot tub, an indoor swimming pool, and it's isolated, so it will be totally safe."

He grabbed the phone from her. "This may do. Let me show Nina."

When he started to walk away with her phone in his hand, she blocked his path and grabbed it back. "I'll let my brother know you'll be moving your things in this afternoon. It has plenty of space. I'll text you the address." She stared at a distinct scar above his left eyebrow. "What's your number?"

"It's private." He snapped his fingers toward Agent J, or was it K? "Give this woman your number. We'll be moving out of the B&B within the hour."

The agent leaned in and gave her a phone number. She punched in the address to her mother's house. "Brady Logerquist will meet you there at two o'clock." She smiled confidently, without knowing if her brother was in a Coast Guard boat somewhere out in the middle of Lake Michigan. "I think you'll find the estate safe and perfect for your needs."

She quickly texted Brady: ***Get to the house ASAP. For Wagner to stay. I'll explain later.***

Kat handed Chris a menu. "Here's tonight's dinner, Mr. Wagner. The entrée tonight is my specialty. Mac and—"

"This looks delicious," he said without looking up from the menu. "It's Kat Orlov, right?"

Kat blushed. "Yes...but...how?"

"I have all my dieticians assess the restaurants and food options before I go on location. They mentioned your place highly."

Maddie interjected, "As you're the guest of honor, I would like to show you to the top of the lighthouse. Are you interested? There are ninety-seven steps, but reaching the top will be worth it. The view of Lake Michigan is spectacular."

"Now I remember you." He snapped his fingers and pointed at her. "Didn't that guy...what was his name...screw around on you? On *Summer Haven*? Alex Martin?"

In the front pockets of her silk shorts, Maddie balled her hands into fists. She wasn't sure how Chris knew what *really* happened between her and her ex, Alex. She glanced at Kat to stay composed.

"Weren't you obsessed with this lighthouse?" Chris asked.

She shrugged. "This place is in my blood. I'm sure I spoke about it a lot while working on the show. It's a clear blue sky, a perfect summer day. Seventy-five degrees." Wisconsin weather talk was always her go-to for diversion. "Do you want to see the view or not?"

"Absolutely." Chris dramatically swept his arm out for her to walk ahead. "I'm honored to get a look at this classic building. Gus spoke so highly about filming on the island. My next gig is a Scorsese film, but we're filming in Chicago. There may be a scene or two perfect for filming at this location. All good for Baileys Harbor."

"This island has become a viable source of income for the town." She texted Graham. **Coming inside**

He sent back an emoji of *The Scream.*

At the lighthouse entrance, she envisioned the check again as Chris passed through the screen door.

"*Summer Haven* screwed you royally," he said.

"That's one way of looking at it." In New York, she'd learned fast about how celebrities operated. Reality TV had nothing to do with reality. It was all about the fans. Alex Martin was the star of *Summer Haven,* and there wouldn't have been another season if fans knew how he'd screwed around behind her back. Even though her relationship with him was pretty superficial due to his intense mirror-gazing habit, they were perceived by viewers as the show's IT couple. Fans had started calling them "MartQuist."

For the sake of the show, an alternative version of the events was released to the media. According to the tabloids, Maddie had been the one to screw around on the set and broke Alex's precious heart. "It's a reality show, so there are bound to be a lot of dustups and messy feels. Besides, I was only in front of the camera for one season and much preferred to be behind the scenes as the show's fashion consultant and stylist."

Her career in New York was more like a patchwork quilt of fashion-focused gig jobs, so even if she'd lost some social media clout because of a fling with Alex, she wasn't going to let the dick take her down. She'd been juggling fashion photography, styling, influencing, and designing for several clients, hard and high enough to pay the bills. *Summer Haven* was only one dropped ball, and having been asked to leave the show was the best thing for her, with ideal timing—her mother had just been moved into a Baileys hospice.

In the souvenir shop, Graham strode up to them. "Fancy

meeting you, Mr. Wagner. I'm Maddie's right-hand mate. Name's Graham Bilby."

"Bilby? As in the British sports car engineer?" Chris gushed. "The designer of the magnificent Austin-Healey?"

A burst of pride smoothed Graham's craggy face. "My gramps Barrie was the genius."

While they chatted about British sports cars, she sensed Graham had entered into a bromance with the Hollywood star but knew it would be fleeting.

Her other most trusted volunteer, Agnes, gazed toward Chris and whispered, "Don't think I've seen such a handsome, tall drink of water in a long time."

Maddie interrupted the men, "Okay, Mr. Wagner. Ready? Let's get up to the bird's nest." She untied her espadrilles, dropped them in a filing cabinet behind her desk, and retrieved her cowboy boots.

"Please, all of you, it's Chris. We're going to be working together closely."

Agnes turned a shade of red darker than Graham's cheeks. Sighing, Maddie grabbed a pair of binoculars off the counter and opened the hand-sewn velvet drapes leading into the light-house vestibule. "Follow me."

Thick cream-colored cinder blocks surrounded them in the damp enclosure. The floor was made of concrete and gravel, and each step of the iron circular staircase was an ornate design of scrolls and curls. "As we climb to the viewing deck, you'll pass portholes. You'll see unique angles of the lake and beach. There are two hatches, so watch your head."

She slung the binocs around her neck, smiled at Chris, and started up the stairs. No matter how many times she made this exhausting trip, the lighthouse centered and grounded her the higher she climbed, providing a genuine sense of home.

Behind her, Chris's breath was steady, but when she turned

back to check on him, he had paused at the porthole at the halfway point. "All right?"

He nodded. "Enjoying the view."

She proceeded to the top and pointed out the prism. "This is what has to be updated. And thanks to you, we'll be closer to the necessary funds."

"My pleasure," he groaned. "It's a good thing I work out twice a day, but stairs? Preparing for them is impossible. God, how in the hell do you all do this every day?"

"We're almost there. Once you're outside, I promise, you'll be able to take in a deep breath of lake air and bask in the sunshine."

"How come you aren't out of breath?"

"I was a swimmer," she said. "It's all in the pacing."

"Makes sense. Long arms. Long legs."

"Yep, my superpower." Just like her height, most people—men and women—regularly noticed her physique. She opened the last hatch and climbed onto the viewing deck. Maddie held out a hand to help Chris through. His tightly cropped hair had been smoothed down flat. Even with beads of sweat clinging to his forehead and hair, he really was handsome.

"Thanks." He squinted as his eyes adjusted to the bright sunlight and then shaded them with his hand. "Once a night? Right? Otherwise, these stairs will kill me."

She chuckled. "Only once, during the fireworks on the night of the 4th. I promise it will be easy."

For just a moment, Maddie looked out at the lake, and her palms grew damp. When would the sight of water stop stressing her out? She handed the binoculars to Chris. "There are a lot of sailboats out on the water today. You should walk around and take a look."

She crouched down against the metal-lined wall of the lighthouse for some shade and checked messages. Brady had texted her. **WTF?**

Had offering her mother's home to a complete stranger been too impulsive? Of course. It was because of this darn lighthouse! She let out a growl and responded.

It seemed necessary, Brady. Please...

An endless ellipsis.

Will be at the house to welcome Wagner. But you need to go meet Rob at the Beacon at 2. Promised him a game.

Her relief came and left as the butterflies in her stomach fluttered about again. Bowling hadn't been on her itinerary today, but a chance to see Rob? She couldn't put on a pair of ugly shoes fast enough.

She texted. **Two is fine**

"There you are." Chris stooped down. "You okay?"

She shielded her eyes and looked up at him. "Yes, of course, just a little warm up here. We should get going. Brady will be meeting you at the house pretty soon."

"Thanks again for the upgrade in accommodations." Grabbing her hand, he pulled her upright. "I learned about a great swimming spot called Cave Point. Any chance you want to cool off and go for a swim with me later?"

"No, thank you. I have to meet another benefactor." She tried not to grimace. He'd squeezed her hand and held it infinitely too long for a normal, friendly gesture. A tinge of the creeps trickling down her spine, she gently dropped his hand and took the binoculars from him. "Make sure to be back here by six. I'm the official photographer for these events, and I'd like to take some pre-dinner shots."

Climbing down the stairs with Wagner ahead of her, she focused on Rob and getting to the Beacon. Finally, they landed in the vestibule, and she had a primal urge to be as far away as possible from the guy.

"Thanks for the private tour," he said, politely drawing the blue curtain open for her. "I'll be on my best behavior tonight for the photos."

Passing by him, she stepped out of the vestibule and into the souvenir shop. At the sight of Agnes and Graham, her skin stopped crawling.

"Agent J or K will contact you if I need anything." Wagner gave her a royal wave and left.

As soon as the screen door slammed shut behind him, Maddie let out a long breath of relief and soaked her hands in sanitizer. Then she rubbed in lavender lotion to calm down.

She retrieved her platforms and a pair of socks from the desk drawer and dropped them into her bag. It was time to go bowling. She'd long despised the sport, if you could even call it that, yet tossing a stinky eight-pound ball down the alleys in the Beacon was an integral part of her history with Rob. Starting in middle school, they played on the same league team every summer. Even after going to Madison, she came home for the summer in order to be near Rob on the team. Then, during her last two years at UW-Madison, when Rob was a freshman and then a sophomore, they met up and played at Dream Lanes. Yep, she'd been bowling for love for quite some time. Maybe even a bowling slut, thanks to Rob.

SIX

After taking his brother's dogs for a run around the park at Cave Point, Rob dropped them at home and headed to the Beacon. He traded in his running shoes for a pair of green-and-gold bowling shoes and glanced around the crowded alleys for Brady, but he wasn't visible. Rob sent him a text. **Where are you?**

With Wagner arriving in Baileys, Rob had been avoiding Main Street to eliminate any chance of running into his most despicable client with whom he had officially broken ties. Rob had all the paperwork—signed, certified, and locked up in the Chicago office—to prove it.

His stomach growled a reminder he hadn't eaten lunch, so he went to sit at the diner's counter. The combo of fried food and a loud bowling alley eased him. More importantly, he was invisible.

He ordered a fish fry as the waitress placed a glass of water in front of him. Rubbing his thumb across the detailed image on the drink coaster, he admired the red die-cut with the Beacon's logo—a 1920s Rambler with a tommy gun propped in the car's window. His phone pinged with a message from Brady. **Something came up. Sending in a proxy.**

He assumed (a lawyer no-no) and hoped (another lawyer no-no) Maddie was on her way.

"Like it?" Maddie asked, sliding onto the seat beside him. "It's one of my designs."

"Yes. Yes...it's lovely." His smile broke loose, making him, undoubtedly, look daft. But hell, he couldn't resist. Maddie's sea-blue eyes once again stole his breath. "Shouldn't you be at the lighthouse? Isn't tonight the first fundraiser?"

She asked the waitress for a Spotted Cow and grabbed a handful of popcorn from the bowl on the bar. "It doesn't start until seven, and I don't have to be there until six. I came directly here from the island, and everything looks fantastic. To top it off, I gave Chris a tour of the lighthouse, and he—"

"Chris? You're on a first-name basis?" He pushed the pic of Wagner's smug face out of his mind. "Aren't you fuzzing up the line between personal and professional?"

"Fuzzing? Is that a legal term? Look, if you want to blame anyone, blame the state. They cut the funding, and I have to do whatever I can to save the lighthouse. It's been part of my family since the 1800s. It's my darn legacy."

He fiddled with the coaster and sighed. "I'm a fan of Baileys' most famous tourist attraction, and believe me, I'm cheering you on along with the Logerquist women from the past.

"It's okay. Taking care of Elsie's town has taught me a lot." She sounded worn-out.

"I sense a *but* coming." He thanked the waitress for his order and dribbled some malt vinegar on his fish.

"The *but* is," she said, staring at his food and taking in a big sniff. "May I?"

He grinned at how easily they fell back into a familiar pattern and pushed the plate toward her. "Go ahead, dig in and have some of the chips. Seems like you need some sustenance before tonight."

"Oy, mate, they're called french fries. Chip chip cheerio. Bob's your uncle..."

Her nervous Cockney wasn't half-bad, and he much preferred it to her big-sister tone. "Nice try. I've been living here in the US for a long time. Tell me. Out with it. What is your big *but?*"

"I *bloody* miss New York." Maddie took a big bite of a chip.

"Who wouldn't? It's a wicked city and has been your home since..." He filled his mouth with a bite of fish and chewed hard to avoid saying it out loud. *Since we lost Tyler.* "A long time."

After an uncomfortable pause, he added, "Lovely fish and chips."

"Don't let it go to your head. Kat cooks a lot for your Uncle Graham."

"Explains why there's a bottle of malt vinegar on the counter in a bowling alley." He dug into his meal and let Maddie have access to his plate. "My uncle deserves it."

"Absolutely. And the lighthouse, you know, I wouldn't have survived running the sucker without all Graham's cheesy British humor. I think he channels *Monty Python* 24/7."

Rob chuckled. As the new kid in Baileys Harbor, he had stuck out like a sore thumb. His red hair, English accent, and gawky stature made him a joke for the plaid-shirted wannabe rednecks in middle school. Uncle Graham, with his love of cars, had been Rob's lifeline, inspiration, and the reason he'd gone to law school.

"Maddie," Rob said cautiously. He had to get it out in the open. "I know your family legacy needs you, but please think of yourself. My dealings with Wagner—a closed chapter now—have been challenging, to say the least. He's a con man who used my brother and me."

"What do you mean? I'm desperate to take in money, not get swindled."

"Whoa, wait, sorry. He conned me, professionally speaking. Typically, I defend people who have been burned by the justice system. There are a lot of folks who are innocent but have been convicted by inadequate representation. But then there are those like Wagner, who take advantage of the system and rip it off." A struggle of conscience had been playing tug-o'-war in his head since Wagner was declared innocent. He'd done his job and scored another win, which usually was good, but for the first time in his career, the coup felt dodgy.

"Chris Wagner was found not guilty," she said. "It's a valid fact, right, Mr. Attorney?"

He briefly wondered if the facts had let him down or wholeheartedly led him on. "There's more to it, and because of client privilege, I can't say much." He let out a long breath. "Except this: Hollywood seems to garner strength from sycophants, and Wagner is a fantastic actor and a liar on the sociopathic level. He has a way of getting exactly what he wants and doesn't give a damn about anyone else."

She stared down at the plate and leisurely dredged a chip through a puddle of malt vinegar. "Don't freak out, but I opened up Elsie's house to him."

"You're joking?" But he knew she wasn't mucking about. Ever since they'd been teens, they were like making taffy. She would *push*, and he would *pull*. "So now you'll be staying under the same roof as him. How bloody fantastic."

"Oh no! I'm not living there!" She pointed toward the ceiling. "I've been rooming with Kat in her place upstairs. The estate, it's way too empty." She glanced at her Apple Watch. "Brady's there now to help him and his entourage move in."

A small sense of relief came and went. "Get Elsie out of there. Your mum's ashes need to be put somewhere safe." He recalled how the wall of trophies had been taken down and wondered if the indoor pool was ever opened. But he wasn't about to ask her. "Anything private or personal on the property?"

"Aren't you overreacting? What's the guy going to do with the remains of my mom? Even I haven't figured out where she wants to be laid to rest."

"What?" He shook his head to stay focused. One thing at a time. "I really don't know what Wagner would do with Elsie, but trust me, if there is something important to you, or a weak spot, he'll figure it out and use it against you."

After crossing one long leg over the other, she clasped her fingers around her knee and dropped her head. "Oh, shit."

"Did you tell him something personal?"

Maddie shook her head.

"Was he belligerent?" Rob couldn't forget how crass Wagner had been toward Fran back in Chicago.

"Not really." She hunched toward him. "It was strange. He knew so many details about all of us. Kat, Graham, and he even charmed Agnes. But then, he knew something about me that wasn't public knowledge. I just figured he had some inside source from *Summer Haven*."

"Wagner thrives on gossip," he said, without thinking too hard about all the lies his former client had told to get him off the hook. "Was it an obscure detail overlooked by *Cue*? I know the industry rag is like his Bible."

"The *Cue*?" she asked, tapping the side of her forehead with one finger.

"You're a celebrity stylist, and you don't read the *Cue*?"

"Yes, occasionally and on a need-to-know basis." She rolled her eyes. "The key word is stylist. I read *WWD* obsessively... *Women's Wear Daily*. But Chris, he knew and was sympathetic about how Alex Martin cheated on me. Even though most of the fans thought I was the cheater. This type of gossip fuels reality shows like *SH*."

Rob wanted to reach out and hug her, but it felt like an act of brotherly support. He was pretty sure about being in the friend zone and wasn't thrilled about it. So, he carefully threaded his fingers between hers and squeezed. "I knew the story was total bullshit."

When she tightened her grip on his hands, the sounds around them muffled. His clearest thoughts contained only Maddie's nearness and presence. He swallowed his breath for fear she'd pull away. The last time he held on too tight, he had saved her life but ultimately lost her.

Right after Tyler died, she left for New York to attend FIT.

"That's because we've been through a lot together." Maddie kept hold of his hand and lightly caressed his jawline. "Even if Chris knew what really happened between Alex and me, it's nothing important. Alex was and is a dolt. We met five years ago through a mutual friend, and he got me the gig as the show stylist. For the first four years, he barely noticed me while in the Hamptons. Then, last year, we had a silly summer fling, nothing serious. Except fans started calling us MartQuist."

"Good to know." He sounded official, but her proximity made it difficult for him to maintain a courtroom demeanor. "But again, I've learned from working with Wagner, he's slippery. And since he's here to fundraise for the lighthouse, he will make sure to know about everything important to you."

"Okay, true, but he doesn't seem to be the brightest bulb in the box. It seems like there isn't a lot going on behind his celebrated blue eyes." She let go of his hands. "Do you know anything about the scar above his eye?"

"No," he said to avoid divulging any details. He'd heard that Wagner had bumped into a corner wall on some set. For the duration of the case, Rob had tried to find out the truth about the scar, but with no success. Only one hint passed across his desk: something had happened in the Hamptons, the location of Wagner's vacation home. "I do know this though. His celebrated blue eyes are another one of his cons. Fake. Colored contacts."

"Disappointing and good to know. Well, if Chris wants something from me, he'll be out of luck. I don't have a pot to piss in, and there are no hidden treasures worth having, at least nothing a mighty megastar would want."

Rob arched his brow as high as possible. "There is the legacy and Baileys. You may not be the keeper of Gotham, but you are Elsie's daughter."

"I'm keeping a sleepy town in business and have to maintain a lot of plants, gardens, and flowers so they don't wind up on the endangered species list. Doesn't sound like any of it would be of interest to Wagner. Besides, he told me his next movie is with Scorsese." She lifted her palms up and down like a scale of justice. "Scorsese? Or lighthouse? Which would you choose if you were a famous actor?"

"Maybe you're right." His first instinct was to dig out all his resources on the case to review and assess. What was Wagner's endgame? Instead, he buried his cold, overactive legal sense. But his reserve of pent-up frustration needed a release. As long as he was at the bowling alley and in the proper shoes, he asked, "Wanna bowl a game?"

"Do I really want to? No. But I will because I want to play... and beat you."

"We're not swimming. You do realize we'll be in the same lane, and timing is inconsequential?"

As they strolled over to the bowling lanes, he kept a foot-long distance between them, to make sure his damn pounding heart couldn't be overheard. Lounging on the leather sofa, he crossed his legs at the ankles to portray a picture of perfect relaxation. *Utter rubbish*, as Uncle Graham would say.

"Just once, I'd love to beat you at something," she said, eyeing the shiny balls spitting out of the chrome mouth. "I'm grabbing the heaviest Brunswick."

"More power, babe. Go for it."

Her first turn, she tumbled all the pins for a strike. He also started off with a strike, but then it went downhill fast. He bowled two gutters but wasn't surprised. It was hard to keep calm, bowling again with Maddie.

Dancing around the lane, Maddie celebrated her streak of strikes. When she teased him and gave him one of her supreme smiles, he finally relaxed.

SEVEN

Savoring the cool breeze on the lighthouse viewing deck, Maddie spotted the Coast Guard boat about a mile away from shore. Through the binoculars, she spied Brady on the rig as the boat meandered around the lake, then circled around the barge loaded with barrels of explosives prepped for tomorrow night's fireworks.

She sent her brother a quick text. ***Ahoy, Captain Logerquist. Thanks***

The first two fundraisers had gone without a hitch, giving her a sense of accomplishment, but it was way too early to get cocky. Guests strolled about the top of the lighthouse and gazed out at the fabulous moonlit view of the lake. When a woman tripped and grabbed hold of the guardrail, Maddie shoved her phone in her back pocket and sucked in a breath. Time to get back to work and take care of the **#LightUP** donors.

"Enjoying yourself?" She glanced at the name tag bouncing on the woman's Harley-Davidson tank top. "Linda?"

She grunted. "Climbing to the top has been a workout. How many stairs?"

"Ninety-seven. Every one of the wrought-iron steps is worth

it." Only the third night, and she had to try like hell not to sound like a robot. "There's nowhere in Door County with such a spectacular view," she said again, for what seemed like the millionth time.

"We're here for the Vintage Boat Festival, and I nearly fell off the motorcycle when I saw the news about Chris Wagner. I couldn't believe it." Linda hastily added, "And you. I wanted to meet you. It really sucked when Alex forced you off *Summer Haven*."

"Really nice of you to say." She'd grown past her one summer on the show and graciously accepted that she and her lighthouse had been upstaged by Chris. It was a brief TV role she was okay with giving up. "Chris Wagner is pretty hot and definitely worth stopping at a lighthouse for. Thanks for coming."

Maddie adjusted her headset to make sure Kat's ETA for the appetizer came in clearly. Linda stepped back and stumbled. Maddie grabbed the woman's elbow and assisted her upright. "You okay?"

"Oh sure, I really didn't need this wine," she said, pulling out a silver flask from her biker bag.

"You'll need to descend immediately," Maddie instructed. "As it states in the waiver you signed, alcohol is not allowed in the lighthouse. The fireman will guide you down to the ground. Hold tight to the railing, please."

"Michael, 9-1-1 on the eastern side," she yelled into her walkie.

"You know, you're really not as pretty as I expected for a star and influencer." Linda's voice had thickened, and Maddie spotted her bloodshot eyes.

"Sorry to disappoint you." How did this woman get past her? The thick black mascara must have hidden them. Maddie swore under her breath. "Please, as soon as you're on the ground, get some water and a snack in the souvenir shop."

"Here," Michael shouted, waving his arms as he approached Linda from behind.

"I'm perfectly fine. These are tough boots." Linda kicked out her foot and swayed backward. Michael swooped in to steady her.

"Perfect timing." Maddie sighed and made a mental note to look closely at each guest, especially their eyes, as they climbed onto the lighthouse deck.

Before escorting Linda down, Michael passed by and mouthed, "It's okay."

At least she worked out this glitch tonight and not tomorrow night when Chris Wagner would be up on the viewing deck. Stepping around the perimeter, she kept her left hand steady on the guardrail. With a plastered-on smile, she shook hands with the rest of the guests and gave her usual speech, then made sure to sniff for any alcohol. After finishing the circle, Kat's voice blasted into her ear. "Harley woman's safe. You can start getting folks down here for my marvelous food."

"Ten-four," Maddie yelled into the walkie. She asked each of the remaining guests, mostly female, to start descending the stairs. "Take your time, folks. Dinner's ready, but if you want to eat dessert first, go ahead. Life is short, and Kat's cherry pie is waiting for you. Then Chris Wagner can be your à la mode."

After the last person climbed through the deck opening and Maddie was alone, the waves of Lake Michigan's waters were illuminated by red lights. Sirens blared from the Coast Guard boat. She peered through her binoculars and saw a sleek red speedboat moving way too fast and too close to the rocky shoreline. Brady's boat pursued and quickly caught up with the renegade boat, and recognition dawned on her.

It was Tyler's Barracuda. Her deceased brother's most valuable possession with Chris Wagner behind the wheel and playing captain.

What the hell?

"Hello, hello, hello." His drawling voice was loud and clear, thanks to a megaphone. "Are we ready to get lit for the lighthouse?"

What is going on? Maddie's fingers trembled as she texted Brady. *How did he get the boat?*

The binoculars pressed hard against her eyes, she saw Wagner, without a shirt, waving at the onlookers on the ground below her. The guy was posing and acting like Matthew McConaughey.

She dropped the binocs and screamed into the walkie, "Mayday, Mayday. Or SOS. What's going on down there, Kat?"

Through the screeching, she heard Kat laughing. "He's a prize ass, and the women are loving it."

Waiting for a response from Brady, she watched as he pulled alongside the speedboat.

"Hey, hey, look who's picking me up," Wagner shouted. "Should I have the mighty Coast Guard bring me to shore?"

Cheers and catcalls came from the invitees on the ground.

Seeing Tyler's precious boat made her want to scream and yell, so she quickly climbed down and paced her breathing to stay calm. Once in the vestibule, she found the emergency first aid kit and swallowed a handful of Tums, and sat down on the bottom step until her stomach stopped churning with anger.

Her phone pinged.

Brady: *We got the douchebag off the boat in a raft and on shore. He's drunk. Not issuing a ticket. Yet. Tell me how you want to roll with this ass.*

Maddie: *Can you get Tyler's boat back to the house safely?*

Yes

Maddie slipped her phone into the side of her cowboy boot and stood. She brushed gravel debris from her bum and strode into the souvenir shop. Graham and Agnes ran up to her.

"What do you want to do to the idiot?" Graham demanded.

"He'd been so charming." Agnes's voice dropped off as if she were in a trance of disbelief.

"The show goes on. If I do anything to make him seem like a bigger dick, it will make me and this darn lighthouse look like complete killjoys. People love him, and we don't want to become the villains. Stay here. If anyone comes in to ask what's going on, just say this is one of Baileys' traditions on the third of July."

She went outside and joined the group of women who'd gathered on the edge of the island, waving excitedly toward the beach and its pier. The dining tent was quiet but for the wait-staff snapping pictures. Maddie strained to see if she could find Chris's PR woman in the crowd of chatting fans, gave up, then ducked between and around the women to get a closer look at the shoreline.

Chris Wagner hopped off the rubber raft and climbed onto the pier, then wrapped his bare arm over Kat's shoulders like a drunken sailor. After they hiked up the embankment, Wagner split from Kat and jogged up to her. "What an amazing, diabolical entrance!"

Before his entourage or guards whisked him away from the fans, Maddie went on the offensive. "Hey, ladies, now's your chance to get one-on-one pics with a bare-chested Chris Wagner. Did someone say romance? Or Matthew McConaughey? Form a line. Linda, you're up first."

When Linda squealed, Wagner scowled and clutched his ear.

"Let's not get too excited. I need to clean up and pose properly for the cameras. Can't be looking like some cliché romance cover. Wouldn't be good for me."

"Impossible. You are beautiful—" Linda pinched his cheek "—with short hair. More like Chris Evans."

Chris reared away as if he'd been branded, but his smile stayed locked across his face.

Maddie suspected that comparisons to any other famous *Chris* had calamitous effects on his fragile ego.

"Smooth move, boss," Kat whispered as she stood beside her. "You think he can handle it?"

"After the completely idiotic move he pulled, he's going to shut up and take photos with everyone here, even if he acts like a drunk shithead. He's our rockstar for the lighthouse, and clearly, he hadn't thought this through." She watched her brother's red boat bounce on the water as the Coast Guard towed it away. "Tonight's event isn't as big as tomorrow's. Thankfully, only a small amount of press are here."

"What a relief. I'll go grab him some water," Kat said, jogging back to the tent.

Agents J and K tried to close in on the superstar, but the women encircled him.

Maddie yelled, "Okay, folks, let's all go into the souvenir shop. There will be plenty of time to meet Chris Wagner...one-on-one."

Maddie caught sight of a demonic leer before it disappeared from the star's face.

Once inside, Graham was holding on to an old Polaroid camera; then he tossed the actor a T-shirt with a picture of a lighthouse on it. "Oy, mate, get by the bookshelf. It makes a lovely step-and-repeat, doesn't it?"

"No need, but thanks, Graham." Maddie snatched the shirt from Chris's hand and decided she would call him Wagner from now on.

With a smirk, the bare-chested Wagner took his place in front of the lighthouse's expansive display of books and lighthouse photos.

One by one, each woman who had paid to see him as he sat at a distance was now able to stand close to him, skin-to-skin, and have a picture taken with him. Every time he smiled, Maddie thought she heard his teeth grinding. While Graham took the Polaroid shots, Maddie found her Canon and started shooting professional pics to use for the lighthouse.

The women were incredibly gracious, smiling and laughing while posing with the celebrity. Maddie relaxed a smidge and laughed a bit. Even if the vibe coming from Wagner wasn't one of joy, he eventually came around and joined in on the schtick, dropping some of the women back like a romance hero but without the long hair.

Afterward, all the women thanked her profusely for one of the best times they'd had in a long time. Maddie wasn't sure how, but she'd come out on top of this fiasco.

Wagner strutted up to her. "Is it okay if I leave and skip dinner?"

"No way. Dinner is waiting, and your golden throne is ready." Maddie crossed her arms and stood to her full height. "And if there's even one teeny tiny scratch on the boat, you'll be getting a bill for extensive repairs from the Logerquist estate."

Nina appeared, handing Wagner a hanger with a dress shirt and a suit coat. "I told you this was a wicked bad idea. For Pete's sake, please take my advice. This is why you pay for a PR specialist."

"I've gotten this far, almost to the moon, without your wise words, Nina," he said, grimacing.

"I'll let you know how much the ticket from the Coast Guard will be ASAP," Maddie declared. "And for tomorrow night, get here safely from land, not water. No more bullshit stunts, please."

"No worries, I'll be on my best behavior."

The balloon in Maddie's chest almost popped but didn't. Someone must have been looking out for her.

EIGHT

Humphrey, the bigger of the two dogs, trapped Rob on the side of the bed. With tired growls coming from both he and the dog, Rob grabbed his phone off the bedside table. The Rolling Stones song "Tumbling Dice" stopped blaring when he answered it.

"This better be important, Graham."

"Oi, boy. Wake up. She's heading your way."

"Is Maddie okay?" Rob jolted upright so fast that Humphrey hopped off the bed. The smaller dog, Bogart, quickly nicked the warm spot. "What did he do?"

"She's fine, but Wagner is a right arse. He stole Tyler's boat out of the Logerquist boathouse and went for a joyride."

With one hand, he clawed on his sweats. "What a complete arse. Where's the boat now?"

"Brady took care of it. He'll let us know if there's any damage." Graham sounded exhausted. "Any chance Gus can get here and take over for the wanker?"

"No idea. Gotta go, I hear her driving up." Rob ended the call and threw on a T-shirt as Humphrey crawled back to bed. When he opened the front door, Maddie marched inside. Her cowboy boots clacked on the wood floor and echoed off the great room's high ceiling. "Hey."

She turned around. "Thank god you're here."

"It's midnight, not sure where else I'd be." He closed the door softly. "What's going on?"

"You don't fool me. I'm sure Graham rang you." She plopped down on the couch and rubbed her chin. Her voice trembled. "Wagner's a bastard. Total dickwad."

Rob's inclination to hug her was replaced with an offer of something to drink. He grabbed a beer out of the refrigerator. "Sam Adams good?"

"Sure, but anything stronger?"

"Sorry, no. It's a dry house. Gus is an—"

"Recovering alcoholic. Yes. I know. Just in a tizzy." She dropped her head back and looked at the ceiling beams. "I think I handled Wagner like a fantastic mob fixer, but I really pissed him off."

Rob handed her the bottle of brew and sank onto the couch beside her.

Crossing her legs, she faced him. "Tyler's red boat. It was like his baby, his pride and joy. How the hell? Wagner's a monster for even looking at my brother's most prized possession."

"I was curious if the Ferrari-on-water was still being stored at the house." He settled back against the cushion, and a small relief crept through him. For the first time, Maddie had said Tyler's name out loud to him. "How's Brady?"

"Shit. I haven't called him yet. He was supposed to update me, but I came right here. During dinner all night, I sewed together stories about Wagner, so the donors thought his arrival by boat was a planned surprise." She guzzled the beer, checked her phone, and dropped it between them. "Nothing."

"Call him. It's important," he said. "Knowing Brady, he's still inspecting every inch of the boat with a magnifying glass."

Gazing at her beer bottle, she remained silent.

His next words and movements collided in his mind. He was a realist when it came to Maddie. It was simplest to accept their relationship for what it was, a deep friendship that began in middle school when they had each other's backs. Passion only entered the equation later, during high school. Then, when it did get hot and heavy, his mum's death hindered most of his emotions. The loss of Tyler squashed what was left. Rob couldn't make sense of the timing and decided not to lose time thinking about it.

"Go ahead, talk to your brother. You'll feel better."

"If that were true, I wouldn't be here talking to you," she said without looking up. "I should have listened closer to your warnings about Wagner. PS, not calling him Chris anymore. You were right."

"Not exactly a feel-good update." He waited for more than a second, then sighed. "I'm sorry. If it's any consolation, Wagner duped me, too."

She lifted an eyebrow toward him. "I have a hard time believing you were 'duped' by the jackass. You're the smartest guy I know."

"Thanks for the vote of confidence, but Wagner swindled me out of my pride. His original story was one of the saddest things I'd ever encountered. About how all his staff and co-stars on the show were out to get him. So, even when one of the former stars on his show came to me accusing him of firing her for no reason...I believed him over her. He'd been so pro-women and so highly regarded in the business, and according to Gus, the guy was one step away from sainthood for all the doors he's opened for women."

"Wagner is a quintessential evil chameleon. He had your

Uncle Graham eating out of his palm. They talked about cars like they were people."

"Well, we are talking about Graham. Thanks to his love of car racing, I survived high school," he said fondly. His uncle had been there for him more often than his father, who had had his hands full taking care of his mum and her addictions.

"What about me? And Brady. And Tyler." She tapped his bottle of beer. "Don't we get some props?"

Rob mashed his lips together. "The Logerquist trio. The only people who would drive to Lake Geneva with me to meet Gary Gygax."

She found a throw pillow and playfully slapped him with it. "You lied to us. Told us we were going to the lake to lie around on the beach."

"I didn't lie. We did go, after—"

"A six-hour game of Dungeons and Dragons? By the time we made it to the beach, it was dark."

"Hey, you took a lot of fantastic photos of the three of us playing D&D with the creator of the game. He died a couple years later, so I bet they're worth something."

"Darn, I better go dig them up. Wagner might find them and sell them or something."

"Not important or flashy enough for him," he said. "At least, I don't think so."

Shaking her head, she gave him a lopsided grin. "It makes me sick thinking about how you were treated when you moved here from England. I never understood cruelty until I witnessed the boys on my own wrestling team and our swimming team tease and bully you about—"

"Everything?" He chuckled. "One time, the worst of them accused me of being a communist because of my red hair."

Laughing, she almost spit out her sip of beer. "Your class of sophomores had to have been full of knuckle draggers. Thank goodness you and the twins yanked up the grade point for the rest of the bozos. Man, I was so glad to graduate."

"You were able to escape the madness two years before me."

"I left you in good hands with Brady and Tyler."

Before Maddie left for Madison, Rob hadn't thought she'd noticed him outside the damn bowling league. She'd been two years older and tight with Gus. As seniors, they were the king and queen of homecoming. He was the nerdy one who followed them around. Like he was still eating paste, and they were sipping champagne. "You three kept me sane back in the day."

"I think Brady and Tyler were less mischievous around you. They were always playing tricks on me and Mom, but with you...they were more serious."

"It's my special sauce. Mix the dork with an upper crusty British know-it-all, and they were easily pacified."

She rolled her eyes. "And your love of all fast-moving things. Especially boats and cars."

"Well, true."

Her phone pinged.

"Brady busted Wagner. Gave him a ticket. Ten grand."

"Wow." Rob dropped his jaw. "A lot of cash. But he's got it."

She read the message aloud. "Cited with reckless endangerment. Fifteen other boats in the water. The barge with the fireworks. Explosives."

His need to protect Maddie was somewhere, but being alone with her after so many years apart, a deep desire pulled... oh hell. His imagination took hold, and he wondered if she still made that cooing sound, like a mourning dove, as he luxuriously planted kisses along the entire length of her neck. *Collo bellissimo.* He cleared his throat and crossed his legs.

"The fine is good," she continued, "but I'm sure a drop in the bucket for the superstar. What about the Fourth celebration? What if he pulls another stunt tomorrow night? Even worse?"

"Probably not." He adjusted the throw pillow on his lap. "Since this PR excursion is being paid for by his studio, most likely his insurance will go up if he doesn't get his act together. He's on very thin ice after the lawsuit and needs to be seen as dependable and trustworthy. His reputation isn't in tatters, but it isn't solid either. Wagner's agent is probably on the phone with him as we speak, reading his contract to him."

"Do you ever get tired of being right all the time?"

"It's exhausting." He stretched out his legs and set his feet on the coffee table, carefully keeping the pillow over his gray workout sweats. "Maybe I should just learn to keep my mouth shut."

"Don't you dare. If it weren't for you, I'd be gone. Dragged under the tow with Tyler."

All the air left his lungs. For the past decade, he'd learned to live with the repercussions of one treacherous night out on the lake. He rubbed his temples. "It's nice when you say Tyler's name."

"I don't mean to ignore it...it's just, I try not to think about that time." She inched closer to him. Her breath warmed his cheek. "The whole day was such a blur. One minute, the four of us were on a boat looking for sunken treasure. I had my tried and true Canon in hand and at the ready. Then Tyler jumped overboard to get a better look at the shipwreck, and he didn't come up."

He swallowed down the lump in his throat. "The day used to play over and over in my mind. Every night. For the longest time."

Being near Maddie, a lightness overcame him. "I think Tyler saw something near the remains of that stupid shipwreck, and he had to have the bloody thing. When he swam after it, the riptide captured him."

She sighed.

When her shoulders trembled, he pulled her into his chest. "There was nothing any of us could do."

"I was a fantastic swimmer... I should have at least...tried." She wiped her nose on his T-shirt.

He buried his chin into her hair. "But Brady was a better swimmer. And he jumped in and immediately came back out. He dove under for less than a second and came up when he didn't see Tyler. Rip currents are invisible monsters."

She wrapped her arms around his waist and said softly, "I've missed you."

Rob wasn't sure how to respond. He'd missed her terribly. There was a hole within him, a place where she had once been part of him, and no matter who he was with, the emptiness never went away. It wasn't like Maddie wasn't accessible. They called and talked, but he hadn't been able to shake off the misery. That his one decision, to hold her tight so she wouldn't jump off the boat to look for Tyler, had been the undoing. Like the rip current yanking Tyler from this earth altered or stole away Rob and Maddie's bond.

"I'm not always right, Maddie. But making sure you didn't jump out of the boat and try to save Tyler was the one decision I won't ever regret. I'm sorry if you ever believed I was guilty of restraining you or making the situation worse. But in my heart of hearts, I knew, Brady and I would have lost you, too. I'm sorry for any pain I unintentionally caused you." He cleared his throat. "And I've missed you, too. Terribly."

NINE

The debris strewn around the tables lightened Maddie's heart. All of the guests had gone home happy. Stars had filled their eyes from watching fireworks and meeting Wagner. She looked around for the man of the day. He might be a wanker, but after all was said and done, the lighthouse would be much closer to getting the necessary repairs after tonight's success. She was on cloud nine.

She checked the grounds to see if anyone was still working and then wandered through the dining tent. Both spaces were deserted. Graham and Agnes, looking exhausted, had left after the fireworks. Only Kat, who was still cleaning dishes, was in the lighthouse kitchen. Maddie grabbed a couple of dishes and forgotten forks off a table and went to meet her. Anything else could be done the next morning, and Maddie wanted to get home and celebrate.

Hopefully, Rob was still up.

She dropped the cutlery in the kitchen sink. Without seeing Kat, she went into the still souvenir shop. "Kat?"

Maybe she'd gone out while Maddie had come in. At her

desk, she peeled off her platforms and dropped them in the filing cabinet under her desk. When her cowboy boots hugged her feet, Maddie sighed. She took in a deep breath and let the scent of sulfur tickle her nose. She laughed out loud. From this morning's parade to the celebrations on Main Street and tonight's fireworks, the holiday had been crowded with delighted people. She couldn't wait to see how much money folks had dug out of their pockets and donated to the lighthouse.

Her phone pinged. It was Rob. ***Up for a nightcap?***

Yes. Thank you. I'll head to you shortly.

He responded. ***Patrón shots are set to go.***

She texted ***Sweet*** and searched for an appropriate emoji but couldn't find one to describe her feelings. After they'd talked last night, it was like a whole new chapter with Rob had opened up. She settled for the *cool* emoji instead of delaying her trip over to him.

"There you are," Wagner drawled. "Thought you'd left."

She wondered if the asshat knew how bad his McConaughey imitation was. "Finishing up a few details."

His arms-across-the-chest posture reminded her of some kind of boy band. Would he break out into dance? She laughed.

"What's so funny?" His eyes slitted.

She was surprised at how he growled at her. "Nothing. It's just...you reminded me of Mark Wahlberg for a second."

He shook his head. "Sure, I get it. The guy is fit."

She wasn't about to admit that it was during Wahlberg's boy band phase. "Thanks, for everything. Did you like the parade? You put on a fantastic show as the Grand Marshal. And riding in Graham's Aston Martin. Pretty sweet, hey?"

"It's a Bond car through and through. Wonder if the old geezer would sell it to me?"

She swallowed hard. The comment ruffled her feathers.

"Not sure Graham wants to be thought of as a *geezer*." She dropped her phone in her bag. "Need a ride back to the house? I'm going—"

"No. Waiting for my security detail. They took Nina back and will be here soon for me."

She ignored his cold tone and fought to stay professional after what had happened last night—stealing Tyler's boat. "Well, okay. Let me know if there's anything else I can do for you. For the next few days, before the next fundraiser, you can enjoy Door County. Check out the other towns. There are fantastic restaurants in Sturgeon Bay. Fair warning, you might have to wear a hat or some kind of disguise. After today, everyone on the peninsula will be coming up to you and asking for a selfie."

"Thanks, but I think I'll be sticking around Baileys. Any chance you want to go get a bite to eat? It's late, but Kat already left and is at the Beacon. She'd open the kitchen for me."

"Really?" His all-knowing or spy-like superpower gave her the jitters. "Kat was pretty tired. I wouldn't want to make her cook again. Raincheck? I have plans."

"Oh, booty call?"

She shuddered and took two long steps away from Wagner. The way his gaze slid over her legs made her regret wearing a skirt. The hair on the back of her neck stood, and she wanted to bolt out the door. Instead, she calmly massaged the back of her neck. "Hey, it's been a long-ass day. I'm sure you need your rest."

"Didn't mean to be so rude." He planted a hip on the corner of her desk. "It's been a thrill, all of the hospitality you've shown me. The studio never even batted an eye when they apologized to you with a hefty donation to the lighthouse. But the red speedboat was irresistible, like a luscious pair of lips. It had my name on it." He gazed around the shop, landing on the velvet curtains that led into the vestibule. "One more trip up the stairs? Tonight's a full moon. Bet it's a gorgeous view at the top of the lighthouse."

"No, it's late. I have to get going." Her mind seemed to buzz and hiss at the thought of her brother's boat in the hands of such a jackass. She was tempted to ask more about the donation from the studio but pushed it out of her mind. Slinging her bag over her shoulder with a heavy thud, she went to the light box and yanked the breaker down, saying, "I'll walk you out." The shop darkened. The red glow from the EXIT lights illuminated the doorways, and the threads of emergency lights brightened the stairs. "I think I hear your ride."

He followed her down the stairs and into the entryway. There wasn't a car nearby at all, but her instincts crept along and warned her. She needed to be out of the dark and away from this man. His kindness had grown as fake as his McConaughey drawl.

"What's the rush? I'm sure there's a cocktail of some sort in the kitchen here."

"No, thanks."

"Don't you think you owe me after yesterday?" He let out an irritated, raspy breath that reeked of rancid whiskey.

"I owe you? After you stole my boat and took it for a joyride?" She clutched onto the handles of her bag and glared at him. "You're joking."

"You forced me to play nice with strangers." He shook his head, and his lips formed a circle. "I had no idea how clever you were."

She felt like a dementor was trying to take her soul. "Isn't that your job as an A-list actor? And this *is* part of your community service." She balled up her fists. "Our community welcomed you in with plenty of red-carpet attitude."

"Mostly everyone," he jeered, "but you."

He thrust out a hand, and she backed up, dropping her bag and stumbling against the door. But he closed the distance between them, and her breath got stuck in her throat. One hand locked onto her shoulder and shoved her against the solid wood door. His other hand reached between her legs, clamped onto her, and squeezed. A sharp pain shot through her.

"What the hell is wrong with you?" She gasped and tried to push him away, but he fell against her chest, pushing his arm against her throat and locking her tighter in place. She struggled for air.

"Come on, you know how fucking hot you are." He licked the length of her neck. "Irresistible. Shaking your ass at me going up those stairs."

Maddie nailed the pointed toe of her boot into his shin.

He yowled and stumbled back, releasing her shoulder. Gagging, she wiped off her neck with the collar of her blouse.

"Can't blame me." Wagner glared at her as he rubbed his shin. "The way you prance around, all regal and shit. It's like you're just asking for it. Tell me you haven't thought about how good it would be. Me fucking you."

Maddie swallowed down bile and glared at the monster before her. Adrenaline sizzled through her nerves. Lunging, he grabbed and pinched her breast. She pivoted around him and kicked the back of his knee. He shifted off-balance, and she locked his head in the crook of her arm. In one swift move, she dropped on her ass, and his body hit the ground.

He lay face down beside her, rigid and moaning.

She slid her arm free from under his neck, got up, bent over, and grabbed her kneecaps to get hold of her breathing. Trying to focus her blurred vision, she spotted splatters of blood on the entryway's concrete flooring.

Wagner crawled up onto his hands and knees and spit. Carried by a waterfall of blood, pieces of his teeth skittered across the floor. His face was transformed into one distinct feature. Blood smeared from between his eyes, down his nose, and ended at his chin.

Stunned and mortified, Maddie automatically offered him a hand to get back on his feet.

He swatted it away. "You cunt! You're going to pay for this."

A sharp pain seared through her butt and lower back as she staggered into the kitchen area, retrieved a towel, and dropped it on the floor in front of him. "Look, you need to get to a doctor. I can call 911, but it's probably faster if I take you."

He took the towel and dabbed at his mouth. Both his top and bottom lips were split open.

Swallowing down a gag, she found her phone and started to hit 911. Wagner snarled, lunged, and snatched it from her hand, chucking it to the ground. Her phone fell with a thwack. She grabbed her purse and swung just as the front door opened.

His two security agents stepped in as her purse connected with Wagner's shoulder.

"You're a fucking lunatic," he yelled, stomping toward the door. "Get me away from this crazy bitch."

The door slammed shut, and her mind struggled to process. What just happened? Wagner had pinched her crotch, licked her neck, grabbed her boob, and cut off her air supply. She defended herself and warded off his attack. Her survival instinct was as sharp as ever, yet she felt devastated and defeated.

Agony ripped through her right elbow when she stretched out her arms. All her muscles began to tighten and protest. With her left hand, she picked up her phone and tried to focus on the webbed screen, but the bits of shiny white teeth lying between spots and smudges of ruby-red blood seized her attention. Uncontrollable chills racked her bones. Had she really taken him down so brutally? It seemed impossible. The man was taller and stronger than her.

In a haze of thoughts, her phone pinged.

Where are you? Everything ok?

She gasped for air as the enormity of her actions became clearer.

No

TEN

The contents of Maddie's stomach swirled about as she pushed herself off the step and slowly stood. She needed some air and had to stop staring at all the blood soaking into the pea gravel. Carefully, she inched around the kidney-shaped smear of red, but it taunted her. Something acidic coated her tongue. Clamping her mouth shut, she pushed the screen door open and went outside to lean over the railing. And threw up.

Headlights wedged her between two beams. A sharp pain emanated from her elbow when she waved, so she stuck two fingers in her mouth and whistled. Relief swept over her as Rob hesitated by the driver's side, disappeared behind the rear of the car, and then came up to her.

"What the hell happened?" Gently, he placed a blanket over her shoulders. "Son of a bitch."

She forced out a guttural sound. "The douchebag thought pinching my vagina was a sure thing...he licked...and then..." As sweat dripped from her forehead, it lingered on her lashes and spilled into her eyes, burning. "It's like a murder scene in the lighthouse. I have no idea why he fell to the ground so hard. It was just a takedown. Kicked his knee in and pushed him over. I'm strong, but not that strong."

"On the way to the hospital, you can tell me everything." He tapped her left forearm. "I'm going to carry you to the car. All right?"

She mustered up a nod as every drop of energy drained from her.

Rob lifted her good arm around his shoulders, picked her up, and cradled her. She dropped her face into the crook of his neck and took in a deep breath. After he'd laid her down in the front seat, she adjusted her right arm and protected it with a corner of the blanket. With her left hand, she grabbed hold of his and squeezed. "What should I do? Wash off the cement and give him his teeth back?"

"We're going to the hospital first." Slowly, he drove away from the lighthouse.

Though he expertly maneuvered the car on the uneven road, it might as well have been a ride in a bumper car. She gritted her teeth to contain the pain shooting through her butt and lower back. "You know, I offered to call 911 for the dick. Actually offered him a ride to the hospital. I can't believe it. After he attacked me! God. This is so messed up."

"Were there any others around at all?"

"I don't think so. I thought Kat was, but she must have left when I came in to close up the lighthouse. Wagner seemed to appear from nowhere. Left his rock and slithered in."

Rob tapped the dashboard and made a call. As he spoke, she hardly heard a word. The car's heated seat warmed her, and the chills started to subside, but she couldn't relax. Every time she closed her eyes, all she saw was the image of Wagner's bloody face.

Someone pushed a wheelchair toward the car as they arrived at the emergency entrance. She was hurt, and she was tired, but she wasn't helpless, so she waved him off. After Rob parked, they entered the building entrance, holding on to one another.

"Thanks for meeting us here, TJ," Rob said to an approaching policeman.

"Hey, Maddie," the cop said, guiding her into the waiting room. "TJ Bender."

"I know you." She pointed at him. "Weren't you at my meeting?"

"Right. Yes. Are you willing to make a statement? Before the doctor sees you?" he asked, then stared at his phone. "I wanna get your side of the story and then head over to the lighthouse. It's a crime scene."

Maddie clutched onto Rob's arm. *Crime scene? Of course.* She had to think, but her thoughts were muddled. "Well, Wagner's a moron. And he..." She started to feel a little light-headed. "First, he grabbed and pinched me between the legs, and then he pressed his forearm against my neck, suffocating me." Shaking her head, she stopped talking. She was babbling. "I defended myself."

"Solid statement." TJ swiped his phone, then tucked one hand under his bulletproof vest. "A female officer will meet you here momentarily."

One woman sat on the bank of gray pleather chairs while CNN droned from the TV hanging in the corner of the room. Rob took out his phone and started making notes. Sniffling, she dropped her head back and closed her eyes to block out the fluorescent ceiling lights. "This is such a cluster, yet I can't believe it. After Wagner left with his security dudes, I thought...how do I get him to finish the fundraisers? What the hell is wrong with me?"

Her phone buzzed, and she flinched; then she put Brady on speaker.

"Where are you? I just got a message from the security system at Ma's house. A guard drove by, and the gate was open and—"

Rob leaned in to say, "Hey, it's me, Rob. I'm with Maddie at the hospital, and there's been a—"

"Hospital? Are you okay, Maddie? What is going on? Never mind. I'm on my way."

"No, don't. Go to the house and check it." To stave off the pain shooting through her lower back, she breathed through her nose. "I'm okay, really."

"Fine." Her brother ended the call.

Swapping glances with TJ, Rob said, "He sexually assaulted you. Tonight will be rough. The more we record about every minute, the better. Okay?"

She nodded.

"I need to warn you, Wagner's here getting medical attention," TJ said.

"That's totally whacked," Maddie gasped. "Ya know, I offered him a ride. Just like a true hospitable Wisconsinite."

Her little joke made her feel human, and she felt a smidge better when the two men grinned.

"Maddie, you need to be examined." Rob stared so intently that she wondered if he had caught a glimpse of her soul. "Anything you want to say can happen later."

"Then you can talk to a female detective. Wagner is filing charges against you," TJ added, sounding embarrassed. "I left his room when Rob called me and immediately sent a team of investigators to the lighthouse."

"What the fuck! He's the one who attacked me."

"He's claiming assault. Bodily injury," TJ announced. "His face is barely recognizable."

"It just looks bad. We all know there's always an extraordinarily large amount of blood with any cut on the lip or nose.

Remember our Red Cross training in school, guys?" Maddie rubbed her upper arms and tilted her head from side to side to get the kinks out of her neck

A nurse pushing a wheelchair came up to her. As if it were the plushest of La-Z-Boys, Maddie folded into the chair and let out a long sigh. A rush of appreciation coursed through every bone in her body as the nurse wheeled her into an examination room.

RUBBING A HAND OVER ONE BREAST, Maddie shifted her butt and hips in the wheelchair as the nurse pushed her down the hall. Wagner was going to pay for this. Every bit of it. "I'm not a witness," Rob said, "but Maddie's the victim. Not Wagner."

"I know," TJ said. "It looks like she used an award-winning wrestling move on him."

"Fucking arse." Rob's mind fought for more expletives, but none seemed to match his utter contempt for Wagner. The man had finagled his way through the court system and come out looking like a saint, but this time, he'd go down. "You know Maddie Logerquist, of all people, would never hurt a fly."

"Oh, *I know*, but Chris Wagner is a cockroach," TJ said. "This isn't my normal detail, but when I advised the best thing for him was to give his statement to a detective from the county, he couldn't wait for an hour. Yelled he wanted his story on record ASAP. He called for the mayor, who's still in there with him. I don't think the dick knows who he messed with and what he's up against. Maddie's the queen of Baileys."

"By any chance, did you do a breathalyzer? Or get a urine specimen?" Rob paced in front of the nurses' station. "And

Maddie mentioned he licked her neck, so make sure you collect her shirt. May have some DNA."

"Joni's our sexual assault specialist and an ace detective. She'll bag it all up. Get the evidence."

"Wagner's a predator. He's a master at manipulation, with Hollywood powermongers having his back. I have no doubt he deserved what Maddie gave him. And more than likely, he was buzzed or high. Slow to react to save himself."

TJ squared his shoulders and stared at him. "Look, Rob, we go back. So, whatever you need from me, it's yours, but I sense, because of Wagner and his demands, we'll have to tread carefully with procedure and protocol."

"Thanks. I suppose I should state here that I'll be taking on Maddie's defense." Rob lowered his voice. "It's all going to be he said, she said, and Wagner smears anyone who threatens him into anonymity. Take note, he loves his whiskey."

"Good to know," TJ said. "I'll head to the lighthouse. Maddie's in good hands, and we'll get this thing figured out."

After TJ took off, Rob texted Gus in LA.

Bro. Mayday. Need you back in Baileys.

He sat on one of the couches in the waiting room and watched the pneumatic doors sweep open and then close. The early morning darkness had at least a couple more hours, but the emergency entrance welcomed a few people who had celebrated too hard with explosives on the Fourth of July. He vaguely wondered how many digits had been lost to firecrackers and then chastised himself. *Think. What does Maddie need?*

Dropping his elbows to his knees, he massaged his temples. When he closed his eyes, all he pictured was a brutal expression stretched across Wagner's face as he callously terrorized Maddie. He dropped back in the chair. Looking up at the fluorescent light, he flexed his hands into fists to calm down. His heart was pounding like a damn freight train.

Definitely counseling. Plenty of downtime. And no way should Maddie step foot in the lighthouse. At least for a while. He knew little about the effects of a sexual assault but enough to know that revisiting the attack site could be detrimental to healing.

Rob scanned his contacts and looked up his Chicago friends. They may have some good therapy referrals. Then he rang his dad in Kohler. George could have some valuable advice, and he needed to hear a steady voice. After a brief conversation with his father, Rob's tension eased. He then texted Graham with an update and told him he'd be popping over as soon as possible for some objectivity and legal coaching. Lastly, he jotted a message and sent it to his law firm to override any ethical considerations concerning his decision to take on Maddie's defense.

When the mayor strode toward the exit, he briefly considered reaching out to her but then tossed the idea aside. Maddie was strong and had the support of most everyone in town. It should be her decision to speak to the mayor.

The nurse approached him. "Are you Rob? She'd love for you to come in."

To keep his mind from reeling, he stared at the nurse's shoes and listened to the squeaks coming from her Crocs hitting the linoleum tiles. The walk was cut short when she pulled back the gray curtain for him. "Go ahead."

He'd been on automatic, checking off items on a horrible list of steps to ensure her safety. Seeing Maddie, he let out a long, hard breath.

"God, I'm glad you're here," Maddie said, looking away from the detective. "This is Joni. She's getting it all down." Lying in the bed, she was covered with blankets up to her waist. Her cheeks had lots of color, and there was a sling on her right arm. The edge of a dark bruise crept out and up her bare neck from beneath the faded hospital gown.

To curtail his rage, he leaned back against the counter and gripped the edge. He greeted the detective, glad to see that she carried a plastic bag with Maddie's clothes. Before she left, he quietly asked about photos. She nodded curtly as she left the room.

He perused every part of Maddie's face for marks or cuts. "Everything okay? I mean, physically? I'm sure...when you're ready, there's more to get a handle on. It's a lot to digest. About your...emotions and, um, mental health."

She held out her left hand. "Get over here, I'm good. Even better since you're here."

He strode to the side of the bed, glad the safety rails were down. He couldn't take another hindrance getting in the way. He carefully hugged Maddie without pressing too hard against her right arm and let out a long sigh.

"Thank you," she whispered in his ear. "For a second time."

Sitting on the edge of the bed, he took hold of her hand. "What do you mean?"

"Saving my life. Again. I'm starting to think you're a lucky charm with all your red hair."

"I'm way too tall to be a leprechaun, and you don't need any luck. You're a badass."

"Maybe, but I sense things will get a lot rougher. I hope you're sticking around."

He kissed her cheek. "Of course."

Again, he and Maddie were thrown together to face the ominous. At least it gave their relationship a tough coat. But would they ever be themselves again?

ELEVEN

Rob and Brady pleaded with Maddie to stay with Kat after her night in the hospital. But learning that Wagner and his entourage had skipped town, she knew that in order to sleep, it was essential to take care of her mother's house.

She carefully settled onto the pile of pillows stacked on a chair in the dining room. An easy landing. The bruised tailbone wasn't awful, but it was darn uncomfortable. A purple splotch had blossomed over Maddie's right elbow, but the sling covered it nicely and kept her arm in place. Flexing her sore hand, she let the sparkles of early afternoon sun on the water soothe her. There were marks on her neck and breast, and she ached everywhere, but her soul took the biggest beating.

Wagner had left her mother's house in disarray. Takeout boxes cluttered every surface, and the pervasive funk of locker room mixed with a sickeningly sweet perfume lingered. When Rob handed her a mug, she grabbed hold of it like a life preserver.

"Thanks for staying," she said, inhaling the scent of coffee, "and for making a fresh pot. I don't want to know, but...how does the kitchen look?"

"It's habitable. Brady is taking video of every room in the guest wing." Rob pulled out the chair kitty-corner to her and brushed crumbs off the seat cushion. "More proof Wagner is rotten to the core."

"I can sense Elsie cringing," she said. Realizing the silver urn with her mother's remains wasn't in sight, Maddie looked wildly around the room. She tried to stand, but her coccyx sent out a painful message to stay put. "Where's Mom?"

She squeezed her eyes shut and tried to keep her composure, but the events of the last twenty-four hours flooded in, threatening to drown her. When Rob took her hand, she cried.

He hugged her loosely. "I'm here for you."

Maddie sagged against his chest, blanketed in the comfort of his words and his presence. The crunch of the muslin sling kept them apart, but his warmth made up for it. She'd been cold for so long and hadn't realized it. Between the lighthouse and the hospital, her lips had to be blue. "You are so kind, but—"

"Yes, I'll go look for your mother's urn. Try and finish your coffee. It'll warm you up." He kissed her forehead and jogged toward the great room.

Brady strode in and set a CVS bag on the table. "How're you doing? Your scripts were just delivered."

"Thanks. Have you seen the urn?"

Brady tapped his shadowed jawline. "Wait a second, I forgot—"

"About Elsie Logerquist? How dare you?" Teasing her brother lifted her heart, but he didn't crack a grin. Standing stiffly, he scratched his unshaven jaw and stared out the window.

"Hey, I could use a hug, bro." As soon as he broke out of his trance and wrapped his arms around her, Maddie used her good arm to clutch him tighter. "Don't worry. I'll be okay. I'm not going anywhere, so you're stuck with me.

His face lit up with one of his big, bold Brady smiles—a crooked grin with every darn tooth straight and sparkling white. He chuckled. "I'll say it again, it's great to have you home, so I'm going to hold you to your word. Wisco needs you more than New York." He stood and kept hold of her hand. "Before I opened the house for Wagner, I made sure all of the valuables were locked up. So Ma's safe and sound. Somewhere," he said.

"In the boathouse?"

"No, not there. I've been taking care of Tyler's boats since..." He cleared his throat. "Since Tyler passed. I always keep the boathouse locked. Wagner must have broken in because when I brought the boat back here the other night, the main door was jimmied open."

"That's theft," she said, dropping her head back. She'd been so naïve to offer up her family's estate to Wagner. "The other rooms? Did he break in anywhere else on the private wing?"

"Our bedrooms are locked and vacuum sealed." Brady crouched down in front of her and patted her knee. "While you were at the hospital, I checked every nook and cranny of this place. It's our home, and nothing's missing." He paced around the table. "Except for Ma's ashes. They're—"

"Found Elsie." Rob came in, cradling the urn in his arms. "She was in—"

"The closet," Brady finished. "I forgot. I was in a rush to make sure Ma's house was in decent condition for the Hollywood douchebag."

"Hey, Rob," Maddie said, letting a wave of relief wash over her as she stared at the shiny urn in his arms. "Is there any way we can charge Wagner for stealing Tyler's boat? Just found out he broke into the boathouse."

"There's a possibility, but let's take one broken law at a time." Rob carefully set the urn in the center of the table. "There's a bigger issue than the boat." He cleared his throat.

"Wagner assaulted you last night, then left the hospital without letting the cops know his whereabouts."

She tore open the bag of pills and examined the three different bottles of meds, unsure which would be the strongest. Of course, none of them would be tough enough to make her sleep, wake up, and forget about everything. For that, she suspected she'd need some solid sleep and, eventually, counseling. "Wagner stole my dignity and defiled our house, so I want to do something useful. What part is the worst? I'd like to start purging by way of deep cleaning."

Brady looked at the ceiling, then said, "Um. The bar is littered with open whiskey bottles and the like...the bar by the pool."

She could take care of that without looking at the pool.

"You've been through a lot already. Why don't you stay at Kat's," Brady proffered. "Until we"—Brady shot an anxious glance at Rob—"get this place showing no hint of Wagner."

"No, I need to stay here for Elsie. Please. I don't want to let her down. I feel like I've failed her and her lighthouse mission." Maddie sighed and lifted her sling. "This reminds me of what little power I have left. I have to think about my family and the Logerquist legacy."

"Okay, okay," Brady said, with the crease in his forehead deepening, "but don't be so hard on yourself. And instead of scouring anything with one arm, get some sleep. I'm sure you'll be able to spit shine something in the near future."

She thought about her mom's collection of books and journals. "I'll take care of Elsie's private library. Okey-dokey?"

"Aye-aye, sis," he teased and left the dining room.

She adjusted her sore tailbone on the cushion under her butt. "Rob, I'm certain you have a plan. Keep in mind, though, I'm not some kind of wounded fawn."

"*SCUSA*, BUT HELL NO." Rob pulled out his laptop, opened it, then closed it because his pragmatic tendencies needed to take a nap. He set his elbows on the table and steepled his fingers, mustering up his most un-lawyerly side to keep Maddie calm.

Wearing a Tom Petty concert T-shirt had to help comfort his closest friend. He considered quoting one of Petty's most appropriate songs, "Love is a Long Road," then tossed the bloody awful idea from his head. He quipped, "You're right, Bambi. A plan came together while I was in the waiting room."

Laughing, her cheeks flushed, and her eyes sparkled.

He would not tell her something defeating. Wanting to be constructive, he went to his favorite legal tool, *The List*, listing five pieces of info from least important to the most important.

"Here's the top five."

"Who are you? David Letterman? Just spill it, please."

"Only five, not ten." He had a hard time keeping a straight face, but this wasn't a good time to laugh. Sealing his lips, he concentrated. "This is one of my best defense tools. So here goes..."

"Five: every inch of the lighthouse interior was photographed by the cops. Number four: TJ will be calling you so you can make an additional statement sometime next week. As long as you're up to it. But the sooner, the better."

"Wait, *Letterman*. Why does this list sound like I'm the criminal and not the victim?"

"Unfortunately, Wagner considers himself a victim, too," he announced. Better to rip off the Band-Aid. "He didn't disappear after he was released from the hospital. Just went back to Chicago and hired a lawyer. This time, a prosecutor. So TJ needs your side of the story."

With this tidbit of info, her face became ghostly, the bruising on her neck dark in comparison. "What the actual fuck is he planning to do to me? As if he hasn't already hurt me?"

He clenched his jaw. "*No one* will hurt you anymore, Maddie. I promise. I've been on the phone all day. And I'll keep tracking his every movement so we can stay ahead of whatever he plans on doing. But at this point, nothing's happened, and it's a good thing."

"Thank god you stayed in town for the darn lighthouse. Continue on, Mr. List."

"The lighthouse is number three. Graham is compiling info from the fundraising guests. He's going to interview them all. Especially the women." He cleared his throat. "And...I think it's best you avoid the lighthouse."

She glared at him.

"Not really *me*, per se, but Graham. And Agnes. Also, Kat and Michael. Of course, Brady. More of a *we*."

She took a sip from the cup of coffee.

Let her process. He knew how the lighthouse, the Logerquist legacy, and Maddie were one inextricable and touchy entity. They ruled like a small-town troika. He fidgeted in his chair until she finally blinked.

"Am I being banned from the lighthouse?"

"Yes. And eventually..." He coughed. "This house."

"What are you talking about? The townspeople all decided to kick me to the curb? Should I be looking for pitchforks outside?"

"Not at all. We want to do everything we can to protect you. Since he's been at the lighthouse and stayed here, we believe he'll worm his way back. And no one wants you to face your attacker again. Ever." He sighed. "It won't be forever. Just until any kind of scandal passes. Or blows through Baileys. Maybe go back to staying at Kat's. You've been sleeping there the past year. Not a big stretch. And if...actually when, the media gets hold of this story, they will be camping out in front of this house and the entrance gate."

She slumped forward. "Can't I just update the security cameras? Get a ding-ring-thing?"

He had to pick out the next item on the list. As long as she stayed away from the lighthouse, it was a win. Wagner's blood had trickled into every crevice of the concrete floor. The sight of it could cause more trauma for Maddie. "Will you agree to stay clear of the lighthouse and Cana Island?"

She dabbed her mouth with a linen napkin embroidered with the family logo. "Wagner isn't a human; he's a misogynistic pig who hates women. When he pushed me up against the door, he was seething with rage." She folded the napkin precisely and laid it next to her cup. "Because I made him get off Tyler's boat. Which he stole. I think if I go to the lighthouse, at this point, I may pass out cold. I can't look at the spot where..."

Rob nodded briskly to control the slow-rolling rage starting to broil inside him. "It's hard to prove misogyny in court. Especially with actors. So, I implore you to help yourself and stay close to us. Number two: there's been no word or statement made to the press from his studio or agency."

"It's been less than forty-eight hours. Give it time." She scoffed. "The *Hollywood Cue* likes to attack when no one's looking."

Even though he agreed, Rob tried to stay upbeat. "Best news, though, is number one: Gus is coming back from LA to take over the lighthouse fundraisers."

"Why do I have to flip my life upside down for the asshole who assaulted me?"

His efforts to mitigate this tragedy seemed painfully useless. He let an idea from the back of his brain break through and ran with it. "How about you stay at our house? It's ideal. Plenty of room. Two guard dogs. Gus and Lucy. Me. You can sleep in the guest room."

"I think not." She shook her head. "This is my home. It's time for me…let's just say I'm comfortable. And there's the pool. Might be good for my butt."

He knew it would be a cold day in hell before she'd go near the Olympic-sized swimming pool on the south end of the estate. "Our house, though, is already tricked out with high-tech security."

"No deal, bud. I'm staying here."

"Okay, then we will increase and update the security cameras around this entire place. I believe there's going to be a storm coming, and it will be a doozy."

"Doozy? Such a show-off with your legal expertise."

A quick smile escaped him.

She rose from the padded chair, bracing on the edge of the table for support. He shot out his arm for her to grab hold of. "Careful. Do you need some pain meds?"

She leaned against his chest and nodded.

"I'll research the best security systems. Then I'll give you a ring."

"Peace. Thanks. But no need to propose."

"Oh…I didn't— Ha, ha. Tomorrow, noon. I'll be here with lunch."

"Thanks. Have a good night, Rob. I'm crashing as soon as you leave."

He was about to walk out the door but hesitated and asked, "Can I kiss you *buona notte*?"

"Please do." Maddie hugged his waist with her good arm, and the slinged one pressed against his chest. "One of these days, you'll have to tell me about your little bits of Italian."

"*Certo.*" He grazed his lips across her cheek, then softly landed on her mouth. Overcome with desire, they kissed hungrily, and then he carefully held her close until they both stopped trembling.

"I'm safe because of you, wherever you are," she whispered, brushing her fingers across his chin. "Thank you."

"Sweet dreams, Maddie." He wanted to stay but needed to give her a dose of space to start healing.

Outside, the summer stars blazed over Moonlight Bay. He stretched out in his Audi, waiting and watching as each of the lights inside the house went off. When all seemed settled in the estate, he reluctantly drove away. Right when he returned to the house on Kangaroo Lake, his phone pinged. It was a message from his firm. ***Wagner's on the warpath***

TWELVE

After Rob left, Maddie locked all the doors, double-checked the windows, and plodded toward the private wing of the house. An unbearable exhaustion crept into her bones, begging her to go to bed, but she froze in front of her old bedroom across the hall from Tyler's. After he died, she'd moved to New York and rarely came home. The pain, permanently etched on her mom's face, had made it grueling for Maddie to return.

No matter how hard she tried, Maddie could never shake off a deep sense of guilt. As if she were responsible for Tyler's accidental drowning. While in the morgue, she barely looked her mom in the eye.

She'd come home from Madison that summer with a shiny new business degree in hand and was prepping for her next degree in fashion design at FIT in New York. Yet, it was nearly impossible to stave off the resentment at having to watch over her mischievous twenty-year-old brothers again. They were grown-ass men, but her mother continually worried about them.

So Maddie begrudgingly went on another one of Tyler and Brady's adventures to search for sunken treasure in Lake Michigan. Having Rob in the boat was definitely a bonus, given the chance they might hook up, but she hated being forced into action by her mother.

Unfortunately, her guilt at letting down Elsie and still being able to take in lots of free air had grown into a jumble of heartaches.

At her mom's deathbed, she had wanted to tell her. Confess her long-ago pent-up frustrations, but she couldn't do it. As cancer was sucking the life from Elsie, all Maddie wanted to do was hold tight to the precious time they had left together.

In New York, Maddie had little time to think about the past and plenty of opportunities to make choices and think about the future. Living in a hectic city kept her busy and exhausted. It protected her and locked the guilt from long ago in a vault. But being home and maybe because of Wagner, the unresolved anger at the loss of her brother broke free and snowballed.

She must have been cuckoo to believe a lighthouse revival could meet all of her mother's expectations posthumously. For a brief second, Maddie actually thought Elsie's particular brand of earthy optimism was within her reach.

The door to Tyler's room eerily grabbed her attention. She took one step and clutched the knob. Without thinking too hard, she turned it and pushed the door open. She'd expected to see her dead brother's room as it once was, the walls covered with posters from *Fast and Furious* movies. But no. She wondered if her pain meds were playing tricks on her. She closed the door and opened it again. Nope.

Lo and behold, in the corner of his old bedroom sat her sewing machine. The one she'd used to sew the designs that got her into FIT. A bulletin board displayed all her scribbles of swimsuit ideas and fabric swatches. Her mom had never really paid attention to her creative endeavors, so why was this room refurbished?

To make sure she wasn't seeing things, she looked closer at

her steady-eddy Singer for any needles or thread. Had her mother been sewing? This was all very strange. She needed to sleep. Tomorrow, she could check again and make sure she wasn't hallucinating.

Completely drained, she dragged herself across the hall and practically stumbled into her own bedroom. Thankfully, her mother had redecorated all the magenta and black décor with subtle shades of gray and blue. The king-sized bed, piled with pillows, seduced Maddie with sweet nothings. Taking off her sling, she slowly crawled into bed and closed her eyes. But sleep avoided her.

Wagner's bloody and battered face kept filtering in and out of her mind. She tossed off one pillow, then another. The horrible pictures of her attacker kept scrolling through her head. She needed a replacement and decided on the Singer sewing machine. It had an endless number of bells and whistles, so she focused on picturing each one and listing them off. First out loud and then slowly, as sleep beckoned her, she mumbled. As she drifted off into a deeper sleep, sensations from that long-ago day on the lake consumed her dreams. They never became nightmares because she was with Tyler. Swimming.

Kicking hard, using her breaststroke, she swam up to her trouble-making brother and grabbed his ankle. Her hand sliced through the water, and a rock glinted as it sank, sparkling in the black water. Just as she reached for it, Tyler swam up and snatched it from her. When she laughed, her lungs filled with air instead of water. With a strong scissor kick, she closed in on him again. Tyler swam away with such force swells of water pushed her toward the surface. She filled her lungs with air until they burned and dove back down, searching for the glimmer in the darkness.

Maddie kicked off the covers to cool down. Drenched with

sweat, she got up to go to the bathroom. With a struggle, she managed to strip off her T-shirt and decided to take a shower. She dredged through her mind to sort out her thoughts as she washed away the grogginess of sleep.

Nothing made sense except a sharp awareness of anger and deep frustration. She carefully turned on her rubbery legs and let the shower soothe the soreness around her tailbone. Slumping against the cold tiles, she sank to the floor. Hugging her knees, she stared as pellets of water puddled and swirled down the drain. When tears fell off her chin, she blinked harder to keep them coming.

THIRTEEN

Ten Days Later

Maddie believed the Singer sped up her healing process. The sewing machine had a few glitches, but as soon as she worked them out, she was able to use it. There were patterns, a lot of fabric, and even batting folded up neatly on a shelf in the bedroom turned craft room. Since sleep had come in spurts for most of the past week, she spent her nights sewing soup bowl cozies for the microwave. Which proved to be better than any of her prescriptions. She would have gladly stayed nestled in the house, doodling ideas for swimsuits and stitching up more cozies; however, today, she had to leave the safe house to meet TJ and make an official statement.

After double-checking all the security pads at each door, she went to the garage and carefully sat in her mom's ancient, two-seater sports car. The low seat was the most comfortable to access. She'd been able to ditch the sling as the swelling and bruising on her elbow dissipated, possibly thanks to her sewing. The bruises on her breast and neck were all but gone, too. But her butt, the bruised tailbone, still gave her a hard time. The doctor suggested swimming to reduce her aches, but Maddie ignored him.

She had to stop and start frequently for pedestrians as she drove through town to reach the police station. With the convertible top down, the sun beat on her face as she waited at the traffic light. Baileys Harbor was hopping mid-morning on a Friday. All up and down the street, the sidewalks were crammed with tourists. When she reached the Beacon, there was a line of people waiting to get inside Kat's restaurant.

She wondered what all the hullabaloo was about until a black Escalade pulled up beside her and parked in front of the Beacon. Darn, she'd really been out of touch for over a week. Of course, Gus Reid, the Hollywood superstar, was in Baileys and appearing around town to support the lighthouse. She beeped and waved at him.

The tinted window opened, and Gus shouted, "Hey! Coming in to see me?"

She shook her head. "Got a meeting. Maybe later?"

"Sure." Holding up the fundraiser instruction binder she'd put together, he gave her a thumbs-up. Before disappearing behind the black glass, he yelled, "The lighthouse is going to be A-OK, Maddie."

#LightUp and Baileys were moving forward without her. Still disjointed after the July Fourth ordeal, Maddie's emotions kept swerving and careening into one another. She'd thought about coming up with her own *Letterman* list, like Rob's, but opted for an easier and more comfortable method for processing —sewing.

Bulletproof-vested officers greeted her as she sat in a cushioned, almost luxurious chair in the waiting room. The cop shop was pristine and—she inhaled the lavender-scented air— calming and comfortable. Opposite of the station in NYC where she'd made statements. Even though the 10th Precinct in

Chelsea was housed in a historical brownstone near her apartment, there was no way to ignore the unique smell of Simple Green trying to mask urine in the front entrance.

From one of the offices behind the main desk, TJ poked out his head and gave her the just-a-minute signal. He had already taken one statement from her over the phone but needed a face-to-face. Maddie looked to see if there were any magazines, then remembered she was in a police station, not a doctor's office. Which should change, as both were top authority figures and could make or break one's life.

A multitude of positive expressions and safety tips that read a lot like motherly advice were framed and hung on the walls. Unfortunately, not even the police department had good advice when it came to sexual harassment. Holding your car keys with your thumb on the alarm button wouldn't work if you didn't own a car like most women in New York.

She became a regular at the 10th Precinct during her time at FIT. Her swimsuit designs earned her acceptance into the Fashion Institute, and needing well-paying part-time employment, Maddie was thrilled to land a modeling job. She was the right height and size to be a swimsuit model for an outdoor clothing brand. Most of the time, she froze while wearing suits at resorts from Bridgehampton to Montauk. The temps didn't matter; it was about the yellow sun and blue sky, and there was always pink lipstick to cover her blue lips.

Her modeling gig, however, stretched until it snapped apart. The photographers, many men with so much slime she wondered how their fingers ever stayed on the lens, liked to paw her up, down, and all around at every available opportunity. Her two co-models suffered through the same game of slippery fingers every time they were on a shoot. Maddie became so disgusted she filed police reports and contacted the company's ad agency. Police helped, but the photographers, the bad ones, did the deed and moved on. Never to be seen again. Thankfully, she pulled out her trusty Canon and once again worked behind the camera to stay sane.

She'd interned with the swimwear company while in Madison and had kept close ties. Eventually, she became Sunkissed's East Coast influencer.

The officer standing behind the counter shouted, "Miss?"

She'd been so lost in thought she didn't hear TJ calling her name. Her bag clutched tightly in her sore arm, she pushed open the swinging gate and went into his office.

"This won't take long, Maddie."

She sat in a surprisingly comfortable desk chair. "Don't get me wrong, but is this station on the take?"

"On the take? Um. No. Maybe you've been watching too many true crime shows." His smile reminded her of her brother's. "It's a new building, thanks to your family. Didn't you know?"

"Not in the least. Darn. When?"

"Three years ago. Your mom wanted the station to be connected to a community building where neighbors and police co-mingled." He pulled out a photo album and showed her pictures of the station during each building phase.

"Great shots," she said, attempting to disguise her surprise. She'd had no clue about Elsie's influence with the new police station. "It's, well, so comfortable for a police station. I'm impressed. It even smells fantastic. Is there a cookie-baking operation in here, too?"

"Not on the premises, but the bakery delivers fresh ones every day. And extras for blood drive days. The scent, normally, is because of Lucy's candle shop on Main. She supplies air fresheners to make sure the community rooms are comfortable for AA meetings or other groups who use the rooms." His gaze dropped to her elbow. "There are a lot of support groups meeting here monthly."

"Thanks, I plan on exploring therapy options. I'm doing okay, but I really want to get back to some solid chunks of sleep." She lifted her elbow to show him. "The purple bruise is now mauve. What sort of details do you need from me?"

TJ held on to a clipboard and tapped his pen on it. "We took pictures of the interior of the lighthouse and think that we created a visual version of events. I have a few questions to confirm this timeline of the incident—"

"Incident? More like felony?"

"If you press charges, then yes, felony. But until you make the decision..." He cleared his throat. "Let me know if any of these questions upset you, and at any point, tell me to shut up."

"Oh." She adjusted her sore bum in the well-cushioned chair. "Go on. Wait. How many questions?"

Tilting his head side to side, he flipped the top sheet of paper over. "Well, let's just take one at a time."

"Shoot." She laughed nervously. "Whoops. Probably shouldn't say *that* in a police station."

TJ snorted and gave her a pistol finger. "Here goes. Time of altercation a week and a half ago, Monday the fourth?"

"This is the first one? The hardest? You know I suck at *Jeopardy* and *Wheel of Fortune*, right?"

He smiled kindly.

Maddie closed her eyes and started the mental recording of what happened with Wagner. "Around eleven that night. I was over the moon because the whole day had gone off without a hitch."

"Who was with you?"

"I thought Kat was in the kitchen, but when I went into the lighthouse and then into the souvenir shop, she wasn't around. Wagner entered from the kitchen area. It was strange."

"Go on..."

"He asked me to go up to the top of the lighthouse again. I think. I remember being creeped out and really pissed." She scratched her wrist. "He drawled like he was some kind of Texas tough guy, and his words ricocheted from slimy to vile. Within seconds, my slime radar was beeping so fast I focused on doing what I had to to get out of there. I turned off the lights and went to the door."

"How did you see what was happening with the lights off."

"It's a lighthouse. The prism glowed, and the emergency lights were on. When I declined his offer to have a drink, he turned cold and started ranting. Told me I had teased him and that I wanted him to fuck me." She let out a ragged breath. "He pushed me against the door and grabbed me. Hard. Pinched my crotch and squeezed. Then he licked my neck."

TJ cleared his throat. "Did you at all tell him to leave you alone?"

Maddie dropped her chin and bugged out her eyes. "You can't be serious? There wasn't a whole lot of time to politely ask him to step aside. Especially when my vulva was being crunched in his viselike grip."

"Right, sorry. Continue." TJ had the sense to sound sheepish.

"Afterward, the blurriest of parts came. A sense of rage came over me when he grabbed my boob. I mean breast. Right side." Her foot started tapping. "First, I kicked out his knee. Then got him in a reverse headlock, fell down on my butt, and slammed his face into the ground."

"Last question, did you, at all, or at any time, accuse Wagner of stealing?"

"No. Stealing what? ...Wait. Yes. He stole Tyler's boat. And I distinctly recall him calling me a cunt." She took in a ragged breath. "Also. When I saw his face—which has stayed with me every night since—I tried to call 911 for him, and he refused. Then his security team came in and took him away."

"Thanks, Maddie. This is all good. As the days go on, you'll remember one detail or another. Why don't you write them down? May help your sleep situation."

She nodded, impressed at TJ's sensitivity. "I'm staying away from the lighthouse. I know it will trigger something. The truth is, I feel guilty. I've never hurt another being, and his bloody face. It won't fade away. Every night, it's like a rerun of a bad movie. Having you, the police, actually take the time and listen and try to do something is refreshing. I've been harassed a lot in New York, but there, the cops did little to nothing to help. And whenever the big boss got word about my complaints, I was blackballed. At least in Baileys, you all can't kick me out of town." She looked around the high-tech office. "Especially since my mother paid for your new digs."

He laughed. "We aren't *city slickers*, but we can make changes faster. We have to because it's important to the people around here." TJ stood and came around his desk. "Maybe this isn't my place, but I have to say, I would have been pissed as hell, too, about stealing Tyler's boat. I miss him a lot."

"He was such a troublemaker, right?" She laughed. "If I had done half the shit Tyler did, my mother would have sent me away to Holy Angels Boarding School. I'm not the goody-goody like everyone thought in high school. Since I was tasked with constantly keeping an eye on Tyler and Brady, I had to be as tough as Elsie. No high-risk adventures for me."

TJ led her out of his office. "Not when you were at Cave Point though?"

The thought of diving headlong into the lake around rocky cliffs made her shudder now. "The past. I'll leave it there."

"Maddie, I know you're tough like your mom, but you should really think about some counseling, as you mentioned, and then pressing charges against Wagner. I get it's a risk. But you're going to have bills from the hospital and any other services you may need. Wagner needs to be held accountable in some way."

She shook her head. "Let me get my thoughts together and let you know. The rumor and smear campaigns are standard fare when women go after men like Wagner. They aren't worth it to me. He's a blowhard, and I believe in karma."

TJ handed her his card as she left. "Call me anytime."

She tucked his card into the sleeve on the back of her phone, and it pinged. A message from Rob popped up on her screen. **Where are you? I'm at the house**.

"Everything all right?" TJ asked.

Nodding, she texted Rob back. **Police Station**.

Good. Stay. Don't move. Be there shortly.

Oh god.

Staring at TJ, she murmured, "Apparently, I need to stay. Rob is heading over."

"Walk this way," he joked as he zigzagged toward the waiting room.

She followed him through the waiting room and a glass hallway and into the community center. The main room was entirely made up of windows and overlooked the bay. A few kids were playing on the jungle gym in the park off the main building.

TJ gazed at his phone. "Let me show you the meditation room."

The cozy room was loaded with overly cushioned chairs and dim lighting. On the bookshelf were stacks of multicolored journals.

"There are pens, pencils, crayons, and as many blank journals as you want. Free for the taking," he said, distracted by his phone. "Relax. I'm going to meet Rob when he gets here. Be right back."

The room had an immediate calming effect on her. Whether it was the blue-and-gray interior like her bedroom or the multicolored binders and books, they both seemed to click into her love of matching and color coordination. She thumbed through the unused journals and selected one with an orange cover and an orange pen. Tapping the pen on the cover, she closed her eyes and took in a multitude of calming breaths. She glanced around the room for a paper bag in case she started to hyperventilate.

It was less than ten minutes but felt like an hour before Rob arrived. He cleared his throat, grabbed her hand, and squeezed. "Wagner's suing you."

FOURTEEN

Rob sat on one of the overstuffed velvet couches in the Zen-like community room. Leaning forward, he set his elbows on his knees and spoke softly. "I'm sorry for being so blunt."

"The asshole is...suing me." Shaking her head, she crossed her arms over her chest. "Darn, the guy has a set. What the hell is he expecting to get from me? I barely have two coins to rub together."

"Let's take this one step at a time." He slid the documents from his backpack and quietly laid them out beside her. The forewarning he received from one of his colleagues had catapulted Rob into overdrive. Wagner escaped without even a hand slap the last time, and Rob had nearly lost his mojo. Now, Wagner's toxicity had oozed over his home, family, and friends. For Maddie's sake, Rob would take him down. "How have you been sleeping the past week?"

She gazed at the legal papers. "Not well. If I'm lucky, I get four hours a night. Every time I close my eyes, I see... I've had trouble concentrating, so I spent a lot of time sewing."

She looked exhausted.

"Is that why no more sling?" he asked, eyeing her free arm.

"I guess so. Back to the basics, sewing must be helping." Her eyes sparkled faintly. "I notified my clients I'm taking a vacation and haven't looked at social media. Probably a dumb idea, but I'm so tired. And every part of me aches."

While rehearsing the night before, he hadn't been able to find a way to spin any of it into a positive. Wagner was going for the jugular. "A friend of mine in Chicago confirmed Wagner has hired an attorney. A woman by the name of Gwen Ridley. She's filing the papers. They should be delivered to you soon." He cleared his increasingly dry throat. "It's somewhat good news that we're in the know ahead of time."

"After all the oversexed, egotistical jerks I dealt with in New York, I come home to sleepy Baileys to get sexually hara— assaulted and now sued." She stood and stretched her arms over her head. "What do you have for me?"

"Before all the facts come out, I'm going to the worst-case scenario." He held up the top sheet and faced it toward her. "This form is all about me." Tilting his head, he gave her a big, slightly over-the-top smile. He absolutely needed her to trust him. "I will be as devoted to you and your case as a golden retriever. I won't leave your side, and my tail will be wagging for you every day until this case is successfully completed. And I'm not asking for one Milk-Bone. I'm here for you, and it's pro-*Bone*-o."

He caught her quick grin before it extinguished. "Please, Golden? All your drooling and panting isn't covering up your anger? Shouldn't you be more like a pit bull? No, I hate dissing the breed...pit bulls have gotten such a bad rap."

So much for trying to act calm and trustworthy. "Yeah, I'm pissed. Really pissed. Let's just say a German shepherd."

"Settled. Is there any way to bury—" She rolled her eyes "—*not* a bone, but the case, before it sees the light of day?" She smiled, small but radiant. "I'm not interested in any kind of courtroom drama. If I never have to see the twat again, I'll be happy."

"Part of my plan," he said, ignoring his trepidation over telling her the rest of Wagner's vile plot.

She took a pen and the form from him and signed it.

"For the sake of my clients, especially Sunkissed, I really need to keep my name out of the news. An influencer complaining isn't a good look to the higher-ups."

"Understandable." Rob held up another form. "Your signature on this one will allow me to get the facts down." Pausing to give her a chance to skim it over, he added, "To get your side of the story. It's like a deposition. Remember though, it's me, Rob. Only me. I won't let you relive your nightmare for anyone other than me, and only when it's absolutely necessary, okay?"

"Talk to TJ. He has a version of the story as well. I just gave it to him, but I'm having a hard time with details," she said, signing the bottom. Then she pointed to his last document. "That's a lot of Roman numerals, outlines, and numbers. Can we use it for kindling?"

"I wish." He looked at her intently, trying to keep the dread out of his voice. He'd finally come to the worst part of this scene —the stunning amount of money Wagner was looking for. "We need to compile your family's net worth."

"Doable," she said, then paused. "I think, but honestly, since the funeral, I haven't been keeping up on organizing Elsie's assets." She closed her eyes and groaned. "Brady and I, we've attended to the most pressing matters first. I guess the lighthouse has taken up most of my brain space."

"Your mom, I'm sure, had an attorney. Don't worry, we'll work through a lot of these questions," he said.

"Mom made sure everything was up-to-date before she passed, but after the will was read, her lawyer died. He was ninety-two years old, for goodness' sake," she said, shaking her head and looking around the room. "I had no idea my mom had splurged for this community room at the cop shop."

She began sounding rushed. He handed her the last of the documents and watched her scrawl her name with a trembling hand, and then he shoved the papers in his backpack.

Almost there.

"Is it safe for me to assume your mom's records are at the house?" He casually glanced around the addition to the police department to curtail his racing thoughts but was unable to vanquish his uneasiness. "Maddie, you'll need, and I'm more than happy to assist you, an appraisal on the house on Moonlight Bay."

"Why? And fess up. What aren't you telling me?"

"Remember, you're the survivor and the person who's in control." Rob really had to work on his poker face around her, although they'd never been able to lie to one another. It seemed like they worked as truth serum. "So there have been some details out there. Nothing has been confirmed or denied. At this point, you may have to get the worth of Moonlight Bay. How many acres?"

"Ten. Spill, Rob. No lists, and don't sugarcoat it with dogs. I'm an adult. I can handle it."

He bolted up from the too-soft sofa. "Wagner's complaint against you is battery and personal injury. He's looking for lost wages, damages, and restitution. Five million."

"Oh my god! How insane. I don't have that kind of money." Her knees buckled, and as she reached out, he grabbed hold of her until she steadied.

The Band-Aid had been ripped off. "Not your money. The Logerquist estate. I'm on your side. It'll be a fight. But I'll be damned if he takes you or anyone in your family down. I promise."

"Fivemillionbucks," she moaned. "I think I'm going to be sick."

He helped her sit down on the sofa and grabbed a wastepaper basket. "Put your head between your knees and breathe. And remember, nothing is confirmed yet. We have to wait until you're served with the papers."

"Easy for you to say. Wagner sucks. He's a tried-and-true vampire. And I'm the one who gets to be his prey." She suddenly straightened and moved the bin away from her. "I'm not getting sick over that piece of shit. But it's not only Wagner," she protested. "It will be his agency, studio, and insurance. They'll all come after me. Only me. Smear the hell out of me on social media and entertainment magazines. It'll be a feeding frenzy. I don't know if I have the stamina."

Rob thought about his first case with Wagner and the out-of-work actress who accused him of sexual harassment. The Hollywood gossip columns and photographers followed Liza Carpenter everywhere, and Wagner's fans had started calling her *She-Lies-A-lot*.

Rob wouldn't let it happen again, to anyone, especially Maddie. He wrapped his arms around her and held her tight. "Wagner isn't going to get one cent from you. He's a bloody bully, and you know what I think about bullies. He's going down."

FIFTEEN

The following day, Maddie opened the door to her mother's library and inhaled the age-old scent of books and paper. Before going inside the room, Rob laid his hand on her shoulder, and a sense of peace passed through her.

"Welcome to where the queen of Baileys Harbor reigned. This is, or was, Elsie's mission control center." She opened the curtains and let the sunlight brighten the dark, wood-paneled room. While she'd avoided the house up until now, Elsie's office was like a dragon's cave—much too frightening.

"Reminds me of Uncle Graham's office." Rob roamed the room, gazing up at the floor-to-ceiling bookshelves. "Quite a collection."

"And then some." Maddie's fingers ached, thinking of how much writing Elsie had done on a daily basis. For her, snail mail proved to be the best way to find clear answers within the convoluted pathways of local government. She'd composed letter after letter to officials and kept daily journals.

"Proof that mother and daughter are polar opposites. I can barely write a birthday card, and I've never had room for books, so only the absolute favorites were placed on a shelf in New

York. Thank goodness for technology." Outside, the gate at the end of the driveway was closed. "When do you think I'll be served? Will I need to go to the gate to let them in, or will Wagner and his MIB agents J and K burst through the gate and rush to the house?"

"Wagner won't come close to Baileys. It will be a court-appointed official who will deliver the case documents." He glanced at a stack of file boxes under the window. "I'll stick around. We have a few items to go through."

"By any chance, could TJ deliver it?" She dropped into the well-worn leather chair behind her mom's desk and rubbed her eyes. One nice long nap and she'd be good to go. It was tempting, especially when Rob laid a blanket over her shoulder. "I'll be fine. May be better if you do all the heavy lifting while I rest my eyes for a second. Yesterday was a long-ass day at the police station."

"Not an issue. Stay put." He shoved an ottoman covered with a faded floral fabric toward her feet. "Now, take a load off. I'm relieved you're home. This is a safe space for you. To answer your question, yes, a policeman like TJ might be coming to your door."

"I hope to get lucky." She wrapped the blanket over her shoulders and stretched her legs over the ottoman. She wondered what possessed men like Chris Wagner. Were they maniacally desperate for attention, complete narcissists, or did they simply lack a soul? She rubbed her bruised elbow and was glad her tailbone only ached sporadically. "Five million bucka-roos," she grunted.

"We don't know for sure." Rob pulled a copy of *Silent Spring* off the shelf behind her head. "Good read."

"My mom's hero. I think one of those boxes by the window may be filled with more copies. She would take a box to every

PTO meeting and give a copy of the book to each board member."

Rob flipped off the top of one of the cardboard boxes. "Now I understand. It seemed odd I had to read it during my high school law class. One of our mock trials revolved around an environmental issue."

"Mind-blowing, right?" She chuckled, and he handed her a copy of the book. She traced the white lettering with a finger. With *Silent Spring* in her hand, she wondered why—as the daughter of Elsie Logerquist—she'd been so shallow?

If she had bothered to listen to Elsie once in a while, maybe she might have gleaned some encouraging words from her mother. The woman knew how to rally. Elsie had campaigned at the high school, a cringeworthy moment during Maddie's freshman year, to make *Silent Spring* required reading for all students. But nature had never been Maddie's jam, and when the school board voted unanimously in agreement, Maddie—in one of her typical acts of defiance—refused to read the book. Instead, she devoured every issue of Glamour, Elle, and Vogue she could get her hands on and read biographies about Diana Vreeland and Coco Chanel.

"Mom and I were opposites. An earth mother and a determined daughter whose hero is Stella McCartney," she said flatly.

"Stella? Great clothes. May I?" Rob pointed to the file cabinets. "If your mom was half as organized as you are, her information will be easy to gather." He pulled a clipboard out of his backpack and showed her the list of forms he needed to collect. "Even though the lawyer passed away, it's nothing to be concerned about. Most likely, all of her paperwork was distributed to her earlier and is here or in a safe deposit box."

She was stunned but relished the fact that Rob recognized

and knew the fashion designer Stella McCartney. "How do you—"

"Fran Marcheti. She's a good friend." He opened the rickety drawer of the 1950s filing cabinet. His face brightened as he scrutinized the contents. "Brilliant. It's here. Assessments. Assets. Deeds. And financials. All alphabetized. Sweet."

"Mom was very old-school." Maddie recalled the famous swimsuit model. Francesca Marcheti and Rob were a thing at one time. She pushed a nebulous swirl of emotions away. Rob was now officially her lawyer. "Oh god, I know this is going to be bad. So many goods for Wagner to get his hands on."

"When did Elsie buy Birdcage Island?" He flipped through an open binder. "Place has to be loaded with snakes."

She slipped off her sandals and tucked one foot under her butt. "Doesn't it say on the deed? When we went to spread her ashes, I checked the will, and it's not mentioned. My first plan to save the lighthouse was to sell the snake-infested island."

While Rob paged through the binder, she hesitantly opened the bottom desk drawer. Instinctively, she glanced at the door to make sure she wouldn't get caught, then shook off the feeling that she had her hand in a cookie jar. The drawer was filled with yellowed letters bundled together with cracking rubber bands. *Old-school.*

She flipped through one bundle, and immediately, the ancient rubber band broke and popped off. Someone or something must have returned the originals since her mom had hand-written the address of the Department of Natural Resources on each envelope. The letters were all typed. They pieced together her mother's campaign to have the land north of Baileys Harbor, now called the Sanctuary, declared a conservation land trust because developers had shown interest in building on it.

Maddie became immersed in her mother's knack for subtle sarcasm and hints of reverence in her sentences. To get the officials to hear her, Elsie had to *kiss the ring* first. Her mom had received many rejections, and although Maddie was rarely allowed into the office, she remembered many spicy words coming from Elsie and bouncing into the hallway.

It must have been hell to convince the bureaucratic old men's league to forgo profit and save the land. Elsie's persistence had paid off, though, when the Sanctuary was officially declared a nonprofit trust. After reading several of the letters, the space between her and Elsie diminished.

The chime announcing someone was at the entry gate rang and broke into her thoughts. She trembled. Rob looked outside. "It's your lucky day. TJ is here. Want me to let him in?"

Shaking her head, she gathered the letters and carefully placed them back into her mother's desk drawer. "No, I'm good to go and ready."

TOP STORY

Where in the World is Chris?

ONE OF THE FIVE FAMOUS CHRISES HAS EXITED STAGE LEFT. WHILE NO *CUTS* WERE YELLED, CHRIS WAGNER'S QUEST TO SAVE A SMALL-TOWN LIGHTHOUSE CAME TO AN ABRUPT HALT. ACTOR AND HOMETOWN HERO GUS REID HAS TAKEN OVER THE FUNDRAISING FESTIVITIES. THE QUESTIONS ARE MULTIPLYING, BUT NO ANSWERS HAVE BEEN FOUND IN BAILEYS HARBOR, WISCONSIN.

BY GEMMA GARNER

JULY

With all the hushed whispers and sideways glances, it seems as if a true crime show has crept into the sleepy lakeside town of Baileys Harbor. The speculation as to why Chris Wagner suddenly left with his entourage in tow has gripped everyone's attention on the Door County Peninsula.

Yet no one's talking.

Wagner was the man of the hour during several highly successful fundraising events, but after the 4th of July, the celebrity seems to have simply disappeared. Though rumors are swirling about, we can only confirm one fact. An intern working the third shift at the hospital recalls seeing some unusual activity. Apparently, "Several security guards, Hollywood types, and a cop rushed through the emergency room," he said. However, since this incident occurred during the early morning hours after the holiday, he believed it was another explosive case. "One of the many injuries sustained from irresponsible use of pyrotechnics."

Did Chris sustain an injury while playing with firecrackers?

If so, will his fans need to adjust to seeing Wagner with a new look? Missing a few digits?

Unlike other small towns I've visited, Bailey Harbor isn't saying much. The local paper barely mentioned the celebrity switcheroo. When I asked the manager of the Harbor—where Wagner was reported to have been staying—she stated, "He checked out."

Did the megastar head home to Chicago to see his wife and two daughters? After telling us that "fundraising and philanthropy—it's my mantra" a few short weeks ago...this girl's gotta wonder. **{GG}**

SIXTEEN

Sweat dripped down the side of Maddie's cheek. *One more selfie.* She sidestepped around the rack of swimwear shipped from Sunkissed. Her *OG* client, the swimwear company, had kept her in the influencing gig with a steady source of income for the past decade. She rearranged the umbrella to block out the heat from the late-afternoon sun. The clear blue sky was a perfect backdrop for her shots.

Over the past year, she'd added other clients onto her roster. A high-end blouse designer, a nonprofit tote bag company, and a woman-owned cowboy boot maker had built up her fledgling influencing business, but Sunkissed was her bread and butter. And now, it was peak season for swimwear. Snapping pics for her small but mighty group of clients made dealing with her mother's affairs less taxing. Influencing didn't pay nearly as well as styling and modeling, but she treasured the autonomy.

She tugged and tussled to strip off the colorful, floral swimsuit top that reminded her of an embroidered peasant top. Perfect for sipping cocktails by the pool, but not a suit to wear for lap swimming. She chugged down a glass of iced tea and chomped on a piece of ice.

When she'd been handed a court document demanding payment to Chris Wagner—five million dollars—it was choreographed perfectly. TJ entered the house, offered her a shot of mezcal, and then gave her the oversized envelope. With Rob as a witness, all the protocol was deemed legal. Even though she'd declined the liquor, she gained a sense of trust from her hometown. Everyone had her back.

The really good news came when Rob learned that the bulk of the Logerquist properties and ownerships were protected by an umbrella LLC. So, Wagner couldn't touch the most financially lucrative parts of her mother's fortune. But this estate, the house Maddie had moved into and fallen in love with again, was worth well over a million. Wagner could go after it and/or the ridiculous island with the broken-down Birdcage lighthouse on it. The last purchase her mother made before she passed away. Maddie realized she was now responsible for two lighthouses, and both were anything but *enlightening*.

Glancing toward the boathouse, she tried to spy a sandy spot with some shade to take more photos near the water, then stayed put on the padded chaise lounge. Tomorrow was right around the corner, and today, at four o'clock on the dot, Rob would make his daily pit stop.

His routine was unfailing. Before coming inside, he walked the perimeter of the property, checked every security camera, and then contacted the security company.

Finally, he'd stroll into the kitchen and make her a delicious cocktail. She wondered what he would mix up for her today. None of his adult beverages had let her down. If his legal career weren't so successful, he'd be a shoo-in for a supper club bartender.

"We're going for a sidecar today," he said, breaking into her meandering thoughts.

She stretched off the chaise and squinted at him. He seemed

to get more freckles every day. And his legs, when he'd arrived in Baileys', she could have sworn they'd been starched white. Now, they were leaner and had a summer glow of pink and caramel from wearing khaki shorts.

"You're early," she said, scrolling through the pics on her phone. "What's the matter?"

"Relax, nothing's wrong." He strolled over to her clothing rack and glanced at the assortment of swimwear hanging on it. "How's it going?"

"Okay, I only have to fiddle with the filters to get the lighting in these shots spot-on. Props to Sunkissed. They're being so supportive and patient."

"They should be since you designed one of their most popular swimsuits," he said.

"Ancient history, and not for sale in the catalogue this year." She stared at him. "What's going on? I can tell something's up."

"I was just at Kat's. Graham was there, and we had some lunch."

"Did you have a meeting about me? Or the lighthouse?"

"It's almost August, and you haven't left this house, Maddie."

"I've been busy working. It's important to focus on work, especially since I might have to shell out five million bucks, right? It's comfortable here. There's the bed, the craft room, and my trusty sewing machine." Her valiant effort to justify her loner-like existence took a nosedive under Rob's suspicious gaze. "Really. And I'm eating."

"Even if it's Kat's fantastic food, taking out and eating in every night isn't the healthiest," he said.

Was she feeling a little trapped? Maybe, but she wouldn't tell him that. Instead, she handed him her phone. "Look at these pics. Like I've said, I've been working. I want to get the Beacon on Instagram and post Kat's dishes. Doesn't the soup look delicious? FYI, it's hard to make broccoli cheese soup look appetizing. There are a lot of filters on this photo."

"Does Kat know about this?"

She shrugged. "Doesn't matter. When she's ready to hire me, I'll be prepared."

As he paced along the patio deck, he randomly knocked the wood railing with his knuckles. Finally, he spoke. "How about we take a road trip?"

"New York? Then yes, absolutely," she announced, hoping to wipe off his serious expression.

"Not quite. I've got some car work to get done in Elkhart. You might like a change of scenery. We could stay at Siebkens. Fran Marcheti is the owner; she's reserved rooms for me."

"How considerate of your girlfriend—"

"We're good friends. Nothing more. She's with Drew, a driver buddy of mine, and they're blissfully happy together. What do you think about a getaway?" He pulled a padded beaded bralette from her rack of Sunkissed beachwear and squinted at it. "Interesting."

Hearing confirmation that his friendship with Fran was purely platonic, surprisingly eased her heart. "It's one of my earlier designs for breast cancer survivors. Every woman who has gone through any kind of surgery and all the tribulations afterward should be able to get outside and enjoy the sunshine and swimming." She took it from his hand, hung it back on the bar, and pushed the whole rack through the open patio doorway. "So, Elkhart Lake and not New York?"

He followed her inside and grabbed two highball glasses from the china cabinet. "Who needs New York when you have Baers, the best bar in Elkhart, where they mix up a stellar sidecar cocktail. Which I'll be concocting for you now." He pulled out bottles of liquor from a grocery bag on the kitchen counter.

Maddie tugged a sarong off one of the hangers, trying to focus and inspect it. Standing near Rob had grown increasingly challenging. Each time he came to the house, her whole body tingled, and when he came near, his lovely scent revived her—fresh-cut grass with a twist of orange juice. "Sounds delicious."

"Do you even know what's in it?" he asked, arching a ginger eyebrow.

"Not really." As her cheeks grew warm, she navigated the awkward clothing rack down the hallway. "Be right back."

She pulled the rack into the craft room and slowly changed into the shorts and T-shirt she'd worn earlier. Her bruised tailbone continued to ache. To ease the twinge of pain, she sat on the club chair piled with multiple pillows and flopped over to stretch out her lower back. Stretching her arms out, she did butterfly strokes as if in water, and the tension eased all along her spine. Her breathing turned rhythmic.

"Wouldn't that be easier in water?" Rob said, sitting on the floor in front of her.

She gulped down some air. "Why do you always smell so good? Like oranges or marmalade."

"Staying with Gus and Lucy has its advantages. Lots of Lucy's scents are in the shower." He held out his hands and took hers in them. "Let me help."

She let him pull her hands to stretch further. Her whole spine giggled and hummed with release. "Mm, wonderful."

"A good swim might work wonders on your coccyx."

"Swimming is overrated," she said, then whined, "Is your plan to get me to Elkhart and go in the lake?"

"Not at all." He tugged on her arms again. "In fact, all concrete and cars. The vintage races are coming up, and I have to get a look at the new tires and the paint job on my Triumph."

She leaned back and adjusted her shoulders. "Running away to Elkhart Lake. At least it's not far away."

"Who's saying you're running away? It's just a getaway."

She glanced around the room. Even if her mom had transformed it into a craft room, Maddie still saw the shelves as they were when Tyler lived in it. Loaded with sports awards. Her brother was a quintessential sports fiend, and one lousy riptide, just like its name, ripped him away from her.

"Maybe I shouldn't go. The shit is hitting the fan with Wagner, and I'm a sliver away from losing my mother's house. *And* if I lose that stupid Birdcage Island, I'm sunk. I wish I knew why the hell Elsie bought the thing. If something happens while I'm gone, I don't think I'll be able to live with myself."

Rob helped her out of the chair. "We'll figure things out, and in the meantime, Graham and Gus can take care of Baileys for you. I suspect Elsie wouldn't want to see you turning into a hermit crab."

"I'm not crabby." She gave him a cheeky grin. "At least when you're around. Where's my drink?"

"Come on." He grabbed her hand and tugged her out of the safe but stifling room.

In the kitchen, he handed her a caramel-colored cocktail with a twist of orange hanging off the edge of the glass. It smelled heavenly and tasted divine. The liquor warmed every part of her. "I appreciate your offer..."

"No butts." He pointed to her backside. "You can leave your mom's house. Brady can move in and take care of it. He's not going to let anything happen to the Logerquist homestead. And the decrepit lighthouse isn't going anywhere. You need a break."

Either he or the drink was heating up her veins too fast, but the thought of Elkhart Lake intrigued her. She hadn't been curious about anything for a long time. "Do you remember when I was the official photographer for the Baileys newspaper?"

"Of course, snapping pictures of me posing around my

Jaguar. Can't forget. You were always in my face with your gigantic camera."

"Maybe this phone"—she waggled it in front of him—"won't be so annoying."

"No one has taken pictures of me or my cars in a long time. What are you saying?" Rob gave her a quick smile, then planted a kiss on her cheek.

"I'd be happy to bring my old Canon along for you." Her skin went from warm to fire-like heat. "I promise I'll be there for you and your cars, but I'll need to work on Sunkissed, too."

"Not a problem. There are plenty of sunny spots for swimsuit pics around Elkhart Lake." He lifted his cocktail. "To *getting* away for a short vacay."

Maddie shuddered. Having been so immersed in her mother's life, she wondered when she'd lost sight of her own. "To Elkhart." She tipped her glass against Rob's. "And fuck Wagner."

SEVENTEEN

Rob pressed down on the gas pedal, his adrenaline kicking up a notch as the Audi hit seventy, then eighty mph. Glancing at Maddie in the passenger seat, gazing out at the passing cornfields, he quickly memorized the curve of her soft pink lips, then turned his eyes back on the road.

Earlier, he was astonished he'd been able to fit Maddie's suitcase, two boxes of swimwear, and a bag full of camera equipment into his trunk. Glancing over at her again, she looked as if she'd dozed off. A sense of relief came over him. He'd done it. He'd been able to persuade her to leave Baileys for her health and sanity and before any gossip column grabbed hold of Wagner's lawsuit.

Passing a billboard announcing the upcoming vintage races at Road America, his pulse quickened. After an entire year of waiting to get his Triumph on the track, he was more than ready.

"Are we there yet?" she whined with lighthearted exaggeration.

"About ten miles to go, then we'll be in the village of Elkhart Lake. It's not as congested as New York, but there may be just as many expensive cars." Rob opened the sunroof an inch, and the warm breeze hit his face. Utter joy invaded all of his senses. "We'll be at Siebkens shortly. How are you doing?"

"What's all the excitement about?" She tapped his thigh. "You look like the kid who won a golden ticket and a tour of a candy factory. What is it about boys and their cars? I really don't get it."

"It's a thing." He attempted to sound bored, with no success. "In most ways, I'm American—baseball and apple pie, but cars? *It's in my blood, love.* Very, very British."

"Oh, I get it. Are you sure it has nothing to do with the fact that your family designed *very, very* sexy cars back in the day? Graham told me the name of the model, but since I have blood in my veins, *not* oil, I forgot the name of it."

"Cheers for remembering, *darling.*" He layered on an extra-thick coat of what was left of his British accent. "The name of the manufacturer and car is Austin-Healey, and it's where Graham's father and grandfather were employed as brilliant engineers."

"Oh my, I think your native tongue tickled me someplace unmentionable." Maddie laughed.

He gave her a sideways glance and noticed her blush. Both cheeks were pink. His first thought was to slather on the Britishisms. Full-on Daniel Craig. His pulse raced faster than his car. He cocked his eyebrow. "It's genetic. The cars and the accent. We're a package deal, fast and sexy."

He concentrated on the road to avoid driving into a corn-field. His thoughts kept swerving toward Maddie, but he had to keep an eye, or two, possibly three, on his job—defending her. His focus would be tested while in Elkhart, but his superpower was concentration. It got him through four years of high school bullying, four years of intense study sessions during his under-grad to get into law school, and three years of sleep deprivation until he graduated with a law degree from the University of Chicago.

Thinking back, how he'd managed to keep up with a personal life mystified him. The only person in his life at the time was Fran. They'd bonded simply because sports cars were in their blood—his English and her Italian. They met during one of his earliest summer hiatuses to Road America's vintage and classics race. Being with Fran was like being with the sister he never had as they dined at her family's Chicago resort, also the home of their car dealership—the place to go in Chicago if you were in the market for a Ferrari. Both having bigger priorities, they had never been anything but good friends.

Long before cancer came knocking, Fran traveled to any available photoshoot to create a compelling modeling portfolio for herself. He was in court, taking on every case thrown his way to advance his career and reputation. It was all about billable hours at the time and evolving into the most wanted defense attorney in Chicago.

Taking Maddie to Elkhart, where she'd meet Fran, could be one of his best ideas or an epic fail. But Fran *had* been badgering him to introduce them.

"Slow down!" Maddie shouted, pointing out the window. "Did you see that sign?"

Rob dropped his foot off the gas pedal, glided, and turned onto a graveled access road to stop. "What? Where?"

"Can you make a u-ey? Turn around?" She got out of the car and went to the rear end. "Pop it open. I need my camera."

He did as he was told. "A farm? A cornfield?"

Maddie returned, opened the case, collected the camera, and spun on a myriad of different lenses. "Go back to the sign. It read, *Cheese Museum*."

"Are you hungry for cheese?" He turned the car around and

saw the sign—Hennings Cheese Museum. Kiel, Wisconsin. Left and Four Miles. "Interesting."

"I know, right?" Her excitement over cheese surpassed his thrill over the smell of a new car.

While she tinkered with her camera, Rob eagerly drove to Kiel to visit the cheese museum. Inside the cheese store and museum was far more enjoyable than the Chicago Art Institute. Having edible art surrounding him was delicious. He grazed on an abundance of cheese samples and gravitated toward the English Stilton while, with her camera in hand, Maddie poked around the refrigerated shelves stocked with blocks of yellow and white cheeses.

"I signed us up for a tour of the Mammoth Wheelhouse," Maddie said, popping a cube of cheddar into her mouth. "It's in one of those steel silos."

"Sounds good." He grabbed a shopping basket off the counter. "Have you taken any photos, or are you too hungry?"

"Not yet. I'm trying to decide what colors will look best in this light." Maddie found a brick of cheese and dropped it into his basket. "Do you like Colby or cheddar better? I'll find some crackers. We'll need nourishment since I'm going underground, and we shouldn't leave Siebkens."

"Not exactly what I had planned. You'll be safe at Elkhart, so you won't have to hide or be afraid. However, some adult liquids are necessary." Rob found a bottle of red wine and placed it in the basket with the other snacks, then added another bottle of white. "Want some cheese curds?"

"As long as they squeak," she said.

The basket grew heavy with Maddie's choices of cheese and more wine. Rob pumped it up and down like a dumbbell for an instant workout while following her around.

At the back of the shop was a life-size statue of a cow painted in bright oranges and reds, wearing a cheesehead: the cheese-shaped wedge of foam worn by fans at every Wisconsin sports event. Rob meandered over to the corner where cheese hats in a variety of styles were displayed. He set down the basket and tried on the Stetson. "What do you think?"

Maddie tilted her head and squinted. "Not sure if the cowboy look suits you. Here." She grabbed another and placed it on his head. "A fedora, like you're a man of mystery."

"It's better than a cowboy." He glanced in a mirror. "I suppose."

She picked out a baseball cap and put it on her head. "Are you a Cubs fan? Maybe this should be your choice?"

"Hella, no. Brewers fan through and through."

"Come on, before we go on the tour, let's make our purchases. But first, a selfie."

"Can't do it," he said. "Man of mystery, like you said." He pulled off the fedora and finger-combed his hair. "It's a lawyer thing. No selfies. They're frowned on and regarded as self-promotion, and worse, it could be bad news for your case if someone noticed it."

"Good call. I'll go with it," she said, setting the hat back on the shelf and grabbing a foam bow tie. "Explains why I've never found you on any social media."

As Maddie stood close to him, his pulse raced. Her fingers glided smoothly across his skin as she put the bow tie around his neck. He swallowed hard. "Have you been cyber-stalking me?"

"Sort of. I mean, more like checking up on you." She blushed. "As an influencer, it is my job to scope out other niches."

Rob rubbed the back of his neck and adjusted the bow tie in place. He contemplated his next words while his gaze locked onto Maddie's face. "Truth? I have an account or maybe two under a pseudonym."

"Ah ha! I knew it!" She took off the bow tie and put the fedora back on his head. "You *are* a man of many mysteries."

More comfortable, he relented. "Okay, one pic of us. But this baby," he said, pointing to the fedora, "will be my mystery man disguise."

As she leaned back against his chest, he took in a deep breath and tilted the brim of the foam hat to cover his face.

"Say cheese." Maddie snapped a few selfies. "I promise these will stay in my phone."

"A solid plan." He threw his hat and hers into the basket. "It's almost one, and we do not want to be late for the cheese wheel tour."

She whispered in his ear, "I'm going to find out who you really are on social media, my friend."

"Good luck," he said, knowing his social media handles were well disguised. But of all the people in the world, Maddie would be the one to figure them out since he'd created handles with their unique history in his brain.

After purchasing their hats and enough cheese and wine to last a month, they went out the back of the store and into the Mammoth Wheelhouse. In a towering silo, they joined a tour group as the guide began explaining the process of making the huge wheels of cheese. Rob was in awe of the size of the circles, which were thick enough to carve images into to promote local businesses.

"These are beautiful." Maddie darted in and out between the wine barrels displaying the carvings and took photos.

Rob spotted a carving resembling a car. Up close, he realized it looked like his vintage Triumph—a cheddar-orange version. The plaque below listed the Throttleshop as the sponsor, the place where he housed his car. He grew more anxious to get to his Triumph. He snapped a few pictures of the cheese version and shoved his phone back into his pocket. He'd post them on his secret Instagram account later when Maddie wasn't around.

He met up with her by his car, where she leaned against the trunk, looking relaxed and almost happy as she reviewed her shots on the camera's screen.

"Did you get some good ones?"

"Yes, some interesting close-ups. I'm excited to get to Siebkens."

"Great, can we make a pit stop to see my car?"

"No prob." Maddie rummaged around their groceries, pulled out the cheese curds, and nibbled on one. "Hey, thanks."

"For what?"

"Pushing me out of Baileys. It's good to be out and about, and I haven't thought once about all the vile bullshit going on."

"Brilliant." It pleased him to have lightened things up for her. "What is your style of communication? A daily update on the case or more? Or less?"

Maddie dug an orange notebook out of her bag as he pulled back onto the highway. "Once a day, but if you have any out-of-the-ordinary updates, please don't hesitate to tell me." She flipped through the journal pages. "This thing has helped tremendously. When are you going to take my deposition?"

"Let's not worry about it until later. Today is all about cheese, wine, and cars."

And with some luck, the deposition wouldn't be needed. Rob planned to get the entire flimflam of a case thrown out before a judge saw or heard any of Wagner's lies.

EIGHTEEN

Maddie's belly barked after eating most of the cheese curds on the way to Siebkens. The match between the coffee and cheese taunted her with a loud gastrointestinal brawl.

Rob grinned as he focused on the road, then pressed the phone button on the steering wheel.

It rang once. "Siebkens, how may I assist you?"

"Drew? It's me, Rob. How's it going?"

"Racin' Rob! Good to hear from you, brother. What's shaking?"

"Almost in town. Any empty tables for two?"

"You and Graham?" Drew asked.

"Not this time. He's in Baileys. I'm here," Rob said, glancing toward her, "with a friend."

"Well, I'll be damned!" Drew bellowed with a hearty Southern twang. "Any chance your *friend* is prettier than Graham?"

"Hell, yeah," Rob laughed, "but her stomach is howling louder than my uncle's. We need some food. I'm willing to postpone seeing my Triumph for Maddie."

"Thanks, I feel special," she said, "and to be fair, Drew, I've been cramped in Rob's car, speeding along with only cheese and coffee for sustenance."

"Glad to meet you, Maddie. You must be exceptional 'cause my man Rob hasn't ever brought anyone to Elkhart other than Graham. Rob's a man of mystery."

"I heard," she added, "and when we meet, I have a few questions for you. Are you a speed racer type, too?"

"Hells yes. NASCAR. Number 43 with Penske." Drew paused. "What's your ETA, bro? I'll get a table for two prepped. Want anything special?"

"Just the usual." Rob turned the Audi onto another county highway. "Any place to park?"

"Main Street is blocked off for pedestrians only. Come around to the back parking lot. I'll have a spot there for you. And Maddie, what are you interested in eating?"

"I'd love a burger." Her mouth watered. "Medium, no cheese, and fries, please and thank you."

"See you in ten." Rob clicked off the phone and slowed down dramatically.

"How do you know Drew?"

"Met him when he raced at Road America a few years back. Now, he's gotten the bug to settle down with Fran. She owns Siebkens, so when Drew isn't racing, he helps her out. You'll like both of them."

The lush cornfields gave way to quaint brick houses and maple trees lining the sidewalks. Suddenly, the road ahead was crammed and full of people. Expensive-looking cars were parked on either side of the narrow residential street, and folks were gazing at the fenders and peering into the windows.

"It's going to be like this all week."

Maddie pressed her nose against the window. The cars had a fascinating beauty, and she understood their appeal to collectors.

Rob relayed the ins and outs of the vintage car celebration. Collectors from all over the world had transported their one-of-a-kind automobiles to the sleepy little town in Wisconsin to show them off. The cars raced on the track, but slowly. Due to their antiquity, most couldn't move faster than forty miles an hour.

The congestion reminded Maddie of New York. Unexpectedly, she was eager as hell to bump into people and talk to strangers. She wanted to study their faces, make guesses about their backstories, and most definitely check out their style choices. She was excited for the first time in a long time and couldn't wait to get out and about in Elkhart.

Rob turned down an alley, pulled past a privacy fence, and parked. Maddie hadn't a clue about the makes or models of the other cars in the lot, but she knew they were expensive from the shiny paint jobs and tiny creatures trying to claw their way off the hoods.

Once out of the car, she stretched and let the afternoon sun heat her aching tailbone. She snapped a pic of the sleek onyx car next to Rob's, sent it to Graham, and asked, "Jaguar?" Then, she notified Brady of her safe arrival.

A fit Black guy strolled out from under a striped awning, and Maddie knew she'd just met Drew. His captivating smile matched his baritone voice.

She was about to grab her gear from the back seat, but Rob swooped in and took care of it for her. The delicious scent of a barbeque grill tickled her nose.

"Looks like you're staying for a month," Drew said, slapping Rob's back. "Good to see you, buddy."

Rob gave him a fist bump. "Ditto. Pretty close. We're here until after Labor Day."

Drew gave him a smirky eyebrow lift. "We? Sounds serious."

Maddie held out her hand to Drew. "Nice to meet you. I'm not sure about the serious part. Rob and I are old friends, and now he's working for me...so as serious as it sounds, it's—" She tripped over her words. "—well, serious, like important. You know?"

Instead of Eleanor, Awkward became her middle name. Apparently, her alone time had eradicated her social skills.

"Friends?" Drew chuckled. "*Suure.* I understand. Your room is ready to go."

Maddie gaped at Rob. "One room?"

"Yes." He hesitated. "With two bedrooms. I thought you'd need your space after—"

She hadn't thought about sleeping arrangements, but Rob had taken the time to plan ahead. Thinking of her needs first. She sighed. After being insulated with Rob in the car, she felt calmer than she'd been in weeks. Running away with him, only an hour and a half away, had been freeing. Not once had she thought about Wagner. "Thank you."

A tall brunette waved from behind the registration desk in the Siebkens lobby and ran up to hug Rob. The fabric of the short, billowy skirt that wrapped around her legs was beautiful, cream-colored with a floral design full of pinks and oranges. Maddie had to find out who made it. Only after registering the woman's perfect cheekbones did she realize it was Francesca Marcheti.

After kissing both of Rob's cheeks, she greeted Maddie, "Hello! I'm Fran. So glad to finally meet you."

Finally?

Did this beautiful woman know her? Maddie had only seen her in ads and cover photos for some of the most exclusive swimsuits. Francesca's image for a swimwear designer lit up Times Square every year.

Maddie swallowed a giggle and graciously accepted Fran's full-on bear hug.

"Have we met?"

Fran laughed. "No, but I feel like I know you from your work. I'm one of your followers on Instagram. When Rob mentioned he knew you, I went all fangirl."

Maddie struggled to contain the joy bouncing around inside her. Francesca Marcheti was one of *her* admirers? And amid her wonderful compliments, she'd said *Rob mentioned you.*

"Thank you. You have no idea how much this means to me." Maddie nodded toward Rob. "You've *mentioned* me?"

Rob's cheeks turned from red to crimson.

Drew chuckled.

Ignoring Rob's embarrassment, Fran continued. "Maybe 'mention' isn't totally right...more like bragged."

Maddie sucked in a deep breath of barbecue-scented air and relished the unique sense of peace coming over her. Coming to Elkhart Lake was exactly what she needed.

"Rob's not exactly a chatterbox," Fran said, "but when he talked about the well-known fashion stylist and influencer Maddie Logerquist, I couldn't get him to shut up. Oh, and by the way, you got totally screwed when *Summer Haven* let you go. I stopped watching after you left."

It was refreshing to hear from another person how unjust her exit from *Summer Haven* had been. Maddie had spent a lot of time burying her anger over how her cheating ex, Alex, had kicked her off the show.

"Well..." Rob said, swinging Maddie's bags to one side of his back. "Maddie's talented. It's easy to discuss her work. May we get settled in our room, please? I'm anxious to eat and see my Triumph."

Drew and Fran glanced at one another and snickered.

Now, Maddie's cheeks warmed up. She stood close to Rob. "I can carry my bags if you want."

"It's no trouble." Rob glared at the couple. "Glad you're able to meet Drew and Fran. They're good friends." Then, humming a familiar-sounding tune, Fran went behind the desk, retrieved two key cards, and handed them to Maddie.

As they strolled to the elevator alcove, Drew and Fran laughed and sang the theme to the ancient cartoon *Speed Racer*.

"Francesca Marcheti." Maddie broke the silence in the elevator. "She's a fan of mine?"

When the elevator opened, Rob ushered her ahead of him. "Yes, absolutely, along with a lot of other women, I'm sure. Your designs and styles are spectacular. Don't let anyone ever make you forget it."

A rush of heat ran through her as she followed Rob into a two-level loft-style room. The exposed cream-colored brick walls showed off the rustic hotel's age. A professional-grade stove top was centered on a granite-covered island in the small kitchen. The room looked like a chef's dream. "This is nuts. It's so tricked out."

Rob set the bags on a butter-colored leather sofa. "Fran just updated the place and gave each room a royal makeover to define itself against the Osthoff, making it the only boutique hotel in Elkhart. Now, chefs from around the world can stay here for cooking contests instead of going to the Osthoff."

"Is it safe to assume Fran's brother is the famous chef Nick Marcheti? Or should I say, *The Italian Scallion*?"

"Spot-on, but don't mention him to Fran. The two siblings aren't exactly on speaking terms."

He pointed toward the bedrooms above. "There's a room on either side of the loft area. One faces the water, and the other is by the track."

"Is it okay if I take the room near the track?" she asked. "Or do you have to sleep near the track? Some kind of superstition?"

"I am known as Speed around these parts." He bobbed his head. "For you though..."

They went upstairs together. He followed her into the bedroom and set her luggage on the king-size bed. She opened the door to the balcony and stepped out to get some fresh air. "Thanks, Speed. I know being around a lake is usually my style, but for once, I'd like to gaze at land, green grass, hills, flowers, and a hint of a racetrack." She used the camera lens of her phone for a closer look at the track. "I can make out the Road America billboard in the distance."

Her skin tingled when Rob laid his hand on her bare shoulder. She let the sun soak into her face and listened to the car engines revving in the distance. A blustery wind whipped around them, bringing the sweet scent of pineapple and honey with it. They stepped close to the railing and took in deep breaths.

Rob said, "A bonus to this room is that it's upstairs from the kitchen. Drew's family BBQ recipe is on the menu daily."

"We should get moving then before my stomach starts hollering. Do you think Drew and Fran would be willing to model for me? Not sure what for, but they are so darn adorable."

"Fran will be over the moon. She's always talking about your Instagram feed, and she hasn't done any modeling since the surgery. Of course, there's another fan in stiff competition with her."

"Who?" She scrolled through her Insta feed to check out her followers. With over 20,000, Maddie instantly felt guilty she hadn't posted enough since the night at the lighthouse. She vowed to reconnect with her fans while in Elkhart.

A message popped up on her screen. The handle messaging her was *Fukumen Rēsā.* She peered closely at the small image and recognized a picture of Racer X, Speed Racer's big brother. "This is your secret account? I love it."

When she accepted Racer X's invite, she scrolled through Rob's photos. Yes, there were many of him with his cars, but there were a few oldies. And goodies. Pictures of the days when they dove into the water at Cave Point and swam around with abandon and sunshine on their backs. What a glorious sensation. She couldn't take her eyes off one in particular. She'd been standing on the cliff, and Rob had taken it from above. Eyes closed, her smile radiating pure joy, and her hair splayed around her shoulders like a black folding fan. A rush of long-held emotions for Rob woke up and bounced about inside her. All she managed to say was, "It's been a while since my hair was long."

"One shot?" She held out her phone. "You take it. You're taller than me, and your arms are longer."

When their fingers touched, a second of heat sizzled through her. This moment wouldn't escape her. She leaned against his chest and pressed her cheek to the soft cotton of his T-shirt and hard strength of his shoulder, then wrapped her arms around his waist.

"One post on your *Fukumen Rēsā* account."

"Sure," he murmured and snapped a picture.

Then he slipped her phone into her back pocket and brushed his lips against her cheek.

She shivered and held him tighter.

He whispered, "I just have to...want to..."

"Kiss me?" She brushed his cheek with one finger, and the space between them evaporated. Since their last kiss, when she was in a sleepy haze, Rob's lips had left her craving for more steamy smooches. "This time, I'm asking you."

He nodded.

Her pulse quickened as he traced his fingers across her arm.

She knew he was hedging. "Is there a rule against client-attorney kissing?"

"Yes, I mean...but it's more about how you're feeling?" He suddenly sounded like her doctor.

She huffed. "Actually, Doctor Hottie, right now I'm amazing." She let his warmth swirl around her. "Better now than ever."

He crushed his lips against hers and held onto her as if making up for a lifetime of lost kisses.

Pulling back, he whispered, "Okay?"

"I could do this all day, like our summers at Cave Point." She nuzzled into his neck, letting the soft stubble scratch the tip of her nose. His heart pounded against hers, and she let out a long sigh. "Perfect."

She stood on her toes, combed her fingers through his thick ginger hair, and kissed his temple, then earlobe, and just as her lips were about to press into his, her stomach growled.

"Hungry?" He chuckled.

"Starving, unfortunately. Can we continue this later?"

He slid his finger across her lower lip. "We'll need to get past this case."

"I get it, I think. Always good to have something to look forward to."

NINETEEN

Rob's original idea was to pick up his newly painted Triumph from the garage, take it for a spin with the top down, and then park it in front of Siebkens for all the onlookers to admire and adore. The plan evaporated because of Maddie. Because of her growling stomach, yes, but more so, their latest brilliant kiss.

She'd bested his car and reminded him of those carefree summers when they were both back in Baileys from UW-Madison. Just before they lost Tyler. The Cave Point park and its bluffs offered a slew of hideaways where they could be alone: playing, touching, kissing, and making love.

Maddie was better for his heart and a lot less maintenance than the car, but after waiting and wanting her for all these years...it was going to be tough. However, he could call to mind every one of her scintillating spots he'd long ago stashed away when his head, and other parts, began to wander. This plan might delay succumbing to his temptations and help him stay focused on her case. He swallowed a groan of pure frustration. *Yeah, right.*

The clattering of ice cubes snapped him back as the waitress refilled their water glasses. From their window seat in the restaurant, he followed Maddie's gaze and watched the people outside bumping into one another to get a closer look at the vintage sports cars parked up and down the street. "This is the first day of Vintage Week, and it's usually the quietest compared to the next few weeks. Get ready, *bella*. The car aficionados will be gathering in *droves*."

Lounging back in a wicker armchair—with ample cushions—Maddie used her knee to table her bottle of beer and pointed outside. "What kind is that convertible? I love the color, almost like a frosty green. Very curvy."

Rob squinted to shield out the midday sun and quickly spotted the green car in the sea of red ones. He whistled under his breath. "It's one of my favorite car designs, a Ferrari." Leaning closer to the window, he added, "It's a 1972 Dino, but unfortunately, the owner is a prize ass. That lovely piece of machinery shouldn't be bathing in the sun without a top."

"You do realize you're talking about a car and not a woman."

"Of course," he said, surprised. "I'm sure I know the difference. At least most of the time. However, when you own a car worth over $200,000, it's an investment that needs a lot of attention. Maybe as much TLC as your significant other." He added, "And the tan leather interior will fade and look like shit. Leave it to Nick the Dick to leave her baking without any sunblock."

"Fran's brother, Nick?" She took a sip from her bottle of Spotted Cow. "Why so much hostility?"

"The *fratello* is full of himself and treats his sister like a child because she's a woman." It still exasperated Rob. Back in the day, when he and Fran hung out, Nick's old way of thinking had an irritating way of popping up. Fran's smarts and success were always ignored at family gatherings, while Nick's cooking show was talked about like he was the Michelangelo of the food world. "Their family is old-school Italian. Nicholas is the oldest, a male, and therefore the golden boy."

"Oh, my gawd. I can just make out his head with all the folks surrounding him. His salt-and-pepper hair and classic 1950s specs? Wow. He's moving through the crowd in this direction," she said excitedly. "This is so freaking cool. Do you think Fran can introduce me to him? I'd love to meet him. He's incredibly talented."

Rob rolled his eyes. "Sure, but don't complain to me when he politely ignores you. Fran's brother is a cocky SOB. She works hard and goes overboard to impress him. After her surgery, Nick made zero time to help her out. She couldn't even lift her arms."

"Fran's a breast cancer survivor?"

Rob nodded. "Double mastectomy. A year ago."

She looked at him in wonder. "Tell me the truth. Were you two ever really dating?"

He picked at the label on his sweating beer bottle. "We were never a couple, never dated, but people liked to guess, which was rather fun. Fran and Drew are great together. I'm their official third wheel. Our love of cars bonded us, and we've always had a strong friendship. When Fran was diagnosed, knowing her family dynamics, there was no way I could let her face surgery alone."

She stared at him with those magnetic and thoughtful azure eyes, and his face grew warm. It was hard not to be distracted by her intense gaze. Their kisses had spearheaded a host of challenges he still had to figure out. Being censured or, worse, disbarred due to an unethical relationship with a client. Neither of them needed that.

"Fran's brother always stays at the Osthoff. Not here at his own sister's hotel. Like his sister owning Siebkens makes her a social outcast."

"Does Fran know how notorious her brother is?"

"Of course. They talk when he makes himself available to her."

"Wanna get going? I have to work off this burger. With a good walk, I can lick my wounds of disappointment away. It must be true. It's not good to meet your heroes."

"Nick the Dick is your hero? Why? How?"

"I saw him in New York. He collects contemporary art and has a photography collection. His food dishes are inspired by pieces of art. As a stylist, I wanted to learn more about his creative process. It's pretty fascinating. I'm disappointed he still lives in the dark ages though."

"You might score some points if you faint when you meet him."

"We both know playing a damsel in distress isn't my forte. Nick's vlog on YouTube, though, is incredibly beautiful. His posts are slick. After I saw him, I was inspired to change up my fashion photos."

Seeing her rise slowly from her chair, he asked, "Are you up for one more stop? I know it's been a long day, so I'll understand if you want to hang back in the room."

"You're stuck with me, buddy," she said as they left the restaurant. She jutted out her hip without a wince and showed off her bag. "I'm prepped and ready to go with my camera. I can take some photos of your Triumph. Also, I still need to know how you've become so adept in Italian."

"*Certo.*" A racy idea struck, and a tiny thrill shot through him. They left the restaurant, and once outside, Rob yanked his baseball cap from the pocket of his khakis and plopped it on. The sun was fierce. "Hey, did you bring any sunscreen?"

She handed him a tube from her bag. "Always stash it for my pale-skinned English mate."

"Ah. Thanks," he said, slightly embarrassed and flattered at the same time.

They strolled away from Siebkens and hiked along the grass-covered railroad ties leading into the tiny town of Elkhart. In fact, town was an exaggeration.

There were three stately homes on the street. Mansions back in the day, and now turned into businesses: a wine shop, a bar, and an antique shop. The remnants of the defunct train station on the other side of the road housed a coffee shop, pastry shop, and an Italian restaurant.

"Hold on," Maddie said, freeing her camera from her bag. "I have to get a shot of this train station. I love the contrast between the red side and the blue sky. It's tremendous. What a charming town. No wonder you come here."

"Truthfully, I've been to the coffee shop once," he said, checking messages on his phone as she clicked photos. "If you want, later we can hit Baers during happy hour. Go in and get a sidecar cocktail."

Out of all his messages, he read only the one from Gus. *So far, so good bro. No Wagner sightings have been reported. Will keep you posted*.

After Maddie put her camera back, she pulled his hand so hard he nearly tripped on one of the railroad ties. "I have to have a sweet, and I see the sign, Pastries by Patrice."

"Sure, sure," Rob said, checking his watch and calculating the time it would take to get his car. Sam would post the Closed sign in a little less than an hour. "Okay if we walk and eat at the same time?"

Playfully, she shoved him. "It can wait. Let's go get your four-wheeled hottie."

"How do you know it has four wheels?" he joked. "Maybe my Triumph is really a Reliant Robin?"

"You're too smart and balanced to invest in a three-wheeled auto," she said, kissing his cheek and jogging toward Main Street. "Come on."

He shouted, "You have no idea where you're going!"

"Tell me," she shouted back. "I'm sure it's one of the other two buildings in sight."

"Turn right at the stop sign," he yelled, amazed at how fast she jogged with a bruised tailbone. Her swimming legs had turned into runner's legs. Long, lean, and gorgeous.

He was out of breath from sprinting to catch up with her.

She laughed without pausing to catch some extra air. "You need to get out and about and flex those muscles of yours," she teased. "Too much office time." Rob swallowed his spit and controlled his breathing. "Hey, you've been hiking up ninety-seven steps several times a day, remember?" Before his next breath escaped him, he pointed ahead. "Throttleshop is up ahead. See the garage?"

Maddie shielded her eyes with her hands. "It's a car garage? It looks like a museum with two levels of windows."

"Actually, three, the first one is underground. It's a storage facility for cars. There is a museum section where they display a lot of Harleys." With his heart pounding from the heat and his short run, he chastised himself for getting out of his running routine. "Let's walk the rest of the way."

The parking lot in front of Throttleshop was full of cars and spectators. More vintage cars were on display for the gawkers, like those by Siebkens.

"No wonder Main Street was quiet." Maddie patted him on his back. "Are you ready, Racer X? Do you have a mask hidden somewhere in the Triumph?"

He wrapped his arm over her shoulders. "You so get me, Trixie."

As they wound around the men, women, and kids circling and gazing at the incredible collection of cars, Rob had to pull Maddie's hand to keep moving. He couldn't blame her. The sleek designs of all the vintage cars were breathtaking. There were lime-green Corvettes from the '60s, a stately forest green Jaguar, an Aston Martin used in a James Bond film, and another one of 007's favorite rides, a silver Bentley.

When an orange BMW convertible held Maddie's attention for more than a minute, Rob surreptitiously glanced at his watch and the front door of the garage. He craned his neck for a clearer glimpse inside to see if Sam was still working.

"Do you think this one is for sale?" Maddie asked. "It's cute. I like it. Maybe I need a new car. Elsie's car isn't as sexy."

He hesitated before taking a closer look at the BMW. "Let's ask."

The air conditioning inside the shop hit him like a cup of ice down his back. He glanced around for Sam as Maddie wandered around the showroom. "While you take care of Ms. Triumph, I'd like to take a few pictures. Who do I need to ask for permission?"

As soon as Rob saw Sam in the corner by the engine museum, he waved. "Over there, you'll need to ask Sam Penske. She's the owner."

"She? Sam is a woman?" Maddie exclaimed. "Another female entrepreneur in Elkhart. This place is amazing."

"She's from a dynasty of race car drivers. Drew drives for Team Penske. We, Graham and I, are indebted to Sam. She's restored over ten cars for us. Haven't you ever listened to Graham's podcast? Sam is a regular."

Maddie ignored his question and nearly bumped into another client while getting over to where Sam was bent under the hood of a vintage, banana-yellow Ford Mustang.

Wanting to properly introduce them, he made a beeline around the bathtub-shaped Porsche roadsters and reached the Mustang as Maddie strode up.

"Out of breath?" she asked.

He cocked his eyebrow and shook his head. If he *had* lost his breath, it would have been only because she stole it. From their tiny race, Maddie's face was flushed. As they stood side by side, he stepped close enough to brush against her bare arm.

Sam released the brace holding up the hood and guided the top slowly down and back into place. She looked at Rob, clearly stunned to see him. "What are you doing here?"

"Sorry, Sam, my plans were rearranged. I should have called and made an official appointment to pick up the car."

"No need to apologize," Sam said, wiping off a bit of grease from her fingers with a Penske monogrammed cloth. She offered her hand to Maddie. "Hey, I'm Samantha. As long as you're a friend of this one"—she pointed to Rob—"you can call me Sam."

Maddie lifted her hand to her chest and nodded toward him. "He's a friend *and* a lifesaver. I'm Maddie Logerquist. Love your..." She looked around with admiration. "Your car museum? An eclectic display of autos and cycles?"

Sam laughed. "I've been running the family business for ten years, so a lot of this collection has been handed down through generations. I'm lucky to have inherited the job of watching over it."

"Sounds like a legacy thing," Maddie said, giving him a sideways glance. "I'm impressed. I know nothing about cars. Would it be all right if I take a few photographs? I'm trying to get back into doing some styling with my camera."

"Sure, sure." Sam smiled at Maddie and flashed him a look of confusion. "We weren't expecting you for another two weeks. Didn't you request them to be ready for the first race?"

The realization he'd screwed up his dates hit him in the gut. Sam's face paled, clearly upset. "You're right, you are absolutely correct," he said, punching his words while chastising himself. *Shit.* "Where are you at with it?"

Sam adjusted the bandana wrapped around her head and

tucked a long strand of blue hair under the scarf. "The DZs are late."

"DZs?" Maddie asked while looking through her camera lens and twisting the focus ring.

"Tires. Dunlop Direzza DZ101. DZs," Rob said glumly, ignoring the seed of frustration planted by his own stupidity. He should have called ahead to get the status of the car work. He should be better at being on top of his schedule. "How long are they out?"

"Should be here by the end of the week," Sam answered. "Come on, let's go look at her. You will love the paint. The British red is spit shined."

Following Sam from the showroom and into the garage, Rob tried like hell to disguise his disappointment with a straight face and lips clamped tight. He wasn't pissed at Sam. It wasn't her fault. But damn, he'd been looking forward to taking Maddie for a spin with the top down. Actually, he'd wanted to take her out on the Road America track. A slow, leisurely ride to get her acquainted with the racetrack.

When they passed through the automatic doors, he spotted his car—like a beacon from above on the hydraulic lift. All the curves were stunning, and the color was glossy cherry red. She looked a bit forlorn, though, without any tires.

Maddie stood beside him. "She is gorgeous. What is her kind again?"

"A Triumph Spitfire. Mark IV. Built in '72. I found her in a junkyard two years ago."

Sam punched the control panel, and the lift lowered the car until it hovered a couple of feet above the cement floor. "When Rob brought it to us, she was rusted and worn. The original blue color had faded away. We rebuilt the engine to a six horsepower." Popping the hood, she added, "Take a look at this engine."

Maddie looked into the open bonnet. "I love it. Such a shiny congregation of lines. Darn it, Rob, you're going to beat anyone on the track with her. Mind if I take a few shots?"

"Go for it." He circled around his car, taking in every single one of the curves and angles. "Any talk from the DZ rep? Is it possible to get an exact arrival date for the tires? If they get here earlier in the week, say Monday or Tuesday, she'll be all done by next weekend. Hey?"

Sam glanced at him with pity. "I'll go call her now. For you. It's great to see you. All week, I've had to deal with Nick the Dick and his Ferrari. He's already been in to have the green color shined up after sitting in the sun."

Rob grunted his agreement. "And the interior? It's going to fade, too. We were just watching him prance around the car like a horse's ass. Dissin' the maker's logo."

"And green? Really?" Sam laughed as she pulled a phone from the side pocket of her overalls. "I tried to tell him that it's a Ferrari and they're meant to be red. But Nick wouldn't have any of it. Who am I? A lowly chick mechanic!" Shaking her head, she walked into her office to talk to the tire rep.

A shutter snapping dragged him out of his self-loathing. Maddie continued to take photos of his car from every angle. When she lay on her back on the floor and lobster-crawled beneath it, he caught sight of silky smooth legs as her skirt shifted up toward her waist.

"Hey, be careful," he said, trying to contain his lustful thoughts. Thankfully, there were few other people in the garage. But since Sam hired mostly women mechanics, he was fairly certain everyone around him would read his smutty thoughts as he stared at Maddie's gorgeous thighs. He sat on the ground next to her bare legs. "Finding what you're looking for under there? Can I be of any assistance? Is your back okay?"

"I'm fine. Under here, I get a great image of the lines and the guts of your car. I think I can create some cool images for you to post on your Racer X Instagram account."

Did she have any idea what that meant to him? Incredibly grateful, he lost his words.

"Hey?" Maddie shouted from underneath the car. "Are you still there?"

"Yeah, bloody fantastic. Since I can't drive her, we can get her noticed on Instagram?"

She scooted out from beneath the car and pushed down her skirt. "Well, of course. I know it's not the same, but at least we can reach a bigger audience than the one surrounding Marcheti's car. It's amazing who you can meet and connect with using hashtags and pics on IG." She stood up, turned her camera over, and let him look at the small screen. "Check these out."

Rob loved every photo Maddie had ever taken. From her shots of the bridges in New York to the lighthouse and now these pics of the underbelly of his car. They weren't too dissimilar. Her eye for metal, lines, and balance created photos that translated into a unique vantage point. "Fashion styling, photography, swimsuit designer extraordinaire. Talk about talent."

Sam strode over to them. "Good news. Your tires will be here Tuesday morning. Installation will take a day or two. So next Friday, your beauty will be road ready and race ready."

Calmer and completely enamored with the photos in Maddie's camera, he forced himself to address Sam. "Wonderful. Thank you so much, Sam. Mind if we hang out for a while? Maddie's going gonzo with photos for me."

TWENTY

In the Brown Baer Tavern, Maddie waited while Rob went to the bar and ordered drinks. She set her elbows on the table—an old electrical wiring spool turned on its end—and scanned through the photos she'd taken at the Throttleshop. Which were the best ones to add to Rob's secret Instagram account?

The crowd in the bar grew as it was happy hour, and the featured cocktail was a sidecar, just as Rob had predicted. Leaning over the bar, he looked at his phone and tapped his toe to the Petty tune playing on the jukebox. She wondered who was on the other end of the messages.

Wagner's attorney?

She squelched the thought, put her camera away, and retrieved her journal. This first day in Elkhart had become one she didn't want to forget, so she started to jot down some notes about the whirlwind that had become her life. She needed to gain some insight into her emotions. When words escaped her, she resorted to doodling and then started drawing a swimsuit design that had been cooking in her brain after taking pics of all the lines, curves, and colors at Sam's Throttleshop. Even the fabric texture and thread colors of Sam's overalls inspired Maddie.

Without looking away from her drawing, she thanked Rob as he set down their drinks. She quickly finished a sketch of a two-piece swimsuit with a curvy cutout on the back and a centered zipper on the front piece. She pictured it with multiple sherbet-colored fabrics circling around the sweetheart neckline.

"Care for some company?" he asked, glancing over her sketches. "Drew just rang. He and Fran are meeting us. Is that all right?"

She yanked her attention away from the suit design and closed the book. "Yeah, I just had an idea I wanted to get out of my mind and down on paper."

"Another one of your award-winning swimsuits?"

She didn't have the cojones to tell him she'd only been awarded once for a swimwear design, and it had long since disappeared into the nether regions of the warehouse owned by her client, Sunkissed. "It is a swimsuit—a loving tribute to our curves and inspired by your Triumph. But maybe even more. I couldn't help but think about how the women in the Throttleshop were roasting in their uniforms. And Sam, a rather styling business owner, might appreciate a fresh look with some breathable fabrics."

He tilted his head and stared at her for so long she noticed the freckles on the tip of his left earlobe. Suddenly, she wanted to kiss and nibble it and then move over to his lips. She took a sip of the cocktail to cool down. "This is delicious. What's in it again?"

"Cognac and Cointreau, an orange liqueur."

The knot of muscles in her shoulders loosened after a few sips of sweet, citrusy goodness melded with brandy, and she relaxed. "How many of these drinks do you think it will take to unwind me? It's better than any of the scripts my doctor gave me."

"Doesn't hurt that you're in a new environment." He tipped his glass against hers. "Cheers. I'm sure you'll take a liking to Elkhart."

"Already done," she said, waving at Fran and Drew as they walked into the bar. "Again, I'm mesmerized by your two friends. They look like a match made in heaven." Fran, with her smooth olive skin kissed by the sun and soaked by the Mediterranean, and Drew's rough-hewn beard and broad smile inspired Maddie. "Has he been playing with cars his whole life?"

"Actually, they both have. Fran's family owns the only Ferrari dealership in the Midwest. In Chicago. Her Italian family is a tough subject."

"As in, brother Nick?"

Nodding, Rob got up to greet the couple and then pulled two stools over to the table. Maddie wanted to get up and hug them but had found a comfortable position on the seat for her butt. She wondered what, or if, Rob had mentioned anything about her predicament to his good friends. As soon as Drew gripped her shoulder and Fran gave her a bear hug, she knew the answer. Nope. They knew nothing. The slight ache, ironically, felt refreshing. The ugliness in Baileys was in the past and a hundred miles away.

"Are you a writer as well as an influencer?" Fran asked, eyeing her journal.

"Oh, no, doodler extraordinaire," she said. "I'm working on some designs. This place has me jazzed." For effect, she added jazz hands. "And I've only been here for one day."

The two men interrupted to ask them about food, then went to the bar to place their order.

Alone, the women sized each other up. As much as Maddie wanted to know more about Fran's health, she didn't want to be intrusive. Knowing a person had a double mastectomy brought about an enormous number of questions. Especially when they were the same age. Fran had probably traveled around the sun as many times as she had.

"I've never loved Rob," Fran said. "I mean...if you were wondering."

She shook her head. "No, not really. I know you two connected in Chicago, and he..."

"Was like a real brother? *Danarre.* Rob's a good guy. Went with me to every chemo treatment."

"Not a surprise. Rob has always been a steady eddy for me, and now...well...he's gone above and beyond."

Fran gave her a naughty grin. "Are we talking about sex?"

Maddie blushed. "Oh, god. No. I just, he's..." She had to stop and think. Who was Rob Reid to her? They'd been connected by tragedy for so long, but now, in Elkhart, they were all about fun. Mostly. Not mired by sad events from the past. She considered this a do-over. A second, clean-slate chance to get it right with Rob. "His cars are an anomaly to me. It's a part of Rob I've never seen and hardly understood. Guys love their wheels. And lots of speed. The faster, the better."

"Fine with me," Fran said, "as long as they're slow in bed."

Maddie let out a chuckle. After their kiss an hour ago, she sensed a luxurious night of pleasure and passion was in her not-so-near future, if not a night and a luxurious day. She knew from history that Rob saved his need for speed for his cars.

"TMI?" Fran smiled. "Sorry, since surgery, there's been a lot of changes, a lot of things to get used to, but then with Drew"—she brushed a long thread of chestnut hair off her face—"I've been acquainting myself with a new normal and finding a lot of fresh thrills because he's the love of my life. Let's just hope it's a long journey we'll be on together."

Maddie tapped her journal. "Can I show you something?"

"Yes! Please," Fran said, clapping her hands together. "Is it something from *Summer Haven*? A new style? I love how you put the outfits together for the women on the show. They always looked cool enough for the beach and totally hot for their men."

Rob and Drew came back with their food.

"My ears are burning." Drew set down a drink and a basket of food in front of Fran.

"How are you two getting on?" Rob asked, sounding a bit nervous. "I mean, I hope you aren't too hungry. Seemed to take forever."

"We're getting along *fantastica*," Fran told him. "We were talking about how fabulous you are in the bedroom."

Two shades of red spread across Rob's cheeks, making his freckles almost disappear. He coughed and combed his fingers through his hair.

Drew punched his arm playfully. "Dude, is there something you want to tell me about?"

"Hell, no, I'm golden."

All four broke out into laughter so loud that the others around them interrupted their own convos to see what was happening.

"I'm going to eat," Rob said amiably. "I don't want to get into any kind of trouble."

"Go ahead." Fran pointed to the journal. "Maddie was about to show me something more important."

Maddie popped a french fry in her mouth and opened the book to the swimsuit design. "It's this swimsuit. When I was in New York, I designed a few suits for women. It was a small clientele, and I never had time to turn it into anything bigger. Don't get me wrong, I love promoting Sunkissed swimwear, but it falls short for a lot of women."

Fran grabbed the book and paged through, looking at her

sketches. "I haven't worn a swimsuit since my nipples disappeared, and I'm taking the reconstruction process slowly. Not one client who I modeled for has asked to retain my services again." She brought the book up to her nose. "I love the design of the back. It's sexier than hell. What are you thinking?"

"A few of my suit designs are for women who've had mastectomies, and I can adjust or accommodate the designs to their individual needs. Would you take a look? Give me your opinion?"

Drew snort-laughed. "Not sure if Francesca is good with opinions."

"Oh yes." Fran pointed to the sketch. "And if you make this piece, I'd model it for you in a heartbeat."

"Really?"

"Absolutely!"

Maddie tucked her journal into her bag and finished her burger. Although the conversation around her was fun and lighthearted, she only listened with one ear. Her mind kept swirling about ideas for her swimsuit designs. Having Francesca Marcheti model swimsuits for her would be a huge boon.

The jukebox became louder as the waitress took their empty baskets away, and a few patrons started dancing in the back of the bar. When Bruce Springsteen's song "Hungry Heart" blared across the room, Maddie couldn't resist. She grabbed Rob's hand and pulled him out to the dance floor. If he was surprised, he didn't show it. When Fran and Drew joined, the four of them swayed and turned to the music until it ended. Sweating, Maddie wanted to take a break, but "Pink Cadillac" came on, and the two men roared. She kept up with everyone, ignoring her growing aches, and then "Moondance" by Van Morrison came on. She wrapped her arms around Rob's shoulders and rested her head against his chest. They swayed to the music. Tired and blissful.

The bar's conga line broke up after the bartender pulled the plug on the jukebox. There was a collective moan from the last of the dancers as they emptied the dance floor. Maddie hugged Drew and Fran goodbye and gave them a bunch of sloppy kisses as the bartender started piling the stools on top of the bar. It was closing time, and she was approaching four sheets to the wind, if not already there. Once they all made it outside, the cool August breeze woke her up.

She tottered a little and bumped into Rob. His voice took on a level of urgency as he cautioned the other couple to take care as they rode home. Maddie admired Fran and Drew's choice of wheels, a bicycle built for two. Donning helmets, Drew took the driver's seat on the front of the tandem, and Fran tucked her scarf into her windbreaker.

"Be careful," Maddie shouted as the couple wheeled off. "Are they okay to drive?"

"Perfect. They drank more water than liquor, and they don't have far to go. They live in a house on the east side of the lake."

"I drank some water, too, but those sidecars really packed a punch." A few deep breaths and the midnight quiet cleared her head. She took hold of Rob's hand, and he entwined his fingers with hers.

"We'll take a slow stroll back to Siebkens."

She carefully handled her steps and managed to avoid tripping on the weathered railroad ties. Still, the uneven ground, combined with her state of giddiness, made her bump into Rob more than once. She apologized the first few times, although it didn't seem to disturb him. Then, he simply draped his arm across her shoulders.

Now steady, she took in the starry night sky and the fireflies. "What a fabulous night."

The cicadas complained when they passed by, waking them

in their hidden homes in the woods and brush on the side of the train track.

"It is peaceful. Although if we go to the lake, I bet the Tiki Bar will be open."

Shaking her head, she felt like a sloth. "There's a double-thick mattress with my name on it. Besides, it's our first night here, and we have to pace ourselves."

"You're right," he said, flashing his phone light onto their path. "Congrats. You'll have a lot of work to do with Fran modeling your swimwear."

A mix of warmth and excitement ran down her spine. "Another reason to get a good night's sleep. I have a lot of designs to think about."

She didn't mention her biggest design...kissing Rob again.

When they reached their room, they awkwardly separated in the foyer. He helped her take off her dainty summer cardigan, carefully keeping it from touching her sore elbow. When his fingers grazed the arm, she broke out in goose bumps. His touch, light as it was, set her pulse racing. She turned to face him and caressed his cheek. "Can we continue what we started earlier? Or have you forgotten about our kiss?"

He took her hand between his and kissed the back of it. "Recorded in my long-term memory, but—"

She held her breath. But what? There was a lot of fuel behind his kiss earlier. Had she imagined it? Or had all the darn sidecars muddled her senses?

Rob tucked her hand against his chest. When she felt his heart pounding, she knew she hadn't imagined any of it. Hugging him, she inhaled a faint scent of orange lingering on him. "You're hot. I mean warm. Like a good space heater."

"Oh, you're right, but here's the deal. I'm your attorney, and for me to give you the best of my services, a solid defense, I have to think with my head, not any other parts."

"Not even some heavy petting, Mr. German Shepherd?" She stifled an adolescent whine. "Can I sign on some dotted line for other services?"

He chuckled. "Nothing I can condone as legal or ethical."

"Not even a kiss?"

"Maddie, one kiss would never be enough for either of us. If it makes you feel any better, I will be taking a lot of swims in a cold lake."

She released a long-suffering sigh. Finally alone with Rob, yet an evil intruder had invaded and thrown out their second chance. Or was it the third? At least she was sure, as she nuzzled her face into his neck, she would be ready and more than willing for the next time.

TWENTY-ONE

Maddie woke up groggy but clearly heard Rob in the other bedroom whisper-bitching about the effing location of his swim trunks and how his workout routine had gone to hell. When the main door slammed shut, she ventured out and glanced into his bedroom. The sheets and comforter were twisted about the bed and splayed out on the carpeting.

How delightful. Rob had slept just as poorly as her. All night, she'd tossed and turned while dreaming about their most recent kiss, and then she'd fantasized about other kisses in a boatload of delectable areas she'd grown anxious to revisit. It may have been a decade ago when they last made love, but she'd fervently memorized his entire repertoire of touches. The sizzling sensation when Rob tickled her inner thigh with his tongue or when he lightly stroked the back of her leg, from ankle to knee and then upward, finishing with a sweet squeeze to her bum. She'd usually sigh and giggle at the same time.

She needed a hit of sugar to douse her lusty cravings, so instead of eating a healthy breakfast, a stop into a pastry shop had her name written all over it. On her way to Main Street, she found a perfect walking stick and poked it around the edges of the rails and ties of the unused railroad. It reminded her of the High Line in Chelsea. She flicked off the white stones, uncovering sections of overgrown moss and grass around the ties. Mushrooms sprouted in clumps and dotted the sides of the track. When the coffee shop came into view, she let out a low whistle. Off the Rail was next to the old feed mill barn where Pastries by Patrice was housed.

She jogged along the inside of the rails and hopped on every other tie. When her bag bounced against her tailbone, she stopped to walk. Damn bruised butt. On the patio surrounding the shops, she set her bag on the only available table and asked a nearby woman to watch it while she went inside to get her pastry and coffee.

The delicious smell of sugar and butter hit her, and her mouth watered as she gazed at the display of chocolate éclairs and croissants. Hungry and excited, she couldn't decide, so she ordered a selection of sweets. Almost a dozen, and most would end up back at Siebkens for Rob. Maybe they could share one later. She fantasized about licking chocolate off his lips, then squashed the thought and sighed.

A man now occupied the table where she'd left her precious camera, and the woman who had agreed to provide surveillance had been replaced by another woman with a little kid.

"Hello?" Warily approaching the table, she set down her box of mini pastries and clutched her camera bag. "Not sure what happened, but I'd reserved this table. This is my stuff."

The man looked up from his phone, and Maddie sucked in her breath. It was Fran's brother, Nick Marcheti. His beard and mustache, a mix of gray and white, were highlighted by his black-rimmed glasses, giving off a hipster vibe. But his full-blown, toothy smile oozed too much happiness, setting her on edge.

"Ahh, I hope you don't mind," he said with a rising Italian

accent. "I saw your camera and bag and wanted to see who owned it. I offered to watch it and wait for you. Sorry to alarm you, yeah?"

Maddie floundered for words as Rob's warnings flooded into her head. Only one word escaped her mouth. "You."

Nick Marcheti bellowed out a laugh. "Please, sit. It's your table. I don't mean to intrude."

Shaking her head, she attempted to get her act together. His fame and talent were well-known but were celebrated to an almost cultish level around the set of *Summer Haven* in the Hamptons. She sat across from him and held out her hand. "It's nice to meet you, Mr. Marcheti. I a...appreciate your work." *Adore* seemed over the top.

"*Nick, per favore.* Many thanks, but you have me at a disadvantage. You are?"

"Maddie Logerquist," she announced, wondering why he'd sat at her table.

"*Che figata!* You *are* the photographer Francesca raves about."

Maddie was unclear about *che figata.* "I met your sister yesterday. Fran and her beau, Drew, are lovely hosts."

"Although hindered, Francesca is the hardest worker in our *famiglia.*" He took a sip from his cup of espresso. "She raved about you yesterday. When I saw this"—he tapped her camera bag—"I had hope."

'Hindered?'

Trying to ignore his smug vibe, she opened the box and offered him a pastry. "They all looked so incredible, I couldn't decide. Please, help yourself."

While Nick appraised the selection of mini sweets, she scoped out the tattoo peeking out from the short sleeve of his black T-shirt. An Italian word or expression with a lot of letter Vs...*Vivi e lascia vivere.*

He gracefully slid a petite chocolate éclair from the box and placed it lovingly on the paper napkin in front of him. "The pastry chef, she is talented. When I arrive in Elkhart, I stop here first."

"I saw you yesterday with your car in front of Siebkens," Maddie said, then grabbed the other mini éclair and popped it whole into her mouth. Nick Marcheti was no rival to her hunger. She barely finished swallowing before asking about his tattoo.

"Live and let live," he responded, then took a dainty nibble of his tiny éclair. "Will you be taking photos of these incredible artisanal creations?"

"I am trying to expand my photo portfolio for my foodie friends, but I'm too hungry this morning. Here in Elkhart, I'm all about the cars and taking photos for a friend."

"So you've seen my Ferrari?" he asked. "It's at the shop today, taking a rest from yesterday's sun."

"Yes, the green one," she said, feeling confident after learning about all the pitfalls of the color from Rob. "It seems like a strange color choice for the car."

"*Mia bella!* She is, ahh, rare. Although Samantha has offered many times to paint her red, I am against it. She is grounded, like Mother Earth. *Verde* for the future."

Okay. This extra-thick layer from this smooth-talking *Italian chef* started to sound phony and was anything but *grounded.* Besides, wasn't he as American as Chef Boyardee? "I'm no expert on cars, vintage, race, or any kind. I've been living in New York and hoofing it for a while."

"You're from New York?"

"No, I grew up in Door County. My accent has slowly developed from a diet of milk, beer, and a lot of cheese. In New York, all my neighbors recognized my Midwest roots when I used the word *bubbler.*"

He chuckled, clearly understanding the Wisconsin term for a water fountain. Instantly, Nick's Italian accent lost its validity. It was a bunch of baloney, or was it bologna?

"What about wine? There are many vineyards in Door County."

"Yes, I enjoy a Cabernet occasionally."

"Have you been to..." He paused to *finally* swallow the last bite of the tiny éclair. "Vintage? It is a gem. Many wines and beers to select from. They have wine tastings and classes. The owner, Jennifer, is a world-renowned sommelier. I'm interviewing her for my show this season, even though she is a... unique in the world of sommeliers."

A woman? Maddie glowered at him. "I'll have to check out her store. I'm impressed with Elkhart. It seems as though most of the businesses here are owned by women. You must be so proud of your sister, Francesca."

"I hear Siebkens is becoming more popular since the rooms have been renovated." He analyzed another pastry and sounded blasé. "She's young and still has so much to learn."

"May I ask why you don't stay at your own sister's resort?" Maddie tried to sound nonchalant, but after talking to Fran only a couple of times, she wanted to shout and scream about her fabulousness from every rooftop. Why and how couldn't Fran's brother see it?

"But how would you know, *cara?*"

She struggled to ignore his condescension. "Another car collector mentioned it to me. I think you may know Rob Reid?"

"Why yes, of course, *Roberto,*" Nick said gleefully. "He is a beautiful driver. Have you experienced a ride in his Jaguar? It is unforgettable, so smooth and effortless with his expertise."

As Nick went on and on complimenting Rob, her irritation turned to frustration. She wanted to tell him to cut the crap and drop the insincere Italian. Why hadn't he regaled his own sister's accomplishments and survival? For goodness' sake, she'd beaten cancer. Sipping her coffee, it seemed like an eternity passed before she could get another word in with this bogus dude. Her experience in the lighthouse must have sharpened her discernment between the beautiful, fake people in the world and the ugly, real ones.

"There's been a delay with Rob's car," she interrupted. "Unfortunately, he won't be able to drive it until next week. I'll be taking some photos of it for him."

"Car photos, fantastic." Nick clapped his hands together. "The Jaguar? It's the roadster that inspired the paint for my Ferrari. It's avocado green; although the shade I chose is darker, any shade of green is *bella*."

"I haven't seen his Jaguar," she said, thinking how Rob's Italian sounded much more authentic than this guy's.

Nick continued talking about Rob's Jaguar as if she hadn't spoken. Then he spewed on about himself and his cars reverently. She wanted to shout, "Amen," to end all his self-worship.

"Rob's *Triumph* is getting a makeover as we speak." She cut him off mid-sentence. "I can't wait to get a ride in *it* when it's finished."

Now she believed everything Rob had told her about Nick the Dick.

"If it's with Samantha, it is in good hands. She is competent as long as he is willing to oversee her decisions," he said haughtily. "I have to tell you, I chose to sit with you today to offer you an opportunity or make you a proposition."

"Proposition?" A distinct stench was wafting out of this conversation. "What do you want from me?"

"I'd like you to take some photographs of Francesca. Whatever she would like, as long as she is dressed. Since her surgery, she can't be seen unclothed. I will buy them from you and give them to her as a surprise."

She swallowed down a gag. What a reprehensible way to regard his own sister. As if her lifesaving operation had turned her into a monster who had to be hidden away. He was a sad excuse for a brother. Thank goodness Fran had Rob. "I'm not really a portrait photographer."

"Of course, Francesca would love any of your current photos...what are they of?"

"I'm a fashion stylist, and lately, I've been working at a lighthouse."

He waved his hand in a whatever gesture. "Maybe, instead, she would like something from around here. Say a bridge? The track?"

She made sure her face didn't give her glee away about the—unknown to him—new adventure with Fran. "Maybe when I get out this week, I can look for something that Fran, your *brilliant* sister, may be interested in."

Nick looked past her shoulder. "Well, speak of the devil."

She watched Rob striding toward them. A turquoise beach towel was draped over his shoulders, and he used one corner of it to towel dry his mop of ginger hair. His wet T-shirt stuck to his abs. Relieved, Maddie waved him over.

Rob greeted her with a hug and scowled at Nick. "Marcheti, what are you up to?"

"Perfect timing," she whispered in his ear.

"So sorry, Rob. I did not mean to offend you," Nick said. "Maddie's work drew me toward her. I'm looking for gifts for Francesca."

"Really? Why don't you just stay at Siebkens instead of the Osthoff? She could really use your patronage. Fran would appreciate it," Rob said, "and she is your *famiglia*."

With just one word, Rob's accent sounded more authentic than Nick's and much sexier. Would there be any ethical concerns if Rob turned her on by reading a car manual to her in romantic Italian? Maddie stood from the rock-hard picnic bench to stretch out her back. "I can't wait to work with Fran."

"Have you been out on the track?" Nick asked her. "The contrast between the hills and the roadway is stunning."

"I haven't been out on the track, but thanks for asking." She added, "Maybe later, we can walk around it?"

"Absolutely." Rob winked at her. "There are food trucks out at the bends in the track. We can get lunch if you want."

"Thank you for the pastry." Nick patted Rob on the back. "So good to see you, *fratello*. We may not agree on much, but hear me when I say that Francesca Marcheti means the world to me. There's much you don't know since you're no longer *famiglia*."

"No longer *famiglia*, my ass," Rob growled after Nick left.

"I don't think I've ever met a bigger ignoramus," she said. "Thank goddess he's not staying at Siebkens—I'm not sure I can be civil around him. What a condescending sexist."

"Told you. He is an old-school egocentric. Drew and I, and now you, are all Fran has as a family." Rob analyzed the box of pastries. "It's such a load of bull when he talks about *famiglia*. If I hadn't been around for Fran's treatment, she would have been all alone. Her brother was too busy to be there for his little sister."

"Oh my god, Nick said a lot of rude things. I was creeped out and frustrated. He is so similar to another..." She couldn't say his name. "Look, I've been dealing with guys like this for so long, I have it down to a science. I don't understand why I went all ballistic at the lighthouse."

"Pent-up fury, perhaps?" Rob picked out a mini tart, took a nibble, then added, "Or rage?"

"Shouldn't you be the one to say bloody mad?" She found her journal and paged through it, the words blurring as she skimmed her lousy handwriting. Then she hit the moment.

She'd scribbled about Wagner pushing her back against the exit door. "Payback."

"Payback? If you're okay, can you elaborate?" Rob said softly. "Only if you're comfortable. Maybe this experience with Nick is creating some PTSD."

A lump snagged her throat. Writing about it was one thing. Talking about it was completely different. "The night he stole Tyler's boat, I wrenched control from Wagner. Right before he attacked me, he said I owed him. *'You made me pose for pictures.'*" She cleared her throat and sat beside Rob. "No, wait, that wasn't it. He said, 'You *forced* me to play nice with strangers.' Yeah, and I was pissed and confused. Wasn't it Wagner's job to act nice among strangers? Then he pushed me so hard against the door that it knocked the breath out of me. I gagged and coughed, and all I could think about was how to get air and survive."

She dropped her forehead on Rob's shoulder. "Thank you. Not just for me but all the women who have had to deal with pricks like Wagner. The list is endless. I bet that if I asked Samantha and Fran or the owner of the wine shop, they would all have stories about guys who refused to listen to them. Hell, I'm sure even Kat and Lucy have harrowing tales to tell."

"I heartily accept your vote of confidence. Although I can only take one case at a time, Wagner's a beast. But your *'it takes a village'* thought gives me an idea. To slay the beast, we may need reinforcements."

"I think *your bloody madness* is showing," she whispered in his ear and quickly pecked him on his cheek.

TWENTY-TWO

Tyler's boat. Talk about a blazing red trigger for Maddie. Rob's thoughts drifted back to the brilliant times they had together, diving and swimming in Cave Point. Had Maddie even dipped her toes in water since her brother died? He highly doubted it.

When he used to jump off the cliffs to swim in the lake, he would always close his eyes. Free-falling was addicting, yet terrifying. And every time Maddie tread water below, she sang... singing, treading harder, and singing louder until her caterwauling echoed between the cliffs. When he hit the water, he let his splash applaud her. Sometimes, she would keep on singing until the end of the chorus, or he slapped enough water at her to douse her horrible, off-key version of "Rolling in the Deep."

Maddie's lungs were her superpower. She held enough air in them to beat all competitors in high school and college. Until Tyler died. She stopped swimming. Which Rob regrettably understood. It was his fault. But Wagner stealing the air from Maddie? Reprehensible and unforgivable.

"Wanna another cup of coffee," she asked, "or more pastries?"

"Just decaf coffee, please." He set his backpack on the table and pulled out his phone. "I'll get a headache from the sugar."

"Okay," she said, standing and walking away.

"Wait, Maddie." He stood to meet her and gave her a hug. It was a friendly, lawyer-like hug, not a bear hug with absolutely no nuzzling. "Last night was a blast. I haven't danced or been in a conga line in forever. Thanks."

"Really? When and where have you last danced in a conga line?" she teased, then touched the tip of one of her cowboy boots against his sneaker. "Any chance we can make it to square dancing? Any hoedowns around here?"

"I'll check."

While she was away, Rob retrieved his messages. It seemed like all the residents of Baileys had messaged him and/or called during his morning swim. After listening to Gus's message and then Graham's, Rob silently congratulated himself. His timing was impeccable.

Shortly after they'd exited Baileys, Wagner had turned up at the lighthouse with his attorney, Gwen Ridley. There were two sides to every story, and he understood Ridley had to ascertain the details from her client's point of view, but Rob was clear on the truth. Wagner was the perpetrator, and Maddie the victim.

As Maddie headed back to the picnic table with coffee, he quickly sent a text to Kat, Graham, and Gus. ***We'll be ringing you shortly. Be ready***.

Instead of sitting across from him, she sat beside him. Her bare thigh pressed against his leg, and he hoped his swim trunks were triple layered. This case, when he got through it, was going to go on his resume as the all-time most difficult and the true test of his willpower.

He sipped his coffee. "Ready for your first daily update? I have Gus, Graham, and Kat waiting. We need to talk to them."

"All set."

"Wagner and his attorney are in Baileys. They got into town yesterday and went to the lighthouse."

She nodded slowly and drank her coffee.

"He needs to show his attorney what happened and give his side of the story."

"I hope his attorney has half a brain and realizes the dickhead doesn't have a side worth defending."

"There are no pictures and no witnesses." Rob added, "Gwen Ridley, his attorney, thinks she has a case because of Wagner's face. There was a lot of blood after it was smashed on the ground."

"The smallest of head and face wounds produce a lot of blood," she argued. "Everyone knows that."

"He underwent several medical treatments to repair his injuries."

"Surgery? Sure, I took him down hard, but except for the teeth..." She let out a long sigh. "And all anyone sees is his face, destroyed by me."

He set his hand on her thigh. "The good news, though, is that Gus, Graham, and Kat were all in the lighthouse with the two of them. Is it okay for them to tell you about it?" He would not force her to listen to anything that could trigger her.

With her approval, he called the trio in Baileys. As soon as their tiny faces lit up the phone screen, Maddie's shoulders dropped, and she visibly relaxed while talking to her three good friends.

Unsurprisingly, Wagner's version of events completely clashed with Maddie's.

As Graham explained it, "The bloody bastard couldn't even remember where you had wrestled him to the ground. The prat wandered around the whole gift shop. At one point, he thought you had attacked him in the lighthouse vestibule."

Rob suspected Wagner had been inebriated and high at the

time, so at this point, he couldn't tell his attorney the basic facts as to why he had stayed late after everyone else left the lighthouse.

"Thanks, Uncle Graham." Gus added, "It's a good thing you know how to speak in plain and salty language. Have you forgotten all your barrister jargon?"

Maddie's brow furrowed, confused. "Graham, you're a lawyer?"

"Another one of my many talents." Graham chuckled. "Yes, back in the day, I wowed the birds with my barrister wig."

With Graham at his side this time, Rob had a solid chance to beat Wagner at his own game. His accusations were piling up to a mountain of lies, and there was a good possibility his attorney would drop the case. Even if she didn't drop the lawsuit, Rob was almost certain no judge would rule in Wagner's favor. But avoiding court altogether was his first course of action. Subjecting Maddie to a face-to-face with Wagner might be traumatic.

From the phone, Kat's voice grew loud, and the two men became quiet. "Though the best news is, I told his lawyer that Wagner came up to thank me right before I left. He hugged me, and as soon as his hands wandered down my back and closer to my ass, I pushed him away. Wagner, of course, denied it. Right in front of me, and his attorney didn't react, but I'd like to think she wasn't pleased with my reveal."

"Gus," Rob interjected, "what do you think about Wagner's story?"

"I'm a terrible judge of character," Gus said. "I'm sorry, Maddie, for getting you mixed up with this total wanker. He's a slippery douchebag and deserved to get his face planted on a concrete floor. Even though his lawyer never asked, I gave her a piece of my mind and spoke the truth. There's no one in Baileys or in all of Door County who would think Maddie Logerquist was some kind of attacker or person who would hurt another without provocation. I hope the attorney sees Wagner for who he really is."

"What's the plan?" Kat asked.

Rob cast a sideways glance at Maddie, who stared at him. "My strategy is to get Gwen to drop this bogus accusation." He took a deep breath. "Then, prove Wagner is a sexual predator so his studio, or any other Hollywood power institution, won't stand behind him."

Maddie's jaw dropped.

"Sounds like you're going after the big one. Moby *Dick*." Graham laughed.

"It's time for Wagner to go down." Rob gazed at Maddie. "He's hurt a lot of people. Women in particular."

"Okay, Captain Ahab," Gus said. "We won't abandon the ship. Tell us what you need. We're all here for you and Maddie."

Graham and Kat chimed in their agreement.

"Thanks. Keep talking to people. You're my boots on the ground while we're in Elkhart. Tell me all you can about Wagner's actions while he stays in town."

Maddie asked, "How does his face look? It's been a month. Is it hard to look at?"

"Actually," Gus said, "his face isn't nearly as rough-looking as I had expected. He did have to have all new caps put on—"

"Wait? Caps?" Maddie scratched her jaw. "You mean, the teeth flying from his mouth were fake?"

"Oh, hell yes," Gus roared. "It's the only way we can have them white enough for the camera."

Maddie grabbed Rob's hand and squeezed.

"TJ is taking statements from everyone who came into contact with Wagner while he was posing for pictures at each of the fundraisers," Graham said. "And I'm shadowing the copper."

"And watch the house, please," Maddie added, "and the lighthouse if he stays in Baileys."

The trio of informants received their missions and said their goodbyes.

"Hey, hey." Maddie tapped the table like a keyboard and sang, "I used to cry, now I hold my head up high. Like Gloria, I will survive."

He held his hand up to stop. "You really need to sing more in the shower."

"I know, I know, I'm a much better dancer." She slapped his shoulder playfully. "By the way, fess up. What's with all your Italian?"

"What? Oh. Um. I took it up to impress the Marcheti family. Learning a new language decreases my stress, helps me to focus. Fran's family wholeheartedly assisted me, except for Nick, of course."

She hugged him, keeping a safe space between them. He glanced around to make sure no one was watching and whispered into her ear, "*Vorrei che questo abbraccio non finisse mai.*"

"I have no clue what you just said, but I'm all hot and tingly."

Rob debated translating it for her, but thought better of it. "I'm sure Google can help out."

"Ah, no. I want *your* voice slathering Italian words all over me, not a bot."

"Okay, well, then, you'll have to wait until the mood strikes next."

TWENTY-THREE

Thanks to the new alarm system, Maddie was able to check all around her house in Baileys Harbor without leaving Elkhart Lake. Since learning Wagner had gone to the lighthouse, she checked and rechecked the video feed on her laptop three times a day. Looking at the grainy footage gave her a sense of control. So far, the ass hadn't gone near her estate. She was certain because her goofball brother also checked. He popped in once a day and waved at her through the dining room camera.

She opened the boxes sent from Sunkissed and arranged the swimwear on the bed. Keeping her favorite client spectacularly happy would be simple since Fran agreed to model for her. It would rock the fashion world when supermodel Francesca Marcheti came out of semi-retirement.

Even better, after a double mastectomy, Fran was willing to pose in some of the pieces Maddie designed and would make with her newly delivered fabrics, threads, and sewing machine. After just one week in Elkhart, she'd created a workstation and was able to sew to her heart's content. This new fuel for her passion was exciting.

"Busy?" Rob asked, knocking on her open bedroom door. "I have big news."

"Come in, but it better not be about the case. I need a happy-hour cocktail before my daily update."

Maddie detested how their relationship had turned luke-warm after one steamy kiss. Rob had gone all professional to maintain their client-lawyer relationship. She'd tried to convince him that sleeping in the same bed, without any sexy shenanigans, would somehow only boost his career, but he didn't buy it.

For her sake, everything had to be aboveboard and not just on top of the sheets but away from the bed. The past five days, it was as if he'd been covering her in bubble wrap when all she wanted to do was roll around, pop out all the air, and jump Rob's bones. At least she had his wooing in Italian to look forward to. Every time he did so, he caught her by surprise. One time, her bum was in the air as she bent over to find something in the fridge. She had no idea what he murmured, but the way he'd said it, the way he'd looked at her when she turned around, made her hot and bothered.

"My tires arrived at the Throttleshop this morning," he said, bouncing from toes to heels. "They'll be installed by this after-noon. Would you like to come to the shop with me?"

"As if I could say no. Who would have thought tires created such a huge stir? Now I know what to get you for Christmas. Thanks for making it easy on me."

"No, I'm not asking for any gifts," he said, sounding as if he'd just walked out of a legal ethics class. "However, with the new tires on the Triumph, we'll be able to drive around the track or wherever you'd like to go."

"Are you asking me on a date?"

"Ah, I can't—" He added, "*il tuo sorriso bellissimo.*"

"Oh, don't you 'beautiful' something me. I know I have to stick to the wheels and be strictly professional. I get it." She grabbed hold of his hand and shook it vigorously. "Darn glad to do business with you. I'll be ready in ten minutes—no, wait, make it twenty. I have to take a cold shower."

Grabbing her phone and a towel, she left him with his mouth agape and went into the bathroom. As soon as the shower heated up—no way would she ever take a cold shower—she hopped in. Washing up, she belted out her version of the Beatles' "Drive My Car," warbling off-key under the shower.

When she got out and dried off, her phone pinged. A call from Alex? What could her ex, the lone thread of her life in New York, possibly want?

"What's up?" She wrapped the towel around her chest and sat on the toilet.

"Why'd you do it?" he screamed.

Immediately, she regretted returning his call as her brain tried to adjust to hearing the first words from Alex Martin in over a year.

"I know you had to take care of things at...wherever it is you are in the middle of nowhere. But there was a chance for you to come back and style for the new winter show. Now, because of Chris Wagner, there's no way."

"Slow down. I didn't do a thing to Wagner. He sexually assaulted *me*, and I vigorously defended myself. I don't appreciate you calling me out of the blue and verbally attacking me."

"That's not the way the story reads in the *Hollywood Cue*."

She'd been so consumed with the lighthouse, protecting herself and living in reality, that Maddie forgot about checking the gossip columns. Besides, there was no way in hell she would go back to the toxic reality show.

"Alex, thanks for the update, but I've been busy recovering

and working in the real world. I'm no longer focusing on the made-up shit on TV."

"As if *real* matters. Did you see Wagner's face?"

"What? How? There are pictures?"

"Yes," Alex huffed. "The pic is grainy, but even so, the man's face looks off. Misshapen or something. He's claiming that you hit him after he turned you down. There's talk he might go into rehab."

"That's utter bullshit."

"Look, clearly, I've been the bearer of bad news. I know we aren't together, but I like you."

"If you like me, why would you assume I'm at fault, and Wagner's the victim?"

His silence spoke volumes.

Disgusted, she shook her head. "I'm the person who is in recovery, thanks to Wagner's attack. I was dismissed as inconsequential by you and the other producers on the show. It's your loss, Alex. Good to hear from you. Ciao."

And the smear campaign begins.

Maddie returned to the shower and let the pellets soothe her bruised ego. What a prick. How had she ever been remotely attracted to him? The guy only thought about one person: Alex.

Dressed in one of Sunkissed's sunny weather ensembles, she packed up her camera and met Rob in the living room. Now, she was more than ready to go for a drive in a cute British sports car with a guy who whispered sexy Italian phrases in her ear.

She also wanted to get info about the *Cue* article, but as soon as she faced Rob, his hazel eyes swept over her, and she forgot. She wasn't sure, but his jaw might have dropped slightly.

He came over and took the camera bag from her shoulder. "Let me carry this for you. How's your butt...I mean, tailbone?"

"Pretty good." She turned around to wiggle her ass. "Wanna see?"

He blushed. "Not what I meant. I, um, just wanted to make sure your body...is better."

She gave him a cheeky smile. "My body is doing quite well after the long shower. But if you really want to know what would—"

"A good long walk to the Throttleshop," he said, jogging to the door and opening it for her. "You are going to want to take so many pictures of my tires and the Triumph."

"My thoughts exactly." *Not really.*

Her face grew warm. She blew out some air and followed Rob out the door. It was nice to feel attractive and to be attracted to a man who always put her first.

Once at the Throttleshop, Maddie wanted to take pictures of Rob, but he insisted she aim her lens at the car. She settled by taking more pictures of the Triumph but tried to get Rob somewhere in the frame.

In the shop's showroom, the Triumph was the center of attention for a small crowd. Sam and Rob circled the metallic masterpiece on wheels, talking about it with the onlookers. Maddie went about her business, snapping pics of every shiny chrome detail for Rob.

From a shadowy corner of the showroom, Nick came up to her and pointed at his Ferrari. "My auto looks as though she is jealous. She is beautiful, ah?" His Italian accent sounded sleazier than a week ago. "Roberto has turned an ugly duck into a magnificent creature."

"Cars are not people. They are inanimate objects." She stepped away from him to create some distance. First Alex, now Nick. She wasn't in the mood to listen to another male speak *at* her. "Cars don't have emotions, and they aren't women."

"I agree, but cars can be, ah, *fedele.* Faithful." He slipped a small cloth out of his pants pocket, took off his trendy specs, and wiped them off. "My little sister, Francesca, is family. It is my duty to look out for her."

"Taking care of siblings, I understand." She held up her camera to cover her face. She didn't want to be rude by rolling her eyes or gagging. "Family is important."

"Then you will understand. I advised Francesca on her choice. Modeling swimwear is not dignified, and she will embarrass our *famiglia*."

A primal anger ignited her cheeks. She gulped some air to stay calm and spoke once her emotions had settled. "I believe the best part of—" She dropped her camera, and it hit her chest. "—family is how they always have your back. The role of a caring family is to support one another. Through the good and bad, no matter what anyone else thinks."

Nick waved at a person who gazed at his Ferrari. The thing looked as if it were ashamed and had to hide in a corner parking spot. "Francesca is in a fragile space. We are only looking out for her. Doing what is best to protect her. As you know, we almost lost her."

Maddie tugged at the skirt she wore. A brightly colored jungle pattern on a silky soft fabric. Like earlier, she felt attractive and powerful.

Since she was well acquainted with miserable losses in life, she sighed and chose to explain. "Fran is a survivor. *Fragile* isn't how I see her. And she's a grown-up. As an older sibling who's experienced tremendous loss, I understand. We want only what's best for our younger siblings. My amazing brother died while on my watch, yet I wouldn't have done anything to take away his choices. He was smart." She chuckled. "Besides, he wouldn't have listened anyway. Totally stubborn. Like me."

Nick tilted his head side to side, clearly unconvinced.

"My client, Sunkissed, supports women. Fran will inspire so many other women who live with cancer." She wanted to shake his shoulders and yell at him to get out of the dark ages. "Sorry if this sounds rude, but you don't own your sister. We've discussed this thoroughly and planned all the promo shoots already. I think I'll speak directly to Fran from now on."

"You go, girlfriend," Sam said, sending her a high five.

"Hey, Nick." Rob stuck out his hand for a shake. "You getting on the track today?"

Maddie's mood improved when they bookended her. She slapped Sam's palm.

"You two have saved me," Nick said smugly. "From what I hear, it's not healthy to be on the receiving end of one of Ms. Logerquist's tantrums."

Maddie bit the inside of her cheek to stay calm. She knew how things would roll once the media got wind of what happened with Wagner.

"Your sources are unreliable." Rob glanced at his Triumph and then at Nick's Ferrari. "Wanna take it out for a race?"

"No, Rob, it's not a challenge. Haven't I beaten you enough?" Nick ambled up to Sam and kissed both her cheeks. "Ciao, *bella*."

After he walked out of the shop, Sam huffed. "Ciao, *bella*? God, the man is straight out of a bad sixties movie. I'm shocked he keeps coming back to my shop with all the estrogen in here."

"Probably because he has no other choice of mechanics in the area." Rob laughed, then turned toward Maddie. "You didn't deserve his trash talk. Like I said, he's a dick."

Maddie was too bothered about what Nick *decided* for Fran that she hadn't thought twice about the Wagner gossip. "Does Nick really have such tight control over his sister's life?"

Sam shrugged and plunged her hands deep into the pockets of her denim overalls. "Nick has a mob-like mentality. I think it's best to stay on his good side."

"He doesn't have a good side," Rob said.

Maddie nibbled on one knuckle. "Son of a bitch. I'm done for. I bet Fran won't pose now. What a weird dynamic. I should have known it was too good to be true when she jumped on board with my plan within seconds."

"Maybe this is different," Rob said. "I mean, Fran and Drew are tight—"

"Yeah," Sam added, "and Drew's in our corner. He doesn't like Nick either. He'll want what's best for Fran."

"Drew *and* Fran," Maddie said. "This is good, there's hope. Thanks, guys. It will be okay, and I'm sure I can handle whatever happens."

"We'll come up with another plan if Fran falls through." Sam waved toward the women mechanics working on the sexy cars. "My crew would kill to get some playtime at the lake wearing anything but greasy overalls."

Maddie turned to look at all of Sam's employees. The variety of shapes and sizes was beautiful, and another idea came to her. "Really? Because I bet Sunkissed would love to supply new summer pieces if they were willing to pose for my Instagram account."

"Really? They might love it. I'll ask around, see what everybody thinks, and get back to you." Sam dropped a set of keys into Rob's hand. "See you later. Have fun with the new wheels."

"Wait..." Maddie pointed to the cute orange BMW on display. "I really think that car would be adorable in my shoots, and it might be time for me to buy my own car."

"Sure, it's perfect for you. I'll get the sales gal to touch base with you." Laughing, Sam strolled up to a couple gaping at a Porsche.

Maddie tipped her head back and thanked the aluminum ceiling. There were two plans. One or both would keep her in business as a stylist and an influencer.

"Ready for a spin in the Triumph?" Rob hooked his arm

through hers. "We can grab dinner at one of the food trucks at the track."

"I thought we couldn't go on a date?"

"It's a business meeting, but fun. Besides, we need to talk about the article in the *Hollywood Cue.*"

TWENTY-FOUR

After Rob opened the Triumph's door for Maddie, she admired the pillow embroidered with Penske, then placed it on the floor. The leather interior warmed her thighs when she slid into the luxurious two-seater convertible. She could have sworn the car had been featured in a Bond movie. Where 007 and the bombshell co-star would hop over the doors and into their seats. Thankfully, a sore tailbone curtailed any Bond-like action sequences.

"What's her name?" she asked, stroking the glossy woodgrain console set in the dashboard. "She is sweet, and bonus, there's enough room for my legs. What a thrill."

"It isn't a *she*." He started the engine, letting it rumble until it hummed, then pulled out of the parking lot. Onlookers gawked as they drove past. "On to Road America. Ready?"

"Any chance there's a scarf in here?" She patted down the threads of hair blowing around her face. "I hadn't considered the wind, even though it's practically cliché in old movies. Scarves and convertibles are inseparable."

"I know. Check the glove box; there should be one tucked inside. Sam likes to give away plenty of her Penske swag."

"This is silk." She turned it into a headband and knotted it at the base of her neck. "Sam Penske knows her cars and her fashion. What a perfect day for triumph. Get it? *Triumph?*"

He shifted the gear stick and drove along a winding neighborhood street. Up and down were parked cars, headlights kissing taillights. They all looked vintage, rare, and sporting brightly colored paint jobs.

"Is that the Osthoff?" she asked when they reached the other side of the lake. A whitewashed resort sprawled over several blocks

"Yes, it's quite posh, but I'd rather support Siebkens."

They drove under a neon sign announcing their arrival at the Road America track and immediately stopped to wait behind a line of other cars. She tightened the scarf over her ears to muffle the sounds of revving engines. The car ahead of them was an antique design that looked like it was the first car off Henry Ford's assembly line. A large puff of exhaust floated around and scratched her nose. "I'm assuming there aren't any clean air activists in the area."

"It will dissipate once we're driving on the track. This waiting in place is bad for everyone around. The track is less than five miles and a bit friendlier for the atmosphere. Here's my short history lesson: The track was built in 1955. It has fourteen turns, a few hills to drive over, one sharp left turn, and one hairpin turn. I love it, and I'll be quizzing you on it later."

The car jerked, moved forward onto the road, and they passed through a pastoral setting. Grass and trees lined the outside of the track. As they drove along, spectators were parked sporadically on the grassy hills, watching the parade of vintage autos while they lounged on the hoods of their cars.

"Hey." She lightly set her hand on his muscular thigh and shuddered. "This is all business, nothing funny about it. But please tell me you aren't going to get all excited about this metal girlfriend of yours."

"Nope. And this Triumph is named Tyler."

Maddie squeezed his thigh. His hand dropping off the steering wheel and landing on top of hers, Rob veered the car to the right side of the road and slowed to a crawl to let the other cars pass by.

"Your brother wasn't the only one who liked to hunt for treasure. He just happened to like the underwater venues, and I liked roving over the land. I found this shell of a car at a junk shop somewhere near Madison. It was like I'd hit pay dirt. Literally. Every piece of it was covered in mud and debris, except the chrome logo on the back end. When I saw the mangled letters, instead of reading TRIUMPH, I read or saw TYLER. It was strange."

"As if a shiny object or something drew you closer." She added, "I know Tyler would love this thing just as much as his boat. And the red paint? An homage to Tyler as well?"

"Tyler's boat is the distinct shade of red we Brits call scarlet. Royal and eye-catching." After they'd been driving on a long straight stretch, the road curved, and she caught the scent of pine from the trees lining this part of the track. With Rob at her side, she knew Tyler was admiring them from above. "Is it true Paul Newman drove here?"

"According to track lore, he raced here once a year and stayed at Siebkens."

"I wonder which room he stayed in?" As they passed by a lot full of parked Corvettes on the inner area of the track, she read out loud, "Corvette Corral. This is like a Disneyland for car lovers."

"It is. There are camping sites around the track because a lot of car aficionados like to wake up to the sounds of revving engines."

Rob drove a little faster, and Maddie grabbed the Penske pillow and adjusted it against her tailbone to absorb the bumps. Footbridges for pedestrians to cross between the inside and outside of the roadway were above the track. When he drove under the Corvette Bridge, he sped up and drove around a circular piece of the track. The fresh breeze cooled her face.

He slowed the car down. "I meant what I said earlier. Ignore Nick. He's an asshat."

"With a lot of control." She dropped her head back and stared at the blue sky and clouds above. "Really pisses me off. Men with money think they have the right to make the rules and bend them however they want." She waved at one of the onlookers, who let out a loud whistle as they drove past. "Sunkissed is my best client, owned by a woman. My designer handbag client dropped me with a succinct message this morning. His polite phrasing hardly disguised that he thinks I attacked Wagner. Such bullshit."

"The piece in the *Cue*, which we'll eventually discuss, is going to be the first of many, I hate to say. He's only starting to blaze a trail of smear and slime."

"Is it true he's going into rehab?" She fiddled with the pillow under her butt.

"Not entirely sure, but Wagner's in Baileys. We'll talk about this later over a cocktail. The rule is one update per day. Would you mind if we speed up? There's a hairpin curve coming up, and it's a kick to go a bit faster around it."

She tightened her scarf. "Bring it on."

The engine hummed, and it sounded like a lullaby trying to soothe her. She tilted her face skyward and relaxed. The breeze cooled her from the late-afternoon sun, and she liked how the line of towering fir trees on a distant hill swayed gently. She murmured, "Heaven on Earth."

ROB'S INTENTIONS WERE FULFILLED. A day on the track always relaxed him, and now, it had worked for Maddie. "Which truck do you want to eat at?"

"I'd love some tacos and tequila."

He drove through the exit gate and parked near a truck marked PocoLoco in red, but then he spotted Nick's green Ferrari. "Second choice?"

She shook her head. "No, I'm not letting him push me around."

He parked on a hill behind the food truck, and as they walked around to the front, he spotted Fran and Drew's tandem bike. With Nick nearby, the siblings in the same space concerned him. Based on his experience, the Marcheti family and its hierarchy could be Machiavellian.

The line of people ordering food crawled back to where picnic tables had been set up. He took hold of Maddie's hand. "*Sono qui per te*. I'm here for you."

"I know." She gave him a smile he'd hold on to for one hell of a long time.

They sat across Fran and Drew and said their hellos. A small group surrounded Nick in the food line and took selfies with the celebrity chef. He had a fan base in the world of foodies, but he'd never be in the same realm as Bourdain.

"I have some mock-ups of my swimsuits," Maddie told Fran. "I'm wondering when and if you're available for me to take your measurements. Please."

Rob disliked the insecure tone in Maddie's voice. Before running into Nick, she'd been ready to color the world with beachwear and swimsuits. He added, "Her room has been turned into an eco-friendly design shop."

"Of course, this is so exciting. How about tomorrow morning? Can you come by our house around ten?" She glanced at Rob. "He knows where to go."

"Absolutely," Maddie gushed. Immediately, he sensed Maddie's enthusiasm return.

Nick set down a plate of nachos and hovered over their table. "Ah, yeah, any takers on this delicious snack? What is the plan tomorrow?"

"I'm meeting with Maddie for measuring. She's designing suits for me." Fran said, staring at the plate of food on the picnic table. "Weren't there any other topping options on the menu? Why didn't you have them put the onions on the side? You know I hate onions."

Nick scoffed. "Onions are very good for you."

Rob dredged up memories of his few family dinners with Fran. They were often followed by an acute case of indigestion from all the bickering between her father and Nick—predictably, her mother remained silent. As a lover of a good argument and a solid debate, he'd despised listening to the Marchetis' petty disagreements. They were one of the wealthiest families in Chicago, flourishing in a bubbled existence, making it all particularly tragic when they abandoned Fran during the worst time in her life.

"Babe," Drew said, "don't bother. We can eat back at our place."

Fran and Drew kissed, then got up to leave.

"Francesca, if you're intending to take off your clothing again, for—" Nick looked down his nose at Maddie. "—for her, you would be doing us—your *famiglia*—a grave *injustice*. Revealing us with your new appearance. Do you really want the world to know about your burden? Think about Mama and Papa. How they would feel, so exposed in the media, left vulnerable to gossipmongers."

Fran burst into laughter. "You're being ridiculous, and you

can stop with the fake Italian accent. Injustice is happening everywhere, and Mama, Papa, and especially you, have all thrived on media attention. Not to mention, our family has never known or understood anything about inequality. I'm a cancer survivor, Nick, and I want to help other women. Get it?"

"Not possible."

Maddie scoffed and got up. As she stepped closer to Nick, Rob went into protective service mode. The article in the *Cue* had nagged at him all day, and the last thing he wanted or needed was a picture of Maddie looking like she was *bloody mad* to circulate. He quickly stood beside her and took her hand. Anger radiated off her, so he draped his arm over her shoulders. "We should head back to Siebkens. Now's a great time to go for a swim or soak in the hot tub."

"I'm not going swimming," Maddie snapped, pulling away from him. "And this guy, Nick the Dick, shouldn't be bossing his sister around. She's an adult, for god's sake. Why do you guys all think you can tell us what to do?"

"Thank you for defending me, my friend," Fran said, hugging Maddie.

Rob and Drew exchanged looks of solidarity, but Nick, having no skin in the game, looked smug. Whether his sister did or didn't model a swimsuit wasn't important to him, Nick only wanted to exert his power. Dominating them with toxicity. It seemed to slime over every courtroom wall Rob walked into. "Look, Nick, I think you'll agree that what's best for Fran isn't really in your jurisdiction at this point, hey?"

Nick gave him a hard look, frowned, and shook his head. "None of this is any of your business. Or Drew's or the *pazza*, Miss Logerquist."

Maddie's lips puckered, and he knew her understanding of Italian had expanded. With her hands balled into fists, she stepped in front of Nick. "I'm not crazy, you bastard."

Before thinking, Rob grabbed Nick's arm, pulled it up behind his back, and hissed, "I think you better leave, Mr. Marcheti."

"Sure, sure, but can we smile for the cameras first?"

Looking around, Rob was mortified to see a few people watching the scene play out. And taking pictures. He dropped Marcheti's arm. "Go away, dude."

Nick flexed his newly released arm and brushed it off as if some dust had gathered on his garish tattoo. "Ciao."

Drew kissed Fran and then addressed the looky-loos. "Hey folks, head over to Siebkens. The cocktails and appetizers are on the house this afternoon. It's the best happy hour in Elkhart."

Cheering, they moved on, but Rob's adrenaline refused to slow down.

"Are you okay?" Maddie asked, taking his hand. "I'm so sorry, but really, if you hadn't stepped in...I was seeing so much red, I don't know, but clearly, I have issues. I definitely see an anger management class in the near future."

"I'm relieved. I know it doesn't look good for me either, strong-arming a famous chef. But from what I've read, chefs can be pretty tough. I'm sure he's in no pain."

They followed Fran and Drew away from the food truck. Rob heard the chatter among the witnesses and wondered not if, but when, a picture displaying his hostility would find its way to Wagner. At least this time, he was in the hot seat. Not Maddie.

TWENTY-FIVE

Twenty-four hours later, Maddie was following Fran into an exquisite bedroom suite. The bed and bathroom were luxurious, picture-perfect for *Architectural Digest*, but the closet knocked Maddie's socks off. The darn thing was twice the size of her entire apartment in New York. She could have spent hours admiring the designer clothing from Fran's modeling days. When she spied a shimmery black-and-white polka-dotted evening gown, Maddie knew her swimwear designs for Fran would work perfectly.

"I thought I lost you." Fran handed her a glass of sparkling water with a twist of lemon. "I'm anxious to see what you brought me."

Maddie sipped some water and went back into the bedroom where she'd set her carry-on and unpacked and laid out the swimsuits. In the earliest phases, they were pieces of cut-out fabric pinned to a tissue paper pattern. For the two-piece designs, there were the front and back of the tops. Then, the front of the bottoms and the tush piece. She repeated the process with her two best designs and then set the one-piece designs at the head of the bed. For now, she wanted to get

Frans's thoughts on the fabric texture, designs, and colors. And most importantly, which styles really resonated with her.

Not wanting Fran to feel pressured, Maddie went to the window and gave her some space. "If you want, I can check on the guys for a couple of minutes."

"No, please stay. I can't do this alone." Fran focused on Maddie's favorite design for an extra second. The material was jaunty, featuring black-and-white polka dots, much like the evening dress.

"Not a problem." Maddie looked around the ornate bedroom. She'd come directly into this room and had no idea where any of the other parts of the expansive house would lead to. All she knew was that Rob and Drew were in the garage looking at cars.

Of course, *garage* was the understatement of the year. Since Drew had been collecting cars for longer than Rob, he had a fleet in the stable-size garage beside the Hamptons-like house. "Ask me any questions. Also, I didn't want to confuse you with too many choices. All the fabric samples can be used on any of the designs. One-piece or two-piece."

Fran pinched the polka dots between two fingers. "This is soft as butter, but—" She grimaced. Then her face turned red, and she wiped a tear from the corner of her eye.

"Oh my gosh, Fran," Maddie said, trying to stay calm. "We don't have to do this today. At all. Or ever. I don't want to upset you."

Fran broke out into a high-pitched laugh. "No, no, it's *bellissima*. It's just, these polka dots remind me of one of my first swimsuits. When I was a little girl, my mother would take me shopping for a new suit every spring. Looking at this...reminded me. I miss the joy of diving and twisting and splashing in water."

Maddie sighed, then wondered about her first swimsuit. Was it a one-piece? It had to be because Elsie wouldn't allow her to have a two-piece until she was thirteen. And by then, she'd been in the pool so often to swim competitively she had no choice but to wear a spandex one-piece. But the fresh feel of water? It hadn't occurred to her in a long-ass time.

A bit shaky at the memory, Maddie plunged into her sales pitch and pointed out all the details about the design for Fran. "The bodice comes up higher with a sweetheart neckline. The straps are haltered, and the bottom piece is an adjustable bikini. It's ruched, so you can lift it or lower it. Any of the tops can be easily fitted and adjusted with the appropriate prosthesis."

Fran grabbed a tissue and wiped her nose. "This is the design. I want it in the black-and-white dots, but I also love the daisy pattern. Can you do it in both?"

Maddie was over the moon. "Yes and yes. I have to take your measurements, and then I can vamp it any way you need or want it." She paused to gather her thoughts. Over the past week, she'd been updating her sewing knowledge to expand it into the realm of breast reconstruction. It was almost ten years ago that she'd designed a mastectomy swimsuit to get into FIT. With all the advancements, it might as well have been a century ago. She was thrilled with the sewing blogs and YouTube videos on swimwear for breast cancer survivors. "The next information I need is personal, but I can sew in prosthesis pockets if you need. Or want."

Fran gave her an easy smile. "My new *foobs* are only in the beginning phase of construction, so I'll need the pockets. Then they'll look like sisters, not twins, but sisters."

"Foobs?" Maddie retrieved her measuring tape. "I can take your numbers over your T-shirts and shorts. Sisters?"

"Fake boobs that don't look exactly alike." Fran gazed at the swimsuits. "Thanks, Maddie. This is like a second chance for me. I never realized how my ta-tas, or lack of them, debilitated my thinking. Don't get me wrong, I'm happier now than I've ever been, but there are some things in life I once took for granted and now have to think too hard about. For instance, a swimsuit. So, thanks, Maddie. For giving me back one of my favorite simple joys."

Nodding, Maddie took Fran's measurements and entered them into her tablet. She would drop them into her pattern-making program later. "I know somewhat how you feel. I would love to get a handle on my plans. Seems like lately, any attempts to strategize my life fall off the cliff, leaving me to deal with only the hard shit. Thank god I have Rob and his lawyerly skills."

"Rob is like my real brother. Nick only thinks of himself and his damn foodie fanatics." Fran shook her head and raised her arms. "I'm so sick of him badgering me, but once August is over, he'll be gone."

"I know I was really riled with your brother yesterday, I hope I didn't upset you. My stubborn feminist streak has been showing up lately." Maddie spun the tape under Fran's armpits and then carefully adjusted it around her chest, above her breastbone. When she lowered it, she hesitated for fear she'd hurt Fran. "Can I go lower?"

"Don't worry about Nick. He deserved it, and yes, it's the spot where I'm looking a bit like the adorable Tig Notaro, flat as the state of Illinois. But the girls will make a comeback, eventually. There's nothing tender or sensitive. You can wrap, measure, and record. No trouble." She chuckled. "Never thought I'd say, *no trouble*. It seemed as if before my surgery, the girls were more trouble than ever and more than they were worth when I modeled."

Maddie gently lowered the tape measure across Fran's chest, where the tape lay flat. She thought of all the times she'd adjusted and manipulated swimsuits on the women starring on *Summer Haven*. As their stylist, she'd arranged and manipulated an assortment of boob sizes, and the one request most often repeated was for cleavage. She wondered if it was a thing that made women or men happier. Maddie glanced down at her own boobs, and a sudden image of Wagner grabbing her breast crossed her mind. Flushed, she stepped back and hid her sudden anxiety by jotting the measurements into her table.

"Are you dizzy?" Fran asked, holding on to her shoulder. "You just swayed back and forth."

"It's getting warm in here," she said, retrieving her water and then quickly emptying the glass. "I'll finish up. I want your waist and hip measurements in case you'd like a swim dress or skort."

Fran's eyes were on her as Maddie finished measuring with mostly steady hands. Their talk about breasts had inadvertently pierced her protective bubble. She'd worked so hard to forget about the night at the lighthouse that she was almost feeling like it hadn't happened. Silly her.

"Are you and Rob getting close?" Fran asked. "I can tell he's incredibly happy."

"Ah, yes. It's more of a business relationship," she said, "but honestly, I hope later, after the case, we can move forward."

"The case? What case?"

Maddie began putting her designs back in the carry-on. "It's a short but sour story. I was sexually assaulted by Chris Wagner, and I fought back. Now, he's suing *me*."

Fran immediately wrapped her arms around her. "Oh, shit. Such a *bestia*."

"All this talk about boobs made me think and remember. What would have happened if, when Wagner had grabbed my breast, he found nothing there? Or if the whole thing had fallen off? Prosthesis and all."

"I can picture the man's jaw dropping off his pitiful face." Fran chuckled. "He's famous, but I've never been a fan. When I met him in Chicago last spring with Rob, Wagner was horribly rude to me. What a tool. You did women of the world a huge favor."

Maddie tilted her head side to side. "My wrestling moves haven't left me, and I took him down face-first."

"You're a hero for what you did, don't forget it. With Rob defending you, the snake will go back under his rock for good. Rob won't let the *bestia* see daylight. I was with Rob during the first case, when he defended the bastard—and only because his brother asked him to help out. At the time, Rob constantly questioned himself. Whether he was right or in the wrong. Talked my ear off during chemo treatments."

Maddie slipped her Tevas back on. "I've taken up enough of your time. Again, I want to thank you so much. Your new suits will be gorgeous, I promise."

"Don't you have some other pieces from Sunkissed for me to model?

"I do, but I wasn't sure if you wanted...I mean, you've done so much for me already. I don't want to burden you."

"Nonsense." Fran grabbed Maddie's carry-on off the bed and pulled it behind her as they left the room. "I built an indoor pool with a sauna and a hot tub. I couldn't have lived without it. Construction finished at the beginning of the summer. It's been a soul saver for me, maybe you, too?"

Her butt had been aching off and on since they'd arrived in Elkhart. Maddie had tried talking herself into getting into a hot tub to soothe it. But she wasn't sure. Hot tubs were generally located close to the pool, and the last time she'd been close to a pool, she'd hyperventilated. It was an extreme reaction and didn't help her job on the show. She'd had to rearrange her styling tent on the side of the house in the Hamptons. She shook her head to clear out the past. This was Elkhart.

Maddie rubbed her shoulders to stay calm as they strolled through the house to get to the pool. When Fran slid the glass doors open, she stepped inside, closed her eyes, and took in a deep breath, expecting a hit of chlorine-scented air. Instead, she didn't smell anything. "Salt water?"

"Of course. I have spent some time in the Mediterranean." Fran showed her to a cute striped tent, like one of those old-fashioned dressing rooms on the beach.

Maddie avoided looking at the pool and scooted into the tent. She changed into an orange and pink striped two-piece swimsuit Sunkissed had sent to her, and when she exited, Fran was nowhere to be found.

With just a glance at the water, Maddie spotted a chaise lounge covered with an ocean-blue cushion. The colorful Mediterranean-tiled deck commanded her full attention as she walked around the pool. Once seated a good distance from the pool's edge, she focused on her phone and checked messages. *So far...so good.* At ease, she turned to look at the backyard and found a beautiful view of Elkhart Lake.

The sliding glass doors opened, and Fran came in carrying a tray with a pitcher of margaritas and glasses. Drew and Rob followed, holding towels and bottles of beer.

"Hey, if you want to swim in the lake," Drew said, "we can do it, but this hot tub is so much warmer."

Rob sat on the end of her lounge chair and stretched out his nice, long legs. "How are you doing ?"

Maddie knew it was a general everyday question for most people, but for her, it was loaded. She wasn't afraid of water; she just couldn't make it into a pool, a hot tub, or, god forbid, a lake without freezing up and running in the other direction. But with Fran, Drew, and Rob...something was different. "I'm next to a pool, and I'm not breaking out into a cold sweat. I can say that the only thing bothering me is the seams of this darn swimsuit. They keep crawling up my butt."

He laughed, the concern in his eyes disappearing. "I'm here for you, but you're on your own about the bum situation."

The hot tub's jets pushed water around, and she stared at Rob's bare chest and defined abs. She'd seen his bare shoulders and chest the other day, but this time, his nearness kept her from spiraling down into her fears. "But aren't you a genius?"

"Yes, that's me—*genio*, like Wile E. Coyote. Super genius, except when it comes to swimsuits." He held out his hand for her. "Come on, let's soak in the hot tub. It will work wonders on your tailbone. And I should know because I am a genius."

Staring at the hot tub, where Drew and Fran were already chumming it up on one side of the oval tub, she paused at the metal railing leading into the swirling water. Rob gave her an *attaboy* look. Clutching his hand for safety, she kicked off her sandals and stepped down, the metal step cold beneath her feet. The foamy water circled her toes, and she took another step, closed her eyes, and moaned in delight at the heat.

As soon as she sat on the tiled bench, she adjusted her back against one of the jets and wondered what the hell was wrong with her. Why had she waited this long for the best therapy ever? Water.

Rob nestled against her. A long-lost sense of awareness found her, and she was beginning to feel like herself again. In the present. In the here and now. Not in the past.

She smiled at Fran and Drew. "Thanks, guys. This is blissful."

Seeing Fran wearing a short-sleeved swim shirt instead of a swimsuit jolted Maddie's excitement at getting her into a real swimsuit. "It should only take me a week to get your new suits ready, Fran."

"Let's enjoy today," she said. "Life is too short. Best to take one day at a time."

Maddie and Rob's thighs touched beneath the water. "This

isn't personal," she said in case he felt obligated or dared move away from her. "My butt *and* thigh need the therapy."

He took her hand and clasped it to his chest. "Whatever you need, I'm here for you. If I triggered anything yesterday, I want you to know that when I suggested swimming, I was trying to get away from Nick, that's all."

She tapped her fingers on his chest in time with his heartbeat. "I was livid. What is it about men who make such demands? Maybe I have a short fuse and never realized it. Thanks for stepping in and making sure I wasn't photographed looking like a mad woman."

"Well, so far, so good. This is today's official business update. None of yesterday's pictures have popped up on social media. Anytime your name, my name, or Wagner's name appears on the internet, my app pings me."

"Fantastic." She bent over to stretch out her back and let the water roll over her outstretched arms. She took in a breath and turned her head, letting her arms form into a crawl stroke. She dipped her face into the water, made a stroke, then came up for air.

When she finished, she smiled. All three stared at her with jaws hanging open.

"What?" She glanced down to make sure her boobs hadn't popped out from her too-tight suit top. "You all look like you've seen a ghost."

Rob started laughing. Then Drew joined him. Fran announced, "If you want to do some laps, the pool is fabulous at eighty degrees."

Maddie had barely been conscious of the movement. It wasn't lost. It hadn't disappeared. She was an ace swimmer and had loved acting like a fish since she was a kid. And now, with a sore butt bone, it was the best choice for physical therapy. This was her chance to make a comeback. So what if her name was about to be smeared by a petty actor; she still had choices, and the easiest choice to make was swimming.

She got out of the hot tub, went to the deep end of the pool, and curled her toes around the tiled ledge. "Anyone up for a game of Marco Polo?"

Without waiting for a response, Maddie held her breath and jumped into the beautiful blue water.

TWENTY-SIX

When the other three wanted to get out of the pool and shower off, Maddie begged for one more game of volleyball. It wasn't her fault Rob and Drew wanted a more challenging game than Marco Polo. They were the ones who'd brought out the volleyball net and strung it across the pool.

After tinkering with her bikini top, she sank down until the water covered her shoulders, then swam over to Rob, who was seated on the edge of the pool, and splashed him. "Wanker, get in. It's one more game, and I get to play while on your shoulders."

"Frankly, I think you've turned into a fish. All afternoon we've been swimming. Did you grow gills?"

She twirled around in the water. "It's been a hell of a long time since I've been in water. I'm not ready to give it up."

Fran swam up to her. "We're done, sweetie. Drew's fingers are pruned, and I'm kind of tired. But my pool is your pool anytime. I'll give you the passcode to get in from the back door."

"All right. You three win. But good to know Fran and I kicked your butts. Three games to one." Maddie took in a deep breath, dropped beneath the surface, and swam to the deep end. She did a somersault, then pulled herself up the ladder.

Rob approached and threw her a towel. "Happy?"

"Over the moon, Mr. G. Shepherd."

"Thanks for the reminder," he said, scowling. "I'm sure if others were around, they might misconstrue some of this pool party's mishaps."

"Like when my bikini bottom turned into a thong?" She gave him a sassy grin. "Or when I spiked the ball to win and my top twisted and tangled, showing off one of my ta-tas?"

"What do you mean? I have no idea what you're talking about." He shaded his eyes with his hands like blinders. "I saw nothing."

She whipped his thigh with the towel. "What are we doing for dinner?"

"Don't care, but it has to be somewhere quiet. We have to do our update and go over the *Cue* article from yesterday."

Even the mention of the case couldn't pull Maddie down. She was ecstatic about actually swimming in a pool. Floating on her back. Kicking and diving around. Her mom had always suspected she was part mermaid, and it didn't help that she'd watched *The Little Mermaid* over and over as a child. "So let's stay in, order pizza, and drink wine."

Now covered from head to toe in a summer dress and wearing designer sandals, Fran came up to them while Drew jogged toward the shower. "Maddie, I know you've been a true gem for designing swimwear for me, so if this is a lot to ask, just say so. I don't want to overwhelm you."

This was the first day she hadn't felt defeated or overcome by frustration. The pool had let her splash out all of her stresses. "It's okay. I'm happy to be working. What's up?"

Fran cleared her throat and fiddled with the strap of her dress. "I have a situation. The town of Elkhart planned a fundraiser for breast cancer awareness and asked me to host it, as I'm the—at least it seems like—the resident poster child for breast cancer."

"It's a great cause, Fran. You've spent a lot of time making the public happy, so tell me, how can I help?"

"Not many know about this house," she said, waving her hand across the pool. "It's been my solace the past year. But my business, Siebkens, got lost in the shuffle and needs to be promoted. Once winter hits, we go into hibernation mode, and it's a struggle to fill any of the rooms. So when the mayor asked me to organize a *Paddle & Party for Pink*, I couldn't say no. There will be designers and some celebrities attending this event, and all I keep thinking about is how I can face everyone? I'm a wreck. But with you..."

Maddie cackled. "Oh, sister, you have no idea how much I understand your dilemma."

"What's a Paddle and Pink party?" Rob asked, blushing. "Sounds kinky."

Maddie took in a deep breath and towel dried her hair. "A paddleboard race. It's an East Coast thing. Every summer in the Hamptons, there's a celebrity-studded competition to raise funds. Honestly, it's huge money. Fashion companies design and donate bright pink paddleboards, and they're auctioned off to the big names attending the party."

"*Sincera*," Fran said, "I suspected you'd know about this fundraiser."

"All of us on *Summer Haven* were invited to the annual event in Montauk. I've been to a few but never attempted paddleboarding."

"Fran, it sounds like a fantastic event, but as Maddie's attorney, it may not be a great idea for her to be in front of cameras." Rob added, "She's here in Elkhart to keep a low, bloody low profile."

As much as she appreciated Rob coming to her rescue, Maddie had to speak for herself. "It's true, I'm not in a great position these days to be schmoozing with A-listers, but I could, if it's okay with my counsel"—she clasped his hand—"work behind the scenes. Out of view from the public."

"Oh, that's all I'm really looking for. It's more about your client, Sunkissed. Is there a chance they'd like to sponsor a paddleboard? Or donate? Of course, I'll continue to wear anything they'd like me to during any summer event."

With a huge wave of relief, Maddie shuddered. This would be good. Karma had taken over. "I'll contact my client today and let you know ASAP." Then, added for Rob's sake, "I'll be undercover. No one will know I'm in the background of your fundraiser. I promise."

On the drive back to Siebkens, she put on her dark sunglasses to evoke her inner Audrey Hepburn, who had once said, "I believe in being strong when everything seems to be going wrong."

"You good with this Pink paddling fundraiser? I mean, really, if it weren't for Wagner, I'd still be hustling for the lighthouse. At least now, if I look at the bright side, I'm selling a cause that means more to me than the lighthouse but would make Elsie just as proud. At least, I'd like to think so."

He pulled to the side of the road and turned off the car's engine. "Between losing your mom to brain cancer and almost losing Fran to breast cancer, I know this is the right thing for you to do. Your mom is definitely rooting for you. And just in case, I'll make sure Maddie Logerquist stays behind the scenes. At least until after the court date."

She gave him a full-on Hepburn-like gaze over the top of her sunglasses and was tempted to use the "L" word. All she said was, "Thank you. For everything."

PARKED IN SIEBKENS' lot, Rob went to unlatch the container holding the car's canvas rooftop while Maddie grabbed hold of her carry-on. "Wait. I'll get it for you, hon."

Hon?

"I can do it. It's not heavy, and my back doesn't ache. Don't stress, sweetie."

He chuckled and stretched the unfolded roof over the Triumph, snapping it into place. "At least let me carry it up to the room. I'm a bit edgy after you and Fran beat us in every game in the pool. Need to dole out some masculine chivalry."

"I think you're being incredibly noble already. Taking on another fundraiser with me is a pure act of courage."

"Or it shows we're both a bit *pazza*." The cover snap above his rearview mirror refused to connect. He pounded at it with the side of his fist. When it clicked in, he sighed. Notions of courage, bravery, and nobility hadn't entered his mind. Maddie needed to do what she did best, swim. More aptly, dive into the deep end without reservation. She had danced at the bar, sang in the shower, and spent the day swimming in a pool. It was progress, a testimonial that she was digging out from the past. Their past.

When he'd held her tight the night Tyler died in the lake, Rob had inadvertently drowned part of Maddie. Now, as she was boldly reemerging into life, he'd fight so neither Wagner nor Nick could ever take any of her courage away. Although, from witnessing Maddie's determination, spirit, and passion, he doubted that any ideas coming from her adversaries would slow her down. Maddie was making a statement for equality and empowerment with each creation. Like she was fighting the patriarchy one swimsuit at a time. Rob had and would always cheer her while making sure she stayed safe. He chuckled.

Huffing, he connected the last two snaps. "It sounds like a solid win, this Pink fundraiser. But I mean this in the kindest way, I'm going to be a stubborn son of a bitch. I'm absolutely disgusted with celebrities and their phony philanthropy."

Dragging the carry-on behind her, she parked it in front of him. "I guess I need a lift. Do you mind?"

"I know I sound like an a-hole, but really, I know the best way to win your case is by making sure it doesn't turn into a wildfire of rumors. If that happens, I can't control what the public thinks." He grabbed the handle of her carry-on, spun it around, and stared at her with wide and, he hoped, threatening eyes. "The facts in your case will come to your rescue, but people love to believe Hollywood gossip. So, I'll be rooting for you as long as you and I both stay away from any cameras."

"I'm feeling you. Hard." She said, completely straight-faced. Then her cheeks turned rosy. "I mean, everything you have to say is important, and I get it."

They'd swum and frolicked in the pool all day, barely clothed. Between fabric slips and the abundance of her exposed bare skin, his self-control had been tested. *Hard.* Maddie acted so freely, but she was...wild...and in her element. Rob wondered how he would contain his own primal thoughts until after the case. He'd have to add on a lot more laps during his morning swims in the lake.

"We have to get to work," he announced as they rode up in the elevator alone. Standing slightly behind her, he leaned against the back of the elevator and focused on the floor numbers lighting up above the door. Suddenly, the elevator jolted to a stop.

"I want some more words from you in Italian," Maddie whispered. "Now."

He sucked in his breath. "We can't...Maddie. It's not that I don't want to. But—"

"Turn around," she ordered. "Face the wall and start talking. Do what you have to, babe, and I'll let you know about every quiver and quake."

He looked at the elevator's big red stop button.

"Don't worry," she said, "there are two elevators. Besides, with this hypercharged state of sex deprivation, we really need some kind of a release."

One hand clutching the railing, his mind raced with possibilities, but in an elevator? It wasn't good enough for Maddie. He turned and jammed his thumb on the emergency stop button and restarted the elevator. As they moved up to their floor, he closed his eyes and thought of her when they were playing Marco Polo in the pool. The water, thankfully, acted as a cool deterrent, but at the same time, his desires for Maddie heated up and sizzled. Now, they were past sizzling and into boiling. "So. *Facciamo un gioco.* But I get to make the rules for this game."

"Of course." She blew warm air all over the back of his neck. "Tell me what to do, Rob."

He grabbed her hand and dragged her out of the elevator. His brain and cock on overdrive, he stumbled back to pull the carry-on out. "I have to take a shower. I'm a bit dirty and need a good wash. But I can't see where to scrub. I'm sure you can coach me. Will you help?" He added an extra-thick layer of his British accent. "For your best defense, however, you'll need to play on the other side of the shower. *Va bene?*"

"Yes," she whispered into the back of his ear. "Absolutely."

A growing hard-on tented his swim trunks as he fumbled with the key card. Once inside their room, he nearly raced to get into the bathroom. She followed close enough for him to feel her rapid breathing.

He opened the shower door, stepped in, and let the warm

droplets splash over his face. If his brain hadn't checked out, he'd turn on the cold water.

Rob felt Maddie's presence on the other side of the glass door. When he turned around, she was bare-breasted, one hand toying with her nipples, the other tucked into her bikini bottom and between her legs.

Moaning louder than the running water, he braced one hand against the door and found his cock with the other. "*Ho una fantasia.* Do you want to hear it?"

Steam rose, clouding over them and turning the door white with condensation. Maddie pressed her breasts against the glass, taunting him with her nearness. Clamping his eyes shut, he moved his hand up and down while telling her in Italian how he wished it were her mouth.

"Do you want to know what I wish for in this *fantasia?*" she murmured. "My eyes are closed, and your fingers are playing deep inside me. All around and up and down." She let out a gasp. "Rob, oh, Rob. Nice job. You found the spot."

His cock hardened. He pushed his swim trunks off and kicked them away. In his mind, he was dipping his fingers into Maddie's wetness and exploring her sweetest bits. His mouth grew dry, and he licked his lips, letting the running water splash his face. The pressure inside him grew. "Your mouth is so soft, Maddie. Will you please keep kissing my cock?"

"For only a little longer," she growled. "It seems like your fingers have made me hungry, no, starving for more...I can't contain myself." She released a muffled cry of total satisfaction, her eyes glued to his face, watching him come.

Shuddering to catch his breath, he pressed his palm against the shower door as she did the same. Their eyes met, and he saw the same longing for more.

"This no-touch orgasming is going to be hard," she said, cutting through the tension with her smart remark.

"Can we avoid that word? Please." His mind reeled as he tried to regain some decorum. At least he'd made it into the privacy of a shower. PDAs were not in his wheelhouse. But Maddie made him crazy with need. He wanted more. "*Voglio fare l'amore con te.*"

"Sounds sexy. What does it mean?" she asked from behind a cloud of steam.

I want to make love to you. "At least we didn't need a condom."

He swallowed, trying to regain his composure, but when Maddie wiped off the condensation, she was completely nude. Her lips were plump, full, and bright pink, and one hand played with her budded nipple. She blew him a kiss, and there was no way to douse this next rush of desire. He squeezed his eyes shut, imagined her legs wrapped around him, and made his dick think he was inside Maddie as he kissed every part of her bare skin.

TWENTY-SEVEN

On rubbery legs, Maddie made her way back to her own room. It was as if all her pent-up emotions for Rob had bubbled to the surface and exploded over and over. If she'd ever questioned her feelings for him, now she was certain Rob made her feel... What? Whole or complete? Too cliché. Maybe it was a combination. A fantastic mashup of senses, feelings, and affections that had been in her since the day they'd first met but were bottled up. They've both grown considerably since their days at Cave Point, and yet that mixture of emotions had only become more potent with age.

Even while he was in another physical space, her mind ignored the reality. Without a doubt, he'd made deep, passionate love to her. He had consumed her thoughts as well as her body. She'd felt the warmth of his skin on hers, and when her core started to burn, it was simple. As if Rob had lifted her onto his hips, she'd wrapped her legs around him, and they were together.

Standing alone under her shower and missing the steam with Rob, she closed her eyes and tried to imagine hearing his words in Italian. She was positive *Voglio fare l'amore con te* had nothing to do with condoms. Most of the world knew what *amore* meant. At least she did from listening to Dean Martin, her mom's favorite. Washing her hair, she hummed, "That's Amore," and then it manifested into a darn earworm. She let the music in her head collide with the soothing sound of the water splashing and echoing off the tiles.

Her thoughts drifted to thinking about swimming. It was hard to believe, but she'd done it—jumped into a pool of refreshing water. Like it had been just yesterday when she'd begged her mom to let her play in the pool instead of diligently finishing her daily laps. And as she stretched her arms out to do the crawl, she massaged her upper arms, letting the dull ache of long-lost muscles throb and tingle. It was such a weird and incredible sensation. And one she'd missed after such a long time.

With "That's Amore" still buzzing in her head, she fast-tracked getting out, dressing, and getting back to Rob.

In the kitchen, she found all the snacks they'd bought at the cheese museum and built a fairly impressive charcuterie board. But really, as a Wisconsin girl, she was merely making a cheese and sausage plate look more stylish. One of those wicker-wrapped Chiantis would have brought out a more Italian vibe, but the bottle on the kitchen counter was red and looked Italian enough.

The pure joy she'd been fancying since getting off the elevator disappeared when she saw Rob sitting outside on the balcony. He wore his khakis, shoes, and...she squinted to get a better look...a dress shirt? While balancing the tray in one hand and the wine with glasses in the other, she pushed the sliding door open with her foot. She gawked at his neck and was completely relieved he wasn't wearing a darn tie.

If it weren't for the noise from the boats and Jet Skis thrashing about in the lake, she could have closed her eyes and imagined them sitting in a law office. It was a complete buzzkill, but "That's Amore" kept on playing. Old Dino just kept singing.

"Hey, I made a mini charcuterie board for us. I must have bought everything at the cheese store. We need some nourishment. Did you order a pizza? When's it coming? I mean...being delivered?"

Could she be any jumpier?

"I ordered a pizza from Ottos. Although most of my go-to dishes come from Siebkens, Osthoff's pizzeria is better than some of my favorite Chicago deep dishes. I ordered—hope it's okay with you—my usual. The cheese, chicken, and pesto."

Clearly, she wasn't the only jumpy one.

He took the bottle of wine and two glasses from her hand, and she set the charcuterie board down on the table. "Spectacular view of the beach. Those bright red umbrellas are spinning. What is it?"

"The Tiki Bar." He poured them each a hefty glass of wine.

She sat in the chair. "This is all my fault. I'm usually not this—"

"Horny?" He sat across from her, grabbed a cube of cheddar, and popped it into his mouth. "Randy?"

"Yes, but I wasn't the only one, dude." She took a gulp of wine. "What's up with your khakis and loafers? Trying to banish any more of my sexy ideas? It probably won't work—I've already been kicking around some more thoughts about us having sex without having sex. Not gonna lie, your Clark Kent glasses are giving me some lusty Superman scenarios, sweetie."

"I wanted to get into a different head space...mind space... after—" He cleared his throat. "After the most lustful shower of my entire life." He took a big sip of wine and rummaged through his backpack, pulling out a file folder. "I printed out the *Cue* bit."

"It doesn't look so menacing, Clark."

"Appearances can be deceiving. I want you to know before-hand, we've got this. When we get into chambers for discovery, you will not have to worry. Without a doubt, your actions were justifiable. You were defending yourself against Wagner. Clear as crystal. So—" He handed her the folder. "—tabloid gossip is irrelevant."

TOP STORY

"Work Ethic and Hope" Guiding Chris Wagner After Attack

THE HOLLYWOOD ICON, STAR OF TV'S *CASE CLOSED*, REFLECTS ON THE HEALING POWERS OF FORGIVENESS.

BY PAUL MURPHY

AUGUST

Chris Wagner is free and ready to show his face again. Released from a month-long stay at Chicago Memorial Hospital, he's talking about his recovery from an altercation with a stalker at a fundraiser in Wisconsin on July 4th. The alleged assailant, Maddie Logerquist, an influencer known for a brief appearance on the popular reality show *Summer Haven*, could not be reached. The show's producer, Alex Martin, told the *Cue* she had been working behind the scenes but was ultimately let go due to what he referred to as *unprofessional behavior*.

A series of reparations and treatments were made to Wagner's disfigured face, and he admits it will be a long road back to the big screen. He believes his "work ethic and hope" will make it happen sooner rather than later. "The good wishes from fans and family support have sped up this excruciating recuperation. I'm ready to, once again, face the world," Wagner said.

Late last year, Wagner was accused of sexual harassment by a cast member working on the set of his popular cop procedural, *Case Closed.* Although he was acquitted on all charges, the top-rated and popular show was canceled. Wagner explained, "I'm innocent. Unfortunately, due to my popularity and compassionate ways, I've become an easy target. This time, however, due to the extensive nature of my injuries, I'll have to seek compensation. However, I harbor no ill will toward my attacker. We all deserve forgiveness."

Despite losing a three-movie deal with Scorsese, he remains unfazed. "My wife and daughters need me, so the timing couldn't be better."

Apex Pictures, Wagner's studio of record, declined to comment. His PR representative, Nina Fleischer, submitted her client's remarks and added she is no longer working for Mr. Wagner.
{PM}

TWENTY-EIGHT

Maddie stared at the piece of paper. It took all of her concentration to focus on the words in front of her, and after reading each paragraph, she rewarded herself with a sip of wine. But when she finished reading, the words *unprofessional* and *behavior* kept nagging her like knives stabbing the back of her eyeballs.

Melded together, the two concepts went against every grain in her being. Referred to as a stalker? How ludicrous. She'd been so busy accounting for her own life and time that other people were barely recognizable unless she was getting them dressed for the set. And goody for Alex Martin...what a complete jerk. Funny how when he called her earlier, he neglected to mention his conversation with the gossip rag.

She was totally relieved her mother was gone and wouldn't see this scathing paper full of lies. Finally, she dragged her focus away from the article and looked at Rob.

He watched her with what she thought of as reassurance, but maybe the Clark Kent glasses were disguising his worry. But then he pulled off the thick lenses, and Superman arrived. Right away, she knew he was solidly on her side; not one sign of worry crossed his handsome face. He popped another cube of cheddar in his mouth. "A sack of shit, hey?"

"Oh, yeah." The dull throb in her left temple subsided, yet she struggled to keep the tears from flowing. To avoid detection, she blinked furiously and then looked at the palm-thatched roof of the Tiki Bar by the lake. She sniffled. "I'll bet not one of those people at the Tiki Bar knows what the *Hollywood Cue* is. They're simply enjoying cocktails served in coconuts. Yes, there are plenty of Wagner fans, but to most people, he's just another TV actor. An image on a small screen they'll never meet and couldn't care less about."

"Cheers." He tapped her wineglass with his. "The best and healthiest way to think about this problematic situation."

"Maybe, but it's a huge freaking mess. And I have never behaved unprofessionally. Wagner and Alex are complete hypocrites and phonies." She recalled Nick's comments with his fake accent and added, "I suppose I'll have to add in Fran's brother, who had the nerve to call me *pazza*. Even in Italian, the term *crazy* is debilitating and dangerous." She handed the paper to Rob. "Can you stash this back in the file? I don't want to see it again."

He grabbed the article from her and crumpled it into a ball. "There may be more pieces coming, but now that we know how Wagner's smears look, we'll have control over his future blathering. We can stay ahead of these dubious quotes. Is there any chance someone still on *Summer Haven* can vouch for you? Or keep tabs on your ex?"

She opened her eyes wide. "'Keep tabs on my ex' sounds like we're breaking the law, Mr. Attorney."

"Hell, no. Nothing nefarious or illegal at all. It would be beneficial to have an insider's look at what was happening with Alex Martin. Admittedly, since your ex spoke to the *Cue*, he's got my knickers in a twist. I'd love to know why he has some skin in this game. Or maybe you already know?"

She waited for him to stuff the ball of paper into his backpack, but he held on to it tightly. Instead of responding, Maddie opened her tablet and scrolled through her saved *Cue* articles. She found the one about Alex and the woman with whom he'd cheated. The couple was in a passionate embrace in the grainy photograph, and their faces were obscured. She handed Rob her tablet. "Read it. The show was almost canceled because of these two. Alex dumped me for this woman and then told the *Cue* I was the one who screwed around behind his back. The dick never said who I'd supposedly screwed around with." She sliced off a wedge of brie and spread it on a cracker. "Wagner knew about Alex's lies. He told me before he...you know... I wonder if they're more than passing acquaintances on the red carpet of delusion. It's been bothering me from the get-go. How the hell did Wagner know so much about all of us? Not just me, but Graham and even Kat."

"So, wait, why was the show almost canceled?" He scanned the article. "It doesn't say in here, or does it? Was there some kind of breach of contract between Alex and this woman? Was she on the show?"

To think, she slowly chewed her brie-covered cracker before swallowing. "No, she wasn't on the show. I'm not 100 percent sure where she came from. A model? I think she accused him of forgetting the *safe* word, if you get my meaning. At the time, I thought it was bullshit and an attention grab on her part. I wasn't with Alex long, but he was never into BDSM. The executives, though, took her seriously—"

"As they should." Rob finally stuffed the ball of paper into the backpack and then proceeded to pile slices of sausage and cheese between two crackers.

"Oh my god. I'm the worst. I was so judgy and dismissed the

woman's accusations. And when they almost shut the show down, Alex managed to talk them out of it. All of it is so sketchy."

"Don't be hard on yourself. Your perspective has shifted, and at the time, you were also a victim of Alex's manipulations." Closing his eyes and tilting his head skyward, he asked, "What was it like working on the set of the show behind the scenes? Were any of the cast members ever upset?"

She thought about her last five summers in the Hamptons. For four summers, she worked as the stylist for the men and women in the "cast" of the reality show, and it was a hoot. Most of them were wonderful people, so when Alex asked her to join the on-screen group of housemates for last summer's filming, she was ecstatic. She would join Alex and the rest of the summer friends on their weekend excursions into town for rosé parties and the weekly extravagantly themed parties at the sprawling Hamptons house. It was while she was still styling the others and influencing, so she was in a frenetic energy mode for two of the three months until it came to an abrupt end. Alex asked her to leave with his pack of lies, and then Brady called to tell her about their mother. Maddie hadn't even watched when the show aired last February. She was just too darn busy in Baileys. "Not once did I get any unhappy vibes. There were the regulars on the show, like Alex and a few others, and then each season, they would change it up and add in a few fresh faces."

"Are you still friends with any of the regulars?"

She shook her head forcefully. "I did not want to drag anyone down. Once I was asked to leave, I barely said goodbye to make sure none of the others would get mixed up with me or the catastrophe Alex created."

He checked his phone. "The pizza should be here soon. What about the Pink fundraisers in the Hamptons? Any funny business?"

"They were actually in Montauk, another lighthouse town—"

He laughed. "You just can't get away from those lighthouses, can you?"

"It's like a curse," she chuckled and pointed toward the lake. "Finally, I can see land, trees, and water, and not a single lighthouse!"

When his phone pinged, he went to get their pizza.

Maddie wasn't sure what to think. Was Alex still harboring some kind of vendetta against her? But it didn't make sense since he was the one who dumped her, for what was her name... it was some kind of birdlike name...Robin? No. Crow? No.

She had to find this woman and apologize to her.

Rob set a plate of pizza slices down in front of her.

The aroma of the pesto must have come from fresh-picked basil. "I'm trying to remember the woman who had the fling with Alex. Her name was some kind of bird." Blowing onto her pizza, it came to her. "Lark! Her name is Lark."

"Where is Lark these days? Still on the show?"

"I have no idea, but I want to find her and show her some support. Now I know firsthand what she went through last year." She grabbed her tablet and googled *Lark* and *Summer Haven*. A small piece came up about Lark Russell. "Her name is Lark Russell, and it says here she's moved on from *SH*." She took a bite of pizza and scanned the article for anything concrete about her whereabouts. "This article says she's *from* the Chicago area, which is helpful."

"I can check it out. You have enough on your plate," Rob said. "I have some sources who might be able to find her. She could be someone you should meet. I'm starting to think Alex and Wagner have more in common than we think."

"I don't know. Alex was okay for the short time we dated. He was..." She gazed off to avoid Rob's eyes. She really didn't want to get into her past love life. It wasn't spectacular, and she'd be happier forgetting all about Alex. "It wasn't special or strange, but he wasn't the one."

Smiling, Rob emptied the rest of the wine from the bottle into their glasses. "It's old news. I get it. But this Lark person has piqued my curiosity. I really think that if you reach out to some of the other women or men who you worked with on the show— on the QT—they may want to come to this Pink and Paddle fundraiser." His amber eyes sparkled in the sun. "I'm guessing, but my instincts have not let me down in a long time. If ever."

It was almost as if a layer of the shields guarding Maddie's heart cracked and crumbled away, allowing her a chance to float for a change. "Don't take this the wrong way or let it go to your head," she said, "but you're totally right."

TWENTY-NINE

With her stomach full of pizza and wine, Maddie couldn't sleep. She tossed and turned for almost an hour, bothered by something unknown. Finally giving up, she sprang out of bed at three in the morning and started digging through the box from Sunkissed. Checking each of the new swimsuits, she was disappointed. Not one was pink. Time to go to work.

Yawning, she grabbed her laptop and started listing suggestions and questions to propose to the company. Then, while searching for information about paddleboard fundraisers, mostly on the East Coast, she was pleasantly surprised to find that one such event had been held in Wisconsin the previous summer. A pitch formed in her head: an opportunity for Sunkissed to support a fantastic cause and give back to the Wisco community. The Paddle and Party for Pink benefit would spotlight Sunkissed and Summer Fun in Elkhart, Wisconsin.

In the dim light on her bedside table, she began to create a presentation for Sunkissed, to urge them to sponsor Fran's fundraiser. Most of the planning was complete since the event was only two weeks away, but any funds from Sunkissed would be amazing. All she had to do was convince her client to get on *board* the paddleboard.

She opened up the file Fran had sent to her, and already, the list of sponsors was formidable. The paddleboards had been donated by many of Fran's former (pre-cancer) clients. Every business in Elkhart was participating. Some minor celebrities, local newscasters, and others would host and act as MCs of the event.

Using pictograms and pictures to depict the basics of stand-up paddleboarding—SUPing—and then finding online images from the event in the Hamptons, she pulled together a presentation showcasing Fran's hard work and then made suggestions on how Sunkissed could make a solid impact. Between pink suits, several logo'd boards, and their line of mastectomy swimwear that Fran was happy to model, it wouldn't be a stretch for Sunkissed. However, as with any company, last-minute adjustments to the budget were never a slam dunk.

Then Maddie discovered an interview Fran had given to a local newspaper at the beginning of the summer. She copied one of her quotes into the presentation on a pink background.

Fran had said, "I struggled after my surgery, but thanks to paddleboarding, I was able to let my mind drift and my body float among the waves. Standing on the board gave me an incredible sense of control, and lounging on it allowed my soul to heal. Making me feel balanced and renewed."

The interview left Maddie in tears. She found a tissue and blew her nose. *What an incredible woman.* She thought about her own mom and what her battle with cancer had been like. Maddie started to cry harder because it was more of a nightmare than a story of inspiration.

By the time Maddie had moved back to Baileys to be with her mother, Elsie was unable to speak. At least in English.

Elsie's brain had reverted back to her first language, Norwegian. While at her bedside in the hospice, Maddie had clung to her mom's hand, caressing her cool, paper-thin skin and desperately trying to decipher her words. Most were in whispers, some were in grunts, and there were plenty of groans between her foreign-sounding words.

Maddie blew her nose harder, took a deep breath, and refocused on her Sunkissed presentation. This definitely wasn't one of her typical business presentations, so she didn't want it to be cold and business-like. It had to come from the heart.

There was a soft knock on her bedroom door. "You all right?"

"Come in. Yes. Sorry to wake you," she said as Rob entered, dressed in a pair of running shorts and a Tom Petty—Damn the Torpedoes—T-shirt.

"I was trying to be quiet," she said, dabbing her eyes with the tissue.

"I didn't hear much, but I couldn't sleep either." He glanced around the room. With every available space taken up with swimsuits, fabrics, and patterns, he sat on the end of the bed. "What are you doing? More importantly, how are you doing?"

She stared at her laptop to stay calm, but she would have loved for Rob to wrap his arms around her and hold her tight until she really was calm. God, how she hated that he was her attorney. "I pulled together a brief presentation for Sunkissed. I was about to send it off."

"Congrats. Fantastic."

"Wanna take a look at it?" she asked, turning the screen toward him. Hopping out of bed, she found a sweatshirt and quickly put it on over her tank top and sweats. "It's pretty basic, but I think Sunkissed has nothing to lose and everything to gain by being part of this fundraiser."

"Blind as a bat, babe. No contacts or glasses." He squinted to focus on the screen. "This looks thorough. I'm impressed."

After she crawled back into bed, she laid the blankets over her lap. "What do I look like? I mean, without your glasses, Clark?"

He slid the laptop back toward her. "Kind of a blob with a wet face. Why were you crying?"

"Was I that obvious? I have always considered myself more of a weeper but never a bawler."

"The walls are thin, I think you were sobbing. Hey, if this shindig with pink paddleboards is too much, I recommend you tell Fran right away."

"Not in the least. It's fun. Really. I started to think about Elsie, that's all." Dropping her head back against the pillows, she closed her eyes. "The last month before she died was tough."

She inhaled Rob's lovely scent of peppermint. It soothed her, but Maddie wasn't sure how much to say. Talking about the last moments she'd had with her mom was still sensitive. Every time she'd even thought about them, it brought on a dread like she was heading to the dentist for a root canal without any numbing meds.

Shivering, she pulled the blankets up and over her shoulders. "Let me ask you, was there a time when you could talk about your mom, after she'd passed away, without shaking or crying? I mean, I don't recall you actually crying, but you're a guy. How did you make it past so much pain without feeling raw and battered?"

Rob lay across the bed at her feet. Looking toward the ceiling, he drummed his fingers on his chest. "It's been almost fifteen years since my mum died, so for me, I've been able to open up with my uncle, Graham. It's strange, but I sense her when he's around."

"At the end of September, it will be the one-year anniversary of Elsie's death, and I still can't find a way to process or actually believe she's not here, stomping around the house..." She chuckled. "I can still hear the clomping of the wooden clogs she wore all summer long. I loved those hand-painted shoes and was thrilled when she bought a pair for me at the gift shop in Al Johnson's restaurant. I wonder if she stored them somewhere?" Then she groaned. "I shouldn't be thinking about our matching clogs when we still don't know where to lay her remains."

"Simple. Next to Tyler on the island with the birdcage lighthouse." His voice was soothing in the near darkness. "It's already a burial site. I think there are other people from your family buried there."

"Wait, Tyler and others are buried on that little snake-infested island?"

"Yeah, it surfaced when I researched all the Logerquist properties. I wanted to make sure Wagner couldn't get his hands on it. Birdcage Island is where Tyler is peacefully resting, so legally speaking, it's a burial site, and there's no way you can sell it, and absolutely impossible for Wagner to acquire it."

"What a huge relief! Those last few days on Earth were tough for Elsie, but now I know her spirit has reached nirvana, and she's at peace. I feel a million times better, thank you."

"Without a doubt, Elsie lived a full and rich life. And raised three great humans. You know, Brady is a great listener, not as good as Graham, but damn close." Rob rose from the bed and turned off the bedside light. "See you in the morning, Maddie. Sweet dreams."

"You, too," she whispered.

After he closed her door, Maddie snuggled under her covers and sent a quick text to Brady. ***Love you bro***.

She wondered again about those darn clogs. Where did Elsie stash them? Often, when they wore them, they would do a little jig together and giggle about how they both lacked coordination. Dancing was never their strong suit, but then again, the old music of the crooners her mother favored wasn't quite made for clog dancing. Maddie chuckled and, before drifting off to sleep, decided a new pair of noisy clogs would be a perfect addition to her wardrobe.

THIRTY

Rob dragged his ass out of the lake after pushing himself to swim another length and reach past a mile. Yesterday, his mind had been clearer, and he'd soared past a mile and hit two miles in the same amount of time. He crawled out of the water and briefly rested on the pier by Siebkens' private stretch of beach until his mojo returned or a coffee fix yelled at him. At least the constant hum and buzz of Maddie's sewing machine wouldn't interrupt his thoughts this early in the morning. The Paddle and Party for Pink fundraiser was one week away, and Maddie had yet to hear from Sunkissed, which was why he suspected she'd taken up a close relationship with her sewing machine.

A bright pink banner for the event hung above Siebkens' coffee hut and flapped in the breeze. He stretched out his sore limbs, found a table, staked it with his towel, and retrieved a java to get going. With the latest *Cue* article, his work had doubled.

The past week, he'd spent hours trying to track down Lark Russell. The search had led him down a dark rabbit hole without any bird in sight. It was as if Alex Martin's fling had disappeared or, more appropriately, decided to fly the coop.

He sat with his coffee, blew over the cup to cool it down, and considered his next steps. As for Maddie's case, it was solid. After speaking with the district attorney and the police in Baileys Harbor, Rob had compiled a stack of evidence and identified enough witnesses to present to the assigned judge. He was fairly certain that after being shown how Maddie had defended herself, the judge would agree her actions were justified. Maddie was the victim, and in this tort case, she should be excused from any liability. In all likelihood, the judge would dismiss the case completely.

But it wasn't enough for Rob. There was something dodgy about the Alex and Lark story, and he couldn't put his finger on it, yet. Maddie may have accidentally stumbled onto it, but somehow, he knew Wagner was involved. Rob sipped his brew and burned his upper lip. "Shit." He had to get hold of this Lark person to make sure she couldn't swoop in at the last minute with some scathing allegation against Maddie. Celebrities, he'd learned, loved to make dramatic entrances.

He rang Graham to make sure he was on the right track. Having such a close relationship with a client was unfamiliar territory, and with Maddie, it seemed like he was constantly hopping around to avoid quicksand. It was nice to have his uncle's stellar legal advice.

"Oi, boy, what's shaking?" his uncle shouted. "Miss you and our beautiful Maddie. When will you be coming home?"

Rob glanced at the pink banner. "In a couple of weeks. There's a lot going on here. All good for Maddie. It was a brilliant idea to get her away from the lighthouse. Any word from our plaintiff?"

"One time only. The sod came with his representation and nosed around the lighthouse and then, just as they left, asked about your whereabouts."

Rob had made sure to list his office address with a Chicago

zip code on any hard-copied correspondence coming from him and going to the county court. For him and Maddie, this time in Elkhart had been a necessary reprieve from their routine. In many ways, it had proven more liberating for him as he'd been able to conduct business without losing sight of his Triumph or leaving Maddie's side. "Good to know we still haven't been discovered."

"It was a close call though," Graham said, "when the PR woman came sniffing around looking for you two. Agnes almost let the cat out of the bag. Didn't recognize her. Good thing your old uncle has a memory like a steel trap. Her face I knew, but her—"

"Nina. Nina Fleischer. Bloody good catch, Graham," he said, quickly pulling up the *Cue* article in his phone and reading to confirm Nina had quit. What was she up to? "If she comes back again, let me know. Or is she still in Baileys Harbor?"

A small group of women sat at the table one over from him. He quickly tapped his phone off speaker and picked it up. "Sorry. What did you say?"

Graham huffed. "I said, she's come and gone, but now she's staying at the Harbor B&B this week. Want me to suss her out?"

"Maybe ask around to find out who she's talking to while in town. I wonder if she's lying and still really working for the asshole. Keep me posted. One more thing, can you be on the lookout for another woman? Her name is Lark Russell. I've been trying to find her, and it wouldn't surprise me if she comes to Baileys looking for Maddie. Watch your back with her, too. Could be another one of Wagner's moles."

They said their goodbyes, and Rob continued writing down case ideas in his phone notes. Absorbed in another version of his opening statement, a nervous giggle from Maddie yanked him away from the screen.

Fran held her elbow as they approached the beach.

Maddie's steps slowed, and Fran tugged her along. When Fran spotted him, she waved, but Maddie stood frozen on the edge of the sand, staring at the lake. Rob couldn't miss her pink shorts and T-shirt, but it was the lack of color in Maddie's face that stuck out like a sore thumb.

He was about to get up and go over to the women, but Fran held up the *wait* finger. Rob scratched at the scruff on his jawline, and his knee bobbed up and down without his okay. He adjusted his glasses to make sure he caught every one of Maddie's movements. It was one thing to swim in a pool, but a lake? It had become her number one enemy since Tyler's death.

Fran pointed toward several spots on the lake. Rob surmised she was talking about details regarding the paddleboard race. Nodding, Maddie dropped her arm, freeing it from Fran's. It was a small but significant movement. When they started walking over to him, Fran was to Maddie's left, and the water was on her right, beside her. As the waves licked at her toes and sandals, she hopped a bit but never strayed away from the water. With two fingers in his mouth, Rob let out a loud whistle to get their attention and waved them over.

He was about to hug Maddie when they got to the table but nixed the idea. Too many people were around, and because of Fran, supermodel extraordinaire, everyone's eyes seemed to be locked on the three of them. Instead, he opted for a lingering handshake with Maddie, feeling her warmth, and winked at Fran, happy she'd been able to get Maddie so close to the beach. "You two better sit down before you fall down from all the happiness radiating off you. Is it safe to say Sunkissed is on *board*," he said with air quotes, "with the Pink fundraiser?"

"Hardy, har, har." Maddie sat next to him and let her thigh rest against his. "Whoever said lawyers don't have a sense of humor?"

He chuckled. "Everyone, because it's true. You're just so happy you'll laugh at anything."

She smiled, and all the color flooded back into her face. Even her lips were gleaming. He said, "*Amo il tuo bel sorriso.*"

Fran's laugh was so loud, she snorted. "You two need to get a room...with one bed."

"What? What did he say?" Maddie looked around, wild-eyed, then played with her tank top, adjusting it high about her breasts. "Bel, it means pretty, right?"

He whispered into her ear. "I love your beautiful smile. Nothing too smutty."

She laughed. "Who says I can't take smut?"

"I'll take my cue," Fran said, rising from the table. At her full height, her head bumped the palm-thatched umbrella and sent it spinning around. "Damn things. Before the Pink party, they will all have to be lifted higher for the celeb guests. Ciao, you two. Talk later, Maddie?"

"Yes, I'll be coming over for a swim, and I'll bring all your new suits. They're just about done."

After Fran left, Rob dropped his chin in his palm and stared at Maddie. "You've been so busy. Why aren't all of Fran's suits finished?"

"Oh, they are," she said, bursting with excitement. "I just received another box from Sunkissed, and I want to prep it for Fran. The company sent me updated versions of my design for breast cancer survivors, which are for the Paddle event." Before running out of breath, she gulped in some air. "Originally, it was a great design, but they've made some incredible modifications. Can you believe it? And the best part, they're all pink. Or pink and white. Some in pink and black. There's even a pink and teal with polka dots." She looked around the table, spotted his coffee cup, and took a sip, the last one left and ice-cold. "Blech, I need some fresh coffee."

"How about some tea instead," he suggested with a sly smile. "I'm sure you won't want a case of the jitters to get in your way."

"Darn, you're right." She held her hands out, palms down. They both quivered and vibrated. "No more coffee. I have to get a grip. It's just so amazing. When I received word from Sunkissed, finally, it was good timing. I was just about to call and give them a few of my thoughts. Nothing too strong, but they needed a nudge."

A waitress came up to their table, and Rob ordered two large cups of chamomile tea and a pitcher of water with fresh lemons.

Maddie continued on as if no one had interrupted her. She proceeded to list off all of Sunkissed's commitments to Fran's fundraiser. Pink swimsuits and T-shirts for all the race participants. A significant donation to the cause. But the best part for Maddie was how the company wanted her to create a pink polka-dotted design for a unique, one-of-a-kind Sunkissed signature paddleboard to be auctioned off to the highest bidder.

"My design will be the same as Fran's suit and will go on the paddleboard. Or maybe it will be contrasting or complementary. I haven't decided yet. All I know is my Instagram followers will double when they see Francesca Marcheti modeling one of my suits, standing next to my paddleboard design."

Rob kept his thoughts from falling behind as she raced on with fundraiser details. When Maddie listed off the celebrities who planned on coming, he made sure to file them in his brain. Later, he'd make sure they weren't involved with any recent smears in *Cue*.

When the waitress set down their tea and waters, Maddie finally took a break from talking and drank an entire glass of water. "Thanks, I needed this. God, sorry, I've been yapping your ear off."

"Not at all. This is fantastic," he said, starting a new note on his phone. With all of Maddie's excitement, he didn't want to miss any details. "Who are the celebs coming? Did Sunkissed ask them to make appearances?"

She wiped a drip of water from her lips. "Yes. They wanted to give the event more exposure. With a few big names, the head honchos thought more cameras would get their eyes on it. Although they assured me, Fran was the biggest celebrity and the MVP for the day."

He jotted down the names of the other stars and was impressed they all had some tie to Wisconsin. And he was relieved. They were well-known but unscathed by the latest Hollywood scandal to make the front page of the *Cue*. "This will be a blast. What a great event for Fran and the cause. Breast cancer awareness is ace. Not to mention our home state getting a nice shout-out. Will Sunkissed be sending over company reps to take photographs since you'll be mainly working behind the scenes?"

Suddenly, the tea bag garnered all of Maddie's attention. She swirled it in the hot water, then wrapped and unwrapped the thread around her index finger. She cleared her throat fiercely as if the chamomile tea had attacked her vocal cords. "Oh, Rob."

This was going to be bad, but how bad? He just needed to be patient. "Hey, it's okay. It's been one win after another since we've been in Elkhart." He glanced at her toes. "You walked on the beach. Let the water splash your feet. And...I know we don't typically go over your case until happy hour, but this is worth breaking the rule. I just talked to Graham, and Wagner hasn't been around Baileys."

"Good deal." She rolled her shoulders like she was prepping to come out of the corner for a boxing match. "It's...this is all about Fran. Did you know that after her surgery, she started to paddleboard to build back her upper arm strength?"

He shook his head. "It does make sense. She was unable to move her arms when she came home from the hospital. Damn, it still baffles me as to how a double mastectomy can be an outpatient procedure."

"No kidding. Another reason why this fundraiser is so critical to Fran. She wants to earmark some of the funds for post-surgery recovery research." She bit the corner of her lower lip. "Sunkissed is being so incredible. With the sponsorship funds, donations, and support, so when they asked me for one small favor in return, I couldn't say no, but..."

"Oh shit. What do they want from you, Maddie? They do know you're about to go up against Wagner, right?"

"Yes, I mean, they are backing me 100 percent, but they know their brand would skyrocket with Fran as the face of their product at this fundraiser. So...they requested," she said, letting out a sigh, "actually demanded Fran get on the Sunkissed paddleboard and participate in the race."

He tilted his head, confused. "Sounds perfect. To me, anyway."

"It would be, except she does not want to get on a paddleboard in a swimsuit and compete in front of a group of strangers. She's still so body-conscious. It's one thing to pose for a picture within her safe zone, but out on the lake with throngs of people watching? When I told Fran what Sunkissed had asked, she cried and nearly passed out."

Fran had never shed a tear, at least while he was around her, during her battle with cancer. She wanted to be seen as a warrior, not a wimp. His patience began to collapse. He took off his glasses and rubbed his eyes. The image of Fran pointing out at the lake for Maddie came to mind. Within seconds, he knew his entire thought process was about to get thrown overboard. "Is Fran okay? She seemed fine earlier."

"She is terrific. You see—"

Maybe. He put his glasses back on reflexively.

"Fran talked to Sunkissed. The CEO and the entire board... and she explained the situation. They were more than understanding, and when Fran suggested I be her proxy for the paddleboard race, they were completely smitten with her idea."

He put his elbows on the table and clasped his hands in prayer. He needed as many prayers as possible. Maybe even a hymn or two. "I want to get the facts straight. During the Pink fundraiser, you will be out on the lake, standing on a paddleboard and rowing frantically to compete in the race in front of all the cameras and all the guests." He stared at her, locking into her gorgeous blue eyes. "How does this constitute lying low or working behind the scenes?"

"I can tell you're concerned—"

"Very."

"I've worked it all out. I can amp up or change my look. People know me as having short hair." She grabbed a bunch of hair from her scalp and tugged it out. "Ow. But I can wear a wig. And not just any wig, but a post-chemo wig, which is another shout-out for cancer awareness."

There was no way he could win with her. He knew her stubborn Norwegian legacy, and if he tried to talk her out of anything, it was a waste of his own damn breath. But alarm bells were going off everywhere in his head. "What about the lake?"

Maddie shifted in her seat and then lightly touched his shoulder. "It's not going to be easy, but I have to do it. For Fran and for me. Do you get it?"

"Honestly, I wish I did, but I don't. This is bad, Maddie. This is just like the damn lighthouse fundraiser. Total déjà vu. There will be so many cameras, more than before, and shit, so much malicious chatter on social media. You shouldn't be on the radar at all..." He clamped his mouth shut so he didn't say something he'd regret.

"Oh, Rob. I know exactly what I'm doing—"

He shook his head, pissed off and perturbed.

"You'll know all that's happening because Fran and I volunteered you to be the official timekeeper for the race. Since you're the most ethical person in the vicinity."

"And what about the crowd? What if someone arrives and makes an unwelcome appearance?"

"There will be a strict enforcement of the guest list. The only person who will need supervision is Nick. Only under duress has he volunteered to help in the kitchen, but even then, he's told Fran he'll support her. And Fran, she'll be busy with hosting duties but will be watching out for me. She promised. Along with Drew."

Trying to ignore the panic swirling through his entire body, he stared at his phone. "I'm going on record as saying this isn't a great idea, Maddie. Not even good. It's a disaster waiting to happen."

"This is good *pazza*," she said.

"Not you. It's an...*idea pazzesca*. I'm..." He laid his hand on his stomach. "My plan didn't include another fundraiser or taking any chances you'd be spotted in public. And the last thing I want to say to you is 'I told you so.'"

"Have faith, it will be okay. I promise, I'll paddle my ass off, get out of the water, and go undercover for the rest of the event. I have to get going to Fran's. See you later for happy hour?"

"Five o'clock," he snapped, then plastered a smile on his face. "Sure."

After she left, he massaged his jaw to relax his grinding molars, then found the note where he'd begun to write his opening argument. He deleted it all, then wrote: TBD.

There weren't a whole lot of things that made him jittery. He'd bitten off most of his nails through law school, and his beginning cases had given him an ulcer, but the Wagner case? It had almost, but not quite, killed his spirit. Now, though, with Maddie standing in the middle with a target on her back...her case might bury him.

THIRTY-ONE

By accident, Maddie picked up her pinking shears, then dropped them on the bed. She rummaged through her tools, found the seam ripper, and tore the box open. As the paddle-board's beautiful design of bright pink with teal polka dots peeked through the swaths of bubble wrap, her heart pounded, and her palms began to sweat.

It scared the shit out of her. The other box leaned against the wall and reached past the height of the bedroom door—the paddle. Without seeing it, she knew it was tall, reedy, frail, and too unsubstantial to guard and protect her from the lake. What the hell had she done?

With her stomach tumbling down to her flip-flops, she quickly looked up videos about paddleboarding. She'd spent most of her life using her own body to move through waves, but standing on a board was an entirely different matter. Each time Maddie tried to use Fran's board in the pool, she'd fallen off. In the pool, where the water lay flat and lifeless.

Maddie stretched out her arms. They'd become shapelier and stronger from swimming laps. A major win. But since that moment with Wagner, when her fear overpowered her and took control of her strength, she kept second-guessing herself. Thankfully, Adele's anthem, "Rolling in the Deep," popped into her head. The song was from a time when she'd never batted an eye about getting into a lake.

The Paddle and Party for Pink race was one day away. She unwrapped the pink paddle, swung it over her head, then jabbed it back and forth like a lightsaber. The race on the lake was about one-half mile. Only a bit more than ten laps in a pool. Maddie laid the board on the floor, fin side up, and stood in the middle. She tethered the safety leash around her ankle. Shifting her hips to search for her fulcrum, she had to find it in less than a heartbeat once she got on the board in the lake.

To make the dry run wetter, she quietly sang some of "Rolling in the Deep." The memories of her and Rob diving off the cliffs at Cave Point rushed through her mind. She imagined the cool water of Lake Michigan swirling around her legs as she treaded water, waiting for him to jump in with her. Then, after, they would swim into one of the caves for a private conversation or, more likely, a hot and heavy make-out session.

She chuckled.

Making love on the rocks in the caves while cold water splashed over them was intense but never lasted long. This was probably why their recent no-touch shower sex had been so steamy and satisfying. They'd been training all along. And as soon as the darn case was in the rearview mirror, she and Rob would be touching and exploring each other without any distractions. She grumbled, "Be patient."

Even though they hadn't had sex for a stretch, Rob had always known when to accelerate, when to slow down, and always teased her about braking. Maddie wondered what new techniques he'd learned over the years, and her cheeks grew warm.

She and Rob had barely spoken over the past week. Their

five o'clock ritual at one of the town's watering holes had become all about business without any fun. She knew he was trying to curtail his frustration over her participation in the paddleboard race, but she could handle it. She tried, repeatedly, to assure him. Promising that she'd finish the race without any gossip-worthy incident. She would just blend in with the other paddleboard racers and then be on her merry way and out of sight.

Maddie sighed as her palms dried. Holding the paddle, her two hands were no longer best friends but colleagues with mutual respect. They worked together to balance her core and create a spot in her brain where she could retrieve balance quickly. The bigger issue was the lake. She was going to get into Elkhart Lake, smaller than Lake Michigan, but it was still a body of water with an agenda of its own.

Maddie ripped off the ankle leash and hopped off the board. Standing against the wall, the board's bright pink colors shouted all the most important messages. She wished like hell they would drown out all her worries about the stupid lake...and Rob.

It was a fundraiser to help women, survivors of cancer. Her client, Sunkissed, was giving them a loud voice, and as an influencer, she could make sure their voices would be seen and heard even louder. Whether she won or lost the race made no difference. And the folks who were going to be attending would be looking at the bigger picture, focusing on cancer awareness, and hardly bothering to notice an unknown like Maddie.

Rob poked his head into her room. "I'm hearing a lot of strange thumping. All right?"

"Yes." She opened the door for him and demanded he sit his butt on the end of the bed. Pacing in front of him, she corralled her thoughts before speaking. Unfortunately, or fortunately, the lyrics of "Rolling" kept racing around in her head. "No. We need to have a conversation."

"I'm sensing more of a lecture," he said, crossing his legs. "But go on, get it out."

Her cheeks grew warm as she caressed the paddleboard. "This thing is beautiful. I love it for Fran. But *I* don't care about it. It's a means to an end." She hesitated. "And above all else, I don't want it to come between us."

It was doubtful that he understood what she really meant because she wasn't quite sure what was going on in her head. One emotion seemed to be overpowering all of them though: amore. "I can't do this race unless I know you're on my side. Without you, I seriously don't think I can get into the lake. And I can forget about staying on top of this massive pink flotation device because I don't have a lick of balance."

THE PAST FEW days had been hellish. Having Maddie as a client was killing him. At first, he blamed one of her swimsuits. When she modeled it for him—a low-cut bikini top with a thong bottom—his cock almost bulged out of his shorts. He understood she wasn't trying to seduce him, only making attempts to converse about the fundraiser. But it wasn't the damn swimwear; it was Maddie. With only a day until the event, Rob had to get a grip and handle this case professionally and honorably, ignoring any distractions coming from below his waist. Keeping his eyes on the paddleboard, he said, "It's *bellissima*."

"That's because you can see it. It's not floating away in the water with me chasing after it like an idiot. Or worse, sinking." She plopped next to him on the bed. "Can you please help? Prevent me from making a complete fool of myself?"

He glanced at her choice of swimwear for today and let out a sigh without a sense of relief. It was more like scuba gear—a tight pink swim shirt with long sleeves and black wet suit pants.

However, her clothing did little to ease his mind about the fundraiser, where she would inevitably be totally exposed in many ways. "Are you still planning to wear a wig?" He hoped for not only a yes, but also blonde, for a response.

His hopes sank when her shoulders slumped forward. Then she scanned the disheveled bedroom and began searching through half-open boxes. "The darn board has taken over my brain. They're here somewhere."

He dropped back on the bed and stared at the crystal chandelier above. His room sported a ceiling fan. *Curious.* He wondered out loud, "How weird."

"Ta-da," she said, pulling his hand and forcing him to sit upright. "There are two. This is the frosty white version."

He blinked and rubbed his cheek. Should he say it? Should he even be thinking it? But with long silver hair, he couldn't help noticing the resemblance. With the silvery hair, Maddie's face radiated the look of her mother and the strength of a Logerquist.

While he gazed at her, she fidgeted. "What's the deal? Do I look ridiculous?"

"No, not at all. It's remarkable how different you look with long white hair. I think it will be perfect for the race." Especially since it will be an unseen barrier for his libido. "Is the other wig pink?"

She yanked off the white wig and replaced it with a pink one. The pink wig was a lighter version of the swim shirt, making her cheeks rosy.

"The white one reminds me of Elsie," he said.

"Right? I ordered it because I'm paddleboarding for breast cancer *and* brain cancer. Frosty white is the color symbol for brain cancer."

"Are there other competitors wearing wigs?" he asked. "I mean, you won't stand out, will you?"

"God, no. Everyone in the race will have a different color. True, most will be pink, but there will be some blue wigs and others." She took off the wig and brushed out her hair with her fingers. "I like the blue for water and because it matched my teal-colored board design, but Elsie wins."

She repackaged the wigs and stood in front of him with her hands clutching her waist. Her bare feet were spread apart, and she stared at him without blinking. Maddie's jaw was set, locked, and she was determined.

He coolly glanced at his watch.

"Too late, happy hour is long over," she said, adding in an extra huff. "What's your choice? Watching me make a spectacle of myself or helping me stay afloat?"

Every day, he swam laps in the lake to stay focused, and every muscle in his body ached. Once, he'd briefly thought about working out with a paddleboard, but he loathed it. "You're right, it's hard to get your balance. I'm not a fan."

"Ah ha! You have done this stand-up paddleboarding thing or, as the cool kids say, SUP, haven't you?"

"Once upon a time." He went over to the patio and opened the door. It was twilight. The air felt thick, and cars rumbled around the track in the distance. "I'll get into my suit, grab some headlamps, and a bottle of bug spray."

She jumped and clapped. "Really? At night?"

"The water's calmer, and fewer people are around. There are spots on the beach where the security lights from the hotel's decks brighten the water."

All was quiet in the lobby. Carrying the pink board, Rob opened the door for Maddie as they made their way out of Siebkens. Maddie looked like Luke Skywalker thrusting the paddle into the sticky night air. He ducked down when she almost hit him in the head. "Hey. I'm no good to you with a concussion."

"Sorry." She tucked the paddle at her side. "You're not pulling my leg, are you? You do know how to work this thing. Right?"

"Yep." He held the board over his head and led the way, following a mulch-covered path to the beach and to a private spot he'd found years ago that was out of sight from the patrons at the Tiki Bar. Between some brush, the path veered left, and they walked toward a wooden pier. At the end of the pier, he set the board down. "It's shallow."

Not hearing a response, he turned around. She stood, unmoving, at the top of the pier. Even in the dim light, he saw she'd turned ghostly white. He dropped the gear bag on the board and jogged up to her. He tried to take the paddle out of her hands, but they were locked onto it. Pressing his hands on her shoulders, he drew her close against him and whispered, "You're here, and you made it. *Brava.*"

THIRTY-TWO

"I think your congratulations are premature." Every nerve ending in Maddie's body sparked and sputtered. She trembled in his arms. Was it only a few days ago she'd walked on the beach and let the water nip at her toes? Now, with only moonlight, the lake looked menacing. As if a big, scaly creature waited to emerge, pull her in, and drag her down to the bottom. "*Brava*, sounds like brave to me. At this moment, I'm only feeling like this is a bad dream, and I can't wake up and escape from it."

"Baby steps. You're taking tiny bites out of your fear. Just walking down to the pier is *brava*, not brave, but bold." He wrested the paddle from her hands, set it on the pier, and held both her hands tightly. "No question, you're brave. You were willing to jump out of the boat and save Tyler without a second thought. Nothing held you back. Except me."

Through her nose, she took in a deep breath, and instead of a dank, fishy smell, she inhaled Rob's citrus aftershave. "We all did the right thing that night. But my heart can't accept losing my brother so savagely. Neither can my brain. Seems like I have the same nightmare. I'm under the water trying to find Tyler, laughing with him, until he disappears, and I don't have any more air."

"My nightmares, Maddie, are about losing you."

His eyes glittered. She squeezed his hands, then stood on her toes and kissed him.

He wrapped her in his arms and matched her kiss with the same urgency. Almost instantly, a long-held burden was lifted. Her shoulders dropped against his chest as she explored his lips with her tongue. She tasted a hint of caramel, or was it butter? Either way, it was important. This kiss filled her with satisfaction. She murmured, "I'm not getting you in any trouble?"

He trailed kisses along her cheek and landed on her earlobe. After a sexy nip, he sighed. "There is trouble brewing, I'm sure. But it isn't going to stop me. Maybe a delay, but I don't think I can hold back anymore."

The sticky night air smothered the world around them until the unmistakable bite from a mosquito killed the serenity. She slapped her arm. Too late. It had already taken her blood. "Ow. Shit." She jogged to the end of the pier, ripped open his bag, and searched for the repellent. "Not donating to another mosquito," she said, spraying every inch of bare skin. When she aimed the bottle toward Rob, she gasped. He hadn't moved from his position, and she was on the opposite end of the pier, surrounded by water.

She circled slowly to gather her surroundings. One wooden plank separated her and the lake. "A little help here? Please."

The pier bounced and shifted beneath her feet as he came closer. At first, she was unsteady, as if the water was moving her, but she jumped up and came down hard. Nothing to freak out about. The wood was heavy, and she was safely clear of any water.

"Now, I can call you brave," he said. "Thanks to that mosquito, you forgot about your fear."

She held his hand and covered his arm with the spray. Glancing at the stretch of beach in the distance, she liked how the torches surrounding the Tiki Bar glowed and the fairy lights glittered from Siebkens' beachside rooms. She found his other arm and repeated the mosquito barrier process. "Thankfully, the clouds are missing the moon."

He took the bottle of bug spray from her and dropped it in the bag at their feet. "Thanks. Remember how you stepped into Fran's hot tub? It was metal, and this," he said, pointing to the ladder sticking out from the water, "is the same thing. Ready?"

He turned and crawled down into the water. "Hand me the paddle."

She did as he asked.

He swished the water around his waist with the pink paddle; the color was so bright it nearly glowed. "The water isn't as warm as the hot tub, but it's perfect for August. I'd guess it's about seventy or so."

Maddie rubbed her palms on her thighs, glad they were covered with a wet suit. Using the tip of one toe, she pressed the edge of the paddleboard. It teetered back and forth. With a gulp of air, she pushed the board toward Rob and let it fall into the lake next to him. Splashing hard, it sprayed her with warm water. The light from a half-moon illuminated them. She gripped the ladder handle and stepped down into the water, facing the lake and keeping her focus on Rob. When her feet hit the sandy bottom, she yelped. It was soft and silky.

"Booyah," Rob shouted, taking hold of the board by grabbing the coiled leash. "In the lake and squishing toes in sand. Nice job."

Taking a bow, she swept her hand across the wet surface

and splashed him. "It's good. Really good." She hopped about and crouched down until the water came up to her neck. The warmth encapsulated her. "Better than good."

Maneuvering the paddle and the board with one hand and holding the leash in the other, Rob waded out farther until the water circled his waist. "We need to clear the pier. Because when you fall, which you will do many times, you need to make sure to hit the water. Only the water."

"You're just luring me into deeper water." She took a step, then lunged, and then another step. The lunge felt strangely better than the step. Balancing herself, she stayed centered as she cut through the water. "Is falling off our first lesson?"

"Absolutely. And with the leash on your ankle."

His voice grew louder as she came up to him. A slight breeze ruffled the placid water. She splashed her arms with water. "How many baby steps will there be?" When she was in front of Rob and the board, she caressed it with her fingertips and took the paddle from him.

Rob proceeded to play an Olympic-style coach for the next hour. Once she was on the board and kneeling by the board's handle, she found her center and managed to stay upright. The harder element was the paddle. Moving it from side to side, she coordinated her hands to keep them in sync.

And fell off immediately.

She rose from the water, sputtering and pushing back her hair, to receive a scrumptious, succulent kiss.

"Good girl," he said. "You didn't hit the board."

With each of her subsequent falls, she made sure to miss the board, land in the water, and receive her reward. His kisses outshone any gold medal.

"You're going to be fine on Saturday," he said as they climbed up the ladder and out of the lake.

Following behind him, she argued, "The wind will be harsher, and the waves will be higher."

"Just fall, Maddie. Then get back up on the board. It's not a race to win. It's a race to simply finish. If you have to, kneel on the thing. No one's going to think twice about it."

Her arms throbbed. Rubbing them, she collapsed and sprawled out on the pier. "I can see why this is a great workout."

After Rob dragged the board and paddle to land, he stretched out beside her. For a minute or two, they stared up at the stars filling the night sky.

"I think you'll sleep like a baby tonight," he said. "No dreams. No nightmares. Paddleboarding is exhausting."

"I can hope," she said, crossing her fingers. "I'm tired, but I know another surefire way to keep the bad dreams away..."

He turned on his side, propped up his elbow, and laid his head in his palm. As he gazed at her, Maddie sensed he was bickering inside. Seeing him so fraught with indecision, she couldn't handle it. "Rob, stop, don't worry. It's just that your kisses have been so delicious, my sweet tooth has taken over. One of these days, when you aren't my legal beagle, will you be willing to take me to bed and kiss me everywhere?" She licked her lips impulsively. "If you want, I can make a list of spots. Even though you know all of them from back in the day, there may be a few new ones."

He rolled and braced himself above her. Inches apart, a heat she'd never experienced raced through her. His lips floated over her neck and then her cheeks. She closed her eyes to fully appreciate the sensation. When his mouth found hers, she arched her back to close the space between them and wrapped her arms around him tightly.

With a groan, he broke off the kiss. "Just making sure. This spot is on the list, right?"

"Of course," she grumbled. "This lawyer-client relationship is really stifling me."

"Good to hear," he said with a hint of a very unsexy avuncular tone.

"Not really," she complained. "I know you're as frustrated as I am."

He combed his fingers through her hair. "Cold showers and swimming a lot of laps in this lake have kept me going. There's no doubt frustration is my middle name. But, Maddie, I want to make sure, after all that has happened, that you're sure. Tonight, you're sexier than hell because of all the confidence you showed on the board, but..." He tapped her heart. "How are you inside? The lighthouse was only two months ago."

"It feels like another lifetime. I haven't been worrying about a thing. I'm sure it's the out-of-sight-out-of-mind syndrome, but so what? I am definitely stronger." She'd acquired a strong sense of purpose since being in Elkhart, which had to count for something, even if a looming court date siphoned off some of her energy. "I'm braver since getting on the paddleboard."

"Did you know there is a difference between bravery and courageousness?" He sounded like a sexy professor. Standing, he grabbed her hand and pulled her up and off the pier. Then he wrapped a pink beach towel over her shoulders.

"Not a clue." She knotted her towel at her neck and let it fall on her back like a cape. "It was probably an area of expertise for my mother though."

He only chuckled and never offered up any kind of explanation.

Carrying the gear, they left the pier and took the path back to Siebkens. Maddie stifled one yawn after another. After each one, she became more certain she'd get a full eight hours of sleep later. There was a crowd in the lobby waiting to get into the bar. "What's going on?"

He pushed the elevator button. "Probably an after-party. Celebrating the parade."

"What parade?" She gave him a laser-beam, deadly stare. "With cars? Or people?"

"The annual parade along Main Street for the vintage owners. Not a big deal."

"Like hell it isn't." She jammed her hand against the elevator door to keep it open. "You should have been in your Triumph and letting all the fans cheer you on. And you missed it because of this?" She shoved the paddle out.

"I didn't miss a damn thing, girlfriend. I was exactly where I needed to be tonight. In the lake with you."

"Wait, did you call me your girlfriend?" She sighed, then murmured, "Girlfriend. It has such a nice ring to it."

"Well, you're a friend, and you're a girl. So yes." He pulled her into the elevator, and they collapsed, both exhausted, against the back wall. "But...*girl* who is a *friend*, I really want —*vorrei alzarmi tutte le mattine accanto a te*. That means I want to wake up with you every morning. I want to be your pool boy. Or your Italian stallion? Maybe even—"

"Sounds delightful." She dropped her head on his shoulder. "Will you woo me with songs in Italian every night?"

"*Certo*, but actually, I was going to add on, *amante*. Lover." He pierced her with his sparkly hazel-eyed gaze. "You can pick whichever role you need and want from me. I'll meet your desire at any moment because no matter what, I'll be here for you."

Mesmerized by his declaration, she nearly buckled over when the elevator doors lurched apart. Maddie opened her mouth to speak, then clamped it shut.

In the room, they discarded the paddle, board, and gear in the center of the living room. They locked eyes and nodded.

Before parting ways, she kissed his cheek and whispered into his ear, "Good night, boyfriend."

She showered—happily replacing the freshwater scent of the lake on her skin with a lavender soap scent—and collapsed into bed.

In her mind, Rob's litany of Italian words crooned her into a nice, deep sleep—lasting the whole darn night.

THIRTY-THREE

Labor Day Weekend

The frosty silver wig needed constant tweaking and tugging, further frazzling Maddie's nerves. Her Audrey Hepburn sunglasses helped shield her from all the cameras and onlookers standing around the beach, and the only thing keeping her racing heart steady was watching Rob. On the patio with his laptop, he checked in the line of paddleboard racers.

The race didn't start for another hour, but Maddie needed to get used to the temperament and mood of the lake, the water, and the wind. Legs crossed, she sat on the board in shallow water and played with the paddle. Water splashed over the top half of the pink paddleboard while the back half, with her butt, had sunk into the sand.

If she had to pick a day for a paddleboard race, it would be this one because it was perfect. A balmy eighty degrees and not a cloud hanging around to hinder the sun. As a soft breeze passed her, her arms broke out into goosebumps. Once out on the water, the breeze would transform into enemy number one, turning and churning the water into bigger and bigger waves.

She held her breath and counted to ten to calm down. All she had to do was finish.

As the variety of pink boards accumulated around her and speckled the beach, she grew more hesitant. The competitors, mostly women, looked like they'd been training for months. Their thighs were thick and sturdy, and their arms were hilly and muscular. Self-conscious, she rubbed her upper arms. They were solid and strong, but were they tough enough?

When a couple of other racers began towing their boards out into the water, she followed along. Dragging the board along the water by using the leash, she held the paddle with her left hand and kept it close to her side.

Farther out in the water, the waves crashed higher, hitting her waist. She was relieved that the suit she wore, the one she'd designed to match the board, had a nice high waist so it met the bottom of the top piece. There was no way any malfunctions could occur out in public.

The sun beat down on her, and the water did feel refreshing, but Rob wasn't close by. There were friendly handshakes and "good lucks" as racers surrounded her, but their well wishes fell on deaf ears; she hadn't considered how crowded and almost claustrophobic it would be out on the lake. Swimming had always been a solo act, and she always had her own lane, free from any hindrance.

Again, she patted her silver wig to make sure she wouldn't lose a lock of the fake hair. When a board bumped into her, she moved quickly to avoid it. The woman, wearing a long pink wig and a gorgeous teal and pink suit, apologized, then added, while keeping her board under control, "Hey, aren't you Maddie Logerquist?"

Maddie tried to get a better look at the woman, but she wore swimming goggles and a pink baseball hat and didn't look familiar. "Sorry, no. Not sure who you're talking about."

She clutched tighter onto the paddleboard leash and pushed through the water to move away from the woman. But when she glanced back, the woman was aiming her phone in Maddie's direction, taking a picture.

Maddie created space between her and the camerawoman and angled herself to discreetly check on the woman's whereabouts. Now, besides focusing on staying upright on a moving paddleboard in the water, she had to be alert to an interloper. As the others around her began to kneel on their boards, she followed their lead.

Her pink board, with teal polka dots, gave her a warm welcome. Maddie sighed as she was able to keep the board straight under her body. She plunged the paddle into the water until the sandy bottom stopped it, then propped herself upright using it like a crutch. Once standing, the board bobbled under her feet, but she found her center of gravity and remained steady. Phase one complete. She stared at the huge pink buoy marking the halfway point of the race. All she had to do was one lap on the board. To the buoy and back to the beach.

A part of her wanted to see what Rob was doing, but the fear of falling kept her from looking back at the Tiki Bar. Fran stood at the end of the Siebkens pier and shouted greetings through a bullhorn to the boarders gathering around. Maddie estimated there were almost a hundred racers along the stretch of water on either side of the pier. No one could miss Fran in her bright pink sleeveless jumpsuit.

There was hardly any wind, the sun warmed her skin, and she stood tall, maintaining her balance, waiting...

Fran fired the starter pistol.

Maddie's meandering thoughts came to a screeching halt, and suddenly, she was on a starting block at the end of a pool that kept shifting under her feet.

Get a grip, girlfriend.

Girlfriend...

Rob...

Carefully dragging the paddle through the water, she moved forward. The other racers were ahead, but she focused on taking it one simple stroke at a time. All she had to do was finish, not win.

Gracefully moving the paddle from side to side wasn't clicking in her brain. She was thinking too hard, so she tried to concentrate on the sun, the warmth, and the laughter surrounding her. Every time the board shifted under her feet, she used her toes, not her legs, and managed to stabilize. And she avoided looking down, a huge no-no.

Using her core strength, Maddie stayed centered on the board and focused on the buoy. It was getting closer, but already, other racers had circled around it and were heading back to the beach.

Frozen by a bout of *analysis paralysis*, she looked down at the board and wobbled. No, she could not look down. She needed a diversion, to think forward and look straight ahead. She remembered Rob telling her about how he'd imagined Wagner's head on a pin when he bowled and then hit strike after strike. Wagner's face flashed across her mind. He looked perfect as ever sitting on top of the pink buoy, and she made it to the halfway point.

Except as she circled around the buoy, Wagner's face flashed in her mind again. This time, his shining, bright white teeth mocked her. Rob waved to her from the beach.

She wanted nothing more than to reach him and put her feet on solid ground. As she shifted her weight and reflexively looked down, the board dipped precariously to one side. She tried to center herself by keeping her eyes on Rob, but another racer sped past, sending water crashing onto her board. The last thing she saw before her board flipped out from under her feet was Rob. She smiled before she fell, but instead of hitting the water, she hit the board.

ADRENALINE PUMPING, Rob hurdled and cleared every wave to get closer to Maddie. The seconds it took to reach her felt like hours. When her head popped up above the surface and she mounted the board, he waved and yelled. The other racers were mostly at the finish line. Only a few other boards, those with fallen riders, were still in the water.

For the last of the hellish distance between them, he crawled and then switched to his butterfly stroke to make it to her faster. Panting and catching his breath, he stammered at the sight of blood, "Let me check your head. Where are you hurt?"

She turned her face to him, revealing a small gash on her lower lip. The blood dripped onto the wet board.

"Ow." She moaned, wiping the blood off her chin. "I bit my lip when I hit the board. Good news, though, I eventually found the water." Her smile turned into a wince.

Holding onto the board with one hand, he pulled a cloth from his waterproof pack. "Hold this against your mouth to stop the bleeding. I'll kick us back to the beach. Go ahead, crawl onto the board."

"I lost the paddle," she said with a slight lisp. "Darn."

"I'm sure someone will get it for you. This crowd has been lovely. I take back my complaints about celebrity fundraisers. I checked in a host of fine people, and all they did was rave about Fran."

She laid her left cheek on the board and closed her eyes. The white cloth was quickly turning bright red. He kept talking in case she had a concussion. "I estimate around a hundred people will be at the party tonight. Plus the extras I registered.

Almost thirty more paddleboard racers." When his toe stubbed into the sand, he stopped kicking. "We're on land, hon. I'll help you to the first aid tent." He tucked her against his chest. "Are you dizzy?"

"A little. I might have hit my forehead, too. It happened so fast. One minute, I was looking at you, and the next, I was face-planting on the board. I wanted to finish, but hey, I managed to stay upright for half of it. Cool beans."

Together, they dragged the board and leaned it against the pier with the others. He glanced at the timing tag stuck to the bottom. "I'm impressed with this timing app. You'll know how long it took for you to get to the half point a little later."

"It will be a kick-ass time," she mumbled. "I turned the buoy into a picture of Wagner. Like you, when you went bowling. Worked like a charm."

They walked toward the first aid tent at the end of the beach. "After getting you fixed up, let's get back to the room. I don't think we should be seen together, and we've finished our jobs for the day."

She nodded, looking pretty wiped out. "Can you make it a double for happy hour...and add in a straw?"

A dozen or so boarders needing help from minor injuries were in the tent. It was quieter, and Rob relaxed. Since all the others had their eyes on their own injuries, he draped his arm over Maddie's shoulders and nestled closer to her.

She collapsed into his chest, and her wig scratched his neck. "Hey, this wig stayed on. It's pretty and tough." He tugged it lightly.

"I'm not sure I'll be able to get it off. Think you'll get used to me as a platinum blonde?"

The first aid volunteer shouted another name, and a woman in a blue wig limped behind the curtain.

"Nope, it reminds me too much of Elsie," he joked.

She faced him and batted his shoulder with her palm. "Maybe it's lucky. I think I'll keep it on until we get back to Baileys. That way, we'll be able to keep away from each other, and your career won't tumble into the garbage because of me."

"Not a bad idea." The other wounded boarders in the waiting area grabbed their phones, and the tent filled with tired mumbles of exclamation. "The times must have just been posted."

Suddenly, Maddie fumbled in her waist pack, grabbed her sunglasses, and put them on. "Who is that person?"

He surreptitiously followed the direction of her gaze and spied a woman wearing a bright pink wig, but no recognition flickered in his brain. "No idea, why?"

"She knows me. When we started the race, she asked me if I was Maddie Logerquist. I told her no, but..."

His Spidey senses jumped into gear. He tugged his shades off his head and wiped them off, inspecting every speck of dirt on the lenses while trying to get a better look at the woman. He tried to picture her with real hair in every color, but nothing stuck out from his memory. As Maddie fidgeted in her chair, he tensed up. "She isn't someone I've seen before, but it's hard to tell with all the pink paraphernalia."

"Maybe she's just someone I forgot about who lives in Baileys," she said. "I'll go over and introduce myself to find out."

"Bad idea." He pressed his hand on her thigh and whispered in her ear, "Horrible."

She stiffened, lifted his hand, and placed it back on his own thigh. "If she's following me, shouldn't we find out right away?"

His back stiffened, and his newly returned hand clutched his kneecap. "If she is following you, she may be stalking you for Wagner." He scanned the people still waiting; there were only about ten left, but all of them, including the pink woman, were holding phones. He quickly imagined how many pictures could be taken if this strange reunion went sideways. "Wagner is desperate, Maddie."

"If that's the case, wouldn't it be better if I put her in her place? She shouldn't be here. I'm sure Fran's guest list didn't include any friends of Wagner," she hissed through her swollen lip.

He wondered if the board had given her a concussion along with a cut lip. It wasn't rational, but then again, Maddie had shown him her less-than-patient side when she'd confronted Nick the Dick. "Again, it's not a scene that should play out here. Good idea though. Let's solve this by simply looking over the guest list. Then we can see if we recognize any names."

"No need to placate me. I'm not a bird with a broken wing."

His shoulders neared his ears and locked. "I'm just trying to stay calm. And really want you to stay calm." Rob's lawyerly demeanor had never let him down. "This situation—"

The first aid volunteer shouted out another name.

"It's complex. There are facts, all of which I can control, and until we get them before the judge, I'd like to do all I can to keep them in a favorable narrative."

She wiped her lower lip. "What about my feelings? I've been trapped in Elkhart while Wagner gets to prance around and show his new face to the world. You have no idea how frustrating it's been to know the douche who attacked me has an unlimited amount of get-out-of-jail cards stuffed in his pockets." She pulled at the wig, then yanked it until it moved. "While I'm back at square one, starting over. Having to build back my business after he, for all intents and purposes, shredded it to pieces." The wig shifted on her head, and she tore it off. "I'm not my mother. I love her, but I don't want to be her. I really want to be Maddie for you."

Rob swiftly glanced around. All the other wounded were looking at their phones while the unknown woman had locked her eyes on them. When she lifted her phone, he panicked and spat out, "Put the wig back on. Now."

"No way, you haven't heard one word I've said. How typical. I'm glad I hit the board. It knocked a lot of sense into me."

"Not in the least. Your head is too damn hard." He cut himself short and stood up. Why was she so bloody stubborn? Could she not see how she was hurting her case? "I told you this was a bad idea."

He strode out of the first aid tent without looking back.

THIRTY-FOUR

Maddie willed her cut lip not to quiver as Rob stomped out of the first aid tent like a petulant child. While adjusting the wig back on her head and still wearing her sunglasses, she was able to freely stare at the unknown woman who was looking down at her phone and texting with both hands. Without Rob by her side, vulnerability crept in. The first aid volunteer called her by the race number on her back, and she nearly jumped out of her skin.

Once behind the curtain, a young man wearing a stethoscope over his pink-and-orange Hawaiian shirt came up to her. Maddie was relieved to be out of view from the pink stalker, or worse, a spy for Wagner.

"Hey," Mr. Hawaiian said. "Can you take off your glasses and the wig? What happened?"

She hesitantly removed her disguise while side-eyeing the curtain to make sure it remained closed. "Last leg of the race... my board jumped in front of me when it tried to get away. Guess I have to kiss it goodbye." She gently pushed her tongue against her lower lip. "I bit my lip and disappointed my trainer."

The volunteer dabbed at her lip with a cloth and used a

light to inspect it closely. He finally said, "Great set of choppers. You're lucky they didn't all break off. Your lip saved your front teeth, but you'll need a couple of stitches."

"Really? Seems so drastic."

He lifted up the blood-soaked cloth she'd used. "It's still pumping hard, which is typical of lip and face wounds. You may not need the stitches, but then I'd tell you to go lie down for the rest of the day." He gently lifted her chin and shined a bright light into her left eye, then her right eye. "How's the head?"

She buried her first response, *mad*, then tilted her head back and forth. "Okay. My pride is mostly bent out of shape. I wanted to finish the race."

"After these stitches, you have my permission to hang out at the party and celebrate. Even if you didn't finish, the word on the beach is Fran's benefiting the awareness fund with a pot of gold, and that's before tonight's silent auction."

"Sweet," she said without closing her lips. "Two stitches it is, then."

"Maybe you'll finish next year. I think this event will become an annual tradition for Elkhart."

She tipped her head back and let him stitch her lip. With eyes closed, she imagined the various sewing stitches she'd used over the years, to forget about each needle stab. It ended up that she needed four stitches.

"Thanks," she mumbled after he adhered the split with a liquid bandage and stepped away from her.

"Good as new. Just avoid talking too much."

"Easy," she said. "Not much to say."

The pink spy was gone when she exited through the waiting area. Back outside and in the sunlight, she felt unhinged. The celebrations had kicked off all around the beach, Siebkens, and the Tiki Bar. What was her plan now? Go back to the room and hide in her bedroom to stay undercover? Worse, face Rob? She touched her stitches and flinched. Any selfies around the board for Sunkissed were out of the question.

Women gathered around the pier, where the racers had parked their boards upright like soldiers. Maddie decided to ask if they'd like to pose with their paddleboards for her. Feeling useful again, she strode across the grassy area and onto the pier without hesitating at the edge. She would have smiled, but her lip ached. At the end of the pier, she asked one woman, who then asked the group, and they let out hollers and cheers. Maddie quickly took a boatload of shots, making sure to get all the pink signage on the beach in the background.

When the group dispersed, she sat on the pier to look through the photos. A tap on her shoulder sent a jolt through her, but she held her phone tight.

"Excuse me? I'm not sure if you remember, but..."

Maddie shaded her eyes to block out the sun and get a better look at the person standing over her. Even without the pink wig and glasses, she recognized the suspicious stalker.

"I'm Lark Russell."

Maddie glanced around and mumbled, "Who's with you?"

"I'm alone." Lark sat down across from her. "I had to find you."

Had to find me? Maybe Rob had been right: she was working for Wagner.

"My lip is broken, so I'm not in a great mood. What do you want from me? Did Alex send you or...someone else?"

"You mean the asshole extraordinaire?" Lark shook her head. "I wanted to talk to you after I read the article in the *Cue*. What Alex is saying is despicable. Such a bastard and...after what they did to me."

They? Maybe her head hit the board harder than her lip. "I'm not following. How did you find out where I am today, right now?"

"The guy you were talking with earlier?" Lark ignored her question. "Is he Rob Reid?"

Maddie tried listening to her gut for some direction, but no luck. Lark's demeanor didn't appear shady, but... So she spit it out: "Are you spying on me? What do you want? Salacious pictures of some sort?"

"Gawd, no!" she said, completely stunned, her body trembling. "Not a spy. I'm not spying on you. But after what happened with Wagner, I have to be careful because Rob Reid is his lawyer."

Maddie tried not to garble her words. "What happened to you with Wagner?"

Lark's blonde hair swayed under her chin as she shook her head. "It was a nightmare. I barely hooked up with Alex, maybe a date or two, but then, when his buddy Wagner showed up on the set—"

"Alex Martin and Chris Wagner are friends?"

Lark nodded. "Oh, yeah. It was more one-sided since Alex hadn't made it past his reality TV fame. I'm sure he hoped Wagner would get him to an A-list spot."

Now closing in on happy hour, the Pink festivities were in full swing. The racers had gathered around the Tiki Bar, and all of the tiki torches were lit. Maddie tried to catch a glimpse of Rob's ginger crown as she absorbed this staggering bit of news. "Of course, Alex and Wagner are like a couple of Hollywood tech bros."

"Last summer, in the Hamptons, all was well on *SH* until Alex, with Wagner at his side—"

"Slow down, Lark."

Lark nodded nervously. "Sorry, I've never told anyone about this and..."

"You're with me, go on."

"They pulled me into the boathouse. Or not the boathouse,

the pool..." Lark sucked in a breath. "Whatever it's called. Sorry, I'm so shaky. This has been bottled up in me for over a year."

Maddie let her guard down and took hold of Lark's hand.

"So the pool equipment storage... They asked me to come, to check on the floats and the kayaks. They made it sound like they needed my expertise since I'm a surfer. Of course, it didn't occur to me that it was one of the few places where no cameras were set up." She scoffed. "So stupid. When I get there, Alex and Wagner are completely blotto. Reeking of whiskey. Alex grabs me in a strangling hug, and then Wagner slurs on about a threesome. After I get free from Alex, the other scum bucket grabs my boob. They're a couple of depraved tools."

Maddie squeezed her hand so she wouldn't drown in the waves of relief crashing over her. "You're not alone. We've got each other, and we need to find Rob."

Lark pulled her hand away. "Hell no. I've been avoiding him like the plague. He's Wagner's right-hand man."

"Not anymore. Wagner is his enemy now, probably archenemy. Rob wants to take the beast down. He's on our side and working as my attorney." *At least he was until he stormed out of the first aid tent.* "Rob was calling you on my behalf, trying to find out where you went after you left *Summer Haven.* I thought you left because of the bizarre BDSM stuff Alex was going on about."

"Total bullshit. I made it up to get the hell out of the Hamptons and go back to LA. Alex is lucky I didn't talk to anyone about him and Wagner. Then, instead of appreciating the fact I didn't go to the cops, he was able to keep the show going and buried the BDSM story with another fictional line of crap. Lying about how his true love, Maddie Logerquist, cheated on him and how his heart will never be the same—"

"From one lie to another. Alex went from villain to hero in

one fell swoop, thanks to *Cue*," Maddie added. "And then my mother was admitted into hospice, and I had to leave the show."

"Right. Talk about having that gossipmongering rag twisted around his finger. Mostly because of his buddy Wagner. Also, Alex made sure to tell me before I got out of there that Wagner had originally asked him to get you to come to the pool storage. Apparently, I wasn't the 'tall one with solid fucking thighs.'"

A wave of nausea came over her. "Wagner wanted me?"

Nodding, Lark groaned in disgust and hugged her. "I'm so sorry, Maddie. If I had said something last year. Maybe what happened wouldn't have. Because of me, Wagner attacked you. And now the ass is suing you."

Maddie fell into her embrace, her emotions in turmoil. "No one should be *coulda*, *shoulda*, or *woulda*'ing. Especially us." She wanted to introduce Lark to Rob ASAP but wasn't sure. "So, if you ignored Rob, how did you find me?"

Lark flinched. "I called the lighthouse in Baileys Harbor and spoke to a sweet, older-sounding lady. I'm sorry, but I lied and told her I was a swimsuit client of yours. She was so thrilled, she told me you had come here to Elkhart."

"Agnes." Maddie suddenly missed her. "You're right, she is a sweet woman."

Her palms had grown sweaty, and her whole body, not just her lip, was one big ache. Lark was like one of those weird messenger pigeons flying secrets back and forth during wartime. Except Maddie wasn't on the home front. She was in Switzerland, without any chocolate. "Lark, I'm so glad you found me. And I know...after everything that's happened to you, this may be a huge ask, but is there any chance you would be willing to come to Baileys Harbor with me? Maybe tell your story because it proves mine?"

"Oh, hell, yes." Lark let out a long sigh. "This is amazing. Finally, this heavy burden has been lifted. *Poof*."

A twinge of jealousy went through her. It seemed as though the safety leash was tightly strapped to her ankle, and she couldn't move away from the board safely. "Rob needs an update. Only if you're comfortable talking to him."

"For you, of course. Do you think my story will be the case's smoking gun?"

"I really hope so." Maddie forced the picture of Wagner's smug face from her mind. "The quicker we get this out in the open, the happier we'll be."

THIRTY-FIVE

Rob shouldn't have left Elkhart before talking to Maddie, but anger had muddled his thoughts beyond repair, and his damn emotions...well, it was a lesson to be learned. Don't represent a woman you're in love with.

With the Pink Party in full motion, he left the envelope for Maddie and slipped out of Siebkens without anyone noticing. His gear, thankfully not much, fit in the Triumph. His only reassurance—Graham was waiting for his arrival in Baileys. Rob considered whether his uncle was more excited about seeing him or the car and concluded the car won.

When he parked in front of his brother's house, Gus and Lucy jogged over to greet him, worry written all over their faces. Graham followed, gave him a wave, and then strode to the car, looking it over. Whistling, he nodded in approval. "Oi boi, the paint job is bloody brilliant."

Enveloped in a bear hug, Rob peered over Gus's shoulder, and his hopes soared. His uncle was a brilliant barrister in the UK and became an attorney in Wisconsin. After hugging Lucy, all four went into the house and grabbed beverages. It was the only time he wished Gus wasn't a teetotaler; Rob needed a stiff cocktail.

Lucy asked the first question, "How's Maddie?"

Staring at Graham, he answered, "Good. It's been a reprieve from all the shit happening since the lighthouse, but I want, actually need some help."

"Bro, we're here for you, no questions asked," Gus said. "The lighthouse is doing well, and I've loved the fundraisers. Not sure, but I think we blew past the amount needed and went well above Maddie's goal a couple weeks back."

"That's good," Rob said, rolling his head around and stretching out his neck. "She'll be happy about that, but I'm in a world of shit. I left Maddie in Elkhart. She doesn't even know I'm gone, I think. But it was too much. I can't continue with her case. If I defend her, she'll lose it all. I can't be the one who sinks her or her family's brilliant legacy."

Graham let out a hoot, followed by a round of congratulations from Gus and Lucy.

"What's going on? I'm in the middle of a crisis, and you three are celebrating?" He sat on the sofa and rubbed his eyes. Maybe this idea of his was a waste of time. "I was hoping Graham could take over for me."

Lucy sat next to him on the couch. "We aren't laughing at you...wait, maybe we are. We're over the moon you're here and that Maddie's back in your life. You two deserve one another and—"

"Lucy, please don't tell me you've been working your *Emma* mojo on us while we've been in Elkhart. Have you?"

Leaning against the fireplace, Gus pointed to the candles on the mantel. "Of course. There's your personalized match-made-in-heaven scent."

"Do they smell like misery?" Rob quipped.

Graham sat on the edge of the coffee table and patted his

knee. "You've already developed a strong case. I'd be honored to take it over the finish line."

Rob's relief was quickly replaced with suspicion. "What's the catch?"

"The Triumph. I get to drive it around Road America when this is all over."

"Whatever you want, it's all yours." Rob went to the kitchen table and retrieved his laptop and files from his backpack. "Here are all my notes, and I'll send you the files."

Once online, Rob retrieved the case number and court record and submitted a request for a change of representation. Then he found the keys to the Triumph and handed them to his uncle. Overcome with emotion, he could barely spit out a thank-you. Maddie's case was now in the best hands.

Gus and Lucy left the two men alone to work on Maddie's case in private. Only the dogs Humphrey and Bogart interrupted them, occasionally looking for belly scratches.

His uncle's legal mind was as sharp as ever, even if he'd been semi-retired the past few years. The man's curiosity, which some might consider nosiness, kept him on top of all his games, whether playing with cars, boats, or lighthouses.

And for Maddie's case, Graham's love of the lighthouse was her golden ticket. Over the past six weeks, he had kept records on the comings and goings of everyone in the lighthouse during the fundraisers and regular visiting hours. Rob was shocked to find out that Wagner had tried to take a lighthouse tour while in disguise.

Graham let out a rich, cackling laugh. "The sod thought I wouldn't recognize him with a full beard and mustache."

Surprised, Rob asked, "Was it real? Or a really good fake?"

"Oh, it was real all right. The man kept rubbing it. I never took my eyes off him. Made the SOB nervous. Even Agnes knew it was him because of his *Cool Hand Luke* eyes."

It took a second to recall his uncle's reference. Then he remembered Wagner had been compared to Paul Newman, the star of the classic movie. "Did he talk to anyone, or how did he behave when you asked him to leave? You did escort Wagner off the premises, right?"

"Actually, I rang the coppers, and TJ came and hauled his ass off the property. Your restraining order worked wonders."

Rob congratulated himself. He wasn't a mind reader, but he knew how Wagner operated. The man had a depraved thirst for control, and while his lawyer was bound by the law, that wasn't good enough for Wagner. He lived by the adage "keep your enemies closer."

"If his face had been injured so bad, how was he able to grow a full beard so fast? I know his teeth are fake. The reason why they flew out of his mouth when Maddie took him down."

"The man is a bag full of gaseous lies." Graham added, "How he's not in jail is bloody hard to believe."

Thinking about Maddie, Rob checked his phone. What would she do when she discovered he'd left? At the slew of ominous thoughts, he physically recoiled, set the phone down, and let out a low groan. "I'm not sure if Maddie will ever speak to me again. However, in my defense, leaving Elkhart has dramatically increased the chances of her case being dismissed. Thanks to you. Especially since Wagner violated the restraining order."

For a brief moment, he envisioned Maddie's cracked lip and silver wig. Her sea-blue eyes had pleaded with him while they waited in the first aid tent. But he was sure that woman was acting suspiciously. At least, he thought so. Had he gone overboard with his vigilance and been too protective? He'd only been thinking about Maddie's safety, but had he become indignant?

When his phone pinged, his heart pounded harder, but the

message came up without Maddie's picture. "Oh shit, this is not good. Lark Russell has finally appeared."

HER LOWER LIP THROBBING, Maddie repeatedly pounded on Rob's bedroom door. When he didn't answer, she flipped him the bird, knocking her middle finger against the wood. She did not need another injury, so she stumbled into her room, shoved all the clothing, wigs, and swimsuits off the bed, and fell into it.

She awoke the next morning with little memory. Yesterday's sugar intake had drained her, allowing deep desolation to course through her. Between the round cookies frosted with pink *nipples*, coconut cups filled with pink lemonade, and the one treat Maddie couldn't get enough of—martini glasses filled with Campari sorbetto, she was sapped.

With a grunt and a reedy moan, she sat up. The damn silver wig was still clinging to her scalp, but it had shifted so far back it looked like a mullet. She needed to clean up and get her thoughts together.

Her pounding head worsened with each step toward Rob's room. She knocked, and while waiting for him to answer, sensed something strange in the suite. She pressed her ear against his door and didn't hear anything, so she padded downstairs to the kitchen. Her suit designs were still spread out on the table, but Rob's backpack was missing.

She spotted a manilla envelope on the hallway table, jogged back upstairs, and busted into his room. The bed was made, and all of his belongings were gone. Her heart sank. Rob had left her.

Her throbbing head and pounding heart made each step downstairs feel like a trek across a desert. Her name was neatly scrolled across the front of the legal-sized envelope in Rob's handwriting. At least he only wrote Maddie and didn't make it colder by adding her last name.

Darn it. Why did she get so pissed yesterday? He was only trying to keep her case in a solid winning position.

She tipped the open envelope on the hall table and let the contents fall out. First, a fob for his Audi, and then, after another shake, a white letter-sized envelope. What was it with Rob's need for envelopes? Holding on to the Audi key, she opened the letter.

Hey Maddie,

You were spectacular in the race. Congrats. I'm giving you the Audi. I wanted to leave the Triumph but wasn't sure if you knew how to drive stick. I think, for the best outcome of your case, I have to leave Elkhart. I'll be in a better position to process the last steps and get the complaint against you dismissed. Please call me as soon as you're back home. Please.

All the best,

R

Maddie's tears spattered on the paper. Trying to wipe them off, she turned the words into black smears. She tore the letter into shreds. Hiding behind his lawyerly duties? What a coward. Wasn't he the one waxing on poetically about courage and bravery? *All the best?* She swept the pieces of the letter off the table and into her palm. Crunching them into a ball, she returned to her room to stuff them into the bottom of her luggage.

Rob, with his rigid regard for the rule of law, had dumped her. *Girlfriend, my ass.* No doubt he had a procedure manual for his life—color-coded and laminated—and her name was conspicuously absent. She filled the carry-on with her personal items and stuffed the rest, including all the sewing paraphernalia, patterns, fabric swatches, and swimwear samples, into the original boxes. Then, she went into the kitchen to call Fran. She needed a friend, and Rob had given up that title and all the others.

In the refrigerator, she found bottles of water and guzzled them all down. Yet, the throbbing in her head still persisted. Maddie swallowed three pills for her headache and lay on the couch, waiting for Fran. Besides all of the Campari, something else about yesterday was pestering her.

She pieced yesterday together, and when the moment after Rob stormed off fell into place, she remembered Lark Russell. Her smoking gun. Lark was going to make the case against Wagner go away forever. But how? Did Lark contact Rob last night?

Grabbing her phone, she started to text him but deleted it. He had probably dropped her case and was heading back to Chicago. She considered asking Lark, scrolled through her phone, and realized she didn't have her contact information.

Fran rushed into the unlocked room wearing the pieces Maddie had created for her: the two-piece polka dot swimsuit and the matching teal cover-up. "Yesterday was superb! I couldn't have done it without you and your brilliant ideas. And all the pictures from the event are being posted and multiplying on the fundraiser's website." Fran zeroed in on her with a look of horror. "What happened to your face?"

Maddie hadn't showered or looked in the mirror for the past twenty-four hours. "It's nothing. My lip split when I fell yesterday."

"No, your eyes. They're all red, and your face is covered with black smudges. Have you been crying?"

Maddie sat up, found her Audrey shades, and plunked them on her face. "It's nothing. I drank too much, and we—I mean Rob...well, he's pissed, and yes, I cried, a lot." She looked at her fingers. They were covered in black ink. "Stupid letter."

"I'm glad you received his letter."

"What? Did you know he ditched me?"

"Nonsense. He has a plan. You know how organized he is. Rob made sure Drew and I would take care of whatever you need before you left for home today."

"How thoughtful of him," Maddie snarked. "I'm like a dirty little secret. The other woman he's been having an illicit affair with while staying at Siebkens."

"Ha! What a hoot." Fran lifted one eyebrow. "You are the *only woman* in Rob's life, *bella*."

"I mean, we've been friends for so long, yet it's almost impossible to talk to him about anything other than the rules of law. His head never gives his heart a chance. Rob pisses me off." She'd never been so bent out of shape over anyone. "I'm sorry, that's harsh."

"Not at all. In fact, I think Rob would agree with you." Fran sat down on the couch. "It's his way of processing feelings because, let's face it, they can be incredibly messy. The truth is, or *verità* is, that Rob has probably spent his life working and processing cases to avoid his feelings for you. He's only ever talked about you."

"We have been through a lot together." Maddie sighed. "Fran, do you need me here? I mean, I know we still need to take some pics for Sunkissed, but is there anything else you need my help with?"

"Not now, and the current total for the fundraiser is—" She

looked down at her phone. "Just passed fifty thousand. The silent auction was a huge success. All the paddleboards sold."

"Who bought the board I designed?" Maddie rubbed her temples, willing her headache to go away.

"I'm not sure who, but it went for a good amount," she said.

"How much?"

"Ten grand."

"Incredible. Why do you sound so sad?"

"It's fantastic, but now you're leaving, and since you've been here...I've felt like I've had a sister."

"Me too." Maddie hugged her. "I'm only an hour away, and I have so many more ideas for you, so don't worry."

Fran helped her pack up the Audi with all of her belongings, and after another long hug and a few tears, she drove away from Siebkens. Passing the entrance to Road America, she blew a kiss and waved goodbye.

THIRTY-SIX

For the third time, Rob's emotions took the driver's seat and steered his mind. First, he had yet to talk to Maddie. Second, he regretted leaving Elkhart, and now this—Monday's issue of the *Cue*.

Splashed across the front page was a scathing photo of Maddie berating Nick the Dick in front of the PocoLoco food truck in Elkhart. All Rob wanted to do was pitch his bloody tablet into Kangaroo Lake in front of him.

It was Fran who informed him that Maddie had returned to Baileys yesterday. Ignoring his texts, she had no idea she was his top priority, and it was his own damn fault. He'd been a *right prat*, as his uncle would say.

For a clean break as her legal representative, he'd created a document voiding the contract. All Maddie had to do was sign the damn thing. Would she ignore him if he were to show up at the Logerquist estate unexpectedly? He re-examined the *Cue* article and decided to do it. Go to Maddie unannounced.

At the wrought-iron entry gate, he punched in the security code but was denied access. *Bloody hell.* Brady had changed all the codes while they were in Elkhart. He rang Maddie while pacing at the end of the driveway. His heart skipped a beat when she answered.

"Fancy that, the incredible Rob Reid makes time to face me. Too bad, Mr. G. Shepherd, but I don't have any treats for you."

He deserved the snark. "Glad you're back in town. Welcome home. Can we please talk?"

With a loud click, the gate opened.

The top was down on the Triumph, so he climbed over the door and drove up to the house. Security cameras mounted on every corner of the low roof buzzed, clicked, and aimed at him. Blue hydrangeas had blossomed along the front windows and swayed out toward the afternoon sun.

He rang the doorbell to stay official and composed, even though his nerves were unraveling at top speed. *Just get the papers signed.* Maddie opened the door, and he swallowed down his surprise. Her lip had swollen to twice its size after Saturday's fall. He wanted to rush in and get ice for it.

She lifted a frosty plastic bag to show him she'd had the same idea. "It's actually working. You should have seen it yesterday." She stood back and gestured for him to enter with a flourish of her hand.

He tugged at his backpack to make sure all of his legal tools were close by, but his composure crashed at the sight of her. A rush of blood pumped in his head, and a riotous gang of feelings raced through him. "Anything else...you need? I mean, the cut didn't seem so bad before...I left—"

"You mean when you ran away from me?" She closed the front door, slammed the dead bolt in place, and walked past him to sit in the dining room.

"About that, yeah..." He followed, wondering if he should be panting, slobbering, and widening his eyes. He nodded toward the lighthouse urn on the table. "Well, that's why I'm here now. So much is going on."

"Want some coffee?" She glanced at her watch, "Or it's five o'clock somewhere—how about a cocktail? But nothing with salt. After four stitches, I'm still not ready for it."

Following her into the kitchen, he dropped the backpack gently on the counter and laid his hand on her shoulder. She shivered. "Maddie, I'm sorry."

She stood so still he wondered if he should slam on the brakes, kill the engine, and make a run for it. Not again. He'd always be her friend, and if the boyfriend label had been peeled off, so be it. But the thought of losing her ratcheted up his heartbeat.

Slowly, he lifted his hand from her shoulder and clutched onto the counter.

Tears were in her eyes when she turned to face him. "I'm really mad at you. Why did you run off like that? You're the last person on Earth—no, scratch that, in the universe—who I..." She sighed. "I never expected you to actually ditch me."

His heart plummeted, and he had no excuses. He didn't deserve to breathe the same air after what he'd done. He shook his head, trying to fight off the awful malaise. "I can't...I don't know what to say to you. Or how. It was too much while we were in Elkhart. My head and heart were at war with one another. One second, I was focused and blazing the trail for a dynamic opening argument for you, and the next second, I'd forget all about it. My mind kept wandering off. All I kept thinking about was you, Maddie. I couldn't sleep while we were at Siebkens, tossing and turning every night like a damn teenager. One cold shower after another and swims in the lake didn't ease my wanting. You consumed my every thought. Nothing was clear in my mind. Then, when you fell off the paddleboard, I cracked."

She wiped off the tears staining her pallid cheeks and sniffed. "It seems as if every time we get close, some outside force rips us apart. But this time, you did it. You separated us."

The sadness in her eyes cut right through him. "You're right. But I needed to turn my frustration into action. I took off with one single thought: getting to Graham and handing him your case."

It gave him a sliver of hope when she took a small step closer, but he didn't want to believe it too quickly. "How can I ever make it up to you? Wait, don't answer. I'll just beg and pant like a German shepherd."

The corner of her mouth lifted.

Hesitantly, he reached for her hand. An hour-long second passed before she took it. His breath whooshed out of him, and his spirits lifted.

"You're on probation, Mr. Shepherd."

"Understandable."

She squeezed his hand, leaned into his chest, and hugged him.

Slowly, he kissed away every one of her tears. The salt was the best he'd tasted in a long time.

She let out a moan and sounded crestfallen. "All I want to do is kiss you, but I can't. My lip still hurts."

"Let's go outside on the patio." Keeping his emerging joy in check, he found a couple of mugs and prepped some coffee. "Where are the straws?"

After a sniff and a crooked smile, she pointed to a drawer.

He threw his backpack over his shoulder, slipped a straw into one of the mugs, grabbed both, and followed her out the back door. The sun made contact with the lake, and the waves glittered. Once they were nestled together on the wicker love seat, he draped his arm over her shoulders. He took a deep breath of her lavender-scented hair and let it out slowly.

For several minutes, he couldn't move. All he wanted to do

was relish Maddie's proximity. Her nearness had become his quickest source of energy. He retrieved the paperwork from his backpack. "Maddie, I refuse to be your lawyer anymore."

The disappointment on her face nearly wrecked him. "So, you ran off and then decided to cast me out like a leper?"

"No, I'm not a complete jerk," he said, setting the form on the table with his pen in front of them. "You need better representation, and Uncle Graham can give it to you."

As she stared at the form, his heartbeat tripled. "Maddie, I can't be, at least around you...professional. Your case is in fantastic shape, especially after I spoke with Lark Russell—"

She turned and hugged him. "You two talked? Oh my gosh. What a relief. It's fantastic, isn't it? Lark and I, we're compadres in the fight against Wagner. I'm not alone."

"I'll tell you all about my conversation with Lark in a minute." He gently adjusted her to look at the form on the table. "You've never been alone, and now, with Graham taking over your case, I can be your friend. Or..." He wanted to say boyfriend, but it seemed too soon.

"I don't know," she said with a slight lift in her eyebrow, then stretched one of her legs across his lap. She slid on top of him, straddling his thighs. "Can friends do this?"

Still wearing his swim trunks, his bare legs heated up from her warmth. He closed his eyes and let her strip off his shirt. The faded Petty tee fell in a ball on the table. "I may need to reassess that label," he whispered while cupping her sweet bum and dragging her closer to his hardening cock. "Boyfriend, lover, and friend, I'll take all of them."

***

MADDIE SIGHED, then let out another long sigh, releasing all the air that had been pent up for the past two nights without

Rob. Sensitive to his southern needs, she caressed his unshaven face and got off his lap. She lifted the pen, admired its heft, and signed her full name on the document. Madeleine Eleanor Logerquist. As usual, the line ran out before the last of her signature landed.

"Have to make it official," she said, returning to perch on Rob's lap, lightly grazing her fingers over the tent in his swim trunks.

"On the record, and formally, I am no longer your legal rep." His words were barely audible and strung through a moan. "Can we move elsewhere? Not a soul around, but a bed is so much—"

She stood up, took his hand, and tugged him through the house and into her bedroom. She shivered when the air conditioning accosted her, but Rob closed the door and softly rubbed her bare arms. "It will be difficult, but I plan to kiss you everywhere, except for your gorgeous mouth, since it's healing."

"There's no one but you who could make such a big declaration with absolute certainty," she teased. "It will take time, of which we have plenty, finally."

They made it to the bed, and Rob delivered on his plans by kissing her shoulder, then lowered her tank top strap and kissed her arm. He dabbed a kiss on the inside of her elbow, and she shivered. The one special spot known only to Rob. Taking each of her fingers in his mouth, he swirled his tongue and kissed the tips.

Wishing she could kiss him and not wanting to disrupt the slow heat building within her, she nibbled his earlobe and nestled into his neck. Leisurely, at a pace that intensified her need for him to be inside her, he freed her of all clothing, bit by bit. By the time he slipped her panties off, they were soaked. Maddie moaned and sat on the end of the bed. Rummaging around the unmade bed, she found a pillow to press into for endurance. When the corner of Rob's mouth lifted into a cheeky grin, she knew she was doomed.

He kneeled in front of her and parted her thighs. "This may take a bit of time…"

Dropping back on the bed, her legs opened wider, giving Rob all the space he needed to get to where she so desperately wanted him. As his tongue swept circles around the tender folds of skin, he clasped her bum, lifting her gently each time his tongue swirled and darted in and out of her.

Finding her clit, he flicked his tongue around her sweetest spot. Maddie's thighs rose up, and she clung onto his hair. The sensations sizzling through her made it hard to catch up with her breathing. Short gasps came out as her whole body tried to explode, yet a tiny voice told her to hold off. She wanted Rob inside her.

"Please," she said, "Rob, I'm finally with you—" Her words were garbled. She dug her elbows into the bed and forced her way up. There was no way she would come alone.

He grunted something foreign-sounding, then crawled over her. With his arms bracketing her sides and his eyes heavy-lidded, he whispered, "*Voglio fare l'amore con te.* I want to make love to you."

"*Amore* is all I need to hear." She fumbled through the drawer of the bedside table and found a strip of condoms. "I'm shaking too hard. Can't bite one open."

While he kissed her breasts, she writhed under him. How he sheathed himself, she didn't know and couldn't care less. His tongue caressed her nipples, trading one bud for another as the ache in her core intensified. She massaged his back, loving the feel of the hills and valleys of his muscles. With one hand, she grazed her fingers over his sleek, hard cock and then lightly brushed them back and forth over his tip.

"No matter how long it takes, I'm determined"—his voice

grew raspy and desperate with each word—"to find each and every one of your sweet bits."

He lowered his chest against hers, and she relished being swathed in his warmth and slightly damp skin. She inhaled his scent, a combo of fresh air and trees. Her body jolted against him when he eased into her, then settled. Like two puzzle pieces coming together after a decade apart.

As their hips rotated together, she locked eyes with his. There was an enormous smile on his face as if he had just won the lottery. Laughing at his goofy expression, she thrust her hips up.

"What?" He shook his head, kissed her cheek, then pushed into her deeper. "Better?"

"The best."

After the tumultuous summer, he made her feel like the most desired being in the world, worshiping her with each kiss. She closed her eyes and sank into the pillows, wrapping her legs around his back and letting her body move with his.

His need took over, and they rocked, casting aside the bedding until it fell to the floor. She clawed his back until his breath, rough and jagged, released in a deep moan of pleasure, and he sighed in her ear.

Waves of heat crashed within every part of her body. Legs locked around him, her toes curled. Her fingers clasped then released the sheet involuntarily, and she trembled as he slowly slipped out of her and shifted to his side. Using two fingers, he traced her entrance and slowly massaged her most tender skin until she gasped. Her body shuddered, her back arched, and her legs shook.

Rob cradled her against him. She laid her head against his chest and listened to his heartbeat as the delightful waves of passion flowed through her.

"I hope I'm number one on your top ten list, sweetie," she said.

"Truth is, you're the only one on my *list*."

Rob's laughter came from deep in his chest, and she held him close to capture all the love vibrating from within him.

TOP STORY

Starving for Attention and Thirsting for *Amore*

CELEBRITY CHEF NICK MARCHETI CONSIDERS HIMSELF FORTUNATE AFTER AN EXPLOSIVE ENCOUNTER WITH CHRIS WAGNER'S ALLEGED ATTACKER.

BY PAUL MURPHY

SEPTEMBER

During his annual pilgrimage to Elkhart, Wisconsin, celebrity chef Nick Marcheti encountered an overzealous fan. The host of the popular cooking show *The Italian Scallion* appears to have much in common with Chris Wagner, as the woman turned out to be Maddie Logerquist, the stalker who ravenously hunted Mr. Wagner in July.

Clearly still hungry, she chased Marcheti through the grounds of Road America, where he exhibited his classic Ferrari during the track's vintage car parade. The established chef and foodie is known and revered for transforming a simple plate of food into an artistic masterpiece. When asked for a comment, Marcheti declined at first, then added with a *vivace* lilt, "Her fiery reaction is typical, hey? A woman with *passione. Amo il mio super-fan*," he gushed in his native tongue. **{PM}**

THIRTY-SEVEN

After a deep sleep, Rob woke and reached over to touch Maddie, but the bed was empty. The smell of coffee dissolved his disappointment. Fumbling into his tee and swim trunks, he grabbed his phone and made a beeline to the kitchen, scrolling through the many messages from Graham. His sex-muddled head cleared in an instant. After all the *amore*, he had yet to tell Maddie about the *Cue* article with Nick.

Detouring into the bathroom, he read his uncle's messages repeatedly and urgently requesting that they meet today. *Damn.* He'd left Graham in a treacherous position. Maddie looked outrageous in the photograph with Nick Marcheti. Any judge could pick up on her antagonism and instantly change the course of the slam-dunk case Rob had delivered to Graham two days ago. What a cluster...*fanculo.* The scales of justice were so mercurial. Rob shot off a message saying he'd be at the lighthouse by noon and hurried to the kitchen.

Right away, he noticed that the award wall leading down to the stairs had been reinstalled. While taking a drink of coffee, Rob stared at the new presentation Maddie had created. Instead of the old swimming awards and plaques, she'd hung up family photographs. Still unfinished, the captured moments were mostly of the three siblings doing what they did best: goofing off and swimming. He was pleased he'd made the cut in a few of the shots. Rob gravitated to the framed and unframed photos stashed in the box on the floor but headed to Maddie instead. He wasn't sure of his exact words but wanted to get this Nick-pic conversation over and done with.

At a picnic table, she sat focused on an open sketchbook, drawing with two colored pencils in one hand. He didn't want to give her a fright, so he shouted, "*Buongiorno*." She acknowledged him with a quick wave, the simple gesture awakening his southern regions. The sight of two long, intertwined strands of pink hair ribbon trailing down her long, gorgeous neck made him swallow down a moan. Last night had been extremely satisfying, yet he craved more. He glanced out at the lake to check if the water was calm enough for a swim.

A brisk breeze smacked his cheek and pushed him off his lusty cloud nine. Drinking his java, he sat across from her and watched her draw. The fluid movement of her hand mesmerized him. Holding two different-colored pencils, pink and blue, she switched back and forth, outlining what looked like a swimsuit. "Another design for Fran?"

"Uh-huh." Her eyes never left the paper. He was left to stare at the pink fabric tied over her crown of sleek, dark chestnut hair. When the tip of one of the pencils broke, she let out an exaggerated sigh. Setting it back in the box, she pulled out another, much lighter shade of pink. "The magenta is telling me it has had enough of me."

This was the view of Maddie that he wanted the whole world to see: a contented, intense artist and designer with a big heart. How could he get *this* image of Maddie into the *Cue?* "Can I take a few shots of you at work? Staying under cover while in Elkhart was difficult, and I want you to know since I'm no longer your lawyer—or warden—I can be your biggest fan."

"Click away," she said with a laugh. "Photoshop my lip, if possible. Or add a lip emoji." It was a relief to see that the swelling had decreased, and her mouth looked less painful, but the healing slash on her lower lip still jutted out. "When are the stitches coming out?"

"They'll dissolve by next week." She turned to a fresh page in her sketchbook, then stared at him with a sultry pucker and arched eyebrow. "Then we—if you want—can have a do-over. Last night was incredible, but you did all the heavy lifting, as I recall." Her cheeks turned a shade darker than her magenta pencil.

He cleared his throat. "About last night—"

"What's wrong? I know I was a bit—as they say in England—randy. But darn, Rob. It was so much fun."

"It was more than fun. Brilliant," he said, crossing his legs and making sure they were under the table. "There's a piece of information, though, that I wasn't able to present to you... before...uh, my thoughts melted, and we rushed into bed."

"Oh, no. What is it? Is it Wagner? Is he here in Baileys?"

He brushed through his matted bed head with shaking fingers, then tapped his phone, scrolling past the damning picture and landing on the content. He gently pushed it toward her. "It's Nick Marcheti. This piece came out yesterday." He made sure to watch her, hoping against hope she would simply read the article and ignore the picture. But no such luck. Of course, she pushed the screen right up to the photograph.

Staring down at the picture of her and Nick, she shook her head in disgust. "I look like a hyena in heat. Dear god. And Nick the Dick looks like he just walked off the cover of *GQ*. How repulsive."

His heart pounded viciously in his chest as all the implications from this single photo mounted in his thoughts. Prioritizing or using his top ten wouldn't minimize the paralyzing effects of this image.

"Well, now the whole world thinks I'm *pazza* because of a douchebag Chicago guy who likes to pretend he's Italian." Her eyes glittered. "What's the worst-case scenario? And please don't tell me you can't discuss it because you're no longer representing me. You were there when this pic was snapped, not Graham."

Her voice was low but earsplitting. He fought the urge to sugarcoat the consequences because, in the final analysis, there would be no benefit to hiding the truth from her. Basically ignoring a growing sense of cataclysmic doom, he retrieved his phone and hid it in his pocket. "We're meeting with Graham this afternoon and—"

"Get to the point." She averted her gaze and focused on arranging the pencils in the box. "Please."

"It doesn't look good, Maddie. This picture, if presented to a judge, can be interpreted in a variety of ways. None of which will help your case." He clenched his jaw, then spoke economically. "The photo will more than likely be used against you. Showing how you might have attacked Wagner intentionally."

"This is bonkers." She closed her sketchbook and organized her supplies into one pile. "So Wagner could win?"

"Well, no... But..." Rob glanced around at the spread of the estate. The house had to be worth over two million. "Just a thought," he pressed on, "the house. Or the boats, not Tyler's, but aren't there others at the marina? Or the winery?" The words tasted venomous. "Pay Wagner the money...so we can get past this and put it behind us."

"Us? Are you speaking as my lawyer? Friend? Lover? Or a man on a deadly mission? Instead of slaying Goliath, you're taking down David?"

He struggled to gather his thoughts, but the truth was dismal. If Maddie's case went to court, she could lose it all. And then he would lose her forever. "All of the above."

A FIERCE SENSE of self-preservation came over her. Maddie glanced around at all her mother had built, which was only a fraction of the total. There wasn't going to be a day cold enough in hell that would force her to surrender to Wagner.

"If it's okay with you, I'd like to meet with Graham. Alone." She had a hard time subduing her growing aggravation until the subtle downturn of Rob's mouth. It pissed her off, so she gazed past him and stared out at the boathouse.

"Whatever you need, it's yours," Rob said. "Don't forget I'm on your side."

"Sounds like you already forgot that little detail," she snapped. Volatile emotions coursed through her. "Wow! Wham, bam, thank you, ma'am. You throw in the towel and give up on me!"

"No, not in the least. It's... I...don't want you to experience any more pain. You've had enough for one lifetime."

Last night with Rob was all she'd expected and more, making love to the one man who seemed to have had her heart from the beginning of time. Today, however, he was abandoning her again. Maddie swallowed a long groan. "I think it may be best if we take a breather from one another. We were together a lot in Elkhart, and since we're back home, I think I need to concentrate." The words stung the back of her throat. "For Elsie's sake."

His mouth opened as if to protest, but then he pressed his lips together and gave her a quick nod. "Of course."

Selling Elsie's property was the last thing she'd do. Her

mother had busted her ass far too long just to give it up to a predator like Wagner.

To curtail the overwhelming frustration, she found the *Cue* article on her tablet. On the bigger screen, in the photo of her berating Nick, she looked diabolical. A far cry from what she'd ever believed about herself. She was glad she'd gone from being in front of the cameras to behind the cameras. She'd mastered a skill many amateur phone snappers missed: *context and situation.* Both were easily overlooked when fear made an appearance.

"Are you certain about seeing Graham alone?"

"Yes, I'll be able to focus better, and I want to explain the photo to him from my perspective."

She had to make it through this nightmare without Rob.

Wagner was the culprit, the celebrity without a conscience. The biggest fake in Hollywood. Rob's position had made it impossible to expose the truth about him the first time around.

From her experience, all the skills she'd learned from being behind the camera could help rebuild her case. And as a designer, she was well acquainted with perception and quite skilled at playing optical tricks. Screw you, *Cue.*

"There's some prep work I want to talk to Graham about." Rob came to her side of the table and kissed her softly on the lips, managing to avoid her stitches. "I'll make sure to be off the island before you meet with him."

After Rob left, Maddie's center of balance seemed to shift. She tapped her feet on the ground as she'd done on the paddleboard to regain her equilibrium and remain settled.

She packed up her sketchbook and retrieved her orange journal. Of all the feelings flurrying inside her, the one sticking out the most was how she missed her mom. She would have loved a few words of wisdom from Elsie, who had a way of taking the direst of situations and making them look easy to solve.

She stared at the orange journal from the police station. The meditation room had been orchestrated by her mother, surely; the journals were one of her ideas. Maddie jogged back into the house and into her mother's office. Maybe journaling was hereditary, and her mother had kept her own journal.

Searching every nook and cranny of the wood-paneled library, she came up empty-handed. She grabbed a copy of *Silent Spring* from the shelf and paged through it to get a glimpse into Elsie's hero.

Maddie was stunned to learn the writer had died of breast cancer. Suddenly, Rachel Carson became a link between her, her mom, and Fran. Maddie browsed through the rest of the book and all the other books by Carson. Immediately, she sensed she'd grown closer to her mother, and this strange connection gave her a smidge of strength.

With *Silent Spring* in hand, she once again looked at her photo in the *Cue* article. It was still hideous. The child in her head whined that it seemed so unfair. She squeezed her eyes almost shut, tilted the laptop in different directions, and squinted, looking for a better angle. No luck. At every turn, she only looked uglier.

She knew there were more layers to her, and unfortunately, her warring emotions were lost in this one image. But then she thought of Wagner. He had already brought out the worst of her *pazza* side, and she'd survived. This picture was just one sliver of her true self. It couldn't diminish or demean her or take away any of the strength she'd gained since coming home to Baileys Harbor.

THIRTY-EIGHT

Already uneasy walking into the lighthouse, a sense of Maddie's fear bulldozed over Rob. In the souvenir shop, he tried to imagine her steps as she fought off Wagner.

He was so deep in thought he didn't hear Graham until he was right in front of him and shouting, "Bloody 'ell, finally. What took you so long, boi?"

Despair settled over him like a heavy blanket. "I've mucked up royally with Maddie and your case."

Graham clasped his shoulder. "Utter madness, there's nothing to lose. Wagner can take a long hike off a short pier. Your defense is brimming with proof that Maddie had ample justification to take Wagner down. And Lark Russell? She's our star witness and plans to testify on Maddie's behalf."

He gave his uncle a quick hug and walked to Maddie's old desk. All of the photos of her and her family had been replaced with PR photos of Gus, playing his role of Nick Parker in his TV series. "I put off telling Maddie about the picture in the *Cue*. She was at her worst, yelling at a celebrity. It's bad."

"Yes, it's a terrible picture," Graham said, tapping the

graying sideburn at his temple, "but you're no longer her lawyer. I am. So let me determine the course of action."

"Maddie looks unbalanced. It won't be hard for Gwen Ridley to inundate the judge with anecdotes, factual or not, full of perceived *emotional imbalances*."

"That's your opinion. Maddie has many good friends in town, and they'll support her. Don't forget, we're not in Chicago, where gossip rags are easy fodder for talk. In Baileys, folks are too busy finding out about the weather and don't have time for the *Cue*. There's more to it though, hey?"

"I'm in a pickle. No longer her lawyer, yet I just had to stick my foot in it and suggest she sell Elsie's house to get past this nightmare."

"Bloody 'ell, Rob. Your knickers aren't just twisted, they're in a damn knot," he said, lowering his readers from his head to his nose and sitting at the desk. "Capitulating to Wagner? It's a doozy. Well, boi, you came up with the brilliant idea for me to take over this case, so there's hope for you. But I suspect you're going to have to do a whole lot of backflips through a fiery hoop for Maddie."

What had he been thinking? The photo of Maddie was explainable, but suggesting she sell the estate was completely daft. He'd let his fears and worries strangle his logic. He dropped down into the chair. "I may have to pack it up and join Cirque du Soleil."

"Oh, rubbish. First things first: the photo." Graham pulled up the *Cue* article on his laptop. "Tsk. Nick the Dick is doing his full-on *Italian Scallion*. What a stupid name for a TV show."

Rob propped his elbows on the desk and massaged his temples. "And his damn Ferrari. It's still green."

"The bloke never had a lick of common sense. Maddie looks enraged, true, but half of those who know Nick find him and his ego appalling. She certainly isn't the first person to go after the macho chef." Graham chuffed.

"In the photo, Maddie is defending Fran. Talk about empowerment. The Marchetis can be harsh. I'd say old school, but it's closer to outdated, if not obsolete. Nick thinks he has to defend the family name."

"Maddie has a bigger family and a longer legacy to protect." Graham eyeballed him over his readers. "Correct me if I'm wrong, but is your arm, an edge of it, on the other side of Nick?"

"Yeah, Nick needed to cool down. After the man tried to sideline Fran, he called Maddie, *pazza...crazy.*"

Graham slid his glasses up onto his head and rubbed his eyes. "It's a bad photo, but I'm relieved you aren't in the frame. Nick needs a wake-up call, a chance to return to Earth. If anything, for the sake of his sister. And if he's so worried about the family image, it's him, not Fran, who looks like a disgrace. Even his quotes in the article make him sound like a patronizing SOB."

"I'm fairly certain Nick's Italian accent is for the show." Rob inspected the photo. His uncle made a good point. So concerned about Maddie's appearance, he'd ignored Nick's. The celebrity chef's face looked bloated, and his cheeks were puffed up. Without the signature glasses, Nick's eyes were bloodshot. "The sod is pissed up!"

"Nick's irrelevant; he won't be an issue. You've been working hard, too hard." Graham tapped at his keyboard. "Developed a bad case of tunnel vision. You have to figure out how to make up with Maddie. She's one in a million." He shook his head, disappointed. "Selling the house? Really?"

"I am such an idiot." Rob pounded his temple with the meat of his thumb.

"Get over yourself. She still needs your logic and the charm you inherited from me. In fact, stay and wait." Graham glanced at his watch. "She'll be here in the next hour or so."

Rob shook his head. The idea was a hard NO. He couldn't trust himself around Maddie right now. Too many worries were running around and yanking him in every direction. "She needs to meet her new lawyer alone." He grabbed hold of his uncle's hand. "We'll talk later. Don't forget all the details from Lark Russell."

"I know, I know." Graham huffed. "Get out. Go. Find something useful to do. Take a drive in that car of yours."

Rob hopped into the Triumph, making sure to go slow across the causeway leading to the mainland. Although the path was dry, waves splashed on either side of him. He'd learned ages ago to respect the powers of Lake Michigan.

Once off the island, he found himself at a loss. No direction. Nowhere to go. It had been a long time since his head wasn't full of plans, negotiations, or court-related speeches. If he wanted, he could take a swim at Cave Point, but then he thought of Maddie and rejected the idea.

It seemed as if any place he thought about reminded him of her. The Beacon, the library, the Sanctuary for a hike, Toft Point for a tour, even the police station, not that he wanted to stop there. The only place free from Maddie was the Harbor B&B.

Finding a spot at the bar was easy since happy hour hadn't kicked off. He planned to eat later, but for now, he would watch the visitors coming and going. With others around, Rob was relieved. He couldn't berate himself or grouse or lament over letting Maddie down.

Unfortunately, without her, it was one of his *unhappiest* hours.

MADDIE PARKED the Audi at the foot of the wooden stairs leading into the lighthouse. She listened to the waves crashing over the boulders surrounding the island and stared at the railing. She had clung onto it after the assault. Until Rob had to peel off each finger of her white-knuckled grip.

The humidity created a slight mist around the lighthouse—closed to the public—giving the island an eerie vibe. She eyed Graham's silver Jaguar, parked next to the supply garage, and let out a slow breath. *Now or never.*

The bell inside the door announced her arrival. She wished she'd been able to talk Graham into meeting her at the Beacon, but he'd insisted she come to the lighthouse. It was futile arguing with the man; his stubborn streak was as long as his nephew's.

Her whole body shuddered as she took in the space. The entryway floor, which was once made of pavers and pea gravel, had been replaced with cream-colored bricks, tightly mortared to maintain a level surface. She squinted to see the spot where Wagner's blood had spilled, but it was smooth and clean. Nothing red.

"Ah, lovely." With open arms, Graham strode up and enclosed her in a comforting hug. "How are you?" He glanced downward at her swollen lip. "From the paddleboard, correct?"

Nodding, she inhaled a calming breath full of Lauren's Polo. "Yep, I fought hard, but the board won."

Maddie hesitantly stepped away from his embrace to look around.

The wooden door, where her shoulders had slammed against, flaunted a fresh coat of white paint. Her hands—snug against her hips—turned into fists repeatedly. Her heart kept booming as if telling her to run and bust out of there. She refused to listen.

"A few changes since I've been gone." Her voice came out

like an awkward teen's. She cleared her throat and locked eyes with Graham. "You and Agnes. Kat, Michael...I can't thank you enough." She paused. "And, of course, Gus and Lucy. I don't think I would have been of use to anyone after what happened with..."

"There's a method to my madness, sweetheart. I wanted you to revisit this spot and get a handle on all the feelings darting about. Because I'm telling you now that when we go to court in the town hall, you'll have to face the bloody sod one last time. And you'll need to find your badass voice in less than a second."

She extended her arms as if holding a paddle to mimic training on the paddleboard. "Seems like I'll have to stand on the board, find my balance, and stay on it."

When his forehead wrinkled, she explained. "Your nephew taught me how to find the center of a paddleboard fast to stay balanced and not fall off. It worked..." She pointed to her lips. "To some degree."

With a quick grin, Graham held up a sheet of paper, facing the image toward her. "This is the look of a badass. Here's who you have to be when you see Wagner again."

She gasped at the ugliest picture she'd ever seen...of herself. "According to my previous lawyer, this photo is going to annihilate my case. His advice, before we parted ways..." Her voice cracked. "Rob recommended selling Elsie's house. He actually thought it was a reasonable solution."

"Damn good lawyer, Rob is." Graham chuffed. "Though his intentions, all well and good, would be better suited for a person unrelated to Elsie Logerquist."

Following him into the souvenir shop, she noticed the shelves had been repainted white, and all the tchotchkes sparkled under new spotlights hanging from the ceiling.

"That photo looks like I let my anger take over my brain. There are other sides of me."

"I know, and if Elsie saw this photo," he said, "she would have cheered you on. You are on fire and telling the world, 'Don't mess with me.'"

"Thanks. I'm just not as patient as my mom. When I see an injustice or crookedness, it's like all the alarms go off in my brain, and the only way I can stop the noise is to spit out my anger and frustration. Writing letters like Elsie did? Hell no! Way too time-consuming for me. By the time I even found a pen, my thoughts and words would be long gone, into the drift of my unconsciousness."

"Cut yourself some slack. Your methods may vary, but you and your mother are both fighters." Graham looked around the lighthouse. "Although I'm not in favor of any kind of physical altercations, Wagner right deserved what he got. And because of what happened here in the lighthouse, you started something. Look at all the updates achieved in two months. The new prism is on order. It came about because the whole town supports you. You stood up for yourself and your home. I'm sure Elsie is proud of her firstborn."

Wearing the same cowboy boots she'd worn when she'd kicked Wagner, she thought back to when she'd been in full self-defense mode. Never had she ever attacked or purposefully hurt another being, but in the *Cue* photograph, she looked like a rabid dog frothing at the mouth. Elsie had probably dealt with men much more powerful than Nick and hadn't lost her cool. She wanted to take the high road. "Maybe a letter? I could write an apology to Nick the...I mean Mr. Marcheti."

"A cracking idea and absolutely not going to happen."

"Buhh...what?" Maddie's head jerked. "Seems a little diplomacy may help with Nick Marcheti. He is old-school, but I'm not sure... Rob seemed to think this photo would sink my case."

"All Nick owes you is a huge apology. Trust me, ever since

I've known him, he's been a wanker and, most often, toward Fran. Don't fret about this *Cue* malarky. I have your back."

"I wish Rob felt the same way. It seems as if he's lost faith in me and this fight against Wagner."

"My nephew has faith in you, Maddie. However, the justice system is a whole other matter. He's been on the losing side often enough to be wary of traitors and treacherous outcomes in court. Tragically, it has affected his belief in the legal process, and now he fights hard to protect his loved ones from experiencing the worst of it."

"Thank you, Graham. For everything." Maddie swiped a wayward tear from her cheek and shook off the lingering fear. She tapped the sole of her boot on the floor. "All right if I take a hike to the top?"

"Thought you'd never ask." He pulled the velvet curtain back to reveal the wrought-iron staircase going to the top of the lighthouse. "It's all yours, sweetheart."

THIRTY-NINE

Alone in the house, Maddie sipped a cup of coffee in the dining room and eyed the waves of Lake Michigan. A sense of gratitude flowed through her. Because of the fundraiser in Elkhart, her design—the pink-and-teal swimsuit—had found its way into several fashion magazines. The higher-ups at Sunkissed were thrilled with the orders coming into the company, and her original mastectomy design was getting some well-deserved new attention.

When *Women's Wear Daily*, the fashion industry guru, contacted Maddie about doing an interview and a photoshoot of Fran modeling her swimsuits, she jumped for joy and then buried herself in work. This past week, all her energy was devoted to the sewing machine, with the goal of completing every design for Fran by today.

On the way to the photoshoot at Cave Point, she had some trepidation about going to the spot where she and Rob had spent so many incredible afternoons. Glancing down at the dashboard's phone in *his* car, she considered calling him. They hadn't spoken for days, but in her defense, she was extremely busy, and his nutty idea of selling her mom's house still irked her...except she missed him. Instead of calling and disrupting her mojo, Maddie drove faster. She and Fran were about to splash onto the cover of *Women's Wear Daily*.

The sun was high in the sky, and the lake sparkled when she arrived. The park area had already been taken over by the magazine crew. There were tripods and umbrellas arranged around the gazebo, and folks sat at the picnic tables, working on their devices.

She strode into the white dressing room tent and found Fran. Ignoring the stylist clipping a pink piece of clothing onto her, Fran came over and hugged Maddie.

"Hey, sis," she said, "Where are my suits?"

"These beauties are all for you." Letting Fran's kindness soak in, Maddie unpacked and hung her designs on a clothing rack. "The gazebo is going to be an amazing stage for you to strut around and show these babies off."

"They'll be taking photos near the cliffs. Any chance you know the best angle?"

"Sure." Rob's photo with her in the water sprang to mind, and she gulped down a sudden lump in her throat. "Will it be on the cliff or in the horseshoe?"

A woman charged into the tent, introducing herself as the *WWD* writer Leigh, and thumbed through the swimsuits hanging on the rack. "These are gorgeous. Where have you been, Maddie Logerquist? Your work is extraordinary."

Maddie laughed. "In the Hamptons, styling others. This is the first time my suits have been noticed."

Leigh took out her phone. "Mind if we talk here? And I record you?"

"Sounds good." Staying in the tent, a distance from the cliffs, worked for Maddie. She nodded toward Fran. "I can adjust you when you change from suit to suit."

"Wait, the horseshoe? What were you going to say?" Fran

let the other stylist adjust her sarong skirt. "I need to let the photographer know where it's best to take pictures. We really want to have the water in the background."

"The well of water surrounded by the cliffs is called the horseshoe. People jump off the edge of the cliff into the well. You can pose anywhere around the cliff, and the lake will be in the background."

"Thanks, but no, thanks." Leigh set her phone onto the table scattered with swatches of clothing and sewing paraphernalia. "Jumping off a cliff? Not my idea of a good time."

Weirdly defensive, Maddie replied, "It's exhilarating. When the water is warm, like now, it's like soaring down into a hot tub. And the horseshoe shape of the cliff is perfect for a good echo. I used to belt out Adele songs when I waited for..."

Fran lifted her model-perfect dark eyebrow. "Waited for who exactly?"

Maddie glanced down at the phone's red square, recording her. "No one in particular. It was a tradition," she lied, "to sing while others leapt off the edge to brave the waters below."

Fran, a supermodel, let out a snort and laughed so loudly that she sounded more like a jet engine than a jetsetter. "Oh, before I forget, Drew will be coming to Baileys. We both wanted to be here for you..." She hesitated, then glanced at Leigh's recording phone. "You know, for the follow-up meeting about the Pink Paddle fundraiser."

Leigh ignored Fran's awkwardness, but Maddie caught on quickly.

She'd been able to keep the court date out of her head, thanks to making a lot of swimsuits. But in two days, Maddie would face Wagner. Graham had assured her this wasn't a typical court case. It was a *procedure*. There wouldn't be any jury, or damning testimonies, or dramatic twists like in *Law &*

Order. In all likelihood, it would be less than an hour long. No doubt the longest hour of her life.

Leigh checked the recorder on her phone. "I know this is a challenging time for you, Maddie, but part of the reason *WWD* asked me to interview you wasn't just for the swimwear. You're showing a side of the fashion world that isn't so glamorous and making the industry accountable and showing off its value. A lot of women will be thanking you because of the Wagner case."

"Thanks for ripping off the Band-Aid," Maddie said. "There isn't a lot I can say about the case right now, but since the initial incident, I've met some incredible women who have been brave enough to share their stories with me. Once we found one another, we were able to draw on each other's strength."

"FYI," Fran added, "if you saw that unglamorous picture of Maddie in the *Cue*, it was taken while she was standing up for me. My brother is in deep doo-doo."

"How so?" Leigh laughed.

"Nick Marcheti has misogynistic tendencies and can be an old-school blowhard. Maddie was able to set him straight and get him to think in the twenty-first century. Otherwise, the Paddle fundraiser might have flopped. Me wearing Maddie's designs opened up a new world for women."

"I've received messages and letters from women full of gratitude for these swimsuits. Telling me they're now more confident and willing to go out in public to a pool or the beach again."

"If Nick wants to avoid a lecture from my mama and papa, he'll be making some face time here in Baileys soon to apologize to you, Maddie." Fran wrapped a pink beach towel over her shoulders, kissed Maddie's cheek, and exited the tent with the stylist. "Ciao."

"Thanks, Fran. Break a leg." Maddie said, then looked at Leigh. "Glad to have this all on record."

"Sure. Can we continue with the interview?"

Leigh's questions gave Maddie the opportunity to talk about her design education in the classroom and the work world. She'd been trained since swimming on the team in high school about the importance of comfort in swimwear, and she learned how wearing a swimsuit made a statement that emboldened women at any age. The last question was, "Who's been the biggest inspiration for your career?"

Maddie thought about all the women she'd worked for, her clients, and the women she'd styled on the *SH* show. Her family had inspired her, but it was Tyler who had inadvertently set her course because she'd run away to New York. She admired the hand-painted clog hanging off her foot. "It's hard to say, as the Logerquist family is like a dynasty in Baileys Harbor. A galvanizing force, for sure. My mom and both my brothers inspired me to keep fighting. If you're taking a risk, it probably means a whole lot more to you than what you may be thinking about in the moment."

IN THE WELL OF the horseshoe, Rob dropped his duffle on a limestone ledge. A modern convenience for swimmers and made from an ice-age rock formation. He'd hiked the trail around Cave Point Park and trekked along the rocky beach to avoid the lights, camera, and action above and near the gazebo. He'd stealthily parked his car in the utility lot, telling himself it was to protect the Triumph's paint job, but he could only maintain the lie for so long. He missed Maddie. After Fran had rung —inviting him to the photoshoot—Rob wanted a second, third, or fourth chance to make up with Maddie.

The water swirled around the base of the bluffs. He plunked his feet into the lake. Expecting a shot of cold, the warm water surprised him. He tilted his face toward the sun and let out a long sigh. Hearing chatter from above bouncing around the U-shaped wall of rocks surrounding him, he slipped on his shades to see if there were any bodies attached to the unfamiliar voices. Not until he saw Maddie's tall, lithe form covered in bright pink did the longing he'd struggled to contain all week subside.

The second she spotted him from above, he waved and shouted, "Wanna jump?"

She disappeared, and Fran appeared, yelling, "Brava!"

Several other unfamiliar people joined Fran on the edge of the bluff, all gawking at him in his favorite spot in Door County.

He dove into the water and swam around the perimeter of the horseshoe. When he looked up, Maddie was standing at the edge and wearing a bright pink racing suit. Before the words became stuck in his throat, he belted out Adele. "Rolling..."

After one word, he dropped under the water to shake off some of his overabundance of nerves. When he came up for air, Maddie waved. Her smile reassured him, so he tried again, searching for the right key. It was more of a chick song. He would be so much better with a Tom Petty tune. Treading hard in the water, he gazed up. "I can see you clear as crystal..."

"You are such a dork," she shouted.

The shell of rocks around him repeated the word *dork* a couple of times for his benefit.

"Thank you." He swam to the limestone landing and held on to the edge. Doing a grand gesture in the water would not have been his first choice, but Fran insisted. He cleared his throat and looked up. Maddie was sitting, not standing, on the edge of the bluff. He wasn't sure if it was his voice or her fear. "Are tears gonna fall?"

Laughing, she stood and stretched her arms over her head in the most beautiful diver's pose he'd ever seen. Then he switched songs. The only one that came to him was Petty's whining beat he would crank up when driving. "Hey, girlfriend, I'm running down a dream," he said, then sang," Woo-hoo...woo-hoo...woo-hoo."

Her body swayed.

"Doo-wop and ditty. I can't do it without you," he shouted, then listened to the 'without you' echo around him.

"I know," she shouted, then jumped off the rocky bluff. Clutching onto her knees, she performed a perfect cannonball and splash landed a short distance away. She swam up, hopped next to him on the ledge, and kissed him. "How's that for a perfect ten?"

"Perhaps, but..." Rob pulled her shivering form tight into his chest. Having Maddie so close after only a few days apart, he concentrated on keeping her warm and safe. "I'm a lousy judge."

A burst of cheers from Fran and the others rang out. He gave them a thumbs-up, and Maddie swatted his shoulder. "When did you and Fran cook this little play date up?"

He shook his head. "Me? I would never..."

"Such a bunch of baloney!" She kissed his temple, then his cheek, and when she found his lips, he returned her kiss with a gentle peck. Instantly, it escalated into a long, feverish kiss.

They finally came up for some air, and thankfully, the spectators had left them alone.

Caressing her arm, still covered in goose bumps, he whispered. "I love you."

"What a relief." She nuzzled into his shoulder and sighed. "For once, we're on the same page, hon. I love you, too. How incredible."

"*Sei la mia vita.* You are my life, Maddie."

FORTY

Maddie's body moved as if on autopilot. With Graham on her right and Rob on her left, she stood straight and tall, facing the judge's bench, waiting and sweating. The quaint town hall used as Baileys' courtroom offered little air on this unseasonably warm September day.

All she wanted to do was jump into the lake and swim...with Rob.

He whispered in her ear, "This won't take more than an hour or two, promise."

She swayed and lightly bumped his shoulder. Wearing a tie, dress shirt, and suit jacket, she was certain a plunge into some cool water had crossed his mind.

A copy of *Silent Spring* sat on the table in front of her. The book locked *empowerment* in her mind. Even though Graham had assured her this wasn't a trial but a "discovery motion," the feeling of her world collapsing stubbornly badgered her, and she had to keep it at bay. Nervously, she tapped the toe of her wooden clog on the floor.

Reviewing notes on his tablet, Graham grabbed her hand and gave it a gentle squeeze. "Relax, you're ready."

Yesterday, Graham and Rob spent the day coaching her. They asked her dicey questions using an accusatory tone to practice steeling her nerves when or if she would respond to Gwen Ridley. They also watched videos of Gwen Ridley's lectures for Maddie to gain a sense of her opponent. It worked to some extent, but Maddie found that binge-watching Olivia Benson and her wise words on SVU made a big difference in bolstering her bravery.

TJ, the cop who had been at the hospital after the assault, entered the stuffy room. He said hello and sat behind her. The padded, collapsible metal chair creaked under his weight. The room had a capacity of fifty people, and so far, only four were occupying it.

While chatting with the bailiff, the judge entered from the side door.

Maddie sucked in the fresh air and caught a glimpse of people gathering around the park outside.

"Good morning. I'm Judge Lewis. I'm glad to see you. Please be seated. Before we proceed with this matter, I've ruled that no cameras or phones will be allowed in the courtroom, and only the court stenographer and a reporter from the Door County Press will be here to document today's proceeding." He glanced at the empty table on the other side of the aisle. "Seems as if the plaintiffs didn't get the message." To deter looky-loos, the judge had requested that all parties involved show up before the session began.

"We will begin in fifteen minutes at 8:00 a.m.," Judge Lewis said, then directed the bailiff to open the front doors.

The noise of high- and low-pitched voices, combined with the shuffling of bodies, filled the room. Too nervous to look around, Maddie listened to her friends chatting. Gus and Lucy. Kat and Michael. Fran and Drew. At the sound of Gwen

Ridley's voice, Maddie turned a smidge for a quick view of Wagner, but only the beast's lawyer strode into the room.

Alone, Gwen Ridley sat straight-backed at the other table. She focused on the judge, said hello, then set both her hands in her lap and picked at a thumbnail.

Brady approached and hugged Maddie. "Hey, sis. I heard about your plunge at Cave Point the other day."

"I was sure it was a ten-point cannonball, but this guy," she gave Rob a sassy grin, "scored it a seven. Yep, there's always a German judge in every crowd."

Maddie held on to her brother a second longer. "Thank you for being such a wonderful brother and friend. And for putting up with me."

"You're welcome, but don't let it happen again," Brady chided, then sat down behind her and quietly spoke to TJ.

"This does not look good," Rob said, staring at Gwen. "I would not want to be in her shoes right now."

On Wagner's side, not even his wife and two daughters had shown up. The chairs behind Gwen Ridley were empty, while all the chairs behind Maddie were filling up.

Where the hell is Wagner?

"Hey, hon." Lark Russell tapped her shoulder and sat in the first row between TJ and Brady.

The three people who might be asked to vouch for her had arrived, and Maddie caught Brady and Lark smiling at one another for a long second. *Interesting.*

The small room grew stuffier, so the judge ordered the bailiff to check the air-conditioning. The elementary school clock clicked loudly. It was closing in on eight o'clock, and all she kept thinking about was getting her sweaty palms on an ice-cold cocktail.

Judge Lewis cleared his throat. "We're almost in session,

Ms. Ridley. Five minutes. Is your client running late? In my courtroom, timely attendance is not only beneficial but most respectful to all of us."

Gwen stood. "I apologize, Your Honor. There was a delay on the freeway. Mr. Wagner should be arriving momentarily."

Maddie's bullshit meter peeled and clanged.

Rob reached around her back and tapped his uncle's shoulder. "Google the Kennedy and County 43. Find the accident. Wagner's up to something, I know it."

The subtle breeze from Rob's whisper made the hair on the back of her neck stand up.

As Graham scrolled through his tablet, the big clock grew loud in the small room.

There was a burst of laughter, followed by the heavy thud of the metal doors opening.

Wagner strolled down the middle aisle, and Maddie couldn't stop staring. Had he just come from a day at the spa? Wearing a crisp white polo shirt, he was practically glowing with relaxation. As if he'd just had a deep-tissue massage. And his face was in pristine condition, all smooth and tan.

What a kick in the teeth, literally. The last time Maddie had seen him, he was bloodied and toothless. She tapped her lip. Even with the stitches gone, it was still a bit puffy. True, Wagner had over two months to heal, but wouldn't there be some indication left from when he was hammered against the concrete ground? Wouldn't it only benefit his case?

Finally facing her attacker, Maddie had expected to be afraid or nervous, but instead, she was annoyed and aggravated. She glanced down at her book.

Empowerment.

Wagner's cockiness, smarm, and swagger were revolting and needed to be stripped away. The world had to know the truth. He was a predator without an ounce of humanity.

Depraved and indifferent. She repeated this in her head and grew bolder.

There was no way she would let this Ken doll without a dick take her down.

"Glad you could join us," the judge stated without disguising his irritation.

Wagner nodded to the judge, then waved to the folks sitting on Maddie's side and sat next to his attorney. He leaned back in the chair and spread his knees far apart—manspreading, staking his territory, and taking no responsibility.

Graham murmured something under his breath that sounded like, "Bloody sod, absolute twat."

In a low hush, Maddie said to Graham, "He must know something we don't. Clearly confident he's already won. What gives?"

The judge cracked his gavel before Graham could answer. "This proceeding is now in session. Mr. Graham Bilby, please state your motion of discovery in the case against Madeleine Eleanor Logerquist."

Graham stood. His chest rose. About to speak—

Loud music blared in the stifling room.

Maddie recognized the ringtone before Wagner picked up the call. The Pachelbel-like, high-pitched strings introduced Adam Levine's song "Memories." A song women loved—at least Maddie did, until now. Unfortunately, Wagner probably used the sentimental song as bait.

Graham glared at the judge. "This is completely inappropriate, Your Honor."

"Ms. Ridley, please contain your client," the judge said, pounding his gavel.

Wagner ignored everyone, greeted the caller, and then held up a hold-on finger. "I apologize, Your Honor, but it's my agent calling from LA. We've been playing phone tag. I promise, this will just take a second. Hollywood meetings, unfortunately, are only scheduled early in the morning. It's their rule, not mine."

Gwen Ridley stood and backed away from the table so forcefully the chair crashed to the floor. "I'm, uh, sorry, Your Honor." She looked around the room, nodding apologetically to everyone, and picked up the chair. "Mr. Wagner has a negotiation call that he was unable to reschedule." The color drained from her face as Wagner continued his conversation in a hushed tone.

The judge dropped his head onto his palm. "Does your client, Ms. Ridley, realize he is making a mockery of this court?"

Shrugging, Gwen Ridley sat back down and grunted.

Maddie, Rob, and Graham, completely gobsmacked by Wagner's arrogance and disrespect, sat frozen and glowered at the opposing side.

"That's enough," Judge Lewis shouted at Wagner. "End the call and hand me your phone immediately, or I'm slapping you with contempt of court and kicking you out of this proceeding."

The noise level in the room zipped over the *indoor voice* requirement.

Wagner slowly stood up, continued to speak, and approached the judge at a snail's pace. He chuckled, ended the call, and handed over his phone. "It's Hollywood. Business as usual."

The judge grabbed the phone, and Wagner sauntered back to his seat.

Judge Lewis hit his gavel again. "This is unheard of in my courtroom. Any other last-minute outbursts from your client, Ms. Ridley, and I'll throw your whole case into the dust file."

"What a smug son of a bitch," Rob muttered.

Maddie was aghast and actually felt a tiny bit sorry for Gwen Ridley.

The murmurs died down in the room, and the judge examined his paperwork. "Ladies and gentlemen, this has been a highly unusual start to this discovery process. We will now continue. Case number 07241100. Filed by Mr. Christopher Wagner. Alleging an attack by Ms. Madelyn Logerquist on July 4 in Baileys Harbor."

Maddie shuddered, thinking about all the *wrong* in the judge's words.

She was attacked. Sexually assaulted. By Wagner.

Rob scribbled down something on the paper in front of her.

I Love you.

She smiled to herself.

Graham tapped her shoulder, a gesture for her to stand up with him, and addressed the judge. "I call Ms. Madelyn Logerquist to the stand, Your Honor."

Maddie glanced back at her cheering section before going to the front of the courtroom. They were all subtly smiling, waving, or giving her a thumbs-up. Catching Lark Russell's eye, they exchanged smiles.

Maddie strode to the makeshift witness stand to the judge's left. She let the cold metal back of the chair cool her down as she stared down her accuser in front of her. Wagner's self-assured smile disgusted her. What a tool.

"Please state your name," Graham said, standing before her and to her right, allowing a clear view of her assailant.

She stated, "Madelyn Eleanor Logerquist."

Empowerment.

Graham continued, using a soft and reassuring voice. "Thank you. As you know, this is a formal disclosure proceeding to assess the encounter between you and Mr. Wagner that occurred on July 4 in the lighthouse on Cana Island. And the subsequent actions you took after said confrontation."

The pieces of the night fell into place perfectly. The picture in her mind was whole and resolute. Maddie kept her icy glare on Wagner's fake blue eyes and spoke.

"After a successful fundraising event to increase monies needed to update the Cana Island lighthouse, I went into the souvenir shop."

"About what time, Ms. Logerquist?" Graham smiled.

She cleared her throat. "Around ten or maybe closer to eleven. I was looking for my friend Kat...Orlov...and Mr. Wagner came into the shop. I discovered Kat had already left."

Wagner leered at her exactly as he had that hot summer night.

On her lap, her open palms turned into fists.

"Continue," Graham said, glancing at Wagner and then back to her. "Take your time."

"Ah, sure. I'd made plans to meet with a friend," she said, side-eyeing Rob, "and was finishing up miscellaneous paperwork at my desk when Wagner perched on the edge. At first, he asked me to dinner, which I declined. Then, he asked if I wanted to hike up to the top of the lighthouse. Again, I declined, saying I had plans."

"What was his response?" Graham asked.

She swallowed hard. "He said, 'Don't you think you owe me?'"

"What was Mr. Wagner referencing? Do you recall?"

She'd rehearsed her answer so many times yesterday, but now she couldn't quite remember. Then she looked at Rob. *Tyler's boat.* "At a previous fundraising event, Mr. Wagner took, actually stole, my deceased brother's precious boat from the boathouse and arrived at Cana Island like some kind of Hollywood action hero. Although he didn't hurt anyone or damage the boat, I decided to play into his celebrity persona and arranged for him to meet and greet all of the patrons who had paid to see him." She cleared her throat. "Unknown to me at the time, I insulted him, and he was angry I'd taken control of his time."

Maddie crossed her legs and sat on her hands. "When I pointed out to him two nights later, the fourth, that this was what he'd volunteered to do for the lighthouse and Baileys Harbor... he clutched onto my shoulders and pushed me up against the entry door."

"That's a lie," Wagner shouted.

The judge pounded his gavel. "Please refrain from outbursts, Mr. Wagner. You're already on thin ice."

Graham addressed the judge. "I'd like to point out the July issue of the *Hollywood Cue*. In it, Mr. Wagner is quoted as saying, 'Fundraising and philanthropy. It's my mantra.'"

"Noted for the record," Judge Lewis replied.

Maddie took a deep, cleansing breath and continued. "After Wagner pressed me against the door, the rest isn't as clear, but I distinctly recall he jammed his forearm against my neck. My airway immediately diminished, and I panicked. The loss of air terrified me. While I was frozen in fear, Wagner viciously grabbed me between the legs and pinched my privates so hard... but with minimal air, I couldn't scream out in pain."

"She's a lunatic, Your Honor," Wagner heckled. "Why would I do something so obviously malicious. This is ludicrous."

Maddie glanced at Lark Russell. She mouthed, "Go."

Emboldened.

Judge Lewis pounded his gavel so hard Maddie heard cracking wood.

"Ms. Ridley, this is my last warning. Contain your client, or this will be the end of his complaint."

Gwen knocked a knuckle on the table and shot her client a look of rage. Whatever she hissed into his ear seemed to mollify Wagner. He grunted, dropped his hands between his outrageously spread legs, and gazed up and off toward the wall clock.

Maddie pulled her hands out from underneath her, recrossed her legs, and smiled at Graham. "Should I continue?"

"Please, continue, Ms. Logerquist."

"There's not a whole lot more to say. After my air supply was nearly shut off, I resorted to my survival instincts. Every move I learned while on the wrestling team came to mind in a rush. I kicked the back of Mr. Wagner's knee to set him off-balance and took my attacker down with a basic headlock. I landed on my butt, and he crashed into the floor face-first."

Nodding, Graham scratched the back of his neck. "Did you, Ms. Logerquist, in any way, deliberately plan or intend to hurt Mr. Wagner?"

Wagner continued staring at the wall as if by avoiding her, Maddie would disappear.

I'm not going anywhere.

"Absolutely not. I have never intentionally or unintentionally hurt or injured another human being. And, in fact, when Mr. Wagner was on the floor—" She stared at Wagner until he realized, from the silence in the room, that she was waiting for his attention. When he looked toward her, he eyed the flag on the wall behind her. "—I retrieved a cloth to stop the bleeding around his nose and offered to call 911. He refused and slapped the phone out of my hand."

"Thank you, Ms. Logerquist. If there's nothing else you'd like to add, you may step back to your seat."

Maddie locked Wagner into her view and glared at him ferociously. She contemplated whether or not she'd gotten everything off her chest. Since finally coming face-to-face with him, she wanted to make sure that after walking away, she wouldn't wake up tomorrow morning and think, *Oh shit, I should have said X, Y, or Z.*

"Judge and Mr. Bilby, I do have one other comment to make. Please."

Graham nodded.

"Mr. Wagner, I can stand tall and freely walk anywhere, and no matter where I go, I will hold my head high, knowing my conscience is clear and sunshine has my back. I am not at fault. You cannot steal my light—sunlight or moonlight—and you will never destroy my empowerment."

There were mumblings of excitement from her cheering section. Her bare arms had broken out with goose bumps.

Judge Lewis asked Gwen Ridley if she had any questions for Maddie. The plaintiff's attorney shook her head and groaned, "No, Your Honor."

Maddie thanked the judge, glanced at the small, petty man in front of her, and sat beside Rob.

"Lovely job," Graham whispered.

Rob pushed his earlier note in front of her. *I Love you.*

Graham then called Lark Russell to the witness stand.

Maddie smiled at Lark as she passed by the table.

Graham scanned his device, asked Lark to answer the standard court questions, and then, instead of requesting that she describe what happened to her in the Hamptons, he asked her to confirm or deny his information.

The judge and Lark both agreed.

Maddie peeked at the predator. He held his head in his palms and looked bored.

"Lark Russell, is it true that last summer, while on the set of the reality show *Summer Haven*, your associate Alex Martin requested you to meet with him in a boathouse, where shortly thereafter, Christopher Wagner confronted and sexually assaulted you?"

"True," Lark stated, then added, "I can confirm this."

Whatever color was left in the predator's over-shined body disappeared.

"Please confirm or deny the following statement. Alex

Martin, your former boyfriend and supervisor, did not come to your aid after Christopher Wagner groped your privates."

"Confirm."

"Ms. Russell, can you tell the judge what Alex Martin told you before you escaped from the two predators in the boathouse?"

Maddie stared at Lark, a bit confused. Up until this moment, she'd known all of Lark's story, and this didn't ring any bells.

"Wagner really wanted," Lark said, "'the tall one with the solid fucking thighs.'"

"And who was this *tall* person Wagner asked for?"

Lark pointed. "Maddie Logerquist."

The lightbulb clicked on...with high wattage. Maddie had been a hot mess the day she'd hit the paddleboard and fallen. Some details of her conversation with Lark were lost in her muddled thoughts. Now, it flooded back into her mind. Alex Martin and Chris Wagner were good friends, and Wagner had also wanted to go after Maddie on that horrible day for Lark.

For all Maddie knew, Wagner had been stalking her for over a year and hit pay dirt in Baileys Harbor. Maddie rubbed her arms and forced the dread out. Her story, now combined with Lark's, was powerful, if not explosive.

Graham concluded his interview with Lark and let her sit back down.

Maddie blew a kiss to Lark as she passed by.

"With providing this information to the court," Graham said to Judge Lewis, "we've shown that there is a pattern of behavior evident on the part of the plaintiff, Christopher Wagner. I would like any and all allegations of wrongdoing by Ms. Madelyn Eleanor Logerquist immediately dismissed and rejected by this court in Baileys Harbor, Wisconsin."

"Your request is accepted and approved," Judge Lewis stated. "Court is dismissed."

He pounded his gavel and let out a sigh of pure relief.

Hugging Graham and swaying so hard, Maddie nearly fell over. But Rob swooped in and held them steady and secure. Maddie relaxed, feeling absolutely loved.

FORTY-ONE

The sun beat down on Rob's back outside the town hall. Maddie's arm was hooked with his, and Fran stood on his other side. As Graham addressed the crowd that had formed while they were inside the courtroom, he vigilantly watched Wagner and his attorney talking to the *Hollywood Cue.*

"Speech, speech," Sam from the Throttleshop shouted from the back of the group on the lawn.

Graham opened his mouth, then shut it when Sam yelled, "Not you, Bilby. We want Rob!"

"Your adoring fans want you," Maddie teased.

Fran kissed his cheek. "You're a good guy, Rob. Thanks for sticking up for us."

Hotter than hell, he wanted to bolt and jump into the lake. Instead, he grinned and waved. "Well, as most of you know, I'm a car guy. But what you may not know is...autos and driving were—"

Graham snorted, and he cheerfully side-eyed his uncle.

"They were my escape from bullying. Back in the day, bullies were easy to detect. They were bigger, and meaner, and had no shame in bragging about their—" He coughed. "—special set of victimizing skills."

Boos and murmurs went through the crowd.

"Woah, hold on, no booing. Today's a victory for everyone because bullies are harder than ever to spot. Even those close to you can be manipulative. Folks who are brave enough and tough enough to stand their ground not only defeat the monsters among us, but they build safety nets for other victims. Because resilience is a mighty force that makes the slimiest bullies retreat under their rocks."

He glanced at Fran, then at Lark, who stood in front of him with Brady, and he tightened his elbow around Maddie's. He whispered in her ear, "No tears, love."

The roar from the crowd was deafening. While court was in session, another hundred people had gathered in the park, waiting for Maddie.

The mechanics from the Throttleshop were dressed in pink overalls. His dad and oldest brother, Sinjin, with his wife, Claire, stood beside Gus and Lucy. Several of the paddle-boarders were in attendance, and Nina, the PR gal, hovered near them. It took him a second to realize that the dark-haired man wearing big pink glasses was Nick Marcheti.

Maddie pulled him close. "The women from the lighthouse —when Wagner stole Tyler's boat—are here. Oh my gosh, there's Linda. Look, she's wearing a pink Harley T-shirt."

As he looked around, Rob sensed he was being watched.

His uncle took the lead and announced that there would be a celebration dinner at the Beacon.

"Brats and burgers are on the house," Kat shouted.

Fran, Drew, Graham, and other folks started to follow Kat and Michael, and Rob spotted Wagner. He'd moved away from the *Cue* reporter and was heading toward him and Maddie.

Instinctively, he pulled Maddie closer to him.

He recalled the moment in Chicago on the courthouse stairs when Wagner ranted and preached about his victory in court. Rob had spent the next six months chastising himself and the role he'd played in freeing a predator, but now he had a sense of relief.

Thanks to Lark and Maddie, he'd received a slew of calls from other victims of Wagner's. Rob had gathered so many testimonials and victim statements that he and Graham were working on a lawsuit to be handed to Wagner in the new year, which would put him away for a long time. And to Rob's absolute relief, Liza Carpenter planned to appeal the first decision, giving him a chance to rewrite history.

Just as Wagner was about to reach them, Gwen Ridley yanked his arm and pulled him away. Rob had a gut feeling that this was the last time Gwen would defend Wagner since hers had been one of the complaints Rob had received—anonymously, of course.

For a second, Rob wanted to rip off his glasses and go all superhero on Wagner for Maddie's sake. But what did it matter? He won. He got the girl.

Suddenly, Wagner broke away from Gwen, ran up to Rob and Maddie, and started screaming in their faces. The rage spewing from Wagner turned Rob's stomach. The onetime Hollywood superstar had devolved into an inhuman caricature.

Maddie clutched onto his arm. "He is the one who is *pazza.*"

Rob really wanted to take a swing at Wagner but opted to protect Maddie. "Take a breath, dude. People are watching you."

Wagner looked around wildly. Inadvertently, Rob had added fuel to the fire. Looking for blood, Wagner drew his arm back, swung his fist, and missed Rob's chin by a sliver. Rob felt his whiskers vibrate. TJ came from nowhere and pounced on Wagner, shoving him into the ground.

"Nice move, TJ," Maddie said and laughed.

Rob let out his breath. "May I suggest a perp walk through this crowd of Maddie fans."

As Wagner swore and spit, TJ lifted him upright and slapped on the handcuffs. "Mr. Chris Wagner, you're under arrest for attempting to cause bodily injury."

Wagner muttered something and called out for Gwen.

She was long gone.

As TJ hauled Wagner's ass off to the police department, the photographer from the *Cue* ran up and took photos from every direction. Wagner tried to headbutt her, and TJ constrained the beast as he yelled, "Fuck off."

Rob was stunned. He'd never witnessed such a demise of human decency. He wrapped his arm around Maddie. "Are you all right?"

"I'm good, just hot as hell. I'd love to strip and go skinny-dipping but don't want to get arrested for indecent exposure. I've had my fill of brushes with the law."

Chuckling, they strolled along with the other folks who were heading toward the Beacon. As if knowing their need for privacy, no one came up to chat with them. Or maybe, like him, they all needed coffee and food and were too hungry to talk. Either way, he relished this time with Maddie.

When they entered the Beacon, he tugged Maddie into the alcove by the restrooms. "Can we make out for a bit?"

She caressed his cheek, slipped her fingers under his belt buckle, and said in a sultry voice, "Of course."

And then the damn bathroom door swung open, and Nick Marcheti appeared.

A COLD BUCKET of water doused Maddie's desire. Thank you, or *grazie*, Nick Marcheti. She calmly unhooked her fingers from Rob's belt and sneered at the *Italian Scallion*. "What are you doing here? Don't you have to be with your precious Ferrari?"

"Did you get hit in the head with a paddleboard, Nick?" Rob grabbed her hand, and they strode into the Beacon. "What's with the new pink glasses?"

The scent of charbroiled hamburgers drifted her way, and her stomach growled. She could not wait to eat, swim, and hop into the sack with Rob. All better choices than seeing Nick the Dick.

"Hello, you two." Nick handed her a copy of the *Cue*. "Maddie and Rob, I wanted to say I'm sorry, and I thought this was the best way."

His over-the-top Italian expressions had gone up in smoke. In fact, Maddie detected a slight Chicago accent. When he said *sorry*, it sounded like *sari*. Vindication coursed through her reptilian brain.

Clutching onto the *Cue*, she scanned the article and the photograph. It was a full, written apology to her *and* Fran. In the photo, she and Fran were arm-in-arm at the Pink Paddle event. Having imbibed one too many Camparis that day, she wasn't sure when the photo was taken, but luckily, they looked beautiful and proud in their Sunkissed swimsuits. The caption under the photo read, "Nick Marcheti donates ten thousand dollars for the Pink cause by purchasing the paddleboard designed by Maddie Logerquist for Sunkissed."

Had Nick Marcheti come to his senses and exited the dark ages?

She couldn't quite wrap her head around this drastic change with the *Italian Scallion*. "What's the catch? Did you print this one and only copy for my benefit?"

"Not in the least. You can confirm with the reporter Gemma Garner."

She glanced down at the name on the byline. "Should I know her?"

He tapped his big, round, and pink eyeglasses. "No, but she knows you. She's been following your story and Wagner's for a while. Gemma contacted me after the release of that cruel photo of you and me. Apparently, Paul Murphy, another *Cue* reporter, was skulking around Road America, looking for ways to defame you. He'd been on Wagner's payroll."

Rob scratched his chin. "I should have known."

"Not at all," Nick said. "We were all so car-happy while in Elkhart, Mr. Murphy blended into the crowd with his vintage Mustang. I imagine it was a down payment from Wagner to dig up some dirt on all of us."

"I'm glad you wised up." She pointed to the article. "It says here you're the proud new owner of a ten-thousand-dollar neon pink paddleboard."

"Yes indeed, and my glasses will match when I get out on the water with it. Funny how Paul Murphy ignored my supportive purchase and released the picture anyway."

Rob shook his head. "Definitely another delay tactic or meant to put the kibosh on today's hearing. Such a crook, Wagner."

Maddie gave Nick a hug. "Thanks for standing up for us female types. So what made you move to the twenty-first century?"

"Seeing you and Fran and all the love happening with the women *and* men at the Pink fundraiser. I was mostly banished to the kitchen, but the enthusiasm and positivity soaked in and reminded me of the good times when Fran and I were growing up. Before *business* overtook and consumed *play*."

"Now you really do sound Italian, *mi amore*." Maddie

chuckled. "Maybe with your new paddleboard, you and Fran can have fun out on the water, playing. Oh, and I'm sure Fran can enlighten you on all the great values of feminism."

"Come on, let's go get something to eat," Rob said. "There may be a Chicago-style hot dog to be had, Nick."

"Sounds *delicioso*, especially with extra relish."

Walking into the Beacon's diner, Maddie said, "How can I reach Gemma Garner to say thank you, Nick?"

Nick's big black eyebrows shot up over his pink specs. "Oh, she's here, somewhere. I'll point her out to you. She was at the Pink fundraiser and wanted to introduce herself but didn't have a chance. Gemma came in first in the paddleboard race. She's a breast cancer survivor, too."

"Wow" was all Maddie could say.

She and Rob left Nick on his own in the dining room, and she finally had a chance to wrangle Rob to herself. There must have been close to a hundred people in the Beacon. So she squeezed Rob's hand and pulled him into the coatroom. She wanted to have a hot and heavy make-out session but had to ask, "Okay, bud. Where do we go from here?"

"Aren't you moving back to New York?" Rob combed his fingers through her hair, jump-starting a flutter of lovely tingles deep within her.

He caressed her cheek, and she mumbled, "I'll only go there if you come along."

"Mmm," he said, sliding his lips along her neck. "New York. Sounds like an adventure. However, I like Baileys better. Less concrete and more water."

Sighing, she laid her head against his chest and hugged him. "Can we just stay put?"

"In the coatroom?"

"Sure, whatever. Maybe there are pillows in here somewhere," she said.

He unhooked her arms, took off his suit coat, and dropped it on the floor. "Here's a soft spot to rest, babe. But first..." He got down on one knee and looked up at her. "This is a proposal. Of sorts. I don't have a ring yet, but I'm not taking any chances. I don't want one more day to go by without you. Maddie Eleanor Logerquist, will you marry me?"

Her heart pounded so hard she got on her knees. "Depends."

Rob lifted one of his adorable ginger eyebrows and held her hands.

"I've never gone swimming in the Mediterranean Sea. How does a honeymoon in Italy sound?"

"*Perfecto.*"

Maddie draped her arms over Rob's shoulders, and they tumbled to the floor together. She kissed him, then sang, "When the moon hits your eye, something, something, not sure..."

"Big pizza pie, babe."

"Okay, Rob. But I know for sure...it's *amore.*"

TOP STORY

Chris Wagner — Never to Get Another Call from Hollywood!

FOLLOWING A DRAMATIC SCENE IN A BAILEYS HARBOR COURTROOM, HOLLYWOOD ICON CHRIS WAGNER HAS RIDDEN OFF INTO A FIERY SUNSET AND CHECKED HIMSELF INTO A CHICAGO REHAB FOR 28 DAYS. AFTER A CAREER MARRED BY ALLEGATIONS AND ACCUSATIONS AGAINST HIM, HIS RECORD OF MANIACAL WRONGDOINGS CAME TO LIGHT FOR THE WORLD TO SEE. THE ONLY ROLE LEFT FOR WAGNER TO PLAY WILL BE IN AN ORANGE JUMPSUIT AS A PRISON INMATE.

BY GEMMA GARNER

SEPTEMBER

As Chris Wagner's career and life imploded, his fall and crash-landing from the stars were celebrated with fireworks exploding through the town of Baileys Harbor, Wisconsin. It echoed around the country for all women to hear.

In the small-town courtroom, it appeared that even his attorney didn't want to sit beside the alleged predator. Most visibly, Wagner had zero support. Empty chairs lined his side of the room, and his wife and two daughters were conspicuously absent.

While Lark Russell described Wagner's sexual assault on her on the set of *Summer Haven*, Wagner could be heard grumbling and gritting his set of new white caps. It took only minutes for the judge to declare Wagner's case worthless and a waste of the court's valuable time.

His famous blue eyes only sparked when he lunged toward his onetime defense attorney, Rob Reid, after the proceeding. Outside the courtroom, Wagner shouted to reporters. "They're all lying. Goddamn slander. A bunch of f#c%@*s."

Basking in the sunny center of the drama and keeping her head held high was Maddie Logerquist. The fashion stylist and swimwear designer for Sunkissed told her empowering story. **{GG}**

The urn stayed safely tucked in Maddie's arms. Settled next to Rob on the back bench, she tucked one foot under her butt as her brother steered away from the house. With Brady piloting Tyler's sleek red boat to Birdcage Island, a deep sense of calm came over her. Finally, she was fulfilling her mom's last wishes.

When they approached the island, the battered bones of a wooden pier jutted into the water. She sighed and laid her head on Rob's shoulder. At the southern end of the island, the ship-wreck of the *Christina Nilsson* lay resting under the dark, verdant, and indigo waters of Lake Michigan, still hiding the elusive gems that Tyler had jumped overboard to find so many years ago. It made perfect sense that Elsie had bought this place and then buried Tyler on it.

Rob rose to help Brady tie the boat to the pier. Handing the urn to her brother, Maddie climbed out of the boat with a helping hand from her boyfriend—no...her fiancé. The worn wooden planks creaked under her feet, making her dread the condition of the lighthouse up ahead. On either side of the sandy path, the trees and foliage were wild and overgrown.

The early morning trip meant more time for the trio to sort

out where to lay Elsie's remains, but it also woke up a lot of unwanted visitors: mosquitoes, sand flies, and gnats. Maddie growled as she, at the front of their line, stopped short before walking through an invisible cloud made of insects. "Why am I in the front?"

"Because you're the oldest." Brady playfully pushed her shoulder, then handed back the urn. "And the leader of our pack."

She hugged the urn and waved off the bugs. Letting them scatter, she wiped her tongue with the back of her hand and then covered her nose to prevent any intruders from making their way into her nose or mouth.

Rob walked alongside her. "I appreciate the invite. Are you sure this isn't a private moment for you and Brady?"

"Not in the least," she said, then blew raspberries. "I wouldn't have been able to make it to this island if it weren't for you freeing me from Baileys for a short time." She shaded her eyes with her hand and gazed at the red shingles on the house ahead on the path. "This whole town—the people and all of Elsie's enhancements—has become a playground bigger than NYC and much, much richer. Also, because you're my fiancé, you're obliged to face the snakes and bugs with me."

"I can deal with it." He gave her a hip bump.

Passing them, Brady said, "I'll scope out the house and clear out all the snakes."

"Thanks, bro," she laughed. "Appreciate it. That means my *fiancé* will take care of the bugs."

When they reached the dilapidated house next to the crumbling lighthouse, she shuddered. What a mess. For a second, she wondered if Elsie had been nuts to buy this island.

Cautiously walking through the overgrown plants and weeds, they reached the old house's front door. The dark wood door was carved with intricate flowers painted with bright colors. It was the only part of the house not decaying.

"Hey, guys," Brady shouted. "Get over here. I found the perfect spot for Ma."

Maddie adjusted her sunhat and strode around the house to where Brady stood, looking at a garden...of rocks. She gasped. "This is beautiful."

The perimeter of river rocks circled around stones and various sizes of succulents. The chicks and hens popped out like fresh greenery wanting to say hello. In the center, a pea gravel path curved out toward an outer edge of limestone boulders. Sprouting from the crevices between the stones was an abundance of pink wildflowers.

On the edge of the garden, Brady stood beside a stack of rocks as tall as him. "It's a no-brainer, sis. This is Ma's final resting place."

With Rob following, she tiptoed through the garden's maze of stone and greenery and reached her brother. In the ground at the base of the stone tower was a patinaed copper plaque with Tyler's name and beside it, another plaque, not yet dated, for her mother.

"Woot!" she hollered. "Finally!"

Rob and Brady gave each other a high five, and Maddie gently slipped the lighthouse urn next to the plaque.

"Shouldn't we get the dates stamped on the plaque?" Brady asked.

"Eventually," Maddie said. "Let's give Elsie a well-deserved rest first."

Holding hands, Maddie and Rob followed Brady back to the pier. When Brady was out of sight, Maddie stopped short.

He faced her. "You all good?"

She paused to make sure the words she'd been practicing came out. "*Sei la metà della mia mela.*"

Flames rose on Rob's cheeks.

She wondered if she'd made a mess of her Italian. "Did I say it right?"

"Oh, yes. I'm impressed by your version of *soulmate* and truly honored."

"Thanks. Being your *half-apple* in Italian is so darn romantic." Maddie squeezed his hand and kissed him. "Come on, let's go. We have plenty of time to get to Cave Point and go for a swim."

THE END

ACKNOWLEDGMENTS

Many thanks to my steadfast critique partner and friend, Carla Luna Cullen. With her weekly encouragement I'm able to stay happy while writing. Sometimes juggling all the balls in the publishing gig can get overwhelming and thanks to Carla, when one ball drops I don't get discouraged. I just keep writing.

> Rest peacefully my writing buddy.
> I know you're watching out for me.

Jennifer Rupp is my endless cheerleader who looks awesome wearing black. Thank you friend for keeping me laughing through the ups and downs of this writing stuff.

Thank you to the crew of professionals who helped get this book out into the world. Lynne Pearson has made sure my characters don't sound like Captain James T. Kirk. Sandra Dee deals with my over abundance of commas. And Sarah Hansen, your artistic vision for all my covers has been brilliant.

To my friends Swati Agterberg and Rachael Herrenbruck. Thank you. I've always admired your wit and wisdom. I'm so thankful for your friendship and support while I tend to disappear for months on end to write another dang book. Here's to our next trip to San Miguel de Allende.

Red Oak Writing has been listening to many of my chapters through the years. Thanks to Kim Suhr and all of the round table writers who have shared their thoughts and given me great advice. I truly value all of your incredible writing skills and insight.

My dearest sisters, Kathy Bender and Jill Lamek, thank you. You two sweethearts lift my spirits daily. I'm so lucky to have your friendship, support, and love.

Special thanks to all of my friends who have shared with me amazing stories of winning their battles with breast cancer. You are truly badass heroines, especially Patti Zinda.

Lastly, the origins of this story came about many years ago at Road America in Plymouth, Wisconsin. My incredibly cool brother-in-law Perry Lamek had asked me, a newbie writer, to write a piece about the vintage sports cars for the official race catalogue. What a treat. The cars and the fun at the vintage races have stuck in my mind ever since. Thank you so much Perry for giving me such a great opportunity. As well, *Freefalling in the Moonlight,* has a distinct musical influence that comes from Perry and his good friend Howie Epstein and Howie's boss Tom Petty. I know the three of you are still jamming your hearts out.

ABOUT THE AUTHOR

Audrey Lynden writes contemporary and swoony women's fiction. Living in Wisconsin, she's inspired by her home state's charming small towns, celebrity residents and the beautiful beaches along Lake Michigan. Because of the many interesting histories and quirky traditions happening all around Wisconsin, her love stories will make you laugh, cry and cheer. With an affinity for British mysteries jaunty capers find a way into her books.

She favors writing hope, empowerment, satisfying endings, and avoids cliffhangers.

Every winter she binge watches all seasons of *Brooklyn Nine-Nine.*

www.ingramcontent.com/pod-product-compliance
Lightning Source LLC
Chambersburg PA
CBHW030929120726
47906CB00002B/544